A MIRROR GREENS IN SPRING

Selina Sen was educated in Shimla and the Delhi University, where she studied Economics. She was inspired to write this, her first novel, based on her mother's reminiscences of her ancestral home lost upon Partition in present-day Bangladesh.

Selina has contributed features and travel writing to most of India's leading newspapers. Until recently, she was the North Indian correspondent for the Hong Kong based Publisher's Representatives Ltd., a group of magazines on Asian economic affairs. She is very widely travelled, being especially keen on river journeys. She has explored rivers as far-flung as the Orinoco in Venezuela, the Jhelum in Kashmir, the Ganges, the Teesta in North Bengal, the Rhine and the Seine.

Her other chief interest is garden design and she maintains a prize-winning water garden at her home in a New Delhi suburb where she lives with her son. She is at present working on a second novel, set in New Delhi and Kashmir.

OTHER INDIAINK TITLES :

A.N.D. Haksar	*Madhav & Kama: A Love Story from Ancient India*
Boman Desai	*Servant, Master, Mistress*
C.P. Surendran	*An Iron Harvest*
I. Allan Sealy	*The Everest Hotel*
I. Allan Sealy	*Trotternama*
Indrajit Hazra	*The Garden of Earthly Delights*
Jaspreet Singh	*17 Tomatoes: Tales from Kashmir*
Jawahara Saidullah	*The Burden of Foreknowledge*
Kalpana Swaminathan	*The Page 3 Murders*
Kamalini Sengupta	*The Top of the Raintree*
Madhavan Kutty	*The Village Before Time*
Pankaj Mishra	*The Romantics*
Paro Anand	*I'm Not Butter Chicken*
Paro Anand	*Wingless*
Paro Anand	*No Guns at My Son's Funeral*
Ramchandra Gandhi	*Muniya's Light: A Narrative of Truth and Myth*
Ranjit Lal	*The Life & Times of Altu-Faltu*
Ranjit Lal	*The Small Tigers of Shergarh*
Raza Mir & Ali Husain Mir	*Anthems of Resistance: A Celebration of Progressive Urdu Poetry*
Sharmistha Mohanty	*New Life*
Shree Ghatage	*Brahma's Dream*
Susan Visvanathan	*Something Barely Remembered*
Susan Visvanathan	*The Visiting Moon*
Tom Alter	*The Longest Race*

FORTHCOMING TITLES :

Anjana Basu	*Black Tongue*
Kalpana Swaminathan	*The Gardener's Song*
Prafulla Roy Tran. John Hood	*Freedom's Ransom*
Shandana Minhas	*Tunnel Vision*
Susan Visvanathan	*The Seine at Noon*

A MIRROR GREENS IN SPRING

SELINA SEN

IndiaInk
ROLI BOOKS

IndiaInk

Although the vanishing of two ships is based on a
real-life incident, all other events and characters, except
for the assassination of Indira Gandhi in 1984 and
the ensuing anti-Sikh riots, are completely fictional.

First published in 2007
IndiaInk
An imprint of
Roli Books Pvt. Ltd.
M-75, G.K. II Market
New Delhi 110 048
Phones: ++91 (011) 2921 2271, 2921 2782
2921 0886, Fax: ++91 (011) 2921 7185
E-mail: roli@vsnl.com; Website: rolibooks.com
Also at
Bangalore, Mumbai, Varanasi, Jaipur, Kolkata, Chennai

Cover Design: Nitisha Mehta
Layout Design: Narendra Shahi
Back cover: Detail from Pahari miniature painting,
         courtesy National Museum, New Delhi

ISBN: 81-86939-33-4

Typeset in AGaramond by Roli Books Pvt. Ltd. and
printed at Anubha Printers, Noida, U.P.

This book is dedicated to the memories of two very special women, Ma and Dida, whose courage and love remain for me a source of strength and inspiration.

To

Esha Sen and Hena Chhobi Halder

CONTENTS

Acknowledgements
ix

BOOK ONE
1

BOOK TWO
137

Credits
305

acknowledgements

This book would never have been completed but for the painstaking feedback of Sunetra Sen Narayan, Ananda Swaroop and Badri Narayan. I am deeply indebted to them.

For help and advice with the manuscript, I must thank Mukul Kesavan and Sam Miller, they have both been very kind and generous.

Sanjiv Saith for invaluable insights, patience and good counsel – a big thank you.

It has been a great pleasure working with Renuka Chatterjee, my editor at Roli Books; I look forward to doing so again.

Sunita Dwivedi, Nayantara and Vikram, many thanks for the enthusiastic encouragement.

I am grateful to my family for their appreciation and support, especially to my father, Maj. Gen. G.K. Sen and to my son Varun, who kept me going through the various drafts with tales of JK Rowling's rags to riches story.

Shanta Ramaswamy for the Krishna prayers and for providing erudite opinion on matters of astrological reference – thank you.

New Delhi   – Selina Sen
December 2006

book one

Would you riddle the miracle of the wind's shaping?
Watch how a mirror greens in spring.

— **Mirza Ghalib**

prologue

As always the old man was dreaming. The power cut woke him, he could dimly see the blades of the fan slowing down and coming to a stop. His wife slept on, sari pallu flung away from her body, sweat glistening in the creases of her neck, arms outflung like a child's. He went out to the verandah where a damp breeze provided some scant relief. Sparse raindrops were striking the dusty earth, the leaves of the kadamba tree. He sat down heavily on the cane chair, tilting his head uncomfortably against the backrest, knees spread apart for coolness. He willed himself back into his dream. It was a dream that recurred. Startling fragments of buried memory more real than his present life.

The boat was gliding through a landscape that all around him was quickening into life. The river swollen with the July rain, in the distance multicoloured paper kites soaring from one level to another. Half submerged reeds, glinting at the water's edge, stretched into flooded jute fields or emerald ripples of rice. A kingfisher perched on the bamboo pole put up to spread the fishing nets, darted with a sudden plunge into the water.

Now the boat was transversing a beel, neither lake nor marshland, unique to the flat Bengal landscape. The river spreading over a patch of lowland into a mirror-flat sheet of water, a shoreless expanse in the monsoon. The water was as clear as glass, the boat skimming the surface, scarcely causing a ripple. Villages, a cluster of huts built on a mound, stood out like islands. Water lilies yellow and white, pink, rarely blue lifted their pointed petalled heads, and waterfowl peculiar to the beels foraged for insects amidst leafy circles.

Slumbering uncomfortably on the chair, the old man's mouth fell open as he gasped for air. He was swimming in the river now, a young man. His dhoti folded above his knees and tucked around his waist, his arms cutting the water in skilful swathes. Twisting and laughing, swimming along with fish that grazed his shoulders, his flanks. Sometimes he had glimpsed the Ganges river dolphin although it was a tributary of the Brahmaputra in which he swam. Like him the long-beaked dolphin would break the water for air. Its flipper would undulate from side to side as it swam in shallow waters, hunting for small fish, using sonar echolocation to navigate. One tip grazing the riverbed for orientation it would seize the fish with a snap of its elongated jaws.

The sand-stirred waters closed over his eyes. The dolphin dream dissolved in a bubbling stream. Each glassy sphere enclosing the aching void inside him. It was almost forty years since he had seen the Brahmaputra. Forty years since he had seen his green, green land, lost forever in Bangladesh.

In the small room towards the front of the house, his granddaughter Chhobi awakened to the sound of thunder. In the still air the mattress so lumpy with retained heat was unbearable and she shifted to the floor. It was that time of year which stretched the limits of endurance, when trying to get cool seemed to be the only preoccupation. That time of tension and expectation before the monsoon their grandfather called Rohini.

A dust storm earlier had left its gritty imprint everywhere and now she felt the sandy grains chafe at her skin. Sprinkling herself and the floor with a mug of tepid water, she hitched her kaftan mid-thigh. Sleep did not return and suddenly she was flashing back to another wakeful night almost exactly a year ago.

A night when irritation had given way to anxiety as the minutes had mounted past eleven, her sister Sonali's deadline. Chhobi remembered with painful clarity lying on a sweat dampened pillow watching the yellow street light outside the gate flickering in the reduced and uncertain voltage, the luminescent minute hand on the bedside clock creeping past forbidden hours. After 3 a.m. she had begun pacing to the window and back. When she had finally heard the gate latch rattle, she had rushed out to see the red Datsun with the musical horn reversing down the lane. Only one car played *Jingle Bells* in June.

Sonali, face half hidden by the cascade of hair had slipped in without speaking, and then begun to undress quickly. Chhobi had felt a flame of outrage then, not untinged with jealousy. She had controlled the urge to grasp Sonali's hair and shake that expression off her face. Secret, mutinous, guilt-edged but superior at unshared pleasures recently experienced.

Like every other night, Sonali had sat on her bed and brushed her hair. Chhobi's flash of rage did not dissolve but seemed to radiate to that river of black streaming down Sonali's back, cool silver bangle rhythmically moving up and down. Her hair in the dark coming alight with static sparks, as though ignited by her sister's anger and a dry as bone June night in Delhi 1983.

It was nearing daybreak when Chhobi heard the first few raindrops striking the windowpane. She drifted between an uneasy sleep and restless wakefulness. This monsoon was not to be a time so much of rejuvenation but of rebirth. Events set in motion by Sonali a year ago would come to their preordained completion and the family would be called on to draw upon hidden resources that they did not even know existed. Pitted against unrelenting circumstances, they would emerge in more powerful avatars, tempered by the fire that was about to rage.

one

The house was a single-storied one, set in the corner of a narrow lane with rows of similar houses. These were lime-washed yellow, rose pink and Mrs Chatterjee's a dubious shade of pistachio green. In the noon haze they seemed to shimmer and melt with the colours running into each other. Theirs was white streaked with grey, half smothered in the grasp of an unruly jasmine. Once a year it was studded with a constellation of fragrant flowers, but mostly it sagged, dusty and unpruned over the verandah.

Like its neighbour, the house was constructed in the prosaic style of colonies hastily built to house refugees at a time when Delhi's population had doubled suddenly after Partition. It had the usual L-shaped living area leading onto the small bedrooms, separated by a kitchen. This connected to the rear courtyard where Dida's pickles in white and ochre earthenware jars followed the path of the winter afternoon sun. Green chillies grew in a discarded washbasin. In the corner flourished a feathery red hibiscus, pistils and petals unfurling in frilly profusion.

When it was still dark the bulbuls warbled their song in the kadamba tree and as it grew light the everyday sounds of waking up took over. The thud of the rolled-up newspaper striking the front door, Dida, clinking the teacups in the kitchen and the distant whine of the trucks changing gear as they lumbered up the new flyover. The background noise was, of course, of the drumming of the taps as the water filled up in the buckets, to be stored till the fresh water was released again in the evening.

Dadu was particular about his first cup of tea. In a ritual almost as exacting as a Japanese tea ceremony, the long leaf Darjeeling tea, Lipton's Green Label, was carefully measured into the warmed porcelain pot. A survivor of Dida's wedding trousseau, it was English, part of a Crown Derby set, stained now with a fine network of crackle underlying the glaze. The sugar bowl and milk jug had slipped through careless fingers long ago, and only one rose-flowered cup reserved for Dadu remained. It was special, translucent and fragile with a tiny rosebud painted midway down the inside of the cup. Hitkari China or even the defunct Bengal Potteries would never have imagined such delicate details. Chhobi always knew when Dadu reached the halfway mark, he would take a big gulp to reveal the whole flower in one go, rather like the receding tide suddenly exposing an iridescent shell on an empty beach.

Dida preferred the strong inky cup she brewed after her bath and puja – it masked the bitter aftertaste of the saccharine she used. She never joined the rest of them at table. Today, like always, Dadu sat at the head half-hidden by *The Statesman*. Ma already bathed and smelling faintly of sandalwood soap in a crisp starched sari was slowly pouring herself a cup. Chhobi tried to read the headlines from across the table, but just then the paper was laid down.

'Meera, listen to this, there has been another murder. In South Delhi this time, a retired bank manager and his wife – she's in a coma, he is dead.' There was a photograph, a pot-bellied policeman in a ransacked room that appeared to have been struck by a hurricane. The rumpled bedclothes were stained dark with blood.

Ma was resigned. 'There's never any good news. I hate to read the newspaper these days. What do the police say?'

'That gypsy tribe suspected again. There are thousands pouring into Delhi every year, Nepalese, Bangladeshis, those construction workers from Bihar and Orissa and the police always suspect some obscure tribe.'

'But don't they always follow the same modus operandi?' Chhobi intervened. 'You know, break in before dawn in naked oiled bodies for that slippery getaway? And don't they always leave a pile of...'

Ma silenced her admonishingly with her eyes.

It was true – the tribe of thieves always left their trademark by defecating by the door as they exited. It was one of those snippets of useless information that Chhobi collected. She had a box in her head crammed with unrelated facts often stranger than fiction. A nonsensical collage, an ill-assorted ragbag where very often stray clippings pulsated with a jabberwocky rhythm of their own.

'We must do something, can't depend on the police. We have to put in those steel grills in the windows this month. All other expenses will have to be postponed,' continued Dadu single-mindedly. 'Delhi has more crime than Bombay, Calcutta and Madras put together.' Of late he had begun reinforcing his opinions with hazy statistics.

Dida overheard that. 'We have nothing worth stealing, as it is the place looks like Red Fort after you raised the boundary walls last year,' she said. 'I can never get used to those ugly glass shards you had embedded on the top.' Glancing at the paper, she said. 'What about the attack on the bus in Punjab? What about the blast in Sri Lanka? It was on TV last night, but that news has become so common that the papers only carry it in their back pages now.' Dida dispersed Dadu's feelings of insecurity at home, spreading them thinly to encompass the whole subcontinent simmering with ethnic tension.

'We have nothing worth stealing but the thieves don't know that. Any way I am talking to my daughter. As for Punjab, do you expect the Sikhs to sit placidly when you demolish their most sacred shrine? And Sri Lanka it is the same policy – double-edged and two-faced.'

'Sonali and her husband are returning soon. We have to buy

gifts for both of them it will be the first visit after her marriage,' continued Dida inexorably.

'When she didn't follow any traditions, why do you have to stick to these one-sided customs? Not only did she marry a non-Bengali, she did not even bother to tell us,' and folding up the newspaper in a tight angry square, Dadu went into the garden leaving his breakfast unfinished. It was one of those frequent moments when injuries were crowding into his mind – he was a refugee, his practice was non-existent, his only daughter was a widow, his wife obstinate, his plants parched and his granddaughters either too promiscuous or not enough.

Ma sighed. 'Non-Bengali, that was the least of it.' Glancing at her watch she picked up her handbag, Dida rushing behind with her polka-dotted parasol and bottle of water. The chartered bus stop was at the corner opposite Mrs Chatterjee's house.

It was the 'non' before Bengali that still disoriented and sometimes frightened Dadu. Despite having spent more than half a lifetime in Delhi, his world was still carefully divided into Bengalis – and everybody else classified by 'Non'. They were Probashis Bengalis – the Bengali diaspora that did not reside in Bengal.

Dadu would sit now for hours on the old cane chair on the verandah. Hands ridged with veins fingered a wen on his chin. His pupils, ringed with a hazy blue would gradually become unfocused, looking back through the distance of the years. It was the blue haze of the lost rivers of his youth and childhood. His very veins seemed to pulsate then, not with life-blood, but with the greenish-brown waters that swept him back and beat against the intervening lifetime.

…Padma, Meghna, Ganga, Madhumati, Dhaleshwari, Mundeshwari… Green the lush, unforgotten landscape criss-crossed with the spun silver sparkle of the deltas. Nostalgia's rose-tinted lenses would allow him only to recall the bounty thrown up by these rivers and not the pitiless havoc wreaked annually by their flooding.

In the early fifties, he had found a pale and insignificant solace in Delhi's Yamuna. The bathing ghats were still peopled by the devout then, the banks forested and cool. In winter, migratory birds brocaded the waters with their rich plumage and fishermen in boats netted heavy catches of mahseer and bhetki. The pilgrims, the birds and the fish had all but vanished today, vanquished by pollution. Only a stubborn strain of Japanese carp survived under the purple mist of the water hyacinth. The boat club at Okhla, once quite a favourite picnic spot, was virtually non-functional now. It was best forgotten that Delhi ever had a river, dismissed Dadu with contempt. The black and dead waters no longer offered any Letheward remedies.

two

At the time of the '71 war with Pakistan, thirteen years ago, Bapi had been stationed in Simla, the old summer capital and the army's western command. After hostilities broke out in East Pakistan, convoys of troops had wound their way down the Simla hills and had occupied posts along India's westernmost borders with Pakistan, leaving behind the women and children and a skeletal staff.

The Commandant's house in Simla, a sprawling British-built bungalow, stood on a high ridge, projecting out through the pines. On a clear day you could see the plains of the Punjab stretching out in an infinite dusty haze. Most evenings the women and children would gather there for news, huddled against the cold, candlelight glimmering on tense faces as the blackout siren sounded. Once they saw the fiery explosions of bombs striking far below and the smaller spurts of returning anti-aircraft fire, like a macabre celebration of Diwali. Years later Chhobi saw the site of the bombing. Only one wall of north India's oldest church remained, miraculously intact like the facade of a movie set.

The news was good, India was winning the war and casualties were much heavier on the Pakistan side. Finally after two days of intermittent rain, on a clean silver morning, cease-fire was declared. Soon the men would be back and things would return to normal.

A week later, returning home from school, Chhobi tugged at dawdling five-year-old Sonali's hand. As usual her grey uniform was grass-stained and she was swishing off dandelion clocks with a stick. Curious to see the knot of people at their gate, Chhobi dragged her along the last two hundred yards. The knot parted before them and there was silence. The silence, more than the soft keening sound they could hear in the background frightened them. Sonali's stick dropped with a clatter. They went upstairs where Ma was sitting up on her bed. Everything appeared normal, except for the frozen look on her face.

Bapi, Major Bhaskar Dutta, had been killed instantly when his Willy's jeep had a head-on collision with a truck on the Grand Trunk highway. The driver was flung clear, and only suffered a broken collarbone. The visibility was poor in the rain, he said, and the truck had been overtaking a bus on the wrong side of the road.

But the war's over, Chhobi remembered thinking incredulously. To die in a road accident on the journey home after passing safely through weeks of action at the front, appeared to her then, as it did today, an incomprehensible anticlimax.

Events moved swiftly after that, like train tracks in a motion picture, or the camera panning leafless trees turning to bud, then bushy foliage in a matter of seconds – to depict the passing years. Bapi's brother and only living relative, a research scientist in America, offered to pay for the girls' schooling. Bapi had saved very little, and Ma, married at eighteen, was ill trained for any employment. However, she had dabbled in paints all her life and was advised by the Commandant's wife to join a textile designing course in the South Delhi Polytechnic, after which she got Ma a job in her brother's garment export factory where the hours were long and the pay inadequate. Ma did her graduation in commerce by correspondence and was now heading the production department. She travelled out of Delhi occasionally to source fabrics, embroidered braids and other trims.

Chhobi continued as a boarder in the school at Simla, run by Catholic Irish nuns while Sonali accompanied Ma to Dadu and Dida's house in New Delhi, and joined a co-educational school. Chhobi was nearly thirteen at the time and Ma nineteen years older.

※

That first summer holiday when she returned from Simla to swelter in that little house with the desiccating garden, Chhobi had struggled to grow used to many things. Her missing father, the fatigue that scored lines on her mother's serene brow, cranky Sonali asleep on Dida's bed, and most of all Dadu's hunched posture. His eyes that grew glazed despite the sun squint. The long day that would drag on until finally, evening slanted over his heartsickness for an idea of home that was always towards the east.

Chhobi, grown older overnight, watched how their grandmother injected a note of festivity at lunch or dinner. She cooked with inspiration, undeterred by the stuffy, poorly ventilated kitchen. Her food was always mouth-watering, a cunning blend of her skill and an innovation born of severe resource constraints. The fish in her kofta curry might turn out to be green plantains in disguise, her dry mutton, jackfruit dressed as lamb.

As her day was governed from meal to meal, so her seasons too were ordered and planned in her kitchen. Winter brought the aroma of guava jelly mingled with ginger flavoured tea. Huge cauldrons of the pale fruit boiled and frothed, then dripped overnight through sieves made from discarded cotton saris tied on legs of upturned dining chairs. The juice that collected was boiled with an equal volume of sugar until it set into a rich deep red jelly, almost wine coloured.

End July and Chhobi and Sonali grated green mangoes for Dida's famous mango chutney spiced with ginger and sprinkled with delicate slices of red chillies. A phalanx of bottles lined the sideboard then, their contents as hot as an embalmed summer. Dida had adopted some north Indian culinary styles and liked to thicken mutton and chicken curries with a purple mince of pungent onions.

Chhobi remembered comparing her to one on occasion. Pink and fragile-skinned on the outside with tight packed layer upon layer of secrets and obsessions right down to the mysterious core. Her words often carried a sting too and made one's eyes water.

She had help in the shape of a withered old woman, Savitri, who swept and swabbed the floor, scrubbed and starched saris and sheets and worked with Dida in the kitchen in orchestrated unison.

Savitri's hands tinkling with her bangles, one red, one white and one iron, as she pounded a blend of spices to a smooth paste on the pitted stone slab. Dida's hands tinkling with her bangles as she stirred the paste in the hot oil, coral, shell and iron bound with a spiral of gold. 'Why do you wear an iron bangle, Dida?' Sonali had asked once.

'It's a shackle,' Dida had replied a little tersely. 'Your husband's family puts it on you when you get married – the Bengali wedding ring.'

Dida's frustrations, heat maddened in that barbecue of a kitchen, erupted that day. Despite resolutions not to burden the girls she spilt out, 'After all why else did we come so far north to Delhi? Soon after we left Mymensingh things were not so bad.' Her indignation stabbed the air with her ladle, spattering the wall with turmeric drops.

For a brief span of six years in the early fifties Dadu's prospects had been more optimistic. He had met Dr Mitra who had been a year senior to him at Calcutta Medical College, and had been easily persuaded to join him in setting up a clinic at Delhi.

The clinic flourished – there was a steady rise in the number of patients. Dadu's excellent diagnostic skills coupled with Dr Mitra's polished bedside manner proved to be a winning combination. Within five years the clinic grew into a white double-storied nursing home with neon-lit red crosses on the roof. The rooms were curtained in hospital green and patients tended by a flock of reassuring Malayali nurses. Dadu was busy and although he remained taciturn and abrupt with his patients, it was for no reason other than that he was simply unable to learn any Hindi beyond a few necessary commands to the staff.

He did complain about the white-hot summers, the dusty landscape, but the long hours he put in at the clinic did not leave time for any real loneliness to intrude. He was, however, unable to even functionally shed his prejudices and could not learn to share his space with others of diverse cultural moorings. Delhi at that time was flooded with refugees from West, not East Pakistan. Dadu did not learn from these uprooted people how to flourish in a place as they did, far away from their natural milieu. The Punjabis, with their huge appetite for everything new, lost no time in occupying the space that belonged to the original inhabitants of Delhi, still governed by the slow refinements of a Mughal heritage. Once occupied, the space was so quickly transformed as to belong to quite another time.

Comfortable workwise at least, everything changed when Dadu made a mistake. A simple, even stupid one, but one for which he was severely punished. As the clinic had grown in importance it had been placed on the panel of several small companies to conduct annual medical examinations of employees, as well as carry out pre-appointment checks.

Late one evening a storekeeper from one of these companies came to him. The man appeared agitated and implored Dadu to give him a medical certificate confirming that he had been admitted to the clinic for a day. He said he had been unable to attend office due to some domestic problems and since this had happened once too often he feared he would lose his job. In a hurry to get home, and without thinking too much about it, Dadu signed a certificate stating the storekeeper had been admitted to the clinic with dehydration, and had been administered two bottles of saline drip.

The next morning all hell broke loose. The man had murdered the company's manager and made off with the payroll, which was to be distributed the next day. Dadu was arrested as an accessory after the fact.

Dida's and Dr Mitra's combined efforts managed to get him released though Dida had to part with her ruby and gold necklace to pay the lawyers.

The stigma of the scandal stuck, and regretfully Dr Mitra asked Dadu to leave. The old workhorse would be difficult to replace. Since then Dadu had worked in a series of smaller and smaller clinics which offered him no more than a rickety security and he came to depend more and more on the kindness or rather the hypocrisy of his wife's rich relatives. Finally, he put himself out to pasture when Meera and her daughters came to live with him, by opening the clinic in the garage.

three

A vague notion of responsibility and a desire not to worry Ma, had prompted Chhobi to speak to Dida when Sonali entered college. Dida was the one who exerted the maximum influence on Sonali.

She was careful to choose a moment when Dida would be at her most receptive. Shrinking slightly for she didn't wish to appear an interfering busybody, Chhobi started up the stairs. It was a flight of stairs leading nowhere. Well, not precisely nowhere, but to the sun-baked terrace with its greying bricked-over surface and piles of dry brown leaves gathered in drifts. In safer summers when the house was first built, the terrace would be sluiced down in the evenings and niwar cots spread with cool white sheets, which glowed in the soft starlight, put out. Nowadays mosquitoes and theiving tribes ensured they all sweltered indoors.

The small landing at the top of the stairs had been converted to Dida's puja room. As always, and today especially, Dida's private space overwhelmed her. Chhobi, who had for years been used to snatching moments of peace in the ordered calm of the school chapel, could never find the same tranquillity here. The multitude of gods contrasted unfamiliarly with the chapel's simple altar with its single crucifix, the tapered glimmering candles, the pristine sprays of peach blossom and waxy aurum lilies.

Dida's puja room seemed so cramped, haphazard and overcrowded, the prayers at first incomprehensible and the gods too numerous to invoke any individual feeling of reverence. There was Saraswati gliding on a swan; Lakshmi the goddess of wealth, resplendent in red and gold; Durga and a pot-bellied Ganesh. In the corner were smaller black and white framed reproductions of Ramkrishna Paramhamsa and a handsome turbaned Swami Vivekananda.

Over this rich panoply loomed Krishna. Dida's preference for him expressed itself in many ways. Given pride of place in the centre was a beautifully carved alabaster statue of Krishna with his peacock plume crown and magical flute. A miniature cradle held a tiny silver image of infant Baal Krishna cast in a traditional crawling posture. A framed calendar print depicted a vivid blue Krishna crushing Kaliya the hydra-headed water serpent who lived in the Yamuna. Chhobi liked best the churning waters with the serpent's mermaid wives thrashing about like a sprinkling of confused commas.

Dida's chores started before dawn but her day began with the intonation *Om Namo Bhagavate Vasudevya* and then the many names of Krishna – Madhavan, Kesavan, Hari, Gopal...

A beautiful woman, she looked her best now, fresh from her bath. Long hair almost untouched by grey lying loose in damp tendrils like an actress in an old Guru Dutt film, skin faintly luminescent and eyes with a dreamy liquid gaze that actually seemed to melt and coalesce under the powerful solvent of her faith. Dida's skin had always been perfect, so smooth in her youth that people commented that should a fly alight on her body, it would lose its footing. Today the fine network of wrinkles was visible only in close-up, and if anything added to her beauty, rather like the patina on the glaze of antique china. She always wore the self-contained look of the very deaf, and at this hour she was able to completely shut out the petty demands of the day.

Gradually Chhobi had begun to appreciate a definite pattern to

Dida's daily ritual. The tinkling of the tiny brass bell to get her senses in tune with Krishna. The ribbons of sandalwood incense which wrapped the images in spirals of devotion. The floral offerings on the shining brass plate, red hibiscus and white jasmine, the sugary batasa and tulsi leaf. All motions were unhurried and graceful. Chhobi once asked Dida what she prayed for. Her reply was vague, the act alone appeared to be of greatest importance. Almost every day Dida would read a passage from the Bhagawad Gita and sometimes from Jaydeva's *Gitagovinda*.

That day Dida had closed Jaydeva's book, placing it on top of a well-worn Gita. Smiling, she had placed a tulsi leaf in Chhobi's mouth, who swallowed, then said, 'I was thinking, Sonali's started college. Psychology Honours. She seems to be far more interested in clothes. Also she comes home quite late. We don't have any idea where she goes, who are her friends. She is always whispering on the phone with some boys.' The last few words sounded so prudishly tale-bearing that Chhobi had immediately wished she could retract them. Tamely, she added, 'At this rate, she won't get through college – and what will she do then?' Dida's reaction had been calm, 'After college? No office job. Not for her. No, no. You are the one, we know you will become a District Collector soon after you clear the exam this year.'

Chhobi, who had, after completing her Masters, been rather half-heartedly preparing for the civil services, flinched a little at the discrimination and at Dida's confidence. She hoped, but didn't realistically expect to clear the exams.

'It is natural for such a beautiful girl to have suitors,' Dida had continued. In Bengali the words '*Ato sundori*', sounded like a title. 'She will make a brilliant match. You will see,' Dida had stated without emphasis but with complete conviction, looking up at the wall glowing blue and gold with her gods.

Suitors for a brilliant match. An ambition quite medieval, Chhobi had thought then, effectively silenced. What about love and emotions that led to a quickening of the heart?

A brilliant match. In retrospect one that had burnt out in a brief sulphurous flare despite the primitive energy with which it had been pursued.

Dida's Krishna wasn't very generous with his boons, Chhobi was to think a few months later when she did not clear the civil service examinations. Reticent Dadu, for whom disappointment had become a permanent state of mind, did not say anything, but the hurt in Ma's eyes filled her with guilt.

'You will make it next time,' Dida had said firmly.

Power and Glory, thought Chhobi whose reading often made her think in book titles. What was it about British bequests that made them so desirable? Prized. Jobs in the Indian Railways and the administrative service. Never mind that corruption and sloth had stained and shrunk them, making them resemble worn hand-me-downs. Defensive then, she was nevertheless resigned to trying again.

Meanwhile, the money was tight. Their father's dwindling gratuity fund was only partially able to offset Dadu's very uncertain earnings. It was Ma's salary that actually tided them over from month to month. Chhobi began to fruitlessly scan the Wednesday papers for part-time employment. Finding nothing suitable, she drifted into an M. Phil. degree in history at Jawaharlal Nehru University, and found she was enjoying it. Months passed before a chance meeting with Rosemary at Janpath found her the job she was looking for.

In search of a wedding present, Chhobi had wandered into the Cottage Emporium, that slightly ramshackle barrack of a place crammed with superior handicrafts. Examining some enamelled brassware she had bumped into an elegant woman. They glanced at one another, looked away, and then as recognition dawned exclaimed simultaneously – 'Aren't you from Simla?'

It was Rosemary D'Mello, four years her senior at school. A little girl tugged at her hand.

'Rosemary D'Mello?'

'Now Coutinho, and you are – wait, don't tell me... I remember – Chandrayee!'

Chhobi smiled in agreement.

'What are you doing these days?'

Chhobi, as usual, felt like an apologist when asked that question and she answered slowly.

'Actually waiting for something to fall into place. I appeared for the civil services last year but I didn't make it. I am trying again. In the meantime I have been doing my M.Phil. from JNU.'

'A jholawali from JNU,' laughed Rosemary.

'Huhnn...' Chhobi nodded in a self-deprecatory way, immediately feeling dowdy. Rosemary, self possessed even in school, was the epitome of good grooming now, the contours of her face enhanced with clever make-up, the rubies clustered in her ears accentuated by the short and expensive hairstyle she sported.

'No seriously, civil services? So iffy! Are you looking for a job?'

'A job... may be part-time. I finished my course work last year and have to write my thesis this year. After that, let's see... I may teach.'

'What's the subject of your dissertation?'

'It's... well, the confluence of Hindu and Islamic styles in Delhi's architecture.'

'Really!'

Chhobi was faintly surprised at the animation she displayed, until Rosemary explained that she was editing a city magazine on New Delhi. It was rather predictably called *The Rajdhani*. Chhobi had seen it a couple of times, an expensive glossy. She did not think the circulation was large. 'Didn't you get the English prize every year?' Then as Chhobi nodded in the affirmative, 'Here's my card, come and write for us, on the monuments of Delhi. We use a lot of freelancers.'

A week later, card in hand, Chhobi had doubtfully entered the tiny office off Bahadur Shah Zafar Marg. At least the locality, the Fleet Street of Delhi, was reassuring.

She submitted her first piece on the Hayat Baksh or The Life-giving Gardens at the Red Fort. Writing came easy to her, she found. She grew lyrical as she described the stone waterways, the pavilions called Sawan and Bhadon appropriately designed to represent the varied flow of the rain during the two phases of the monsoon. Here a torrent rushing over marble slabs in sheets, there a tinkling trickle. Hollowed recesses in the stone behind the cataracts had contained camphor candles illuminating the falling water beautifully during Emperor Shah Jehan's times.

Rosemary was so pleased with her work, made striking with a pen and ink sketch done by the magazine's art department, that she offered Chhobi a regular column. From a single piece submitted once a month, Chhobi had rapidly started doing interviews and book reviews. Six months later she had joined as a regular employee with the informal understanding that she would get time off to complete her dissertation. The money she earned was very useful in supplementing the mounting household expenses.

❧

August and the monsoon seemed to have passed Delhi by, save for a brief outburst that had flashed like a solitary bolt of lightning. Even the neighbouring Rajasthan desert had received more rain. Six-thirty in the evening and everyone at the bus stop was visibly wilting as they waited for the chartered bus. It sounded grand, like a chartered plane, Chhobi thought as she squeezed into her usual place. The rexine upholstery was sticky and warm. The assistant engineer smiled as he sat down, the corner of his black hard-topped vinyl briefcase striking her right knee. She pushed herself further into the corner to get away from the ripe smell of sweat mingled with the perfumed hair oil he favoured. She wished he would stick to pure cotton and not synthetic shirts in summer.

At India Gate they were stuck in a traffic jam. As they sluggishly circled the stone cupola where George V had once stood, monarch in marble drapery, Chhobi idly imagined the bus losing its moorings with a sudden loss of centrifugal force. Depending on which tangential path it took, they could hurtle past the magnificent ruins of the citadels of Delhi's various rulers.

Briefly appeared the vision of Mughal grandeur epitomised by Shah Jehan seated on his peacock throne. The striped dome of the

Jama Masjid flanked him. Shah Jehan, Queen Razia, and Sher Shah. Other rulers, shadowy but grand, were all pinpoints like so many satellites separated by time revolving on axes of different dimensions around a shifting centre point, Delhi. Chhobi closed her eyes against the heat and seemed to be whirling in a merry-go-round along with Queen Razia, Delhi's only woman ruler before Indira Gandhi. It would be a good idea to do a short sketch on her for the next issue, she thought, wiping the sweat gathered on her neck with her chunni. She opened her bag to look for her diary but failed to find it in the jumble of old pamphlets and letters... She pulled out some stiff folded cards to write on. Smoothing them open she saw they were old passes for an Odissi recital. The months fell away as she fingered them.

The bus moved forward as she remembered the last time the three of them, Ma, Dida and she had gone out together.

It was when Rosemary had handed out these passes for an Odissi dance recital choreographed to Jaydeva's verses that they had made the long journey to Kamani Auditorium, hurrying in as the lights had dimmed.

The MC for the evening had spoken from a spotlit rostrum, the mike amplifying her accent carefully cultured for the benefit of the many European tourists who filled the hall. No sooner had she begun quoting from an English translation of the twelfth century poet's verses, than Dida started chanting the same verse from the Sanskrit version. Normally when she spoke she reduced the volume of her voice to an almost inaudible pitch as though to compensate for the amplification of tone that was required to reach her own tympanum, but today she was excited and spoke loudly. Heads turned to stare as Ma, smiling in embarrassment, shushed her.

Soon after that Chhobi had borrowed the Stoler Miller translation of the *Gitagovinda* from the library, pouring over it in office.

...Make a mark with liquid deer musk on my moonlit brow!
Make a moon shadow, Krishna! The sweat drops are dried.
She told the joyful Yadu hero, playing to delight her heart.

Fix flowers in shining hair loosened by loveplay, Krishna!
Make a fly whisk outshining peacock plumage to be the banner of
love.
She told the joyful Yadu hero, playing to delight her heart.
My beautiful loins are a deep cavern to take the thrusts of love-
Cover them with jewelled girdles, cloths, and ornaments, Krishna!
She told the joyful Yadu hero, playing to delight her heart.
(The Twenty-fourth Song, sung with Raga Ramakari)

Chhobi, who   muttered the Lord's Prayer when in trouble or
secretly repeated a string of Hail Mary's, read her grandmother's
prayers in confusion. Schooled in the absolute perfection of the
Immaculate Conception the song shocked Chhobi – what was
physical or metaphysical, divine love or erotic mysticism?

Rosemary looking over her shoulder commented, 'Reading
erotica?'

'No, no… It's actually about divine love,' answered Chhobi
with a slight stutter. 'The *Gita Govinda*.'

'Let's see… humm…,' there was silence as she read on, 'quite
beautiful actually, reminds me of the Song of Solomon.'

'Whose song?'

'Solomon's – from the Old Testament.'

'Oh, the Canticles.'

'Hmm… Same thing…' Rosemary began to recite
dramatically:

'How beautiful are thy feet with shoes, O prince's daughter!
The joints of thy thighs are like jewels, the work of the hands of a
cunning workman.

Thy navel is like a round goblet, which wanteth not liquor: thy
belly is like an heap of wheat set about with lilies.

Thy two breasts are like two young roes that are twins.

Thy neck is as a tower of ivory; thine eyes like the fishpools in
Heshbon.

Thy nose…

something, Lebanon – I forget… It was part of the English

literature course in college. It's the same thing you know… earthly passion used as an example to express the complexities of divine love.'

'How do *you* know all this?'

'I do have a Masters you know,' Rosemary answered, a little annoyed at the emphasis. 'You know your problem?'

'No – what?'

'You need to forget all this divine love business… and get rid of it.'

'I am just reading, my grandmother feels very strongly about Jaydeva.'

'I wasn't referring the book, *you* need some earthly passion. I was talking about that little bit of intact tissue – don't make a big issue of it.' She grinned as she walked back to her cubbyhole, leaving a brick-red Chhobi speechless, shuffling the papers on her table.

Today Dida was waiting at the gate for her, smiling, fanning herself with a large manila envelope gaily pasted with unfamiliar stamps. 'Letter from Sonali,' she hailed, 'photographs too.' While her love for Krishna, the dark Lord, superseded other passions, she had two other obsessions, collecting family photo albums, and the Nehru clan.

While less enthusiastic about the Nehrus, as children Sonali and Chhobi had loved to look at Dida's collection of photographs. On rainy days she would let them take out the albums and examine long gone faces. They would snigger at the crimped hair lines and frilled necklines of their great-aunts. The older albums were thickly covered in umbrella black, each photograph painstakingly affixed with tiny triangular corners pasted on to the page. The pictures were almost all stiffly posed studio portraits where no one smiled. Taking a picture in those days was a solemn occasion. A tissue-thin sheet of misty paper veiled each page of photographs as though the subjects were in purdah.

Today Sonali's album was opened out on the dining table. Beginning with her Annaprasanna at six months – recognisably her, a fair baby, eyes heavily outlined with kohl and a black spot on her cheek to ward off evil eyes, the album recorded almost every event of her brief life till 1971, the year Bapi died. He was the family photographer, the keeper of their collective memories, so that Sonali and Chhobi did not actually so much remember events, but rather his black and white snapshots of them. Since he was the one usually holding the camera there were very few photographs of him. Even these were mostly shadowed or out of focus and gradually that is the image of him that they recalled.

These latest snapshots were vivid Kodakrome. As though by turning the pages of her album, Sonali had made her escape from this hot little house, so discoloured by neglect, to escape into a world of glorious Technicolour. Ma reached home as Chhobi began Sonali's letter. Flinging her bag on the table, she pulled a chair directly under the fan and collapsed into it, using a familiar motion to smooth a furrow between her eyes. 'No rain...' she said plaintively, thinking of the roads trembling with heat.

Handing her a steaming cup of tea, panacea for all ills, Dida said, 'The weather's perfect in Greece. Sonali's finished her cruise, Hong Kong, Istanbul and Piraeus. Cities we don't even visit in our dreams.'

Looking at Dida's enthusiasm for the photographs, Chhobi wondered why Ma never looked at old pictures. There were no photographs of their father around the house, save for one framed portrait by Ma's bedside. It was as though she preferred not to look back upon the past, so obviously a period when she had seen better times.

Chhobi went to the bedroom and rummaged through the old bookshelf under the window, pulling out a tattered school atlas. Bringing it to the dining table she and Dida charted the course the ship had taken. Geography in real life seemed so much more exciting than the dry lessons in school.

'It's not a cruise, Dida, it's a cargo ship carrying tapioca meal for pigs,' Chhobi corrected. She put out her hand for the thin airmail sheets, scrawled in Sonali's careless back-slant writing the nuns would never have tolerated. The pictures were of Istanbul and

Greece. Sonali smiling against a background of sunlit minarets and crumbling forts framed by the soaring arch of the bridge the ship was passing under. On the reverse of the photograph she had written, 'Istanbul view from the port wing.'

'Very nautical,' Chhobi commented, 'port is left side of the ship, isn't it?'

'She was very seasick in the Arabian Sea, they had force eight gale winds,' said Dida knowledgeably. Chhobi grinned, 'How many times have you read the letter?' she teased.

Sonali and Dadu might have occupied enemy camps in the war of the generations, but she was Dida's favourite and Chhobi knew that Sonali sent these photographs and long descriptive letters mainly for her. Dida missed her terribly. They were alike in so many ways, both beautiful and headstrong, and lived very much in the present. They loved to laugh. Sometimes both of them would be watching the Sunday evening movie on TV, Dida rubbing oil into Sonali's scalp and the rest of them would hear their laughter, wheeling, swooping and dashing against the walls. 'What's so funny?' Chhobi would ask, but they never explained.

Dida, whose hopes for the future had been so illumined by the bright flame of Sonali's beauty. A hope she had nurtured carefully between cupped palms.

Dida might now colour Sonali's unexpected marriage in the most optimistic shades but she had been terribly disappointed. She had harboured great hopes of utilising her beauty to forge an impressive alliance.

Sonali and Chandrayee. Chhobi had been born on a full moon night and given a fanciful name. The nuns had pronounced it as Shandrayee, but here in Delhi it had been abbreviated to Chand. She was Chhobi at home. Nothing very moonlight or quicksilver about her, except that she often felt like a watery reflection of Sonali, the golden girl – gold of skin with her large dark fringed eyes also shot with gold. Now Chhobi was the focus of Dida's ambitions. It was difficult taking on the role of silver lining in a cloud of Sonali's making. Dida used to look at her with such impatience at times. She was always handing Chhobi little steel bowls of herbal concoctions for lightening her skin or adding lustre to her hair. Lime juice mixed with top of the milk and besan, pounded hibiscus leaves, coconut milk. If only she could transmogrify Chhobi from lead to gold by some magical alchemy.

It was not as though Chhobi were plain or even 'homely', that favourite requirement in *The Times of India's* advertisements for brides from grooms requiring efficient homemakers. No, she had a shapely figure and large intelligent eyes, but she tended to disguise her shape in ill-tailored handloom kurtas and constant reading by dim light late into the night had given those eyes a slightly strained and myopic look. As Dida complained, she did her best to look anything *but* her best. The chief drawback was that looking at Sonali, her truly exceptional beauty, people's expectations were pitched too high.

four

An irritated expression crossed Dida's face now and Ma turned to see Mrs Chatterjee moving heavily towards the screen door. Ma and Chhobi exchanged an exasperated look as Ma got up to let her in. Chhobi rushed to the other end of the room to switch on the fan in the dining area. The last time, Mrs Chatterjee had commented on the dirty blades. Dida need not flinch now as Chhobi turned the regulator to full speed and the dirt disappeared in the whirr of the blades.

'You can get me a cold glass of water, if there's any lime I will have some sherbet,' Mrs Chatterjee declared, lowering her massive frame onto the faded sofa that creaked in protest. Her fat beringed fingers were spread on her corpulent thighs, and her many chins gave her a marked resemblance to Queen Victoria – or rather her snowy hair and dark skin made her look more like a negative of the old Queen. Her white sari proclaimed her widowed stage. Her husband had been for many years a tea taster in London and had died there. Both her sons were doctors with the National Health in the UK, and visited India infrequently. Her elder son had just made one of these rare trips and they knew they were in for a blow-by-blow account of it. Neither of her daughters-in-law could get along with her and so she lived alone. As though in compensation her sons showered her with gifts, most of which remained untouched in their original packing. Her cupboards were stacked with food processors, electric steam irons and pop-up toasters. She truly enjoyed two gifts, the large colour TV that was sent during the Asian Games and the tribal maid supplied by the convent at South Extension.

'These visits of Montu are so exhausting, he always arrives and departs in the middle of night,' she said pointedly.

'Oh, he's left, has he? We didn't get to meet him this time. How is your daughter-in-law?' asked Ma politely.

'Mishti is fine, she couldn't come as she had to visit her parents in Calcutta, but she sent me something very, very expensive,' boomed Mrs Chatterjee, who always used foghorn tones when talking to Dida. Now she'll drone on about some gadget or the other, Chhobi thought, viciously squeezing a dry, hard lime into the glass. Always bragging or grumbling.

'It is a VCR, the latest model,' she said proudly. They were impressed – nobody in the colony had one, as far as they knew. She cast a disparaging look at their black and white set, where very often the reception was so bad that the newscaster peered out of the screen as though through a blizzard.

'That's very generous, we must come over to watch a film, Montu must have brought you some tapes as well,' said Ma who was secretly a little sorry for the old lady.

'We got a letter from Sonali,' said Dida, 'she is enjoying her cruise in the Mediterranean.' Dida, Chhobi knew, had introduced Sonali as a diversionary countermove to deflect from Mrs Chatterjee's expensive imported possessions. Dida still had illusions of keeping up with the Joneses, or in this case the Chatterjees, the Dases, the Ghoshes or in fact nearly any of their neighbours, since almost all of them were better off than them.

'How is that Punjabi husband of hers, it was such a sudden wedding. Not very good-looking or qualified. In us Brahmins we don't give our girls so much liberty. He must be at least ten years older too, much more suitable agewise for our Chhobi here. How old is she now? Twenty-three?'

'She is only twenty-two,' Dida replied a little defensively. Ma and Chhobi looked at each other. She was twenty-four.

'Why don't you move with the times?' Mrs Chatterjee was relentless, 'these days it's so convenient, you can advertise in *The Times of India*. Has she got her horoscope papers? My niece got married through the matrimonial columns. She had to provide the boy's people with a computer horoscope. They don't want the old-fashioned janam patris anymore.'

'Chhobi is doing an interesting job, we will be introducing her to some good eligible boys soon,' Ma said, cutting her short. 'I only wish Sonali had got her degree.'

'I think I will see if Dadu has finished for the day,' said Chhobi, making her escape. Ma always made matters worse by springing to her defence. Ma should not worry, she was getting quite thick-skinned. Swiftly replaiting her hair in the bedroom, she could hear Mrs Chatterjee still bellowing at Dida, 'When is Sonali coming home? I need something from Europe. Can you write and ask her to get it?'

'She is returning in November. I hope it's nothing heavy,' Dida replied reluctantly.

'No, no, Montu forgot to bring it, I need it for the VCR, it's so dusty in Delhi, he said I must use it regularly.'

'What? What do you need to use so slowly?' Dida had a selective deafness that allowed her to switch off conversations that didn't really interest her. Chhobi sometimes wondered exactly how deaf she was, she had seen her drop her ladle in the kitchen when the old Bakelite radiogram played *Bageshri*, her favourite raga.

'It's something called head cleaning spray,' Mrs Chatterjee was continuing.

'Head cleaning? You mean shampoo. I never use it, full of harmful chemicals. Reetha soap nuts are the best. Just look at my hair, scarcely any grey in it,' Dida said proudly. It would probably take all night to sort that out, Chhobi thought with a wry smile.

Chhobi ran out of the drawing room to her grandfather's clinic across the small garden, where Dadu was reading an old *Reader's Digest* magazine.

Clinic. It was, in the circumstances, an ambitious, euphemistic word matching up only to the grandeur of the name painted in old-fashioned italics on the board outside – Dr Dharani Dhar Talukdar, MBBS. Dusty yellow curtains block printed with maroon camels partitioned half the garage. The curtains were from Sanganer and had bled in the first wash, making the camels turn blurry as though lashed by a sandstorm. Behind them were stacked black painted wooden packing boxes, which contained most of their possessions. These were stencilled in white with their father's name and the military APO address. Dida and their neighbours had packed them thirteen years ago in Simla. They numbered 1 to 41.

Yesterday's newspapers piled on the floor grew in stalagmite configurations until the kabadiwala's next visit. In front of the curtains there was a metal table with a laminated top and two chairs of bent steel pipes with plastic cane work. On the wall were framed some gory pages pulled from a pharmaceutical calendar depicting scenes of medieval surgery. Pictures of surgeons in blood-stained leather aprons holding down screaming patients like inept butchers were enough to turn the stomachs of all but the most stoic of Dadu's visitors. Several generations of geckoes, some pale brown, others mottled black lived behind these illustrations.

Dadu put down the magazine and began to lock up once Chhobi called him. He did all the kitchen shopping and meal times were practically the only times when he could whip up any *joie de vivre*. On the rare occasions when a dish was indifferently prepared he would conduct an incisive post-mortem of what had gone wrong. A short man, a truly hearty appetite had added layers of bulk, and the girls had been amused to discover that his pants measured length 40", waist 40".

The market was close by, just a ten-minute walk. On the way they met Ratan Kaku, Dadu's childhood friend, several years younger than him. His was the sole exception that preserved Dadu from the exclusive company of women. He was just emerging from a meeting of the EPDP Society.

'What actually does EPDP stand for?' Chhobi had once asked Ratan Kaku.

'It's what we are,' replied Kaku simply, 'East Pakistan Displaced Persons.'

'East Pakistan? But there's no such place anymore,' Chhobi had objected, refusing to be identified by such an anachronistic acronym.

'The death of East Pakistan was inevitable, the defect lay in the conception, in Jinnah's two-nation theory. Bengalis would belong to Bangladesh sooner rather than later.' Ratan Kaku employed a pedantic turn of phrase.

'We would never have left our home if it had become Bangladesh in 1947,' Dadu had added a little bitterly. EPDP, an ironical sobriquet in the circumstances, considering they had forsaken everything to avoid being labelled Pakistani in the first place. Being Hindu in a Muslim State, could it be any harder than feeling so foreign in this land-locked aggressive city? Dadu had left behind his home, his estates, his dreams and aspirations when he fled Mymensingh in 1947. Although he carried with him nothing, he was considered luckier than others, because he had a medical degree and was married to the daughter of a rich man from Calcutta.

⁂

The market came alive at dusk when it was cooler. Vegetables gleamed fresh and typical to the Bengali palate – bunches of puce coloured banana flowers, stringy bundles of drumsticks, fat striated potols – vegetables difficult to find in any other market in Delhi. A long string of hissing petromax lanterns lit up the fish stalls, spilling onto the narrow sidewalk. Perched behind blocks of cooling ice, the mongers shouted prices in hoarse voices, their wares spread before them in piscatorial plenty – bhetki, rohu, ilish, koi, katla and other smaller fry. The white lights reflected off scales that shimmered and changed hue, mostly silver but sometimes lead, sometimes pewter.

Dadu must have actually had a couple of patients today. They were heading towards the fish quite purposefully. Chhobi almost stumbled over a tin tub containing small brown crabs that stiffly clambered over one another, too tiny for any real meat in their claws. Inspecting a large rohu carefully to see how fresh it was, Dadu examined the eye, prodded the belly and lifted the fan-shaped gill to confirm the unspoiled redness underneath. Satisfied as all his tests passed muster, he nodded and the vendor cut off a one-kilo chunk, gutting it with care so as not to puncture the bile sac. They watched as he deftly sloughed off the iridescent scales, the sickle-shaped blade of the sharp knife held upright on his foot, gripped firmly by his big toe.

'Good fish,' said Ratan Kaku. He had a long history of chronic stomach complaints and survived on dull boiled fare, chiefly vegetarian in content. He would vicariously spice up his meals with daily trips to the market, where he stared at the gleaming fish or the plump tandoori chickens roasting at the roadside dhaba. A gastronomic voyeur.

Today he authoritatively asked the fish-monger prices of bhetki and rohu. The man was rude, and quoted impossibly inflated prices, dismissing Ratan Kaku, muttering offensively under his breath that he never ever bought anything, merely wasted his time. Dadu and Chhobi hurriedly steered him away before an ugly argument ensued.

Ratan Kaku's other pastime was drafting letters to editors. As a retired bachelor, he had plenty of time to spare. He was presently waging a war against the land developers who threatened to turn their modest colony into a so far imaginary jungle of gimcrack apartment blocks.

'Look out tomorrow,' he confided, taking a furtive sip from a bottle of milky pink antacid, which he carried in a packet, almost surreptitiously like a secret tippler. 'I am sure it will be published.'

'What is it now?' Dadu was impatient, thinking of the fish. Dadu abhorred change too but believed he was helpless to prevent it. He felt Ratan Kaku's ravings were futile.

'That man Goel, who bought the Bose's house, I have found out he is a building contractor, suppose he puts up a five storey block of flats? What will happen to my light and my air? As it is the Asian Games have ruined my rent prospects.'

'Asian Games?' Chhobi found the sudden mention of the event Indira Gandhi had used to beautify Delhi hard to reconcile with a reduction in property values.

'What's the matter?' asked Dadu quietly. Kaku did appear to be more than usually agitated.

Ratan Kaku did not receive any pension, but managed to live comfortably off the rent he received from his first floor. He, like many Delhi landlords, had a simple but inflexible rule about tenants. They must be South Indian and employed by a public limited company.

'You know my tenants, the Menons, had signed a three-year lease, but now with a year still to go Mrs Menon is talking of moving somewhere quieter and less polluted. Their six-year-old has started wheezing ever since the flyover came up in front of the house. She also complained that she is kept awake most of the night with the traffic noises. Now if we have an apartment block next door, I will be stifled. That Goel is also bound to install a booster pump in my water line and suck me dry.' He winced as a stomach cramp twisted his insides.

'Don't worry so much, Kaku, things will work out,' Chhobi interjected placatingly, but Dadu was stern. 'All this worrying will give you ulcers, why don't you just ask Mr Goel?'

'I don't speak to him, the one time I did he asked me if my house was for sale.'

'You had better wait until you're sure of his intentions, it's not right to make false allegations in the newspapers.'

Chhobi left them arguing there and ran to the sweet shop. The glass fronted shelves displayed trays piled high with sugary delights.

Flies buzzed in frustration and greed, as the sweets temptingly garnished with saffron, almonds and beaten silver leaf remained tantalisingly out of reach. She asked for an earthenware pot of mishti doi and bought a smaller one for Ratan Kaku. Yoghurt couldn't harm his stomach.

⁂

Returning home, it was fish that set Dadu off. 'In our home, I never saw anyone buy a piece of fish,' said Dadu. 'Our home' to him was always the rambling joint family estate in Mymensingh. The land the family had owned stretched beyond the line of vision in softly rippling paddy fields, now lost forever in Bangladesh.

'We never bought fish. We had our own ponds and used a net to scoop them out by the score,' he continued, swimming back into the great stream of his reminiscence.

'Tell me about the mangoes, Dadu.' Chhobi had heard it all before, but she loved to hear him describe the sheer abundance of the times he had grown up in.

'Why mangoes, the orchards surrounding our house would yield bushels of purple jamun, jackfruits bigger than babies, seedless guavas pink fleshed, coconuts...' shifting the stained cloth shopping bag to his other hand, he continued, 'during the mango season the fruit arrived in big baskets cushioned with straw. Some from our own orchards and some sent over from my mother's family. The big deep verandah at the back was stacked with these baskets. The whole house would smell of the ripening fruit. I would eat no rice, only fruit until I grew sick of the taste.'

'What mangoes were your favourite, Dadu?'

'Himsagar, pale fleshed langras and chousas. Mangoes were served as snacks, for breakfast and for jalkhabar, our afternoon tea. The best was mango pulp mixed with creamy thick khir. We had a big brass tub, we would fill it with water. The iceman always delivered blocks of ice wrapped in jute cloth in the mornings. We would float a big block together with a bushel of mangoes in the tub. Then we would sit around it, gorging ourselves till the juice ran

~ 36 ~

down our chins and dripped in sticky rivers from wrist to elbow,' he said, lapsing into silence.

He began thinking of the light, in the end he did not know what he missed more, the light or the water. That sparkling riverine landscape.

The harsh flat white of Delhi's summers, so blinded him that he could scarcely focus on the dwarf shadows that followed behind him and made him long for the light of Mymensingh. Diffused, green, a liquid light that brightened each day with a lambent quality and allowed his gaze to travel beyond the far stretching fields to where the clumps of bamboo formed a tossing palisade.

Although he might have escaped the bloody carnage that followed Partition physically unscathed, the uprooting had so traumatised him that he remained forever in exile, a prisoner of his own memories.

Once removed from the protective glow of Dr Mitra's polished bedside manner he could never recover professionally and his patients continued to dwindle. Most of them were poor migrant labour, and they usually left it so late that they required to be immediately hospitalised, never to make a repeat visit. The unfamiliar burden of balancing the household budget was proving too much for him, until Ma took over.

Dida and Ma managed things far more efficiently now, but both of them were careful to disguise any major purchases as a decision of Dadu's making.

There was one area of his life that Dadu guarded fiercely. He would brook no interference in the garden, where he carefully nurtured shrubs and trees which produced only white or cream blossoms, almost all chosen for their perfume rather than the beauty of their flowers. Perhaps it was a lost purity he hankered for, as all colours converged to white through the prism of his lens.

Flanking the gate were Chandini and Kamini, like two sirens of the silver screen, waiting in the wings. Close by was the temperamental gandharaj or gardenia that responded to his touch by producing a profusion of layered blooms. The flowerbed leading to the main door was thickly planted with tuberoses whose scent Chhobi found too overpowering. There was a champa tree in the corner, surviving despite the merciless amputation of its limbs to make way for the winter sun every year. The gold-centred fleshy flowers were her favourite, bunches of them fringed with whorls of dark green leaves that turned glossy when the dust was washed off. Outside the boundary wall glinting with jagged glass, flourished a kadamba tree planted many years ago at Dida's request. The tree was rooted in mythology, for under it Lord Krishna had dallied with his maidens and played his flute. The tree thrilled into blossom at the first sound of thunder, in July when Delhi turned green, freshly washed with rain. The flowers like fist-sized golden orbs closely studded with white stamens as though rolled in confectioner's sugar, attracted clouds of bees and butterflies, a rare sight in the midst of South Delhi.

He had also planted in the backyard a seoli tree. Chootu, their twice-weekly teenage gardener called it haar singaar, so much more lyrical, it looked like a poem too. The tree shed its fragrant flowers, white with their brilliant orange carpels twice a year. The girls used to sometimes spread an old sheet under the tree, when in bloom, and gather the sweet-smelling flowers that were shed overnight – they would then thread them into garlands for Dida's Krishna.

Dadu was a taciturn apolitical man – he didn't indulge in any adda discussions. He might blame the British for Partition, but he didn't particularly dislike them. In fact, there were many spheres in which he compared their functioning very favourably to the present Indian government. His swadeshi effort was confined to one area. He loathed English flowers – gaudy and scentless, he called them.

It was the first real difference he had with his daughter. Used to cantonment gardens vivid with annuals, she had, in the first year she returned to live with them, planted asters, stocks, sweet william and hollyhocks. Ma had been well pleased with her efforts until looking out from the window one day she had seen Dadu swish viciously with his walking stick at a dahlia of prize-winning dimensions. That was the only time she put down any winter flowers.

Chhobi enjoyed Dadu's fragrant night garden. It reminded her of Shah Jehan's Mahtab Garden at the Red Fort which had been planted with select aromatic shrubs that bloomed only by the light of the moon. She wondered if Ma felt it wore a funereal air. White widow's weeds. Ma did wear colours, though nothing bright and nothing red. In gardens she still longed for the entire vibgyor spectrum, instead of these pallid flowers, palely visible. She satisfied herself with looking at the roundabouts in Lutyen's Delhi on the way to work.

five

The taps made a hollow gurgling sound the next morning and ran dry. The water pressure was sufficient only to reach upto the garden tap. Dadu stood sentinel next to it, patiently watching the thin stream leak sluggishly into the galvanised metal bucket. A blotched neem leaf from an overhanging branch spun lazily down and drifted into the bucket where it undulated gently on the water's surface. A scimitar-shaped leaf, the outer edge of the arc wilted yellow, blending to a glowing green. Sunlight soaked into the webbing of the bitter-sap veins. Dadu's eye glanced off the arc at a familiar tangent.

The curve recreated as a yellow tangail sari bordered in green billowed like the sail on an eighteenth-century galleon. Mymensingh and the many ponds of his estate flashing silver like mirrors embedded in the mind. His mother, bathing in the pond, or *pukur* as they called it, reserved solely for women. The edges of the circumference fringed with tall reeds. Just the entrance to the water's edge screened by the sari stretched across bamboo poles. Liquid splashes alight with radiance borrowed from the sun. Water – so much of it. A shout from Dida snapped him back into the present. The bucket was full, overflowing. He closed the tap and tightened it so as not to waste a drop. Slowly he picked out the neem leaf and put it in his mouth. Chewing deliberately he savoured the leaf's bitter astringent taste.

Chhobi missed her chartered bus that day due to her much-delayed bath. The overhead tank was adequate only for the kitchen where the dirty gaping mouths of last night's pots and pans required quenching, only after which a scant half a bucket could be spared for her. Dadu had used up two buckets to water his precious plants, reluctantly leaving a little for Ma.

The minibus Chhobi squeezed into soon had her bathed in sweat. She did not need to add to the jungle of upraised arms clinging to the overhead straps for support. So firmly wedged was she that the hot press of bodies from every side ensured she could not fall no matter how sharp the turn. The rank hairy stench emanating from a multiple of exposed armpits forced her to take very shallow breaths.

It was with relief that she found a seat after three stops. Black and white notices pasted above the windows caught her eye. They were warnings issued by the Delhi Police. The crude artwork illustrating them were a grim reminder of how troubled times were. The notices exhorted citizens to 'Look under their bus/train seats for explosives', 'Beware of suspicious packages' or 'Avoid strangers offering food and drinks'. Chhobi shifted gingerly to peer under the seat in front of her, but all she could see were some torn-up scraps of paper, and burnt-out bidi stubs.

Rosemary called Chhobi into her office that afternoon. The incipient disgust on her face made Chhobi exchange a look of dismay with the copy editor who had also been summoned. Mrs Iyer, tired, menopausal but one who still measured her month with the ticking regularity of deadlines.

Outside the white heat was deranging and they did not have the energy to cope with Rosemary's ire. She gestured at a pile of letters on her desk, 'They all say the same thing, how can a magazine on Delhi ignore politics? What about Punjab? We should deal with serious issues such as ethnic tension, separatism… and so on and on and on.'

'It's this Blue Star, Indira Gandhi made a huge mistake with Bhindranwale,' murmured Mrs Iyer, referring to the almost daily terrorist incidents where Hindus were offloaded buses and shot at point blank range. Chhobi nodded. Certainly since the sixth of June, when the army had entered the Golden Temple and desecrated the holiest shrine of the Sikhs, life in the Punjab had become even more violent.

'Overconfident she is after creating Bangladesh, she is meddling in Sri Lanka as well, supporting the LTTE, another Frankenstein in the making,' she offered.

Mrs Iyer added, forehead breaking into a frown, 'It was the LTTE that blew up a part of Madras Airport last week, that's more or less confirmed. My husband was at that airport only a day before the blast. An article on terrorism would be very topical.'

Rosemary wanted to edit an inconsequential thing of beauty, an ode to Delhi, with soft focus on weathered monuments, cultural events and artists with an 'e'. She chafed at reality that turned poetry into politics. She glared at both of them.

'We are supposed to promote tourism. Five-star hotels keep our magazine in their rooms. Do you imagine it's going to boosts sales if readers expect to be blown apart by bombs?'

'But... They may have a point... I think it is our duty to warn our readers... I mean they should at least become more vigilant,' said Chhobi.

'Our duty! Chandrayee, that still small voice of yours, it's deafening. I haven't taken on the burden of a saviour. Who do you think you are? Mother Teresa? —Get a life!'

Chhobi smarted at Rosemary's words, she was sick of being described as a repressed puritan. It was the reference to Mother Teresa that rankled, raking up a tiff she had had with Sonali many months ago. Back at her desk, she was unable to continue work on another piece eulogising one of Delhi's beautiful monuments. She began to doodle a string of explosive stars. Glaring at the page, she relived the squabble.

It had begun with Sonali snipping away at a black T-shirt she had bought at Janpath. Swiftly edging the altered neckline with a silver trim, she tried it on.

'What do you think?'

Trying her best to sound casual, Chhobi remarked, 'Isn't the neckline a bit too plunging?'

Sonali twirled around the room sinuous in a black and silver dervish dance – 'V in the front,' and picking up her plait, 'V at the back – two V's make a W – W for wow!' The front V an arrowhead, a sexual signpost pointing straight down, between those high breasts that wobbled slightly as she struck a pose.

'It's about as subtle as a DTC bus!'

'I suppose you think a nun's habit with that blinker headgear is subtle. That's why you always dress in grey or beige. It makes your skin look like mud. Remember that even Mother Teresa left your stooopid school because she preferred the sari,' grinned Sonali, the little snort of laughter an additional barb.

'That's hardly the reason why she left,' muttered Chhobi furious, at the same time suddenly doubtful that she was, as usual, letting sense overrule sensibility. It was sometimes so tiring maintaining her balance on this pedestal of surrogate motherhood she had placed herself on.

six

It was exactly six months ago, that Chhobi learnt about Sonny's identity. A whole lifetime ago. Sonali's lifetime. Her previous life wiped clean in one smooth swipe.

They were all sitting together on the verandah where the cane chairs needed urgent repair. The girls preferred to sit on the ground, where the cement floor met the singed lawn. Afternoon was dwindling to evening, but the summer's day was long enough for Dida to read by the fading light. The empty teacups attracted a couple of lethargic flies. A pigeon fluttered softly as it alighted on the dusty wall light. It was an hour of the day when Dida could relax, a lull between meals. Sonali was pestering Ma for a pair of dark green dark glasses with metal frames.

'Goggles' Dida called dark glasses.

'Why do you need goggles?' she asked Sonali sharply for once. 'With the hours you are keeping, and the shadows under your eyes, you are wearing god-given ones. Meera, do you know what she is up to?' Sonali's face took on a blank switched-off expression like the TV screen when the power went.

The furrow between Ma's eyebrows grew deeper. Chhobi tried to change the subject. 'What are you reading Dida? Must be on

Nehru.' In Dida's mind Nehru occupied a space only slightly less elevated than Lord Krishna's. She collected all books on and by him. After his death, the same feelings of hero worship had extended to include his daughter Indira.

'*The Return of the Red Rose.*'

'Sounds like a cross between Louis L' amour and the Scarlet Pimpernel.'

'It's on Indira Gandhi's life.'

'Why Red Rose? What a stupid title.'

'Because her father always wore a red rose on his lapel,' Dida explained a little severely.

Dida admired Nehru's writing and his chiselled features, that urbane upper class Brahmin look. If the father and daughter had been ugly, Chhobi doubted that she would have followed their lives with such extreme attention. A highly developed aesthetic sense had always been Dida's Achilles heel.

Dadu, who had been worrying if termites had attacked the champa tree in the corner of the garden, suddenly joined in the conversation.

'I am not even going to mention the Emergency, but just that name Gandhi... always coupled with Mahatma... Suppose she had had some other Parsi surname – like Sodabottleopnerwala or Daruwala? No one would have voted for her... relied on the magic names totally – Nehru and Gandhi.'

Dida did not deign to answer. In a show of temper she shut the book with a snap and stalked indoors, the lightness of the evening evaporating with the sound.

Late at night, Chhobi who still hadn't questioned her sister looked at her listening to Kishore Kumar songs on All India Radio. There were numerous requests coming in from some very idle people in Jhumritalaya.

Convinced she could no longer turn a blind eye towards Sonali's frequent absences, she propped herself on one elbow and switched on the bedside lamp.

'Who is he?' she asked quietly.

For a long time only Kishore Kumar was heard singing:

Mera jeevan kora kaagaz
Kora he rah gaya...

'His name is Sonny,' Sonali answered finally. 'Sonny Talwar.'

Punjabi, thought Chhobi with extreme prejudice. Punjabis were usually so overwhelmed at producing a male child that they had to reinforce the fact by giving the baby names like Sonny. Chhobi had only glimpsed a red imported car, his view through the rear window receding down the road. Fair-skinned with longish hair.

'Where did you meet him? What does he do? How old is he? Are you serious about him?'

The questions stacked up, a teetering house of cards.

'I met him at Ghungroo.' Sonali had a watchful expression on her face.

'Ghungroo! The disco... When did you go there? Isn't it very expensive?'

'Don't be silly, I don't ever pay.'

'Never pay – Have you been there often? What is it like? Is it nice?' Chhobi's voice grew a little shrill, amazed at the life her younger sister was leading... so far removed from her own.

'Nice? No, it is not *nice*. It's very dark – darkness you can feel, like sinking into black velvet.' Sonali's metaphors usually drew on fabrics and garments for inspiration. 'The floor is made up of glass squares which light up in tune to the music.' She began to smile dreamily. She was thinking back to the night that she had first met Sonny. His face appearing alternately red or yellow under the spinning strobe lights. All she could see clearly were his teeth flashing with the lights, head moving easily in tune to the music despite the crush of the gyrating crowd

'Is he Indu's friend?'

Chhobi reflected, although she realised that she was too late in doing so, that perhaps Indu was not the most appropriate friend for Sonali. Indu belonged to a closely-knit and very large family. Her parents allowed her a great deal of freedom, cocooned as she was in the safety of the numerous and burly cousins who always accompanied her. Dida was very fond of her and never worried about Sonali when she was with Indu.

'Who introduced you?'

'Nobody did – he asked me for a dance. Indu had taken us there for her birthday.'

'How could you dance with a perfect stranger?'

'He is very good looking' Sonali said as though that explained everything, then she added softly, 'and very rich.' Sonali was prattling on, the enforced secrecy of so many months spilt out, split open. 'Royal Bengali Tigress, he calls me. My eyes you know, like a cat's he says. He wants to meet you and Ma.'

But Chhobi scarcely heard anything beyond that 'very rich'. The words filled her with foreboding and a plummeting sense of fear, an indefinable danger she felt unable to forestall. The house of cards tumbling down. As for Sonali, she remained secretive no longer, convincing Dida she had found the ideal suitor.

⁕

It was winter when Chhobi finally met Sonny.

Mid January and on some days car headlights on till noon as Delhi shivered, shrouded in fog and the smoke of fallen leaves burning at every other crossing, swept into shifting pyramids and set alight by the municipal sweepers. On the rare sunny days, Dida would rush to spread out the quilts in the backyard where they would puff up with warmth and fade in uneven streaks. Savitri brought powdered wood ash from her home to fortify the detergent she used to scrub the congealed greasy vessels. Her hands red in the icy water, a fistful of bee-stings. Ratan Kaku donned his brown knitted balaclava cap, leaving just a circle of face visible, a dyspeptic langur. Chhobi wore Simla-acquired long johns under her salwar, and woollen army issue olive green socks. The gaps between hairwash days grew longer and herbal remedies for dandruff were debated.

The Talwars, Sonny's large family, always celebrated Lohri, symbolically the end of winter. Sonny invited them all, Ma and Chhobi along with Sonali. Ma refused to go but insisted a very reluctant Chhobi accompany Sonali.

The house was thrown into a flurry of activity about what the girls should wear Sonali wanted to wear her rather form-fitting black dress, but Dida told her to wear something more traditional.

Ma's saris. They would cut them up into salwar kameez outfits.

Sonali poured over Ma's lists, neatly written contents packed into forty-one black wooden boxes, thirteen years ago, stacked in the garage-cum-clinic. Annually aired and moth balled with the help of Savitri and Chootu.

Boxes thirty-seven and twenty-six contained Ma's wedding saris. Brocades from Benares, Baluchoris, Kanthas intricately worked in running stitch from Shantiniketan, heavy silks from the south and gossamer tissues. Saris all richly embroidered or woven with leaves, tendrils and vines, blossoms, elephants and peacocks. Saris Dida had collected painstakingly since Ma was born. Worn for so short a season, then carefully preserved with layers of dried neem leaves, wrapped in white muslin – a shrouded youth.

Along with Savitri the girls heaved at the stacked boxes in the garage, and dragged numbers thirty-seven and twenty-six to Dida's bedroom. Ma, Dida and Savitri crowded around as Chhobi unlocked the boxes and carefully unpacked the shimmering contents, spilling them on to the bed. The colours were fit for a bride – ruby, garnet and plum, peach, claret and rose. Colours Ma could not, would not ever wear. The air took on the slightly bitter acrid smell of the interspersed layers of dried neem leaves. The bitter smell of loneliness and disuse.

Sonali instinctively knew what suited her – burnished her skin with a golden lustre, brought out the liquid amber tones of her eyes, set off her slender form with surprisingly heavy breasts and delicate wrists and ankles. She turned heads even when casually clad in jeans and T-shirt, her normal garb, but when she did bother to dress in something more elaborate, she filled the house with excitement and pride. Dour Dadu smiling and Dida and Ma mirroring each other's proud expressions. Chhobi not really into appearances, but basically appreciative.

Her inbuilt sense of style had been sharpened further by her own efforts. She could talk fabric drape and fall for hours with Ma, something that didn't interest Chhobi at all. Sonali would often make forays to the Sunday market pavement stalls at Darya Ganj and pick up outdated copies of *Vogue* and *Harpers*. She learnt to accessorise effectively and recognised how to look expensive with the minimum of outlay.

Sonali shook her head dismissively as Dida draped a maroon brocade around her and instinctively picked up another from the pile. It was a sari in shot silk, the warp of the thread apricot and the weft a beautiful salmon pink, unravelling into a galaxy of tiny silver and gold stars. A dawn sky with night stars still shimmering. Wrapping it around herself, she moved to Dida's dressing table – a heavy piece of furniture with bevelled mirrors in three wings. The rest of them moved with her like ladies-in-waiting.

Sonali multiplied. Sonali reflected back at them in a series of infinite images, each smaller image seemingly more gorgeous than the first. Ma, Dida, Savitri and Chhobi all smiling – this was the one. Savitri rushed to the kitchen and came back with some smoking chillies, which she circled around Sonali to take care of all evil eyes.

Ma picked out a blue Bangalore silk for Chhobi, the colour of a peacock's feather, edged with a narrow gold border. Chhobi moved to the mirror too, wrapping the pallu across her shoulders. She peered into the mirror, a little myopically, and it grew foggy with her warm breath – Chhobi reflected back in a hazy image as though from a great distance.

Sonali's preparations for the party were those of a bride for her wedding. For half an hour she suffered one of Dida's herbal face packs, cold and dripping – until it slowly hardened into a stiff mask. Her hair, normally swinging in a heavy plait was left loose, blow-dried at the beauty parlour, gleaming as blue-black as a Simla sky by night. Each strand glittering individually and falling heavy to her hips as though weighted with a plumb line.

Sonny was to pick them up in twenty minutes. Spreading her fingers in a wide arc to let the paint dry, she asked Chhobi to do up the hooks on her kurta. Chhobi complied with hands that trembled a little, 'What's wrong?' queried Sonali, 'hasn't he fixed the hooks properly?'

'Tenterhooks,' replied Chhobi, 'the tailor's done a good job, it's just my tenterhooks.'

Although ill at ease Chhobi was looking unusually chic in the straight lines of the silk that showed up her slim figure to advantage. Her hair was glossy in a bun, not her usual unkempt plait with wispy strands escaping in a ragged frame around her face, on which she chewed in absent-minded fashion while reading..

They were all very curious about Sonny, but he did not come in, merely blew loudly on the car horn from the gate. Sonali giving a last satisfied look at her reflection in the mirror flew out when she heard, hair and dupatta streaming behind. Chhobi followed more slowly, she thought it rude that he did not come in to meet Ma. Dida was exclaiming about what a beautiful granddaughter she had. Chhobi smiled to hear Dadu correct her, *two beautiful granddaughters,* he said. At the gate she turned back to look towards the house. She could sense rather than see Dida watching them from behind a chink in the parted curtains.

At first glance he seemed very handsome, although quite a bit older than Sonali, at least twenty-six or seven.

'Hi,' he said casually, his eyes on Sonali as she introduced Chhobi, referring to her as Chandrayee. Chhobi got into the back seat, looking at him from under lowered brows. Yes, there was a definite air of a peacock about him, everything just a shade too fashionable. The cut of his jacket slightly too sharp, his shoes a trifle too prominently stitched along the vamp, the perfume he exuded a bit too overpowering. He wore his hair long. It was expensively cut in layers to add thickness, and lifted when he turned his head, settling back on his scalp with an easy assurance. A close trimmed brown moustache accentuated the sensuous line of his upper lip. She noticed how he used the rear-view mirror, not to check on the traffic behind him but to view himself in satisfaction. A Michael Douglas chin.

The Talwars lived in a bungalow in Friends Colony. As they entered into the curving drive, Chhobi looked at the house, all lit up for the party. The Mughal monuments she had studied had honed her taste in architecture, and she couldn't help wrinkling her nose at the misalliance of East and West the house represented. Mediterranean balconies had been married with corbelled arches and sandstone fretwork jaalis. Heavy-duty air conditioners installed in a multiple of windows gave the house a closed in, secretive look.

Soft murmuring voices, garden lights glinting on hand-cut crystal glasses and on the diamonds clustered on ear lobes and fingers, gloved waiters like portly penguins circulating silently with bottles of Scotch whiskey. In the centre of the driveway curving past the circular lawn, was the bonfire. Not lit yet, two servants were piling more and more logs onto it. The stack was almost six feet high.

This was not what Chhobi had expected. Lohri, a purely North Indian festival, was normally more like a friendly neighbourhood affair where everyone lounged around packing case bonfires, cracking jokes and peanuts. She was conscious of the fact that Sonali had taken pains to ensure they were not dressed for some informal neighbourhood celebration. The mandatory peanuts, puffed cereal and rewri were there on hand-painted trays, but the guests ignored them, helping themselves instead to miniature mushroom vol-au-vents, chilli paneer cubed with green pepper and charcoal grilled chicken tikkas melting in the mouth. Celebrating the passing of winter's longest night.

Sonny's mother came to greet them – a thin elegant woman, she was simply but expensively dressed with a shahtoosh shawl over one shoulder hiding the beautiful Kashmiri embroidery on her beige satin sari. Her smile did not reach her eyes, merely touched her mouth with the cold graciousness of condescension. Chhobi glanced apprehensively at Sonali's clothes – suddenly the stars on it seemed to flash a little tawdry, twinkle a little too bright. She tried unobtrusively to wrap her sensible black shawl around the gold edging of her own kurta neckline. Sonali had refused to carry any woollens and seemed to have no doubts about her apparel. Or her appearance.

She was on good terms with several of Sonny's school friends. Typically boarding school educated and obviously used to money, the air was loud with school nicknames and back-slapping in the cause of bonhomie. Sonny was nicknamed 'Chut Dodo,' a name Chhobi thought most unsuitable for a six-footer – Chut meaning tiny. Sonali explained later, Dodo was his elder brother, five years his senior at school, now running the shipping wing of the business in Bombay. Sonny was Chut Dodo.

Sonali waved at Chhobi, allowing herself to be steered in the direction of the house by Sonny. Chhobi looked around uncomfortably. Sonny's father and uncle lacked the elegance his mother had displayed. They looked what they were, brothers and prosperous businessmen held together by their shared need to make more and more money. Both were dressed in dark grey or black Nehru-collared coats.

The uncle, referred to almost reverentially by everyone as Bhai Sahib, being the elder brother, was seated on a sofa facing the unlit bonfire, next to a man draped in a shawl. His height was apparent even while sitting down, for he dwarfed those near him. He gesticulated vigorously as he talked, wrist wrapped in sacred red thread and fingers flashing with several rings set with stones of astrological importance – emerald for health and sapphire for wealth. Gold-rimmed spectacles glinted on his nose. Stray snatches of conversation drifted across to Chhobi as she stood helping herself to chicken tikkas, dunking them in green coriander chutney.

'Location, that's the only thing that matters in real estate, not construction, nothing but location.'

Bhai Sahib beckoned at the waiter, who hurried over and bent to refill his companion's glass with Scotch whiskey. More Scotch is drunk annually in India than Scotland is capable of producing,

Chhobi remembered reading that somewhere. Sonny's father joined Bhai Sahib who, Chhobi realised, was looking after a minor politician from the Punjab. He had links to a cabinet minister, someone was whispering.

Now the waiter offered Chhobi a glass of white wine, a first for her. The only alcohol she had imbibed till now was some rather unpalatable rum punch at college parties. The wine tasted good, not intoxicating at all. It stopped her shivering. Sonali was nowhere to be seen. Tired of teetering on high heels, borrowed from Ma, Chhobi perched on a garden chair. She took a second glass of wine, downing the first almost in one go. Sonny's mother sat on a sofa nearby listening to a man in a purplish blazer, a shade too tight. Staring into her glass Chhobi concentrated on their conversation.

'Madam, I have understood your requirement exactly.'

'Really? And what is that?'

'You need a decor that is constantly changing, so that you are never bored. I know just the thing, I suggest you convert one wall into an aquarium, floor to ceiling. It will be full of movement, always changing.'

'A bit like one of those James Bond movie sets,' Sonny's mother replied, the disparaging note coming through.

They were going to light the fire now, a servant was pushing in the kindling – crumpled newspapers soaked in kerosene. The wood caught with a loud crackle and Chhobi could no longer hear Sonny's mother.

Bhai Sahib's wife joined the circle, seating herself with her two friends to the right of Chhobi. An obese woman, wealth had not added anything but weight to her appearance. She had badly dyed coal black hair with an Indira Gandhi streak in white above her temple. Dark lipstick stained her teeth with maroon, like the tidemarks of a receding smile. She was talking to another woman in Punjabi. Chhobi concentrating on her third glass of wine could follow the gist of the conversation. The fire was smoking badly, her eyes watered. She wished she were back at home, in bed with a book, tucked into a warm quilt. *Where was* Sonali?

Mrs Bhai Sahib was commenting about the many entrepreneurial pies the brothers had thrust their fingers into. It was very creditable, the listener commented, to build up such an empire after losing so much during Partition.

Mrs Bhai Sahib laughed – apparently the family had lost nothing in Partition but gained a great deal. Sonny's grandfather used to own a small business in Sialkot, Pakistan before Partition. The family was comfortable, though not wealthy. It was Partition that had made them. Bhai Sahib had gambled every penny by taking a room at Imperial Hotel, then Delhi's most expensive hotel. Here he had mingled with the most influential displaced families from Lahore.

The hotel stay was to prove a wise investment. Contacts made there had helped him and he had seized every opportunity. He had acquired a thriving agricultural implement factory left by a fleeing Muslim household in Old Delhi, for a song. The brothers had dealt in emergency supplies to refugees camped in Delhi, and Sonny's father had travelled throughout North India earmarking handsome properties belonging to wealthy Muslims which had been abandoned as they fled to Pakistan. He had then systematically cut corners and tape until he acquired four such mansions for a pittance. Location was the key. They had all appreciated manifold by the time he had disposed of them. So he had wooed and won Sonny's mother too. She was from one of Delhi's old families with far-reaching connections that touched the right places.

Both Mrs Bhai Sahib and her companion seemed to think the brother's business acumen laudable.

'Opportunism in the extreme,' thought Chhobi in distaste. She had a sudden bleak picture of Dadu and Dida fleeing their beautiful colonnaded family home in Mymensingh, with brigand bands like the Talwars waiting to pounce – to plunder. She felt a little sick, and rather unwisely helped herself to more chicken tikkas.

Sonny and Sonali drifted back and joined the circle around the fire, which was blazing now. Sonali seemed to be floating, very happy, lit up from inside with a wonderful radiance. Sonny sat next to her, and laid his arm in a proprietorial manner over the back of her chair, a circlet of desire. Sonali looked sideways at the arm, smiled, then gazed at the blazing logs. Firelight turned her clothes and skin a warm hue of apricot outlined by a thread of flame. A glow emanated from her – an effluence. She seemed so outstanding in that crowd – a tropical butterfly wandered in amongst so many drab moths.

Mrs Bhai Sahib was asking who was the 'soni kudi'. Chhobi was about to answer when she caught sight of Bhai Sahib staring at Sonali. It may have been a trick of light, just an illusion, the flames reflecting off the lenses of the gold-rimmed spectacles, but the sudden roaring crackle of the fire drowned out all rational thought. A spasm of pain twisted her gut as the fear and apprehension of so many months erupted. The reflection of the flames appeared so that it seemed as though the fire was raging inside Bhai Sahib's head. Flames licking at the circumference of his eyes – a rage, fiery, spreading, destroying.

The shifting pain in Chhobi's stomach intensified. She had a fierce urge to throw up and defecate at the same time. She tightened her muscles desperately, clenching her jaw shut. The spasm slowly passed but left her mouth sour and dry, with a cold sweat starting out all over her skin.

She got up from her chair and stumbled away a little blindly. Her high heels dug into the soft manicured lawn. Then there was somebody at her elbow.

'Are you okay?'

Chhobi turned covering her mouth with her shawl and dimly registered a tall figure, longish face, slightly pitted with old acne marks.

'Bathroom,' she croaked, stumbling faster over the unending lawn, wrenching her heels out of the ground at every step. Behind her was the bonfire – a bright warm oasis.

The figure took her elbow, hurried her through a long fern-filled verandah and through the massive hand-carved teakwood doors.

A guest bathroom was tucked away in the corner of the wide expanse of entrance hall, staircase dividing in two, chandelier and cut-glass vases capturing rainbow prisms of light.

Chhobi staggered in and clutched at the wash basin inset into a slab of black granite. The nausea seemed a bit better, but it was momentary respite. Bhai Sahib's eyes burned at her, she peered at her face reflected in the big gilt framed mirror – no peacock this – bilious green and cyan blue – more like a poisoned crow. Her stomach heaved again and she retched, bringing it all up, spattering the spotless basin and clogging the drain. Belatedly she wished she had had the presence of mind to puke in the WC. She cleaned the basin with a lace-edged, cross-stitched hand towel, hiding the soiled thing behind the looped curtains and washed her face. A sour taste and smell lingered.

'How are you feeling now? Better sit here,' said the tall man, guiding her to an armchair. 'I am Karan,' he introduced himself. She noticed him better now. Thick hair cut so short that the scalp showed in places, and a concerned face.

'Are you with anyone?' Then to the attendant servant hovering around, '*Memsahib ke leye coffee lao.*'

'My sister... I came with her.'

'Who is she? I will fetch her. I think you need to go home and lie down.'

'Sonali ... she is wearing orange, with Sonny.'

'That girl! The girl with the long hair.'

'Yes.'

They left soon after, Karan locating Sonali who was a mixture of concern and remorse for having neglected Chhobi, not untinged with irritation at having to make an early hasty exit.

Karan accompanied them on the drive home with Sonny. For most of the journey he was twisted around in the front seat to stare at Sonali who sat at the back with Chhobi. He seemed almost transfixed by her.

They did not know it then but he was a man whose absence was to take on an unshakeable presence in their lives.

seven

Chhobi had resolved to speak to Ma about the unsuitability of Sonny first thing the next morning. The next morning, however, there was a minor crisis of Ratan Kaku's making.

Dadi and Ratan Kaku were part of a yoga group that met in one of the central leafy parks, surrounded by houses on all sides. This particular park was not very well maintained, the ground dry with a worn out cricket pitch marked by running feet. The park was a bone of contention between two rival groups of teenage boys since it served too as a football ground. There were frequent altercations between the two teams for the preferred use of the ground. All was quiet at 6 a.m. however when the yoga group met.

There were about twenty of them, all men over sixty-five. They began with the chanting of 'Om', the syllable that, when pronounced with concentration, was so laden with spiritual energy that the three elements Brahma, Vishnu and Mahesh were represented. The 'm' of the Om ended in a prolonged sound that resonated around the park.

It had been Ratan Kaku's idea to join. He looked like a thin stork doing his asanas. In summer he wore very wide starched half-pants that retained their own shape, no matter how contorted the posture. His skinny legs moved inside like the clapper in a bell. Dadu's trousers, waist forty inches and length forty inches, strained at his belly. The session always ended with the laughing exercise: 'Open wide your arms, flinging them away from your chest, throw back your head and laugh with a loud Ha Ha Ha, bring your arms to your side.' Milkmen and newspaper boys on their cycles stopped to snigger. It was infectious laughter, even though fake.

Curious Chhobi had walked by once to see. The last time she had seen all of Dadu's teeth was when she had glimpsed his dentures in an eerie smile, floating in a glass by his bedside.

The crisis occurred today – during the Ha Ha Ha exercise. Ratan Kaku just could not stop laughing. He laughed and he laughed, forgetting to lower his arms, which were frozen in a posture of crucifixion. He laughed till the tears rolled down his cheeks. Dadu muttered some excuse at the rest of them, gaping in astonishment, and dragged him away, shocked and alarmed at this unaccustomed unstoppable mirth.

Ratan Kaku slumped in a chair on their verandah. Dadu as always when confronted with a problem shouted for Dida. Ma, Dida and Chhobi gathered around. Chhobi had a splitting headache from last night. Coaxed into a semblance of composure after drinking some sweet gingered tea, Kaku's bottled up worries spilt out. It was a full four months since the Menons had prematurely vacated his house. Despite having spent on paint and polish, he was simply unable to find a suitable replacement. Meanwhile Goel's bulldozers were demolishing the house next door, all surfaces in Kaku's home were covered in a thick blanket of cement and brick dust. There was a constant noise of destruction. Worse, every other day some sinisterly smiling man who either wanted to rent or buy his house would accost him. He was convinced they were Goel's men. For the past two days he had been getting blank telephone calls synchronised with the hour. Whenever he picked up the phone, there was no answer, but a faint sound of breathing like a threat transmitting itself down the wire.

The huddled group on the verandah froze, hairs prickling on Chhobi's neck, as the phone rang. A sleepy Sonali finally answered it. It was for her. Karan calling to find out if they were feeling fine. She stumbled out, pushing the sleep out of her eyes, a little indignant at being woken up.

'Who is Karan now?' asked Dida sharply.

'Oh no one, just a poor relative, a sailor,' said Sonali dismissively. 'Chaa, Dida.' She smiled at Ratan Kaku without noticing the state he was in and went in again.

One fallout of the morning's mini breakdown was that Ratan Kaku dropped out of the yoga group, and very soon Dadu followed suit.

The second was that in the face of such real distress, Chhobi felt her own fears fade away. Once removed from last night's flickering firelight, Chhobi was a little embarrassed and ashamed as well. Sonali was quiet about the wine Chhobi had drunk, the mess she had created. She decided to talk to Sonali herself, or tackle her when Sonny renewed his invitation. Chhobi felt too that maybe her doubts were exaggerated when she observed Dida's shining satisfaction as she heard about the huge house, the many servants, the diamonds and the impressive garden.

But although they met often Sonny did not invite Sonali to his house again.

Chhobi decided to broach the topic with Sonali on a trip to Chandni Chowk the very next day. Sonali had cajoled Ma for extra spending money and now she planned the excursion with a definite sense of purpose.

'But what do you want to buy that's not available in Lajpat Nagar or Connaught Place?' protested Chhobi.

'You'll see,' said Sonali.

'No, I have to know, I can't rattle all the way squeezed and pinched in a DTC bus until you tell me. What do you need that's only sold in Old Delhi?'

'We will take a DTC bus only till it's bearable, we will get off when the crowd gets too much and then take a scooty.'

Chhobi was firm. 'Stop acting mysterious and tell me. I am not going until I know.'

'I cannot go to that area alone and Indu won't come.'

'Then tell me.'

'I want to buy some ittar, I would prefer French perfume but the smugglers' prices are beyond reach.'

'What ?!'

Sonali danced a little pirouette around the room, and began intoning dramatically in mock baritone, '*Hawa ka jhoka hai, ya tere badan ki khushboo...*'

Used to three generations of women who smelt only of Mysore Sandalwood soap, Lakme talc and Jabakusm hair oil, the compelling need for ittar had Chhobi nonplussed. The word immediately conjured up courtesans who smiled coquettishly, nautch girls who beckoned the nawabs of Lucknow and Hyderabad reclining in white bolstered bordellos. Empress Noorjehan, who had originally discovered ittar of roses, floated by in a scented bath, a ghostly legend.

'Talcum is good enough for all of us,' said Chhobi feebly.

Sonali was uncompromising, jutting out her chin a little. Chhobi knew she would have to go.

The blue green bus with the yellow band was only half full as theirs was one of the initial stops. The logo of the back-to-back double arrows pulling in opposite directions seem to indicate that one remained stationary rather than that one could travel in all directions. It was cold. Chhobi was well wrapped in her thick red shawl, Sonali wore her multicoloured Nepali jacket, like Joseph's coat of many colours, Chhobi said, but Sonali was ignorant of Biblical allusions.

Near the Purana Quila zoo, now the home of the real Royal Bengal Tiger, they got off, struggling past protruding arms and legs, a forest of limbs, thorny elbows, bony knees. Punching, prodding, Sonali used her crooked elbows like oars, chopping at the city louts, the roadside Romeos, Chhobi guarding her breasts with a handbag clutched like armour plate across her chest, completely regretting the expedition. As they disembarked they saw the bus careening crazily round the corner at an angle of sixty degrees, centre of gravity askew with the hanging crowd on both the doors.

The driver of the auto they hailed was young and seemed only interested in the cricket commentary crackling out of the tiny radio on the dashboard, which also held a small brass statue of Hanuman. Soon they were weaving in and out of the Darya Ganj traffic as though dodging invisible gunfire. Catching a glimpse of her tense face in the projecting rear-view mirror, eyes narrowed against the buffeting cold, head wrapped in the vermilion shawl, Chhobi thought she looked like Phoolan Devi, the bandit queen. Grim and at this moment a victim of her own destiny or rather her sister's destiny. Carried along on a mission of enticement.

Off a side lane branching off the main road by Shah Jehan's Red Fort was the perfumery. Chhobi looked around, alive to history. It was close by here that Nadir Shah had entered Delhi, on that plundering trip when he took away the peacock throne, in the early eighteenth century. It was here that a riot had started after a musket was fired at him and narrowly missed him. It was here that he gave orders for a massacre that spread from the Jewellers' Bazaar to the old Idgah, a hundred thousand people were killed, and in commemoration a gate close to the area was named Khuni Darwaza – Bloody Gate.

Stepping off the noise and clamour of the street, they were transported back to Mughal times. It was not a large shop, but old and enjoyed brisk custom. On one side of the counter was an impressive chest, carved and inlaid with ivory birds on ivory trees. It had tiny partitions holding small cut-glass bottles. These were filled with fluids, containing, as the man explained, traditional scents in oil-based formulae. French perfumes were alcohol-based and evaporated rapidly. Ittars lingered.

Sonali asked to try. Extend your hand, she was told, palm down. He dabbed it just above the wrist with the glass stopper.

'Most famous – ittar of roses.'

She inhaled. Chhobi inhaled too, nodding in appreciation.

'Too obvious,' said Sonali

'Extend the other hand – ittar of Queen of the Night.' And so onto jasmine, vetiver, khusgrass. But Sonali shook her head, Chhobi's reeling from the giant bouquet of aromas she had inhaled.

'Oh, for God's sake, Sonali, what kind of perfume are you looking for?'

'... something ... hot and spicy.'

'Hot? Spicy? Sounds like garam masala.'

Finally honey-coloured kasturi, distilled from the musk deer – 'This is the one, just right – it must excite the senses.' Sonali smiled at the shopkeeper, patient in the face of such a particular beauty. He decanted some into a small glass vial, careful not to spill a drop.

Chhobi bought 'gil'. When unstoppered it released the smell of wet earth. Wet with rain after a drought or very long summer. It was distilled from the early morning dew that gathered on such recently quenched earth – a monsoon smell.

It had been a long journey, this one, in search of a scent. Chhobi flopped down on her bed exhausted, and watched her sister daub herself with the perfume – behind the ears, on the pulse beating on her wrists, between her breasts. Scent of enticement.

'Try out yours,' suggested Sonali

'I am saving it for a special occasion. I want to talk to you about Sonny.'

'What about him? If you don't use it will harden and become useless.' Getting Sonali to attend was sometimes like boxing with shadows.

'Do you know what you are doing with Sonny?' Chhobi persisted.

'I haven't done much yet.'

'They're not our kind of people.'

'No thank God, look stop nagging. He *loves* me,' said she with utmost conviction. Looking at Chhobi's doubtful worried face, Sonali repeated, 'He is in love with me, get it.'

'I think he is just having a good time – be careful he doesn't, you know, use you – abuse you – lose you. ... Besides I am sure they have black money.'

At that Chhobi was buried under an avalanche of vituperation.

'Why are you always so pious? Just like those horrible nuns from your school with their white moustaches. Always sitting in judgment, preaching. You think it's wrong to enjoy yourself... what do you know about use and abuse? When you were relaxing in cool old Simla, I was with Ma. I used to watch her studying for her BA, sometimes all night. Now she always pays for everything but has to pretend that it's actually Dadu's money. Black money! Money is money, any money is better than this, this way we are living! I don't need your sanctimonious, holier-than-thou attitude. I cannot be like you, you are like those Bronte sisters you're so fond of reading. Squashed between the pages of a book like a dead silverfish.'

Rage flared in Chhobi as dry timber sparked by her words. Her breath came out – short and ragged... the insult of it... and she the elder... only trying to warn her... so different – how did they occupy the same room? The same womb?

'Shut your mouth,' she cried inarticulate in her anger, clenching on the small glass vial in her hand. The bottle flew and hit the wall, a blind bird dashing to its death. Glass shattering on the wall, leaving an amber jagged stain shaped like a tear, a rent that could not be repaired or camouflaged.

And the smell. A whole monsoon of tension, a torrent of tears. An overpowering squall of distilled dewdrops, that left them both gagging, speechless and gasping for air. Gil.

A deluge wet enough to drown out the scent of enticement.

Almost.

But not quite.

eight

S onali's birthday.
Dida finished her puja that day with a reading from the
Gitagovinda.

> Fix flowers in shining hair loosened by loveplay, Krishna!
> Make a fly whisk outshining peacock plumage to be the banner of
> love.
> She told the joyful Yadu hero, playing to delight her heart.
> My beautiful loins are a deep cavern to take the thrusts of love –
> Cover them with jewelled girdles, cloths, and ornaments, Krishna!
> She told the joyful Yadu hero, playing to delight her heart.

It was to be a day of earthly passions. A day towards the end of April
when Chhobi's fears came true, just before summer ripened to its
full heat.

Sonali's birthday. The red Datsun sped away from Delhi
towards the road that led to Simla, the Grand Trunk highway to
Ambala. The back seat of the car held dark truffle chocolate cake
from Wenger's, pizzas from Nirula's and an icebox of Kingfisher
beer. The glove compartment held Sonali's favourite Kishore
Kumar, Simon and Garfunkel and Cat Stevens tapes. Sonny was

taking her for a drive. A long ride. He was looking for a place to picnic beyond the grim concrete apartments, the bright mustard fields. Under an old mango tree perhaps, with a deep deep shade and boughs weighted with bronze coloured blooms, zardozi embroidered efflorescence. A dust storm during the night had considerably lowered temperatures and so the picnic.

They were leaving behind the Rajghat, the flower clock on the small grassy hillock, hoardings that advertised 'Suitings and Shirtings' and even one that incredibly drew attention to 'Superior Pantings'. At the Inter State Bus Terminus their speed dropped to a crawl. All around them were buses and trucks, rickshaws and cycles and, holding up the traffic, an ancient modified bullock cart drawn by a camel, haughty and unconcerned, led by an equally unconcerned owner from Rajasthan, earrings glinting below his turban. The car's AC purred, blocking out the smells – diesel fumes, bidi smoke, sweat mingled with the smell of bread pakoras fried in cheap oil. All the while, Cat Stevens was singing, 'I'm being followed by a moon shadow, moon shadow, moon shadow.'

Sonali felt real, not shadowy at all. Glancing down at her hands resting on her lap, she imagined them adorned with rings like Sonny's mother's. Not too many of them but set with stones that flashed with a blue fire trapped deep inside. A rust-haired urchin scratched at the windowpane, then pointing to the cardboard cases from Wenger's and Nirula's on the back seat, opened wide his mouth and made a gesture of cramming it with food. Sonali ignored him.

She wore a white kurta and salwar embroidered with Lucknow chikan work – a delicate tracery of flowers enclosed by interlocking paisleys. Around her neck was a golden yellow dupatta that brought out the colour of her eyes. Her hair was pulled tight in a topknot that set off the contours of her neck. Sonny was in his usual garb of jeans and check shirt, a thick new gold chain showing on his neck. She had touched it lightly when she saw it but he offered no explanation.

In front of their car slept a man uncomfortably perched on projecting spears of steel reinforcement. A tattered tarpaulin afforded him little shade, but he lay oblivious in exhausted stupor. The truck had two eyes painted on the back flap, large obsidian Egyptian eyes, and the message *Buri nazaar wale tera muh kala* – if your gaze be evil let your face turn black.

Eyes, Sonali thought idly, eyes were so important. She would rather be deaf like Dida, than ever have to suffer with her eyes. Most un-Sonali-like she remembered Chhobi underlining bits in some article on mortality. The *Rig Veda*, Chhobi had read out, suggests that at the time of one's death, the soul detaches from the body by escaping through the eyes and then merges with the sun.

Sonali began to smile secretly to herself at the thought of merging with Sonny. She glanced at him and suddenly thought of the importance of eyes in the Bengali marriage ceremony. The moment when the bride, perched aloft on the shoulders of her male relatives, unveils her eyes by dropping the protective green lids of heart-shaped betel leaf and gazes at her husband. A gaze that was supposed to invoke an abundance of children, riches and also spiritual fulfilment, Ma had explained to her and Chhobi at a wedding. Dida overhearing that had snorted.

They found their tree off a dirt track leading from the Grand Trunk Highway, an hour's drive out of Delhi. Not one but four trees, old, gnarled marking the junction between neighbouring fields. Under the thick canopy, which but for a stray beam the sun was unable to penetrate, the ground was cushioned with fallen leaves collected between skeins of roots exposed by the eroded soil. They were screened from the main road by a wall of keekar, wicked white thorns surrounding a single laburnum tree yellow with pendant clusters of flowers, just opening, like gilded grapes. A tall clump of knife-edged sarkanda grass hid them from the dirt track. A light breeze stirred the shadows, rustled the leaves and blossoms wafting a faint mango fragrance down to them. An insect hum buzzed in Sonali's ear as she reclined on the dhurries, soft as a bed, woven in a medallion pattern in indigo, rose and ivory. A row of glistening red ants marched up the tree in crocodile formation.

Sonny opened the icebox and took out a bottle of Kingfisher

beer. The green glass bottle was misty with cold, the contents shaken on the long drive. The liquid foamed out in a rope of bubbles winking with elliptical windows. Sonali didn't really like beer, she found it bitter, she had it to keep Sonny company. Today joy brewed inside her welling up in a frothing spasm, and she began to imagine it was champagne she was drinking. Easy to substitute bubbly for beer if you had never tasted any before.

Beer and chocolate truffle cake piped with pink marzipan roses and sugary white cursive script that slanted to the right. Her body, so deliciously cool in pure white muslin in the shade of the mango tree. A languor crept through her limbs.

Sonny brushed a brown crumb of chocolate truffle cake sticking to the corner of her mouth. He reached up and one by one pulled out the wavy V-shaped black hairpins securing her hair, there were seven in all. One by one he laid them on the medallion- patterned dhurries, three-inch victory signs that had drunk too much Kingfisher beer.

Sonali sat up, forehead colliding with Sonny's. Topknot opening, sliding down her back – a blue black python uncoiling.

'What – what's wrong?'

'Ant in my pant,' and pulling up her kurta urgently searched the spot where her hips began their flare. The cord of her salwar gripped her waist marking it with a ridged indentation. She pinched an ant. An angry ant. Sonny rubbed at the flesh above her salwar, his glancing fingers moving in a widening arc. Now there were ants all over the dhurrie. Red, frantic searching for chocolate truffle cake crumbs.

Sonny got up, pulling her up with him. He lifted the dhurrie, shaking it, an ivory indigo and rose wave scattering hairpins, cake crumbs and angry ants.

Now he was spreading it under the farthest tree, where the ground was more cushioned, the leaves piled up from last year, the shade not quite as deep. There were no ants. The sun reaching down through the overhead leaves in shifting shards of light tattooed Sonali with a tiger skin of markings. She lay down again. Her lids felt heavy. Sonny wandered off in the direction of the clump of keekar.

Sonali opened her eyes to see Sonny in splendid chiaroscuro frame, only the burden in his arms sunlit, spilling over with gold. Gift of the Golden Fleece. The laburnum tree was stripped of its just opening yellow pendulous blooms, carried in arms scratched with the wicked white thorns of the keekar trees. Sonny turned poet, inspired solely by a desperate desire.

Sonny's gaze was insistent as he knelt before her, tipping his offering of flowers onto her lap. A stray hair on his moustache glinted as he smiled. Sonali felt a sense of detachment as though she was outside her own body, looking down on the two of them from high above. As Sonny's hand went up to flick his hair in that peacock gesture she knew so well, she snapped out of the exquisite torpor that encased her.

The branches of the mango tree seemed almost animate, darkness velvet in the shadows of the leaves, staining his face with a dusky bluish tint. Beyond the shade of the trees the sarkanda grass seemed to float into the dazzling distance, into the timelessness of a summer afternoon, into the illumination that was as though a hundred lamps were lit behind his head.

He pulled off the golden yellow dupatta, gently spreading her hair, twining it with flowers. Sonali's eyes gold, opened wide, and as his eyes held them in urgent communication, a slight shudder of fear ran through her. She wished her underclothes were delicate wisps of silk and lace, not sturdy cotton Maidenform with circular stitching. His hand held her left breast through the white kurta with its embroidered paisleys, through the Maidenform bra with the circular stitching. He kissed her, tongue tangling on a silk smooth skein of hair that lay across her cheek. His other hand pushed her flat against the fallen leaves of last winter and he positioned himself over her pulling off his T-shirt in a single motion. Sweat shadowed his chest.

She recoiled involuntarily as his hand fumbled at the cord of her salwar, opening it with a tug. She was naked now, golden on the ivory, indigo and rose. He laid the flowers, girdling her hips, upon her breasts, twisted around her arms and ankles. Golden chains, tiger stripes of his desire.

His body appeared at once large and unfamiliar and threatening. He began to stroke her with practised ease, brushing his lips over her cheeks, her hands, her eyelids, her breasts. Fear left her then yielding to the pleasure of it, she wanted it to reach that deep unknown part of her, secret and mossed, moist and velvet. She matched his rhythm, synchronised.

The pain plunged through her – a knife thrust.

A faintly bitter smell, like a poisonous herb, filled her nostrils. She was speckled with torn fragments of golden petals. It was clear suddenly why wedding beds were strewn with rose petals and jasmine flowers, it was for the fragrance that was released when two bodies entwined, crushing the blossoms under them. Laburnum blossoms when bruised scattered such bitterness, an odour like a premonition.

Sonny slept, lulled into lassitude after passion peaked. Sonali watched him. A squirrel high above on the mango tree watched her watch him. Conscious of her nakedness, she pulled on her kurta and her salwar. She covered Sonny with the golden yellow dupatta. Sweat mingled with kasturi, musk deer ittar.

She had done it. Wrapped herself about him with chords of desire, chords of love. He was hers forever. A feeling of happy contentment rose up like a cloud to the canopy of dark leaves under which they lay. She felt a little blurred around the edges, as though her body and his had fused together. Again that too green sharp smell. Wrinkling her nose, she lifted her wrist and inhaled the ittar.

Sonny awoke, glanced at her and then at his watch. Flinging aside the golden dupatta, he dressed rapidly.

'Let's go.'

Sonali smiled at him then rolled into the hot hollow left by his body. She pressed her nose against the dhurrie and inhaled a mango mold, his sweat, her kasturi ittar and again the mangled poison smell. Sonny was ferrying the icebox, the wicker basket with the plates and glasses to the car, moving quickly, suddenly very hurried.

'Let's go.'

Rolling up the dhurrie – ivory and rose and indigo blotched with red. Blood red turning to rust already. Sonali knelt amongst the rotting leaves, the smashed golden blossoms, the satiated ants and looked in vain for her hair pins. Seven of them in wavy V shapes. V for virgin.

nine

Sonny told her as they were nearing the outskirts of Delhi, the grey concrete blocks with the ugly water tanks, the treeless roads and rush of traffic. Told her he had promised to marry Bhai Sahib's business associate's daughter. A girl from Ludhiana who had booked him with the gold chain like a Maruti 800, an Ansal's flat. Down payment made. The marriage was next month, in May. A purely business arrangement. He would always be her friend, he said, any time she needed him she just had to call. Throughout the little speech he could not meet her eyes, his words were pat, rehearsed, a faintly self-sacrificing note underlining them.

Sonali felt white and bloodless. Felt the blood drain out of her face, out of her fingers and toes, out of the not-so-secret place between her legs.

'Stop the car,' she fumbled with the door, crouching in a posture as though to ready to leap out of the running car. Sonny abruptly pulled up at the side of the road. Nearby lay the flattened carcass of a dog that had been too slow to dodge the traffic. Sonny reached over to pull her door shut. Reason with her, placating, explaining.

She drew her arm back, pushing tangled blue-black hair out of the way, hooked her fingers into a tiger's claw, nails unsheathed, and struck. Four vertical stripes ran down Sonny's face, white stripes turning to blood red. He reared back, clutching his cheek, disbelieving. Anger chased shock and regret across his face.

She stepped out, on to the end of the Grand Trunk highway, hair eddying around her in a whirlpool gust of wind. Bending down she leaned in through the open door and said with dignity, '*Buri nazar wale, tera muh kala.*'

The Datsun drew away. Sonali sat on a white painted stone and divided her tangled hair into three sections, plaiting them in an untidy rope. It was hot. No AC car, no mango tree shade. She wrapped the dupatta around herself and walked.

Walked right past the NDMC city dump. It was like a Daliesque depiction of Hades, and matched her mood exactly. Stench rose bubbling from fly-encrusted columns and pools. The sun was almost obscured through layers and layers of dirt suspended in the air. Dumper trucks negotiating the growing mounds tipped out mountains of refuse. Hundreds of vultures tore apart decaying filth with bloodied beaks. Kites wheeled a watchful calligraphy in the grey-white sky. Rats and ragpickers scavenged together. All feeding on Dead Sea fruit.

Sonali felt weak, her head whirling with the circling birds in contracting and expanding spheres. She noticed her right hand encrusted with Sonny's blood, tarnished blood. She stuck it out to thumb a ride. A middle-aged couple in a white Fiat stopped, the woman reluctant, the man eager.

'Just till the Inter State Bus Terminus,' she whispered.

They badgered her with questions – where was she going? Alone? In the middle of the afternoon heat? What was her name? What did she do? Where did she live? How many brothers and sisters were they? Did she want water? Was she feeling well?

Sonali answered in mumbling monosyllables, till they fell silent. She shared the back seat with a red VIP vanity case and a steel tiffin carrier with three stackable containers. What had those containers contained – pizza and chocolate truffle cake, she wondered hysterically. Her eyes pricked, she looked down at her hands resting in her lap. Tear drops sparkled on them like precious stones burning with a deep fire, then slipped and trickled through her fingers as water. Like a moon shadow at mid afternoon.

Happy birthday, Sonali.

Chhobi knocked on the bathroom door. The furious splashing sounds continued, tap drumming steadily into the bucket. Sonali had been in there for almost an hour, washing herself, watching her dreams swirl away with the grey water down the drain protected by the steel perforated lid.

'Hurry up, you will empty the water tank. What are you doing? Don't you remember we are invited to Mrs Chatterjee's for dinner?'

Sonali did not answer, merely rubbed, scrubbed at the soft skin of her thighs with renewed vigour.

Normally Sonali's birthday saw a group of giggling girls at the table, gorging themselves on Dida's lunch, a gastronomic triumph that she and Savitri would slave over from dawn, only to see it disappear in a trice.

But this year Sonali had not wanted any of it, she would rather go out with her friends, she said, unwrapping the diaphanous white chikan work salwar kurta with the delicate embroidery, a gift from Ma. 'I will wear it with the golden yellow dupatta and gold embroidered jutis.' Dida had given her tiny star shaped earrings, her own. Sonali had left fresh and pure and beautiful, eyes sparkling like the stars in her ears.

She had returned, grimy and dishevelled, stumbling on comatose feet and unable to speak. Two semicircular ridges of tension marred the beauty of her soft mouth. Plait untangling in fat tangles down her back and kajal smudged about her eyes like bruises. The eyes themselves looked lifeless, lightless.

'What happened? Didn't Sonny drop you?' they had asked as she had entered. Mumbling some vague answer about an accident, she had bolted herself in the bathroom and was there still. Almost a full hour later she emerged, white-faced. She pulled on a pair of jeans and an old T-shirt, soft and faded, and began to dry her hair.

Tipping her head over till the dripping ends almost touched the ground, she whipped her hair with a tightly rolled pipe of towelling. Beat it like Savitri beat the doormat with the broom every morning, almost savagely. Whirled her head around, hair swinging from side to side, scattering tear-shaped drops. She refused to change into something more suitable. Chhobi picked up the soiled white salwar, discarded in the bathroom where Sonali had stepped out of it.

Dida looked as though it was her own birthday. A festive red bindi glowed like the dawn sun on her forehead, and she wore a red-bordered tangail sari with an edging design of gold dogteeth. She had been saving up a knob of toffee-coloured patali gur from Calcutta, wrapped in wax paper and hidden in the refrigerator for Sonali's birthday. Today she carried the rich caramel pink khir to Mrs Chatterjee's like a trophy, studded with raisins, fragrant with basmati, redolent with cardamom, with cream that settled in a thick wrinkled sheet on the surface.

Mrs Chatterjee had invited them for dinner and a movie on her new VCR, a tape her son Montu had bought in London. They were going to watch Ritwik Ghatak's *Meghe Dhaka Tara*, not a recent release but acclaimed by the critics.

The area around Mrs Chatterjee's gate was cemented in black and white crazy paving. It was being hosed down by her Adivasi Christian maid from Bihar – Helen. A most unsuitable name, thought Chhobi. Helen – there was only one Helen. At the very sound of the name a chinky-eyed vamp danced in on graceful feet, posturing and pouting – bad girl of so many movies. Mrs Chatterjee's Helen was dark and thickset, covered in a dusting of talcum like a snowfall.

Inside was a pervading smell of panch phoron, five spice... a medley of onion seed, fennel, mustard seed, cumin and fenugreek. Sputtering, spattering in mustard oil, flavouring cauliflower, bitter gourd, tiny new potatoes, broad bean and aubergine. Everywhere in the room loomed artefacts and wall hangings from Calcutta. Overstuffed sofa sets, hot and springy were draped with white Calcutta cutwork antimacassars. On one wall, a mustard yellow Jamini Roy reproduction of three women with their buns coiled like Olive Oyle's on the napes of their neck, heavy-lidded eyes curving out of their heads. On the opposite wall, fashioned out of shola pith as intricate as lace filigree, was a Durga head in a glass box. This same shola was used by the British to make sola topees, said Chhobi to a lacklustre Sonali.

A curtained alcove was fitted with a white ceramic washbasin, rolled up carpets were stacked like logs behind the sofa.

Mrs Chatterjee was watching the movie for the first time. She squatted importantly on a cane moora in front of the VCR, going through the motions her son Montu had rehearsed with her as she put in the tape. The movie was poetic in patches, grim on the whole. The life of a beautiful girl from a lower middle-class family, plagued by ill health. It was essentially the story of a life unredeemed by the slightest happiness or hope. Mrs Chatterjee preferred Calcutta potboilers and Bollywood melodramas and said so, displeased with Montu's choice.

'That Nargis Dutt was right. These directors exploit India's poverty and dirt. These sell very well in the west. That's why this tape is not available in Delhi, but in London. Foreigners only want to see us going backwards, negative views of India make them very happy.'

She had a point, smilingly concurred Chhobi, who had quite enjoyed the movie. 'It's like those foreign tourists who ignore the Qutab Minar and stop the car to click pictures of some lazy cows holding up the traffic.'

'I hated the film,' said Sonali violently, the first words she had spoken. Dida shushed her. Chhobi and Ma's eyes met in anxious appraisal. Ma put her palm against Sonali's forehead who pushed it away impatiently. Smiling apologetically at Mrs Chatterjee, Ma said, 'Sonali's tired and not too well.'

Ma and Chhobi enjoyed the film. Dida enjoyed tearing Mrs Chatterjee's cooking to shreds – not enough flavour, mustard ground with such a heavy hand, the whole fish curry turned bitter – tch tch – must always grind mustard with a pinch of salt. Dadu enjoyed the khir. Sonali enjoyed nothing.

Later that night Chhobi was trying to read, distracted by Sonali lying on the bed, coiling and uncoiling her still tangled hair with her fingers, just gazing at the ceiling.

'Did you have a fight with Sonny?'

'No.' Just that one terse monosyllable.

'What's wrong then? What happened today? You look bad... so tense.'

Sonali looked at her lips twisting, trembling.

'Actually I am past tense.'

Chhobi picked up her wide-toothed comb, told Sonali to sit on the floor and sat behind her, spreading the blue-black hair over her shoulders down to her hips.

'What have you done? It's like a sadhu's matted in ropes.'

With slow patient gentle strokes she began to comb, starting from the left, dividing the hair into manageable sections. Slowly trying to remove obstinate tangles with her fingers.

'Sonny's getting married,' Sonali announced a note of despair threading her voice, 'to some behenji from Ludhiana.'

A cold hand clutched at Chhobi. It was doomed, she had known from the start but now saying 'I told you so' wouldn't help.

'Royal Bengali Tigress he called me,' whispered Sonali, every word punctuated by pauses in slow and painful enunciation, still so childishly pleased with that term of endearment. She had been prey to such teenage temptations, chocolate cake and fast air-conditioned cars.

'He was the hunter, and I the hunted. His shikar. What chance did I have? I hang now like one of those stuffed tiger heads mounted on the wall. Foolish dead tigress.'

'Don't talk like that. Melodramatic. You are only eighteen. Somebody much better will come along, forget him.'

'Nineteen, today was my coming of age birthday...'

'Don't take it so hard. He was no Prince Charming,' then catching sight of Sonali's expression – defeated, bereft, Chhobi said in a violent uncharacteristic burst of invective, 'Balls to him. Fuck him.'

'I just did. Today.'

The comb stopped its downward motion, Chhobi's hands tightened on her hair. 'You didn't. Why did you allow it... Oh you didn't... You didn't. You fool!'

'I should have saved myself as a gift for my future husband! I thought I was gifting it to my future husband.' Tears tinctured by irony.

'The bastard, he has been leading up to this for two years.'

Chhobi, stirred into a storm of fulmination, was tugging at Sonali's head, snapping off stray wisps, tearing roughly through knots, one hand pulling tight at her whole head. Sonali's body took on the posture of a figurehead on a ships prow, a back to front C shape – hair pulled backwards so that the taut strands were slanting her eyes into Chinese ones, straining at her temples. Sonali didn't complain but the tears were starting to flow now – squeezing out of those Chinese eyes. She could see herself, gold-dusted and naked on an ivory indigo and rose dhurrie, strewn with blossoms, watched by a solitary witness squirrel high up on a mango tree.

The comb paused its harsh assault. Chhobi asked, struck by a fresh horror, 'Did he use anything?'

Sonali cried harder, shoulders shaking. 'This is not some Hindi movie. Of course he didn't... but I am not going to get pregnant like Asha Parekh or Sharmila Tagore, that would be really too much...'

Tigress... Tigress, a helpless cat, an endangered species, soon to be extinct. Sonali was uncontrollable, inconsolable, tears like dissolving dreams running in rivulets down her cheeks.

Chhobi dropped the comb and stumbled out of the room, collecting herself as she silently entered her mother's room. Ma was asleep, curled in a foetal position. Chhobi searched in the mirrored cabinet above her washbasin in the bathroom. Medicines for Ma's insomnia, for Ma's migraines, Ma's sadness, Ma's sometimes lonely madness.

During the fumbling search she wondered about the pain. The older one got, the more painful it was she had heard, unless one went bareback horse riding, or practised gymnastic splits. She did neither.

Tearing open the foil wrapping, she handed Sonali a glass of water, anger making her spill a little, her rage trembling on the surface as an unsteady meniscus.

'Take this,' she said, 'and don't ever tell anyone. Do you hear me? NO ONE. Promise me, not Ma, not Indu... Especially not Indu... What's done is done.' It was comforting to take refuge in clichés. They implied that others had passed that way before them and survived – 'No good crying over spilt milk' or spilt blood – precious blood red tarnished to rust on an ivory, indigo and rose dhurrie.

Chhobi popped a pill too. Her sister, younger by nearly six years, had just pole vaulted, leap-frogged over her, jumped another of life's milestones.

Chhobi continued to comb, not tugging now, gentle in calm unhurried strokes. She began to recount a documentary she had watched on the Bengal Tiger. She spoke in a soothing, bland voiceover.

'The Tiger only attacks from the rear, it is scared of man's face. The big cat is already terribly handicapped, its natural habitat shrunk, forests denuded. The mangrove swamps are almost all the area left to the tiger. You know what the poachers of the Sunderbans do? They have worked out a cunning method for hunting the tiger. They wear masks, boldly painted papier-mache masks on the back of the heads. The tiger is fooled by the two-faced hunter, and too scared to defend itself. It is already weak as there is little to eat, no wild animals left for it to hunt. But the latest study has shown a slight increase in the number of tigers in that area, a rise not a fall. The tiger has learnt to survive, to adapt. It is too smart – some have turned into maneaters, unfazed by the two-faced poachers. Others have learnt to swim and fish and hide in the swamps, surviving mainly on aquatic game,' Chhobi smiled.

Sonali still white-lipped, attempted a wan smile. 'What do you want me to do? A Gloria Gaynor, start singing "I will survive"?'

'It's better than crying.'

Now her hair gleamed like satin, divided into three and woven into a plait. Light bounced off the three sections – onyx, jet and darkest sapphire. Tidied, cleared up.

ten

Two days later the red Datsun was at the gate. Not right in front of it, but just beyond, out of sight from the house, parked under a neem tree. Sonny sat inside, windows down, and waiting. Ma saw him first, on the way to office. She paused by his window, but he looked straight ahead, unmoving, and she passed by. Ma had only been told that he was getting married. It was almost an hour later that she was able to phone Chhobi to warn her. Chhobi was at home, hard at work – she had a deadline to meet... a short historical piece on Jehanara, Emperor Shah Jehan's daughter. Through the half-open bedroom door, she could see Sonali lying on her bed, listening to the tape recorder playing sad songs of Kishore Kumar. She looked ill. For the past two days she had done nothing but watch all the programmes on TV including *Krishi Darshan*. Today she would attend her afternoon classes in college.

Chhobi put the receiver down and walked out to see if Sonny was still there. He was, sitting in his red car, sweat beading his upper lip and forehead, dark glasses shielding his eyes. The marks on his cheek had faded, so that he merely looked as though he had disentangled himself from some wild creeper – a briar rose perhaps, a purple passionflower?

'What do you want?' Anger made her voice harsh, a note of panic underlining it at the thought of Dida or Dadu coming out and seeing him there. They hadn't been told about Sonny's impending marriage. 'Why are you making a tamasha? You've got what you wanted, leave us alone.' Sonny made no response, staring fixedly at their gate. 'What's the matter? It cannot be an attack of conscience, since you don't have any.'

He looked beyond her, over her shoulder, and stiffened. She heard the click of the latch and the creak of the gate on its inward arc as it opened. She turned to see Sonali in her faded green batik kaftan, plait swinging, mouth pinched with tension, coming out of the gate. Sonny got out of the car. He stood next to Chhobi, but unaware of her presence, looking at Sonali walking towards him. Chhobi felt she was part of a film, one of those moments when all movements were fluid and languid in slow motion. Sonali coming towards them in a waft of forest bloom – mingled mango blossom, laburnum and musk deer kasturi ittar.

She stood in front of Sonny and looked at him. No one spoke in this frozen tableau until Sonali reached up and removed his dark glasses. Looked into his eyes, dark shadowed and regretful, bloodshot and yearning. A new realisation had struck, it was as if possessing her had not slaked him at all, only whetted his desire, engulfing his senses with an enormous thirst.

Sonali tossed the dark glasses on the road where they smashed, and walked back. As Chhobi began to follow her, Sonny thrust a slim envelope at her. For Sonali, he said urgently.

The red car reversed, tooting a raucous Jingle Bells in April, turned and raced off, running over the smashed Ray Ban dark glasses, grinding them to black dust.

Sonali did not read the letter then, but put it away under her pillow. She left for her afternoon classes, face expressionless.

After dinner Chhobi was writing the final draft of her piece on Jehanara. She was glad to escape to another time, a time when women were all unseen eyes, hidden behind purdahs of reed curtains, stone jaali fretwork, and lace windowed veils. The Mughal emperors had produced such dutiful daughters. Shah Jehan, she had read somewhere, had got rid of unwanted suitors, and they were all unwanted, by offering them poisoned paans.

Jehanara had held the position of first lady at Shah Jehan's court, after her mother Mumtaz Mahal's death. She shared her father's captivity in Agra and it was only after his death that she moved to Delhi to live with her brother Aurangzeb. She was buried near the tomb of Nizamuddin. No elaborate domes for her, no marble cenotaphs with pietra dura inlay in precious stones. A simple enclosure and a grass covered grave with the small inscription, so stark when compared to the Taj Mahal, her mother's grave.

Chhobi had gone to see her grave. Standing in silence she could hear the trains pulling out of Nizamuddin station, whistling down the track to Agra where Jehanara had spent her youth. Jehanara – light of the world. Someone had scattered a few dark pink rose petals on the grass. She began to check her punctuation. Her sentences tended to be too long, sometimes running to a whole paragraph of convoluted syntax. She was peppering her prose now with little pauses – commas and semicolons. Every now and again heads other than those of the Mughals crept into the tiny pauses. Ma at dinner – half head hammered by a migraine, Sonali resting hers on an unread missive, her own head shutting out a vision of two naked bodies, twined and entwined. All three of them pulling down shutters, retreating behind screens and facades like the Mughal women in purdah.

Toward the early hours of the morning Chhobi was awakened by Sonali switching on the bedside lamp. Chhobi faced the wall, shielding her eyes from the light by throwing an arm across her face. She heard Sonali tear open the envelope. The minutes ticked by on the luminescent clock. There was a faint rustle of paper, half an hour went by. Chhobi turned to look at Sonali, scanning the letter, searching for shades, inflections, nuances. Pouring over the secret signals that must lie concealed in the words.

'Reading between the lines, Sonali?' she asked

Sonali looked up at her, then folded the two pages in four, across and across again, replaced them in the envelope, tucked it beneath her pillow again.

'No,' she replied, 'between the lies.'

❦

While Sonali's plans for her future collapsed like a house of cards, Chhobi too changed her mind, although the alacrity with which her sense of purpose was diverted by Rosemary's suggestions was to surprise her for a long time.

'What's this?' Rosemary had inquired looking at the pile of books on Chhobi's desk.

'Just organising things. I have to start mugging for the civil service exams in earnest. I didn't even make it to the interview last year,' Chhobi had replied somewhat dolefully.

'What if you *don't* make it. I mean most people *never* do.'

'Hunhh,' Chhobi had dithered, unable to link never to now. Her spirit shrivelled a little in advance, at the thought of the future going up in smoke given the midnight oil she was preparing to burn.

'Forget the stereotype, in any case you're not focused enough. My husband's brother is in the foreign service. He worked night and day for two years, joined competitive classes, was coached intensively for the interview. You don't want it badly enough.'

Rosemary had warmed to the theme. 'I know what you are completely suited for... it's academics. Go away to good old US of A. Do your Ph.D... In something to do with Delhi's history, I should think. With your marks, getting a research assistantship should be easy. You could end up writing papers, teaching a small group of students, become an authority on a certain historical period...' But Chhobi was no longer listening, Rosemary's ideas so exactly what she wanted for herself that she had thrilled to a kind of exultation.

Wretchedly she had been plucked back into the circle of books on her table. 'But...' she said, 'my family, I mean, they need...'

Rosemary had been firm. 'Look, just sit for the GRE exam, apply to a few universities, admission should be very possible, probable. As for your family, something will work out, leave something to destiny.'

It was on a Sunday morning that Sonny's wedding card was delivered. Large, cream and gold with an embossed Ganesha tied with auspicious red silken cord. Delivered by Karan along with a kilogram box of almond barfis, layers of thin diamond shapes covered in beaten silver. Sonali answered the doorbell and as she turned to face them colour drained from her face. Ma and Chhobi's faces grew grim and still in sympathy. Karan, at the door, was serious and unsmiling. He followed her in, unable to take his eyes off her, despite her faded kaftan, the shadows under her eyes.

Dida pulling up the sleeve of her sari blouse was readying herself for her daily shot of insulin. It was about to be administered by Dadu who always boiled the syringe and needle in a small saucepan for twenty minutes to sterilise them. Dida felt the sudden tension, palpable in the air and bunched her arm stiffly. Dadu concentrating on the injection admonished her as the needle resisted and drew blood.

Karan wanted to touch Sonali's hand, to express his sympathy, uncomfortable that Sonny had put him in this position. They were all so white-faced, so shocked, hadn't Sonny told them before – were they still hoping against hope. Chhobi came forward, murmuring platitudes, trying to edge him out of the room. Asking him to call later, she saw him to the gate.

The room was very quiet. Dadu vaguely questioning Dida if anything had happened. Dida not replying, but stretching out her hand to read the card lying under the red and gold sweet box on the table. Ma, Chhobi and Sonali not saying a word, the room overcast with their thoughts gathered in cloud-shaped blurbs above their heads like characters in a comic book. Colliding with a crack of despair, a clamour ringing in their ears like thunder. Still no one spoke.

Dida's look said it all as she read the card. Her priceless girl, her great bright hope – dashed, smashed. For an instant Dida's shoulders slumped and Chhobi saw her resemblance to Ma, that same look of surrender, of defeat. Her natural optimism draining away as she saw the future, a constant effort to make ever shortening ends meet. Ships, servants, air-conditioned mansions, diamonds, the grand life disintegrating in a heap of fallen hubris. Then she pulled herself together, literally straightened her back and looked proud.

'The card is addressed to Dr Dharani Dhar Talukdar and family. It's very nice of the Talwars to invite us all. I don't like these Punjabi functions, I feel out of place, but of course the girls will be attending... look there are all these little cards inside,' her voice shook slightly. 'The wedding is at Taj Man Singh hotel, but a week earlier is the sangeet in Friends Colony and the day after the wedding is the reception at Ashoka Hotel. He has invited us for everything. Look Meera...'

She fanned out the smaller cards. Ma took them as though in a stupor, blindly holding this Delhi trick of a selective guest list staggered over several pre- and post-wedding functions. Dida sampled an almond burfi, and then ate another, diabetes notwithstanding. Through silver-encrusted lips, she said, 'The cream of Delhi will be there. You girls must dress well.' Chhobi and Sonali stared at her. She was incorrigible.

A Simla moral science class unfolded like a banner in Chhobi's mind.

Hope deferred maketh the heart sick: but when the desire cometh
it is a tree of life (Proverbs 13.12)

Then the vision of two bodies, Sonali's and Sonny's, twined and entwined, flashed before her and she felt a fresh humiliation.

'What cheek, inviting her, rubbing salt... I am definitely not going and nor should Sonali. She can't be so shameless, so... desperate. As for the cream of Delhi, it will be full of corrupt netas and unscrupulous businessmen.'

Dida's Bengali was suddenly stern and formal.

'You are not everyone's collective conscience.'

Chhobi knew then with a cold certainty. Knew that Dida knew, knew about Sonny and Sonali, knew about the sweat-slicked tangling of limbs, that deflowering amongst the flowers. Knew about Sonali's year-long late nights, her missed classes. Dida had gambled and lost, and now like Sonali was hoping against hope.

Sonali did attend the sangeet, accompanied not by Chhobi but by her friend Indu.

Dida supervised her clothes. Dressed Sonali in one of her own wedding saris with an antique pattern, a gossamer weave with threads so fine that the colour was hard to define. It shimmered, unravelling like a length of moonlight, a wisp of morning mist, a sparkle like twilight rain on peepul leaves. It was cobwebbed with real zari flowers, old gold thread work blooming forth as hope resurrected.

Ma and Chhobi were helpless bystanders, Ma actively passive silent, Chhobi seething. Sonali looked like a beautiful wraith, an illusion. Dida opened her grey steel Godrej cupboard and took out a flat jewellery case. 'This was given to me by my mother-in-law,' she said, as she took out a never seen before choker. Secret stree dhan. Finely wrought gold flowers, seven in all, held six strands of Basra pearls together. Small gold and pearl jhumkas and her hair twisted in an elegant chignon on top of her head. The three-winged dressing table mirrored multiples of so many angles, facets and planes - Sonali and Dida essentially the same.

It finally slipped out - 'Stand tall and be proud. Make him sorry.' It was Dida's first acknowledgement that Sonny was something more than Indu, more than just a friend. 'There must be no loss of face,' Dida finished, directing Savitri to crouch down and straighten the pleats of the sari.

What about loss of ass? thought Chhobi hysterically, Rosemary's speech rubbing off on her.

Don't make a spectacle of yourself, she warned Sonali as she left.

The park in front of Sonny's house had been cordoned off. A bright wall of shamianas in geometric patterns – royal blue and orange, white and green, surrounded it. There was a terrible crush of cars, blocking other people's gates, climbing on to the sidewalk reversing into sandwich slice spaces. Sonny's house was outlined with strings of white miniature lights, the trees around the park wrapped in festoons of blue and green lights that blinked on and off, off and on. The whole vibrated with the subterranean hum of two giant generators.

Sonny's relatives from Hoshiarpur and Ferozepur, those rice and sugarcane-growing farmers, had completely taken over the evening. It was hot. Sonny's mother and her sisters, elegant in pastel chiffons, wilted and dissolved along with abstract ice sculptures that were rapidly dripping into steel trays. Oversized noisy fans revolved behind the ice, cooling people in brief rhythmic gusts so that before the sweat had a chance to dry, the fan swivelled away to whip at somebody else's hair or sequinned dupatta. Guests congregated in little islands around these fans.

Mrs Bhai Sahib was resplendent in a parrot green silk suit marked by huge half moons of perspiration. Her lips were dark red and she smiled her trademark vampire smile. She was seated with a group of brightly dressed middle-aged women on a white-sheeted dais. She was singing, rapping out the tune with a spoon, striking it on the body of a dholak that a woman in an incandescent pink sari was beating vigorously, both of them sitting cross-legged on either side of the dholak.

Her voice was melodious and old-fashioned like Shamshad Begum's. It was in strong contrast to her appearance, issuing forth sweetly from those heavily lipsticked lips. The song too floated out in phrases of incongruity, at odds with that sweet voice. Other voices cordant and discordant joined in the chorus. It was a gaudy bawdy song, as was the occasion, one that called for ribald lyrics – cohabitation, copulation implied in sly innuendo.

Jiske Bibi Moti
Uska bhi bara kaam hai
Jiske Bibi Moti

Moti Moti ...
Bistar pe leta do
Gadde ka kya kaam hai?

The one whose wife is fat is fortunate too,
What use a mattress?
Just lay her on the bed ...

An old folk song made famous by Amitabh Bachchan's drag rendering of it.

Sonali and Indu sat quietly on a sofa at the edge of the white dais. Indu looked flushed and pretty in spangled peach, eyes darting in search of Sonny. Sonali was still except for the cloud of butterflies beating against the very pit of her stomach. Indu nudged Sonali as she spotted Sonny with a crowd of his friends near the drinks counter, where Scotch whiskey was being imbibed in gallons. He looked thinner, dressed in a simple white kurta pajama.

Sonali felt asphyxiated by the festivities, the bright lights and bawdy songs. It was a huge mistake to have come. He didn't have the power or the courage to claim her. She saw that now. When it came to marriage only a chaperoned virgin from a business clan would do. A lump rose in her throat, choking and terrible. She would at that moment have given anything to escape to another time, another place.

Karan got them both fresh lime sodas. Sonali looked down into the misty glass with its rising threads of bubbles, a twist of lemon magnified at the bottom. It was like looking into Dadu's heavy glass paperweight. She could see herself encased by a bubble, rising up to the top and vanishing in a tiny explosion. Sonny saw her before she vanished. His mouth froze in mid-smile and grew straight and grim. The bride's male relatives from Ludhiana were present. One of them, uncomfortable and constricted in an unaccustomed bow tie as though Ludhiana was Louisiana, was slapping Sonny on the back, urging another drink on him. Sonny turned his head and glared at him, wrenching away from the unwanted familiarity. Bhai Sahib's son frowned at him, drawing him aside and murmuring in his ear. Sonny did not approach her but looked at her with hungry eyes,

eyes that reached across the wide expanse of space and held her in tight embrace. Indu giggled annoyingly.

On the outer fringes of the crowd were Bhai Sahib and his attendant brother, Sonny's father, both of them talking serious business in a small coterie which included the minor politician who had been guest of honour at the winter Lohri party. Bhai Sahib's son left Sonny and walked across to join them along with Sonny's elder brother, who was down for the wedding from Bombay. They were all in a self-congratulatory mood. The new Ludhiana alliance had helped them land a string of lucrative contracts in so far untapped South India. The Ludhiana family had been supplying hosiery and blankets to Tamil Nadu and Karnataka for the past two decades. New connections that dialled the right numbers. Sonny's would be the last wedding in the family, as he was the youngest of his generation.

Now the song being sung grew loud, it was the old sentimental number sung at all sangeets. The men joined the women singing around the fiercely beating dholak, upper lips and foreheads beaded with perspiration. A double ring of clapping hands, bangles jangling in tune encircled the singers in widening ripples of sound. They were singling out members of the family in specific relation to the bridegroom, pulling them into the tight circle, into its very centre, and clapping harder whilst urging them to dance. The steps were ancient bhangra ones. Everybody danced in turn, from Sonny's patrician maternal grandmother to his three-year-old nephew.

Nache Munde de Nani
Clap clap clap.
Nache Munde de Bhabhi
Clap clap clap.
Nache Munde da Baap
Clap clap clap.
Nache Munde de Dost
Clap clap clap.

A whole host of Sonny's school friends took the floor, nearly all of them inebriated. One of them, more valiant than the rest, pulled

Sonali into the circle, forcing her to dance, shooting slightly unfocused looks at Sonny and finally in a drunken haze, yanking him into the circle next to her. The clapping became rapid, dholak beating in sharp staccato sounds – *shawa, shawa.*

Sonny looked at Sonali, moved up close to her, the yearning strong in his eyes, then reached past her diaphanous sari and locked his thumb in her navel, swivelling his fingers downwards with an unlocking motion. Sonali gasped. She felt split wide open, surrounded by a cloud of fluttering butterflies released from the pit of her stomach.

Sonny's school friends stopped dancing. The clapping ceased. The song was over. The dancers dispersed, joining the ring of spectators, leaving the two of them standing alone. There was a small pause, and then a cackling new voice began another song, a song thick with suggestion. A song just for the two of them.

Aish karni hai to vakhra
kamra lay le ...

If you want to have fun rent
a spare room ...

'Don't make a spectacle of yourself.' Chhobi's warning rang in her ears.

She turned to leave, Sonny's arm shooting out to bracelet her wrist, tightening to a handcuff. Sonali quelled him with a look and wrenched free, Karan and Indu suddenly by her side. She left. Melted away like a morning mist, a wraith, like twilight rain on a peepul leaf, an illusion.

Four days later, and a day before Sonny's wedding, Sonali married Karan at a civil magistrate's office. She called to inform her astounded family and as she rang off after her brief message, the phone went dead.

eleven

Months passed. On a Wednesday evening just after 7 p.m., Dida and Chhobi were sitting on the sofa with the sagging seat, Savitri squatting at their feet, cubing yellow potatoes and purple aubergines onto a newspaper. They were all waiting for *Chitrahaar*. Savitri would spread a mat and sleep in the rear verandah tonight. Dida and she had been hard at work making malpuas for Janmashtami. In fact Dida would be sleeping late, only after the midnight puja.

Dida was irritable and hungry, fasting, despite the diabetes, for Krishna's birth. Dadu was hovering around like every year, telling her it was so dangerous for her not to eat. His objections fell on her deaf ear.

Savitri normally left for home before dark. She lived with her son and daughter-in-law in a squatter's colony near Nehru Place. Her son worked in a small teashop in the crowded office complex and her daughter-in-law swept and swabbed offices. Savitri had one of the best views in towns for next to her shack was the pristine white marble Ba'hai temple. She could see it through the chinks in the mud-plastered brick wall covered with the tarpaulin that made up her shack. The view was slightly obscured by a snarl of tangled wires illegally tapping the overhead high tension cables for light and power. Hundreds of jutting TV antennae looked like a futuristic flock of birds perched on those tattered roofs. Beyond them was the surreal scene of the half open lotus blooming in a dusty landscape.

Earlier Chhobi had peeped into Ma's room. Ma was home early. She had her feet up, reclining on a cane-backed planter's chair, another of Dida's father's gifts. Flanking it was a tall standing lamp with a fringed shade, a memento of their army days, the body of the lamp fashioned out of a brass ammunition shell. The red silk shade cast a pink pond of light. Light which bathed Ma in a soft glow and washed away the furrows between her eyes. She was reading a Dick Francis novel. She had turned forty-three last week. In this light she could easily pass for thirty-three. She loved British thrillers, they were so far removed from her real life that they created a buffer zone between mundane routine and gut-wrenching memories.

Today, Ma had come home early to decorate Dida's puja room with an alpana. As she had knelt to draw the intricate patterns in powdered rice paste, Dida had come up to watch her. She was in an unusually nostalgic frame of mind. She normally never mentioned Mymensingh, but today she was thinking of the blue water lilies she had had planted in one of the ponds on their estate. Lilies, the colour of Krishna's skin, lilies that were picked in armloads for Janmashtami and offered before the idol of baby Krishna.

A birthday card from Sonali stood on Ma's bedside table. It was an extravagant one a foot tall, all red hearts and teddy bears encrusted with silver glitter. It dwarfed a framed black and white photograph of their father. Bapi was in full uniform, Sam Browne belt crossing him in a leather diagonal. Peak cap shading his eyes, chest heavy with ribbons. The photograph was so much a fixture of Ma's room that nobody noticed it any more than they noticed the light switch or faded dhurrie on the floor.

Along with Sonali's card came a letter airily informing them that she and Karan would be returning home two months earlier, in the beginning of September. She gave no reasons. Ma had told no one yet; Dida's finely balanced budget would be upset. She had planned on a celebration with gifts of clothes and jewellery. Money was being put aside every month for this purpose.

⁂

In those first days before the shock of Sonali's marriage percolated to conscious levels of acceptance, the sudden loss of her filled the house like an element. And if that element was water, they were all drowning in it while Sonali, a fresh green spring, had adroitly found the path of least resistance.

Ma took to her bed for two days. Chhobi and Dida tried to coax her to eat, Chhobi flashing back to 1971 when the dead look first crept into her eyes. Now Ma blamed herself, it was the first time she acknowledged the loss of Bapi as a father to Sonali. She worried incessantly about whether Karan, completely unknown, would make her happy.

Dida was caustic, hiding her own disappointment. 'Happiness. Are you happy? Am I happy? Happiness comes and it goes. It is not necessary.'

Chhobi secretly preferred Karan to Sonny, she thought him kind. She also thought that Sonali *would* be happy. Sonali… Sonali so propelled by inner impulse and outer stimuli, so buoyed by her own youth and beauty.

The introduction of Karan leached like sea-salt into their lives. From a ship owner to a ship's mate, for that was the position held by him, Dida was required to bridge a huge gap. Enforced optimism and a determination not to lose face made Dida view him as a balmy sea breeze, maybe tinged with tar but also fragrant with exotic cargoes to far-flung ports. Karan was on his second contract with a British-owned shipping company that was headquartered in Hull on the east coast of Britain. His wages when translated from pounds into rupees were undeniably good, but it was a contractual job without any real security. Sonali and he had left in June for a six-month contract and were to return in November in time for her to prepare for her final year B.A. examination.

The merchant navy as a profession was one that was unknown to the family. Doctors, engineers, scientists and professors – vocations that called for professional degrees that added a comet's tail of letters after one's name, these were desirable. Even Bapi although an army man had been a sapper, an engineer. In land-locked Delhi merchant marine smacked unpleasantly of trade, the word merchant somehow being a diminishing one to the family.

When Dida talked about Sonali's marriage it was in a skittering fashion, skimming over half submerged, murky realities. Dadu and Ma were mostly silent, although the former's disapproval and the latter's guilt sometimes showed in stray comments. Chhobi meanwhile began to read up on shipping. For the present she left Beryl Bainridge and Iris Murdoch, her favourites, quite untouched on the shelves of the British Council Library, delving instead into the history of shipping.

Chhobi being Chhobi, she began at the very beginning. She moved back several millennia in time and started with the ancient mariners; she sat up late reading about the Minoan explorations; the first discovered boat – the royal barge of the Egyptian Pharaoh Cheops. She confused myth with reality and read on about Jason and the Argonauts, blended fact and fiction with the expeditions of Odysseus, driven by the gods and the winds.

At the second-hand bookseller behind Plaza Cinema at Connaught Place, she unearthed an absolute gem. The leather-bound, gilt-edged volume was expensive. Inside the pages were slightly marked with holes burrowed by silver fish like coded messages penned by previous owners, but these were few and did not detract from the beauty of the sixteenth century maps of sea routes from Europe to India. Mosques, fortresses, wild beasts and warriors decorated the maps, crosses and crescents marked Portuguese and Muslim ships. She discovered the excitement of the days when trade between east and west first opened. Spices and silk, calico and indigo, hurricanes, scurvy and pirates – commerce stirred by ambition, greed, fear, danger and disease.

Late into the night, she lay in bed and wondered how it was for Sonali... long voyages when life contracted to the confines of a small cabin, outside the immeasurable ocean, sometimes mirror smooth glass, sometimes white whipped turbulent, stretching beyond the vision of the eye, to unfamiliar shores and unknown people.

⁕

Chitrahaar, today almost entirely devotional, began, startling Chhobi out of her brine flavoured reverie.

The doorbell rang insistently. Savitri went to check, closing down the sharp blade of her sickle-shaped knife mounted on the wooden stand. She came back with an incoherent message about Ratan Kaku.

'Doctor Sahib is still in his clinic,' Dida said dismissively. Ratan Kaku dropping in at meal times was always a problem. Dida had to hurriedly cook up some insipid stew for him, no chillies, and no fried onions, very little oil. The most irritating part of this unannounced dinnertime visit was the misplaced sense of guilt he evoked in them all. They hated to see his eyes gleam as he hungrily peered at their plates, salivating almost visibly, followed by his gaze of mournful dissatisfaction as he looked down at his own. Now an agitated Savitri was muttering something about a man speaking Hindi and refusing to move. Chhobi picked up her dupatta reluctantly and went to the gate.

A sweat-stained man stood there, carrying with him a powerful odour of onions and stale oil, his shirt so spattered with turmeric and grease that the original colour was scarcely discernible. He was from Bihar and addressed Chhobi in hesitant broken Bengali, relieved when she answered in Hindi. He worked in the main dhaba near the market, he said. He had for the past three weeks been supplying Ratan Kaku with food twice a day, carrying it to his house in a steel tiffin carrier, and waiting till he finished transferring it to a plate, then bringing back the order for the next meal along with the empty carrier.

The order was normally unvarying – butter chicken masala with vegetable pulao in the afternoon and mutton do piaza with egg paratha in the evening.

'Dhaba food! Butter chicken, Ratan Kaku? Do you mean that double-storied corner house on the main road?'

'Yes, yes, the one with the big building coming up next door.'

'But what happened to the maid who used to cook for him?'

Savitri piped in rapid Bengali, 'He kicked her out almost two months ago. Might be Meshomoshai's friend but his behaviour is peculiar, I was going to tell you all, nobody cleans his house anymore either.'

'But what has happened?'

'Today when I went to hand over the tiffin carrier the door was open, Sahib was crouching in his bed in pain, and in my presence he started vomiting blood. Somehow I got Doctor Sahib's house number. He is sick, very sick,' said the man.

Chhobi stared at him, then said, 'Okay, we will see to it, you go back.' She went to speak to Dadu who was reading a newspaper in his empty clinic.

They tried to phone Ratan Kaku but couldn't get through. Dadu picked up his bag and accompanied by Chhobi began to hurry to Kaku's house, shouting for Savitri to lock up the clinic.

It was a beautiful evening. The sky was streaked orange, slightly overcast with the promise of rain, trees green and sprouting new leaves. The boys were still playing cricket in the fading light, they could hear the thwack of the ball hitting the bat, the cheers of the fielders hidden behind the screen of shrubs that encircled the park. The streetlights had not yet been switched on. They passed a long line of cars outside the homeopath doctor's clinic. Chhobi couldn't help thinking wryly about Dadu's Calcutta Medical College degree and his lack of patients.

Rectangular stacks of rectangular bricks, four feet high, pyramids of river sand and assorted rubble almost blocked the access to Kaku's gate. Inside there were no signs of life. A padlock hung on the door. Several newspapers still tightly rolled into cylinders restrained by black rubber bands, lay tossed in an untidy heap on the verandah. With one accord Dadu and Chhobi turned their heads to look next door, but there wasn't much activity at the Goels. A solitary mason was watering the freshly laid brickwork with a hosepipe.

'Kaku?'

'Ratan, Ratan!' they both hailed, Chhobi peeping in from between a chink in the drawn curtains, rubbing at the smeared glass pane with a corner of her dupatta. It was quite dark inside. Dim light filtering in from a split cane chik screening the window revealed a scene of incredible disorder and filth. Soiled clothes and unwashed dishes lay tumbled together across the floor. The phone receiver dangled in mid air from a coiled wire. Although it was too dark to see clearly, she could see a large spreading stain of water seeping across the wall adjoining Goel's.

Dadu went to the back door and found it was bolted. The paved walkway leading to the rear was thickly covered with splatters of congealed cement and plaster. He stumbled over piles of broken brick rubble, half obscured by drifts of small yellow leaves shed by the gulmohar tree just outside the gate. The tree was normally pruned back, but had now thrust its boughs across the gate casting a dark shadow. Dadu was aghast – Ratan abhorred a mess.

He looked at the building coming up next door. It was obviously a block of flats. So far only the construction of a basement and ground floor had been completed, but the length of the house extended almost till the main road, flouting all the guidelines laid down by the Municipal Corporation.

Chhobi craned her neck to look at the first floor and saw a light burning in one of the rooms. Yelling for Dadu, she ran upstairs, skidding a little on the stairs that were slippery with patches of dark-green slime. The door was slightly ajar. She hesitated, nervous suddenly of what she would find. Some trick of acoustics, maybe an echo effect, amplified the whine of the traffic moving across the flyover. It was no wonder Mrs Menon had moved. A discordant cacophony, the constant blare of the horns of assorted automobiles, resounded in her ears. Buses seemed to rumble across her chest. The headlights of a truck, blinding in full beam, swung in a moving arc across her face and the half open door, then grew diffused as the street lights came on.

'Kaku?'

Dadu reached the landing, panting slightly. He pushed her aside, swinging the door wide open. The light was on in the front room that was as bare as when the Menons had vacated it six months ago. They found Kaku in the rear bedroom. The room was empty of any furniture save a folding cot with an aluminium frame upon which he lay. His face, half turned towards the door wasn't clearly visible. As light receded rapidly from the brilliant evening, it was as though darkness had steeped into his skin turning it to twilight.

Dadu fumbled for the light switch, clicking it on. Both he and Chhobi flinched at Kaku's face so terrible to behold in the sudden bright illumination. His breathing was laboured, each inhalation a visible effort, exhalation a wheeze. His eyelids were sunk shut in a face that was ash-coloured. A grey-white stubble filled the hollows of his cheeks, his head was uncomfortably twisted on the soiled pillow.

The air was fetid and sour. A tap in the adjoining bathroom dripped with metronomic monotony. Chhobi moved to open one of the tightly shut windows, recoiling as cobwebs clung to her face and clotted in her hair. Dust balls bowled across the floor near the window and came to rest against a blue plastic bucket that was being used as a slop pail. Chhobi gazed in fascination at the area under the bed. It was marked with several six-inch concentric spirals of ash, the burnt remnants of mosquito repelling smoke coils, as bizarre as the funeral pyres of some unknown crustaceans.

Dadu's face as he turned from his brief examination was urgent and grim. 'Wait here,' he ordered and then went downstairs to use the phone, picking up a bunch of keys dangling from a nail on the wall. He returned ten minutes later. He had called Dr Mitra who was arranging everything.

'Perforated ulcer,' said Dadu tersely, 'we need help to carry him downstairs. Who should we ask...?' precious minutes ticked by.

'The cricket team, I will ask the cricket team.' Chhobi was already slipping and sliding down the stairs in her haste, turning to give a backward glance at Dadu who was feverish in his efforts to infuse some life into that face of gloaming.

The game was over. The park was still ringing with the voices of the boys as they debated cricket and shared cigarettes. One of them was wiping the muddy wickets with a rag. Chhobi recognised some of them, they did the rounds of the houses collecting donations for Durga Puja. The average age must have been eighteen.

'Sonali's sister,' she heard them say as she approached. She spoke to one of the boys whom she recognised. Khokon, perhaps the captain of the team, took charge, trying to conceal his cigarette behind his back; a blue-grey tell-tale plume rose up almost perpendicular as no breeze stirred. One of the boys was despatched to the taxi stand near the market, and two of the taller ones accompanied Khokon and Chhobi to Kaku's.

Chhobi found herself telling them about Kaku's trouble as they waited for the taxi. She saw Khokon's jaw jut out as she described Goel's smiling threats.

The black and yellow Ambassador with its turbaned driver drew up at the gate. Dr Mitra's son, recently returned from the UK with the letters FRCS after his name, was going to operate. He had asked for two blood donors. Khokon and his friend volunteered. The other boy fetched a padlock from home to lock up Kaku's gate. Kaku had been vomiting again. A thin streak of blood had dribbled on his chest. Dadu somehow managed to put a shirt on over his soiled vest. The taxi left, the two boys sitting in the front with the driver, Dadu and Kaku in the rear seat. Chhobi returned home. It was a long journey to Dr Mitra's, she would have to inform Dida.

Dida had begun her midnight puja by the time a tired and dispirited Dadu returned home. Ma and Chhobi sitting behind Dida in the richly decorated puja room, wanted to question him, but waited for Dida to finish the hymn she was chanting. One from the *Brahma Samhita*, which contained verses sung by Lord Brahma in praise of Lord Krishna:

> I worship Govinda, the primeval Lord, who is adept at playing on His flute, who has blooming eyes like lotus petals, whose head is decked with a peacock's feather, whose beautiful body is tinged with the hue of blue clouds, and whose unique loveliness charms millions of cupids. Around His neck swings a garland of flowers graced with a moon-locket; jewelled ornaments adorn His two hands in which He hold His flute.

The sequel to the events that occurred on Janmashtami was that the cricket team took up the case of Ratan Kaku as common cause... picked up Goel's gauntlet as it were.

The emergency operation had saved Kaku's life. Khokon appeared on Saturday morning. He had come to take Dadu to Dr Mitra's nursing home. Dadu looked doubtfully at the battered old Royal Enfield motorcycle parked outside the gate. It belonged to Khokon's elder brother, a commercial artist in an advertising company.

Chhobi and Dida stood at the gate watching the motorcycle recede down the road. Chhobi fought down the urge to laugh until she heard a snort of laughter from Dida. Then they both giggled loudly watching Dadu's tense figure, uncomfortably perched and clutching at Khokon's helmeted body, grow smaller and smaller down the road. The clear acrylic visor that encased Khokon's face gave him an astronaut appearance, and Dadu had had to literally ready himself for take-off.

Kaku was sitting up in bed, looking much better despite the many tubes and dangling drains dripping blood-tinged fluids. A Malayali nurse was taking his blood pressure as they entered. Kaku was worrying about his medical bills, but Dr Mitra assured Dadu that payment could be somewhat deferred.

Though he didn't wish to upset him, Dadu just had to ask him a few questions – why had he moved upstairs to an unfurnished room? What had happened downstairs?

For a long time Kaku just fidgeted with the edge of his sheet. When he looked up at them, they were startled to see a cunning, almost sly expression cross his face. Goel's men were breaking in, he said. Bit by bit they were edging themselves in and squeezing him out.

'Nonsense,' said Dadu robustly.

But Kaku looked old and ill and frail again, when he spoke it was a querulous quaver. Turning his face to the wall, he said, 'I want to sleep, I won't talk about it.'

Nevertheless he did. He was prolix as words rushed forth as waters in a breached dam, pressing down on the crumbled wall of his defences.

Khokon was a silent observer, sitting on a plastic chair with his helmet on his knees. He rose now at Dadu's signal to leave, looking obstinate and angry, his chin, its outline blurred with a still downy beard, jutting in a characteristic look of belligerence which they would come to recognise.

On dropping Dadu safely home, Dida asked him to wait, warming up the remains of her famous malpuas – aniseed flavoured dumplings with lacy brown edges, dripping with syrup and melting in the mouth. She watched him clean up the large helping; it was pleasant having a mobile man of action around, even if he didn't shave as yet and was preoccupied mostly with cricket and motorbikes.

'Do you have Kaku's keys?' he asked Dadu, who replied in the affirmative. 'Good, let's examine the house and see what this Goel is up to. This evening after cricket,' he waved and was gone.

twelve

There was no cricket that evening. By mid-afternoon there was a big cloud build up and by 4 p.m. it was as though the sun had been extinguished. At first the air was uncomfortably still, and then deafening thunderclaps that seemed to originate from the ground not the sky announced the arrival of the heaviest rainfall of the monsoon. Chhobi and Dida began to hurriedly pick up the clothes from the clothesline, snatching at the saris so stiff with starch. They had sent Savitri home early when the sky grew so dark. Dida was fretting about Ma who hadn't carried her umbrella to office today. As Chhobi began to shut the windows, she could see the broad leaves of the kadamba tree tossing and shivering. The tree had just put out a profusion of golden orbs, blossoms as sweet as laddoos. The extreme corner of the small lawn was strewn with fallen champa flowers. Lightening crackled, clouds burst. There was such a roaring rush of sound and water, that Chhobi scarcely heard the doorbell ring. She opened the door to find a grinning Khokon and his friend, their shirts soaked and clinging to them as hot rods of rain slashed the air and struck their bodies.

'Let's go,' they said.

'In this rain?' she objected, but the boys had spotted Dadu in his clinic and were already dashing across the small patch of grass. Dadu gazing at the rain with unfocused eyes was still more reluctant. Already the water was collecting everywhere, churning into muddy whirlpools, skipping and frothing into coffee coloured bubbles where the bullet rain hit the puddles.

The boys were insistent. 'We have to tackle Goel before Kaku is discharged and that's going to be the end of the week. We must check the house today.'

Dadu had to bow down in the face of such teenage enthusiasm, reinforced as it was by the guilt of not visiting Ratan Kaku earlier and allowing him to reach such life-threatening deterioration. Grumbling a little under his breath, Dadu rolled up his trouser bottoms, put on his rubber Bata chappals and picked up the wide black umbrella with the curved wooden handle. It was so large it could almost substitute for a garden umbrella. Dida didn't want Chhobi to go, but Dadu gave her such a look of helpless entreaty that Chhobi took Ma's forgotten polka-dotted parasol and followed him. Her salwar bottoms were almost instantly caked with mud. Khokon and his friend led the way, without umbrellas, laughing, water in their eyes. Hair and wispy beards streaming.

A rank and mouldy odour greeted them at Kaku's. Even while unlocking the padlock on the gate they could see water rushing in a boiling stream down the stairs. A drain was blocked somewhere. Khokon kicked the rolled-up newspapers on the verandah, pushing them in deeper with his foot, where it was dry. Dadu was searching for the right key on the heavy bunch. The bottoms of his trousers were stained with dark tidemarks. Chhobi involuntarily stepped back as they clicked on the light. Huge cockroaches glittered as they shot for cover. The wall adjoining Goel's was peeling plaster, beaded with moisture in patches. The damp was a spreading peninsula, shaped like the outline of India, strongly defined. Soiled bed clothes lay jumbled with the dishes adding to the stale odour. It was oppressingly hot as all windows were tightly shut. A snowfall of torn scraps of paper, closely covered with Kaku's tiny writing, lay in the

SELINA SEN

corner. A file lay dumped on top of it. Chhobi picked it up, dusting it gingerly. In the kitchen, water and sludge had entered from beneath the door leading to the small backyard, sliding into the dining area like thick custard.

There was something strange about the walls. All pictures and hangings were missing. Kaku used to have a large mirror on the wall opposite the main entrance, now there was only a rectangular clean patch of plaster. In every room, square and oblong patches of brighter unfaded wall showed like the footprints of runaway illustrations.

Kaku's bedroom was at the rear, just behind the dining area that opened on to a small passage which led to the kitchen and then beyond to the second bedroom. A heavy desk had been dragged in front of the locked door. The boys heaved it aside while Dadu tried the keys. Everybody was silent, subdued in that sad, stale sodden house.

The door when it opened, opened onto a pit of madness. For a moment they stood stock-still, unable to enter into the room where paranoia crackled and fizzed like electricity. All the furniture – bed, chairs, TV, bookcase – had been dragged to the wall common with Goel's and stacked higgledy- piggledy. A crack in the wall, livid as a bolt of lightning, spread diagonally from floor to ceiling. In places it was two inches wide and they could glimpse a black space beyond.

Kaku had gathered every wall hanging and picture in the house and hung them from nails hammered above the crack as though to conceal it. The pictures hung anyhow, askew, even upside down. A large black and white official group photograph of Kaku at some seminar, a line drawing of Tagore, two mountainscapes, old calendars and a macramé jute elephant jostled for space. In the centre, the only picture hanging absolutely straight was one of Kali. Devi Uma at her most ferocious and terrifying, with blazing bloodthirsty eyes, red protruding tongue, adorned with a garland of human skulls, each of her ten hands armed with sharp weapons, unable however, to keep Kaku's fears, real and phantom, at bay.

'Cracked, yaar,' said Khokon's friend, voice trailing to a little squeak.

'Mindgobbling,' said Khokon to Chhobi who had a sudden insane desire to laugh at the malapropism, which somehow made perfect sense.

Dadu was pale, shamefaced, and unable to look at them as he herded them out and relocked the door. The rain had thinned to a fine drizzle. It was quite dark, the sky as though washed by ink. The boys went upstairs to locate the blocked drain. Khokon returned almost immediately saying he needed some light. He lit up the evening with a flaming torch fashioned from the rolled up newspapers on the verandah, but the terrace was so dumped with rubble from next door that they couldn't find the drain. Dadu was all for taking an official stand, complaining to the authorities, the powers that be. In this case the question was also *who were* they? It was Kaku's file discarded on the heap of waste paper that defeated him. It contained carbon copies of Kaku's correspondence, in chronological sequence. He had written first to the Municipal Corporation of Delhi, the Central Grievances Cell, the Resident, Welfare Association, *The Times of India*, *The Hindustan Times* and *The Statesman*. The tone and handwriting of those letters had changed as the months had passed. From an upright hand, 't's' crossed and 'i's' meticulously dotted, the writing had changed to a crazy wavering slant. The few sentences that could be deciphered seemed incoherent and meaningless.

※

Goel normally visited the construction site before noon. He arrived in a black Ambassador car, sitting on the back seat with his briefcase. A tiny bright blue fan rotated near his head. He parked in the shade of a neem tree just down the road from Kaku's.

For two days Khokon had waited and watched. On Saturday he acted. He gathered both teams and more. Twenty-four boys aged thirteen to nineteen, crouched behind the brick wall of Kaku's house. A solitary fellow lolled against the neem tree.

As the Ambassador drew up, the boy put both fingers in his mouth and gave a short signalling whistle. It was well timed, the ambush, a *coup d'etat*. The boys moved swiftly in answer to that summons, propelled by scenes from old western movies. Each of them carried a wicket, a bat, or fisted a hard scuffed ball. Khokon's latent Robin Hood qualities had surfaced.

Goel was tearing open a blue and silver foil packet of betel nut spiked with tobacco when he became aware of this human blockade in front of his car. Suddenly faces were pressed against the windowpanes, the windscreen, squashed grinning, grimacing faces, misting the glass with their breath. Most of them were weedy and awkward, chins covered with unimpressive peach fuzz – it was the sheer numbers that overwhelmed.

Khokon tapped on the window and as Goel gave a look of startled inquiry spoke in a voice silk smooth with insolence…

'Your car ran over my foot.'

Two of the tallest boys had begun to slowly whirl their bats, steadily stepping up the pace.

'Which foot? You were nowhere near my car.'

Khokon raised his foot clad in a fake Adidas, looked at it then shook his head. He repeated the motions in exaggerated mime actions with the other leg.

'Not my foot, must be his,' pointing towards his small army with a wicket. The point glinted in the sunlight. The boys had begun to whistle now, just a flat note, dappled sun gleaming on a thicket of arms and legs, bats and wickets. The bellicose jut to Khokon's chin very pronounced.

Goel started to bluster, his habitual smile dripping off his face as the sweat dripped off his liver-coloured safari suit. The driver, rattled and uncomprehending, got out of the car.

'*Chalo, chalo, yeh kya bakwas…*' and broke off in mid sentence, clutching his head as a ball bounced off it with a hard thud. There was a loud hissing sound. All four tyre valves had been unscrewed, the tail lights smashed with a splintering sound. Goel like the typical bully he was, was getting rapidly deflated along with his tyres. His driver, a man with a cleaner conscience but feeling frighteningly hemmed in, tried to raise his voice. '*Yeh ball marne ka kya mattalab?*' he shouted snatching at a ball and hurling it over their heads.

'Let's get rid of his balls,' said one of them, prodding him low in the stomach with a bat. The man suddenly made a dash for it, breaking through the imprisoning suffocating girdle.

'*Jaane do yaar*, let him go, Goel *er* balls bounce *koro*.'

'Goel's? Bloody eunuch, he has no balls.'

'*Oye hijra.*'

'No ball, no ball,' yelled an excited six-year-old who had tagged along with his elder brother and thought this was about cricket.

Khokon wanted to end it – the driver was bound to raise an alarm. He put his hand in through the half-open window and unlocked the door. Goel cowered back, his smile, now a grimace, pasted on his face, clinging on to his briefcase as a placebo.

Khokon gave the signal to disperse. The boys scattered in all directions, running swiftly as the dispersing fragments of an explosion. He leaned right into the car for a parting shot, 'We are not going to hurt you... as yet. Your neighbour, Mr Ratan Bose... Put his house in order, without delay.'

The driver returned with the chowkidar and two masons armed with pickaxes and shovels. They found Goel all alone, still clutching his briefcase. All four tyres were flat; he was speechless, stumped.

thirteen

Kaku's discharge from the hospital was something of an anti-climax, eclipsed by Sonali and Karan's sudden return, earlier even than Ma had expected.

It was a still airless day in early September. Not a leaf on the kadamba tree stirred. Chhobi and Ma were both at work. Dadu and Dida were sitting down to a rather frugal lunch of bhatey. The five-litre pressure cooker was dumped on the dining table, and steaming on their thalis were mounds of sticky rice surrounded by smaller pyramids of mashed boiled egg, potato and yellow dal, all garnished with green chilli and raw mustard oil.

Just as she was about to start eating Dida was surprised by the taxi that drew up at their gate. The yellow roof was piled with suitcases colourful with luggage tags fluttering like pennants. Incredulous, she caught a glimpse of Sonali at the gate. A glamorous Sonali, eyebrows thinned to a delicate arch and mouth glossy red. Hissing at Dadu, Dida shouted for Savitri, rushing to hide the pressure cooker in the kitchen. Her joy at being reunited with her favourite grandchild marred by the unexpectedness of it all, she hated surprises. Already her mind was ticking away, what would she offer them. The lunch they were eating was tasty enough, but made her cringe. Ideally she would have liked to have been caught unawares dining on saffron-flavoured biryani or coral-coloured prawns floating in a coconut-cream curry.

Karan refused lunch, insisting they had eaten the airline meal on the plane. He would be leaving for Hoshiarpur that very day by the night bus. His father was ailing. Sonali would be staying behind in Delhi. Even as Dida was calling up Ma and Chhobi to inform them of this sudden arrival, Karan was supervising the unloading of the luggage.

Dida was shooting covert looks at him. Her earlier impression was reinforced – he was quite dark-skinned for a Punjabi. Perhaps it was because he was so hirsute, quite a bonmanush. A blue-black five o' clock shadow appeared on his chin by noon. His forearms and the digits of his fingers were covered with silky black hair and curls clustered in the V-neck of his shirt. His best feature apart from his height, were his eyes, small but smiling with a fan light of crinkles at the corners. Lines acquired by hours of vigilance at sea, lonely navigational watches on the bridge, the constant scanning gaze, far-reaching to the shining line of the horizon.

They spent two weeks house-hunting before renting a two-bedroom flat. It was small and hot and on the third floor, sun beating down relentlessly on the roof. At first Sonali kept getting lost. The Delhi Development Authority Colony was a warren of a place, clusters of identical flats branching out from too-narrow lanes. A garbage dump just outside the entrance of the colony usually had the hindquarters of an undernourished cow protruding out from the overflowing enclosure in which skinny-shanked pi-dogs also foraged.

They had chosen the flat because it was close to Dida's house and also because it overlooked a bare patch of land with a TV transmission tower. The area would never be built upon and the air in the flat should be fresher than that in others.

'Our green lung,' Karan called it. The TV transmission tower looked like the Eiffel tower, he thought. Chhobi thought otherwise. What did flash through her mind as she trudged up the narrow stairs with the crumbling treads was the sweeping marble staircase in Sonny's house, dividing into two midway and lit up by the glittering chandelier.

It was a Sunday. Sonali had asked her to come and help put things in order. On the second floor below Sonali were the Kumars who had moved in only last month. Mr Kumar had retired from the Indian Railways. He must have been used to a lot of flunkeys, thought Chhobi, weren't the railways the largest employer of manpower in India, larger in numbers even than the Indian Army? She had read that somewhere. There was a mess on the Kumar's landing, who were owners not tenants of their flat and were getting the floors redone in marble tiles. Three Pomeranians yipped and yapped as Chhobi approached their landing. Mrs Kumar appeared to have moved half her garden from the sprawling British-built bungalow she had earlier occupied. Plants in cement tubs took up most of the landing and part of the narrow stairs. A fishtail palm almost smacked her in the eye, purple dracaenas and a yellow striped Song of India looked woebegone and wilted, money plants and monesteras drooped listlessly, much like their owners, disconsolate in their new habitat.

Sonali seemed to be adapting quite well to hers. She had spent the last two weeks shopping. Chhobi rang the bell, Sonali opened the door a crack on its safety chain and peeped out.

'I am a bit nervous when Karan is not at home. Not used to staying all alone. Dadu must have rubbed off on me. Look what I keep next to the door.' She showed her a plastic jar of chilli powder, glowing red embers in its depth.

'Where is Karan?'

'Out somewhere, fixing this or that, probably looking for a plumber. The water in the bathroom doesn't drain out, the floor slopes the wrong way.'

'How is his father? Shouldn't you have gone to Hoshiarpur to see him?'

Sonali gave a small shudder.

'I went there for three days, didn't I, just after our marriage. Luckily most of the family was in Delhi for the other wedding. It was so hot, I had to wear a thick silk salwar suit and eat pure ghee pinnis. His mother only speaks Punjabi. She doesn't like me. Not one bit.'

'The other wedding? Oh, Sonny.'

For an instant Sonali was back under the mango trees with Sonny, twined and entwined. Chhobi saw a flash ignite the gold in her eyes. It was a small glimpse but what Chhobi saw was unadulterated anger. Just a momentary spark, then it was gone.

Sonali looked different. Her hair was more elegant. She had swept it up above her ears, anchoring it with two faux tortoiseshell combs and twisting it into a chignon like a figure of eight. She wore a thin blouse soft as a rose petal and linen trousers. Gold flowers bloomed in her ears. She looked older, the newly thinned brows adding a certain sophistication to her expression, but the radiance she had worn during the Sonny days was extinguished.

'Come into the kitchen,' she said as she, drew Chhobi into the bright space where new pots and pans gleamed.

'Taste this – I tried to make a chicken curry. It is smelling a bit odd.' It was very over-cooked. The meat had left the bones and disintegrated into stringy fibres lost in the watery brown curry. Burnt cumin floated on the surface like dead midges. She dipped in a ladle and asked Chhobi to taste.

'Too much salt,' said Chhobi wrinkling her nose, 'tastes funny, not like chicken at all.'

'What then?'

'I don't know – neither fish nor flesh nor fowl! Why don't you learn from Dida? Chicken is expensive.'

Sonali shrugged, 'Karan will have to take us out. Forget cooking. Where should we put these?'

Everyone had imagined they had returned home two months earlier because Karan's father was ailing. The truth was the ship had been sold. In fact the company had gone into liquidation. Karan had embarked on a lengthy explanation about world recession, lack of charters, lack of cargoes, a conversation that had left Ma with a lingering sense of disquiet. They had stayed two weeks in Tokyo while the sale was being finalised. Two weeks that had appeared to have had a profound impact on Sonali. She had gone all stark and minimalist.

She had put down chattai matting all over the living room floor. A golden grass weave that hid the mottled, unevenly finished floor. Tatami mats, she called it after Tokyo. Seating was floor cushions covered in a black and white and charcoal weave. The sole illumination was the diffused globes of rice paper shades suspended from the corner. These gave such an insufficient light that the corners of the room melted to darkness and mystery.

'Are those from Japan?'

'Japan – no, no, they are from that joint Bhagirath Place, close to Red Fort.'

'Not place but palace. It was the old palace of Begum Samru. I did a short piece on her. She was a nautch girl who married a mercenary soldier, Walter Sombre, distorted to Samru. She later became holder of the fiefdom in Sardhana, near Meerut. She became a devout Christian and built the church in Sardhana, where they still have an annual pilgrimage. I went to see. Fascinating woman.'

'Why? Because she built a church?'

'Oh... forget it.' Sonali didn't really find other women interesting, especially not long dead ones. She wanted Chhobi's help to put up two posters she had bought in London, from a shop in Covent Garden. The Kiss by Austrian artist Klimt – all contorted passion and mingled drapery, a mosaic of glimmering gold squares, was pinned up above their bed.

The poster in the living room was a four-foot black and white print of a waiter in a hurry, bow tie flapping, coat tails flying, holding aloft an enormous platter. Upon that platter and simulated into a Little Mermaid posture was the Mona Lisa. La Gioconda on a silver dish, smiling. Chhobi spread it smooth while Sonali stood on a stool and hammered in tiny nails, holding them in her mouth like a carpenter.

'I am not sure I like it. Mona Lisa on a plate. Why?'

'I like the plate bit, Karan thinks I smile like her.'

'You? What do they say? Enigmatic. I believe she was actually trying to hide her black ugly teeth. Karan probably likes the plate too if he thinks she smiles like you – hungry for you?'

'Ya, ya, you know me – a tasty dish to set before the king.'

'More like King Kong, I mean he is so hairy.'

Sonali burst into a peal of laughter, stepping off the stool and collapsing on a cushion.

'King Kong! I like that, I am going to tell him. I call him Teddy Bear but King Kong… I have to tell him.'

'Don't be silly.' Chhobi had stepped back looking at the poster critically, she felt it was a bit lopsided, 'after all he is Jamai Babu.'

'What is Jamai Babu?' asked Karan, coming into the room, nodding indulgently at the poster, then smiling at Chhobi. 'I have something for you.' He disappeared into the bedroom.

'What, more things?'

They had all been inundated by Sonali's gifts – unsuitable and impractical objects – pink lacy cardigan for Ma encrusted with tiny seed pearls, a colour Ma would never wear. For Chhobi a make-up kit by Elizabeth Arden, and slim fit Levis that left her gasping for air after she had finished with her struggle to pull up the zipper. The sight of her round bottom straining at the cloth made her put it away in the deep recesses of her cupboard. Dida and Dadu had stared dumbfounded at theirs. His and Her matching quilted dressing gowns. How could Sonali forget that Dida wore no garment other than a sari? She had remembered to get Dida a bottle of Spanish saffron and a jar of dark California raisins that had pleased her, a saving grace.

Karan emerged now with a bottle of red Italian wine, grinning at Chhobi. 'Remember the first day we met?' The lines around his eyes fanning out when he smiled, deeply etched into his skin, not like crow's feet at all, but like the wings of a bird.

'The curry is a disaster. Karan, you will have to get some naans and kebabs. Don't give her too much wine, it goes to her head.'

'My wife is such an unusual Bong. Not interested in fish, or cooking, her favourite food is kadhi chawal.'

'That's true, she is not typical at all, dislikes Rabindra Sangeet, prefers to listen to Kishore Kumar yodelling.'

'Aha... but you can't deny that Kishore Kumar is also a Bong. A Bong's song.'

There were no wine glasses, so Sonali produced three ordinary Yera water glasses. Chhobi watched Karan grip the bottle between his knees and struggle with a too small corkscrew, an attachment on his red Swiss army knife.

The bottle in that position was like a phallic symbol, Chhobi thought, she seemed to have sex on her brain. Sex, such a mysterious word in her lexicon, a reflection of her own virgin state. Karan seemed to have it too. Sex on the brain. Not mystical in his case, but unslaked, unsatisfied. She noticed the way he constantly needed to touch Sonali – tuck back a stray wisp of hair, snake an arm about her waist, rest his palm on the back of her neck, fingers playing a silent medley on the fragile knobs of her spine. He was still very much a unidimensional figure to them all. A bedazzled, besotted, bewitched man, she thought wryly, pardoning herself the alliteration.

The wine was sweet and fruity.

'Our captain, British fellow, was a bit of a connoisseur, he really scoffed at this wine. Plonk, he called it. I like it better sweet otherwise it tastes like medicine. When we were buying this I tasted a wine called Lachryma Christi – tears of Christ. I wanted to buy for you, but it wasn't sweet at all. Sour tears. This is better, red wine, and today is Sunday, drinking the blood of Christ.' Sonali shot a sideways glance at Chhobi from her half-reclining posture on the heap of cushions, she was making a sly reference to Chhobi's oft-muttered Hail Mary.

Chhobi changed the subject. 'What about some proper arm chairs? Dadu cannot lower himself on to these cushions.'

Sonali shrugged, 'No money for sofa sets. We want to buy a car.' Karan's eyebrows knitted together, then as he saw Chhobi watching him, said with a laugh, 'Your sister will send me back to sea by tomorrow.'

'You will have to look for a new job, I mean a new company won't you?'

'That's right. The job situation is very tight right now with the slump. I have already put out some feelers. I met my batch mate yesterday, my batch mate from our training ship Rajendra. He spent the last two weeks job-hunting in Bombay without finding anything. It is so bad, he was saying, that the marine engineers are settling for jobs as maintenance engineers in three-star hotels. For navigators it's worse, there are no shore jobs for them. Anyway, not to worry, something will turn up.' Looking at Sonali he added, 'But the car will have to be an old, really old, second-hand one.' Then seeing Chhobi's worried expression, refilled her glass.

'Come on, come on, cheer up. Something will work out.'

The glasses jingled, Karan produced a tin of pink Spam, a jar of stuffed olives, spoils from the ship's store. Palates tingled. The girls relaxed, helping themselves to a loaf of bread. Karan started telling them not-so-funny Khalistan jokes.

'What is the national airline of Khalistan?... Give up?'

'Kithey Pacific!'

'What is the national bird of Khalistan?'

'Tandoori Chicken.'

fourteen

For long Dida had planned an elaborate meal for the ritual feeding of her new son-in-law. Chhobi had seen her scribble the menu on the back of a used envelope. It was an organised list with the ingredients required posted next to each entrée. The month of Jaishtha, mid-May to mid-June when summer was at its most terrible, was significant in Bengal for the observance of Jamai shashti, on the sixth day after the new moon. That was the time when Dida made her list, a time when the Jamai Babu was tossing about in the tumultuous waters of the Bay of Biscay.

Tradition required that on this day sons-in-law were given gifts and ceremoniously fed an elaborate meal, a kind of ritual offering by the in-laws to the mortal who held the well-being of their daughter in his hands. Now three months too late, but better than never, Dida was going ahead with her Jamai shashti celebrations.

Sonali looked at the table groaning with dishes, rolled her eyes heavenwards and said it was lucky Karan liked fish. Karan was used to fried fish made by the ship's cook, batter-fried filets English style. He was looking shy and embarrassed, dressed in a silk kurta with Bapi's gold buttons gifted to him by Ma. Ma had given Sonali part of her own wedding jewellery. Kaan balas, intricately wrought ears of gold to clip on over her own, dangling three tiered jhumkas like chandeliers. Six gold bangles and long chain punctuated with filigreed gold balls. Dida and Ma had presented her with eleven saris, four of them Dida's own, rich with real gold zariwork. Dida had given Karan a gold ring and a watch.

The power went as Karan and Dadu sat down to lunch. Chhobi, clicking snapshots for Dida's album with Karan's auto focus camera, thought the scene straight out of a Sharat Chandra novel. Karan in the centre in ghee-coloured silk, Ma flanking him on one side, Dida on the other. Barking short commands to Savitri in the kitchen as she fried luchis, Dida was rotating a palm leaf fan with a hollow reed handle, revolving it close to Karan's head. The sweat still dripped off his brow in the humid air and stained his kurta with irregular dark patches.

He broke into a fresh sweat when the laden bell metal thali was placed before him. The mandatory bitter vegetable, sour-sweet chutney, wedges of lime and tiny pyramid of salt were all present. Fishy concoctions were ranged all around the thali in bowls according to size, as varied as the jaltarang, ode to a watery zoo.

Pride of place had been given to a huge rui fish head. Thwack, smack right in the middle of the thali, dead eye looking reproachfully at Karan, fish lips turned down sadly. Both Chhobi and Ma had demurred at the fish head, but Dida insisted it was traditional. She had reluctantly relinquished ilish, agreeing Karan would not be able to debone this extremely bony delicacy. Dida whirred the fan faster, closer to his head, urging him to 'eat eat'.

Every time Savitri's luchis were less than perfect little balloons, Dida would rasp a warning 'Savitri!'

There was fish cooked with curd and raisins, fish koftas in a rich sauce redolent with garam masala, tapashe maach fried crisp in a spiced batter. The last procured with great difficulty and so named because the fish had a face sprouting droopy wise man's whiskers giving it a meditative air. Such a preponderance of frills and gills. Dida's dishes were a fine test of any man's mettle.

Sonali giggled at him from across the table, looking bridal in pink tissue. 'Eat eat,' she echoed Dida. It was one of those occasions when the women would eat later.

Karan tried to leaven the atmosphere with humour. He attempted to crack a few jokes, but these uneasy sallies did not fall on receptive ears. Dida continued to load his thali, piling it high with fluffy luchis that emitted savoury puffs of steam as they broke open.

'*Bas, bas,*' he exclaimed at this unaccustomed gluttony, but his protests fell on Dida's deaf ear. He carried on bravely in the battle of wills, baulking only at the sweets at the end of the meal. He wasn't blessed with the Bengali sweet tooth, he protested.

Dadu seated opposite had been eating silently and with relish unaffected by the lack of the fan. He was looking distinguished today in a dhoti kurta, not his usual pants, waist 40 inches, length 40 inches. He cradled a morsel of kofta with his tongue. It was a meal like those enjoyed in Mymensingh – lost forever in Bangladesh. A memory lingering still on his palate like taste. '*Madhurena samapayet,*' he interjected suddenly in Sanskrit – a meal should be finished with something sweet.

Karan managed to avoid the earthenware containers of rosogollas swimming in syrup and the pink sweet curd, both bought from the sweet shop in the market, but he couldn't refuse one of Dida's specialities – pati shapta. Coconut and caramelised sugar filled crepes that she normally made only during Durga Puja. He ate two, praising them effusively, rewarded by the smiles on the faces of the women, Savitri's beaming in the background, teeth black-stained with betel.

It was almost time for tea when Savitri sat down to eat in the kitchen, mopping her plate with the now cold and flat luchis. The power had returned and everybody was lethargic after such a gargantuan repast. Ma, Sonali and Chhobi chatted about clothes; Sonali began telling them about life on the ship. Karan dozed on the sagging sofa, he had an enviable capacity to catnap anywhere, anytime, waking up in an instant refreshed.

Sonali went in to lie down next to Dida and Dadu on the their high wide bed. Dida's hair was uncoiled spilling in tendrils across the pillow. Sonali nestled close to her, inhaling the old familiar scent, a mingling of Jabakusum hair oil and starched sari permeated through with the spice smell of the long hours in the kitchen. She began to tinkle Dida's bangles, one red, one white and one iron bound with gold. Made them speak to her in childhood voices. She had always played with the bangles. Ever since she was six and used to creep in to lie down with Dida in the afternoons, begging for fairy tales about princesses to which she listened enthralled.

By the time Sonali and Karan prepared to leave, it was raining again. Late evening and the light draining from the sky. It was to be one of the last heavy downpours of the season. Sonali pouted, she had had enough of the monsoons. She began to needle Karan about a car. Karan was in turn placatory, then promising, suddenly in a hurry to leave. He borrowed Dadu's big black umbrella and left to fetch an auto rickshaw from the stand. He was scarcely out of the room when Ma brought up the topic, so worrying her.

'Sona, what about your degree? You must rejoin classes and make up notes for lectures you have missed. It's only two months, thank god for the summer break.'

'Indu is xeroxing them for me,' Sonali's voice was sulky.

'And stop hounding Karan,' reproved Chhobi.

Sonali replied plaintively, 'But he promised me, he promised me that he would teach me to drive.'

Dadu was curiously restive, eager for them to leave. He wanted to visit Ratan Kaku whom he hadn't seen for almost a week. Kaku had moved upstairs to Mrs Menon's vacated apartment. His old maid was back, Savitri had fetched her. Goel had sent his masons to clear the rubble from the roof and fix the blocked drain. But Kaku so far had refused to live on the ground floor again where the cracked walls still wept with condensation.

Kaku had phoned that morning. He sounded much stronger. A vibrating under-current of excitement almost jerked the telephone wire. He was insistent that they visit in the evening. All of them including Ma and Dida.

They knew something was afoot, when a mysterious Khokon had dropped in a week ago. Between demolishing a bowl of Dida's khir he had triumphantly scattered words like checkmate and bowled out, cryptic but telling.

Dida refused to go till the rain stopped. It was almost eight o' clock when they finally stepped out. The downpour had left a coolness in the air, puddles on the edges of the lane. Ma upset over her little altercation with Sonali was lying down. She could feel the throbbing onset of a migraine.

At the mouth of the crossing where their lane met Kaku's at right angles they stopped short. Kaku's house was no longer a short and shabby dwelling, dwarfed by the scaffolding next door.

Stretching skywards on Kaku's rooftop was an iron grid framework as massive as a dinosaur's skeleton. It held in its arms a blue neon highway stretching towards a point in the infinite distance. Flashing on that highway was a red tyre on the fast track, accelerating up the fluorescent road in an impressive welter of discs and treads. Foot-high white-lit letters that spelled the name of a well-known brand in automobile tyres surmounted the illumined road. The letters blinked on and off. It was an arresting display.

A small figure sat on the upstairs balcony, face and shirt turning pink, blue, and incandescent white in turn. Puddles of water near the gate winked blue and red. As a scooter splashed through the water, the colours shimmered and melted together, spraying up in diamond and sapphire sparkles.

For an instant Chhobi felt a little dizzy underneath that sky with the whirling wheel. Upwards it travelled on a road that dazzled, a soundless song climbing an invisible stair, turning past into future, despondency into joy.

Providence had intervened in the form of Khokon riding on his battered and borrowed Enfield bike. Khokon's elder brother in advertising had taken a look at the place. It was the perfect site for a hoarding he said, and had immediately, easily rented the roof top space. The rush of traffic rising on the new flyover couldn't escape the hoarding. Facing the commuters at the highest point of their road was this illusionary track of coloured lights suspended on iron ribs, a wheel endlessly, effortlessly spinning heavenwards.

'How much? How much? Ask him how much?' was Dida's urgent query.

'How much... What?' said a dazed and dazzled Dadu.

'Tchh! How much rent is he getting for that, of course.'

Ratan Kaku was being paid fifteen thousand rupees a month for the skywriting on his roof, more than double the rent the Menons had given him. By those standards he was a rich man indeed.

Dida gave a little sigh. 'I would hate to have that ugly contraption on my roof,' she said.

fifteen

It was a twelve-year-old grey Fiat they bought. Karan took a car mechanic from the neighbourhood garage along with him, after cutting out the advertisements from the Sunday classifieds. It was the third car on his list. The first impression made Karan believe it would break down before starting up. The body was badly dented, the rear bumper held up by a loop of wire and the paintwork patchy. The doors were disintegrating, the seat covers so worn out that the padding spilled out in places.

The mechanic's black-rimmed fingers were busy checking, sounding and rechecking. He prodded the tyres, recently retreaded and firm, and then started the engine, cocking his head to listen to the whine.

'*Theek hai*, tuning *chahiye*,' he said, then disappeared behind the bonnet, giving Karan an affirmatory nod when he emerged. The owner had received an early allotment of a new Maruti and was eager to sell. Karan and he shook hands in mutual satisfaction as they quickly agreed on a price.

Sonali, waiting impatiently at home, almost burst into tears when she saw the car.

'You've been swindled,' she said, voice shrill with

disappointment. 'Look at the dents,' petulantly kicking at a tyre which held firm. 'The seats are torn, the doors are showering rust,' banging a door violently. 'This thing… this bumper is hanging on with a piece of string.'

'Wire,' corrected Karan quietly. 'The engine, tyres and suspension are all good. The rest is cosmetic stuff we will fix it slowly. It is a bargain.'

'Yes, a bargain for the guy who palmed it off on you.'

It was the worst fight they had had. But by evening Sonali had recovered, keen to start her first lesson in driving.

It soon became apparent that she had little mechanical aptitude and less judgment of space and distance.

The first problem was that the car wouldn't start unless the choke was pulled out. Sonali could never remember to do this, pumping instead on the accelerator in frenzy. Coordination of clutch and gear was another thing she found difficult to synchronise. Every time she pressed the pedals to change gear the car either stalled or surged forward in a sudden violent leap, making Karan bang his head on the windscreen. The progress they made down the road was in hiccoughs, stopping and starting, starting and stopping.

Tired of involuntarily pressing an imaginary brake on his side of the car, Karan blamed her ineptitude on his poor teaching and arranged for her to have driving lessons from the Mahindra Driving School.

For the next two weeks, every evening an even more battered Fiat would toot its horn outside their flat and Sonali would run down for her half-hour class. On the first day, Karan had taken one look at the bell-bottom sideburns of the instructor and decided to accompany them. Like a dog guarding a bone. After the first few lessons, however, he relaxed. The man was decent even if he did look like a minor villain from a Mumbai film. The driving school car had rectangular banners on the roof with the legend Mahindra Driving in italics. The car was fitted with a parallel set of pedals for the instructor to control the gear and brake.

The instructor was obviously a cinema addict for matching his mode of dress, he was given to spouting dialogue from well-known potboilers, imbuing an ordinary zebra crossing with a dramatic turn.

'*Bilkul bindaas ho ke chaliye*,' he said, indicating she should blow the horn incessantly, ploughing through cyclists and pedestrians. The changing of gears was still difficult but eased somewhat by his advice to ride the clutch.

Sholay must have been his favourite film for he referred to the car as Dhanno and Dhanno would roar past other vehicles, overtaking them by a mere hair's breadth. '*Tera kya hoga*, Kaaliya,' was another of his favourite lines. It was delivered in the soft-spoken menace underlying his Gabbar Singh impersonation. Kaaliya would be some precariously perched pillion rider or a Saturday beggar with his tin can, swerving away in a narrow escape.

The last four lessons were reserved for parking and reverse gear. For these they went down to the open spaces of Tughlakabad, a couple of kilometres beyond their apartment.

Tughlakabad, the abandoned citadel built with great velocity by Tughlak Shah in the fourteenth century. Chhobi came along for one lesson. She loved the Tughlakabad area and had worked on a story about it, a longish piece that had received some appreciative letters from readers.

Tughlak Shah was accustomed to the constant attacks of enemies in the frontier provinces where he had been before invading Delhi. Dissatisfied with the low walls of Old Delhi he had built this fort with towering walls half way up and around a rocky hill. Although he had built within the fort great reservoirs for the entrapment of rainwater, the inhabitants found this water sufficed only for emergencies, and so could not live within the fort.

Another reason for the desertion of Tughlakabad was a curse uttered against it by the Sufi saint Nizamuddin, a contemporary of Tughlak Shah, and daggers drawn with him. Nizamuddin was also engaged at the same time in the building of his own dwelling in the city. The king Tughlak Shah wanted every mason for the construction of his fort, and forbade anyone to work for Nizamuddin. The saint circumvented this problem by building at night, but the king got to hear of it and cut off his supplies of oil so there was no light to work by.

The saint was so furious that he cursed the new city. 'May it remain deserted or only a habitation for Gujjars,' he pronounced. And so it was, the fort now a crumbling ruin remained uninhabited forever. The only creatures multiplying within it were the peacocks and the monkeys.

The setting sun was limning the rising and crumbling walls in a brilliant wash of orange light. Peepul trees grew from crevices between the stones where birds had deposited the seeds. Sonali was trying to get the car to move backwards. She was spinning the wheel with an unfamiliar effort, brow knitted in concentration, struggling to coordinate the opposite motions of the wheel and the car. It stalled after a jerky and zigzag backward movement.

Chhobi got out. She supposed Sonali's car was an improvement on the auto rickshaw, an escape from those low level vehicles with high level pollution. She climbed upward towards the entrance of the fort. The huge stones were still arranged in a perfect arch. A wild mehndi bush was releasing its fragrance in the air. Last time she had come here, she had met a research scholar who was doing her doctorate on the Tughlakabad monkeys. They were much less aggressive than the Simla ones.

A peacock screeched on the ramparts., Chhobi caught her breath as it suddenly spread its tail feathers. It was a rare sight. The warm orange light of the dying sun lit up the iridescent greens and blues, a multitude of winking eyes. A good omen. She could not see its ugly feet. It screeched again its name in Hindi...

Mayur... mayur!

This gave the word onomatopoeia quite a new meaning, Chhobi grinned to herself, thinking suddenly of Sister Agnes spelling it out, her chalk scraping on the blackboard. She had tried illustrating the meaning with another bird, the cuckoo. Chhobi remembered her freckled face looking at a class of thirty bemused schoolgirls, none of whom had seen, leave alone heard a cuckoo.

She felt happy, engulfed with the feeling that landmark events were about to take place in her life. Chhobi hugged her secret close to her with an increasingly wonderful sense of possession. It was her fortress, one to which she could retreat, not like Tughlak Shah's Tughlakabad. Ever since the first letter had arrived a week ago, she had performed her daily tasks in a perfunctory and distracted fashion, all the while nursing her glorious secret. Though she was not normally conspiratorial by nature, she felt so liberated by it.

It was lucky that she and not Dida had received the mail. Had Dida seen the letter with the American stamps, she would have had to answer a hundred different questions. Dida would have immediately built up towering castles, Chhobi wanted to wait until she could be sure of more concrete foundations

She had taken the letter into the bathroom when it arrived, put down the lid of the WC, sat down and opened it with fingers that were clumsy and fumbling. She could hear her pulse beat, uneven and staccato. The letter was from the admissions committee of the UCLA:

Dear Ms Chandrayee Dutt,
We have pleasure in offering you a place in our doctoral programme, we offer also a research assistantship. Although there was a lot of competition, the admissions committee was impressed with the quality of your work in the paper submitted along with your application…

For a moment after reading the letter she went completely blank, the Lord's Prayer jumbling through her mind. Then a gulf spanning the Atlantic and Pacific Oceans yawned between her and Delhi.

Putting the letter down, she began to wash her hands and face. The water suddenly seemed a very different element, a substance of magic – breaking, running, shining, frothing and bubbling. It gathered in her cupped palms in pure blue gulps, sparkling like the liquid sky. A sky on which a jet plane streaked westwards.

She imagined the Golden Gate Bridge, the Statue of Liberty,

Mount Rushmore. In the background, vividly backlit, fluttered an enormous flag – stars and stripes. America for her was so coloured by Hollywood's lenses. For an instant she paused mid-flight in England. She would have felt less of a stranger there, she knew, tied to it by history, the years of schooling by the Irish, by British writers, their words collected in the stack of orange spined paperbacks by her bedside.

Now, she turned to watch Sonali somehow execute an almost perfect parallel parking between two stones placed at a car's breadth by the instructor. Unfortunately she could not repeat that performance, shrugging as she gave up. What Sonali lacked in ability, the instructor taught her to more than compensate with a huge dose of overconfidence. He turned her into a reckless road hog.

Chhobi told Rosemary the news, still quiet about it at home. Rosemary, although very glad for her sake, wanted her to postpone her departure by another term. The magazine would be celebrating its tenth anniversary next year and they were bringing out a commemorative book on Delhi. A tobacco company was sponsoring it and Rosemary wanted Chhobi to write the text, very much on the lines of the historical sketches she had already been doing. Flattered but doubtful, Chhobi agreed to write to UCLA for permission, which was granted. The delay in departure was to be a blessing in disguise.

sixteen

While a glad abundance of opportunities were opening up for Chhobi, doors were shutting tight for Karan. With every passing day, his face grew thinner, lined and grim.

The money earned from his last contract was almost finished. Besides furnishing and renting a flat, he had had hospital bills to clear. Soon after their return, his father had been referred to a hospital in Jalandhar where the spasms of excruciating stomach pain had been diagnosed as gall bladder stones. He had been admitted for a week post surgery before the doctors pronounced him fit enough to travel back to Hoshiarpur. The bill had been hefty.

Every morning Karan would go down to the nearby public phone booth and call up companies in Bombay and Calcutta. There were no jobs. He had sent his CV to all the overseas offices he had collected addresses of, but so far – nothing. At first he had applied only to representatives of foreign companies in India – the wages were in dollars. But now as pointed tongues of desperation began licking at him he was driven to Indian companies plying small ships along the coast, some of them scarcely better than tramp trawlers.

Of late he had been thinking of those three days just after his sudden wedding when he had taken Sonali to Hoshiarpur to meet Beeji, his mother. He was not very attached to her, she was an austere superstitious woman much given to fasts and purifying pujas. On the second day she had taken both Karan and Sonali to the family astrologer. Sonali knew the exact time of her birth although the horoscope made for her by Bapi had been misplaced in one of their frequent army transfers. Neither Ma nor Dida believed in trying to divine the future.

Karan recalled the astrologer's room clearly. He had had to stoop to enter through the doorway with the depressed lintel. The room was small, freshly whitewashed and very bare. It was furnished only with a woven dhurrie covered with a white sheet and a low munimji's desk. Karan had been there twice earlier. The last time was when he had decided to join the merchant navy. A decision vehemently opposed by his Beeji. The astrologer had strongly reinforced her negative views on his choice of profession, shaking his head and insisting that the element water was inauspicious for him.

Now this fresh calamity. He was her only son, born after three daughters and years of penance and prayers. Beeji was unable to hide her bitterness over his unexpected marriage, but was prepared to forgive all if Sonali's horoscope should prove favourable. Beeji had nurtured such hopes of Kulwanti's daughter, strapping girl and such a strong fate line! This Sonali was pretty she couldn't dispute that but so thin, she looked as if she would blow away if you breathed on her. And her son such an embarrassment, bewitched, how his eyes followed her every movement. Even so, now if her stars were to prove propitious she would overlook everything.

The astrologer, a man in his mid-fifties had the most beautiful hands, thin and tapered with skin so fine, the fingers appeared translucent. They watched those hands make rapid calculations on a sheet of paper. Then they drew a chart for Sonali with intersecting triangles and diamonds. After studying it for a while, he took out Karan's horoscope, a much worn piece of paper. He finally asked

Sonali in Punjabi to show him her palm. She extended a slim hand, fingernails painted a pearly pink. Beeji gave her a look of distaste, and with her own prosaic and work worn one twisted Sonali's so it was palm upwards. There was silence, then Sonali nudged Karan in a sibilant whisper,'What do my lines say? Ask him, no, ask him?'

The astrologer told them both to wait outside on the verandah while he conferred with Beeji.

'Obviously nothing very good,' deduced Sonali, then shrugged, 'I don't believe in all this anyway.'

'Nor do I, in any case my stars are supposed to be very inauspicious for the next year or so, Beeji's hoping your horoscope will have a beneficial influence and counter my bad luck.'

'Bad luck! She must be thinking it's me that's brought it – bad lines, bad stars, bad girl… Bad Bong girl.'

'Of course not,' Karan said his hand shooting out to cover her delicate one like a hot hairy animal. The astrologer's daughter bringing them tall tumblers of foaming lassi was scandalised at this open show of affection.

Sonali, city girl, wasn't used to the silence, punctuated only by the steady throb of a tube well pumping, far away.

'I miss it,' she told Karan. He leaned towards her and wiped her white moustache with his finger, licking the froth from the tip. A gasp behind the doorway informed them they were being observed, but they didn't care. The crinkles around Karan's eyes deepened as he contained his laughter.

'What do you miss?'

'The lovely Delhi noises – traffic, subziwala shouting for Dida, slogans screamed by rallying workers… Everything.'

Beeji emerged. She looked very agitated as she thanked the astrologer. Obviously payments had been made inside.

Sonali's stars, Saturn in particular, were inauspiciously aligned with Rahu and Ketu. The negative impact was very strong on Karan's already jinxed chart. The astrologer had suggested some solutions for countering his malefic predictions. Damage control. The first was to perform the navgraha or nine planets puja every

Saturday for the entire period. He prescribed that Sonali should wear a ruby ring of a certain weight on her ring finger. The third safeguard was a special sloka, which they were both to repeat one hundred and eight times every morning.

'Rahu, Ketu... what exactly is that?' Sonali's tone was impatient bordering on impertinence. Karan explained, he knew only too well how the forces of Rahu and Ketu had governed his mother's life.

'Hasn't Dida told you about Rahu?'

'My Dida is not superstitious, she does puja because it makes her happy, she doesn't ask anything of her Krishna, she told me.'

'Okay, okay, you know the story when the gods churned the oceans to obtain amrit or the elixir of immortality?'

'Vaguely.'

'Anyway Rahu and Ketu are two shadow planets. They were originally monster demons with tails like comets. One day when the gods were drinking amrit, or ambrosia, they became jealous and disguising themselves as gods began guzzling the amrit like a river. The sun and moon saw them and reported them to Vishnu, for only the gods may imbibe this wine of immortality. Vishnu took his discus and sliced through their necks. Their bodies fell to the ground uprooting rivers and mountains, but their heads stayed alive. They rose up in the sky devouring the moon in revenge every month, and less frequently the sun, when they cause eclipses.'

'What has all this to do with me or my horoscope?'

'Well I don't know... the alignment of Rahu and Ketu along with other stars, it's like an eclipse in one's personal life, I guess.'

Sonali's faced darkened with distress. The shadow that was cast over her sun... Sonny. That was her eclipse. Sonny ditching her... what had Chhobi's advice been... Balls to him, she repeated the words to herself, shaking off that black penumbral spot.

'An eclipse is a brief phenomenon, isn't it? Anyway I don't believe in all this mumbo-jumbo mantras one hundred and eight times a day, she must be joking.' Sonali had finished softly but firmly, looking at Beeji defiantly.

Karan was carefully sticking capital 'Ls' on both windscreens with red scotch tape. Today was Sonali's driving test. It was only a formality, the Mahendra Driving School had assured her. For a fee of Rs 800 they would arrange for her to receive her licence, in fact her presence was little more than a token one. Even so Karan was a bit worried, Sonali hadn't learnt how to reverse. She had driven alone to Dida's house one day and circled the entire block of houses to return without reversing. She felt she could manage quite well without that fourth gear.

An avenue of ancient gnarled tamarind trees led the way to the Road Transport Office, a foliage of fine leaves a grey-green shade like the lichen on Simla's rocks. Outside the drab building were a cluster of touts and contact men, communicating with each other in mysterious ways. Like a multitude of other subsystems in Delhi, born out of a need for corner-cutting through the myriad of bureaucratic ceremonies festooning even a simple procedure like getting a cooking gas connection, it worked well.

A doctor with a genuine MBBS degree was signing certificates of medical fitness, resting them on his hard-topped briefcase placed on the pillion seat of his scooter. His makeshift portable chambers.

Mahendra's man found them, and returned in a few minutes. His contacts must have been the best for they were jumping the queue, moving up to the very top of the line. Sonali was required only to drive around the field in second gear and within the hour she had her licence.

Whooping with self-congratulatory exclamations, Sonali drove them to Chhobi's office nearby, and swept in, hair and dupatta flying, a diffident Karan following in the wake of such exuberance. Shushing her and observing Rosemary circling like a watchful cheel, Chhobi looked at her watch, half an hour to go. She picked up her green plastic tiffin box and prepared to carry her work home with her. People in the office were looking curiously at Sonali, the beautiful younger sister who had eloped.

It was just before five and the home rush of commuters had yet to swell to their full peak. Sonali was going to drive all the way home. Karan disappeared for a moment and returned handing Chhobi a tall paper cone of roasted peanuts, warm and fresh. The first that season, nuts flaking papery pink inner skins. Sonali began to incline her head towards Karan who would pop in a peanut between her parted lips. She was flushed with excitement as she manoeuvred the grey Fiat into a gap between a bus and a rickshaw.

'Not bad,' commented Chhobi, then looking at Karan's face so wan and withdrawn, asked him, 'What's wrong Karan?'

He looked startled for a moment at her quick perception, and then smiled. His wife had so far noticed little amiss, despite his inertia in bed.

'It's that same old story, you know – apply, apply, no reply.'

He was half twisted in the front seat and glancing at both of them, addressing Chhobi but including Sonali in the conversation.

'I went to Talwar Shipping yesterday. Actually they had heard I was looking for a job, and had sent for me.'

For a moment Chhobi couldn't connect – Talwar Shipping?

Then she remembered and gave Karan a penetrating stare. Sonali had registered at once, the knuckles gripping the steering wheel had turned white with tension. For one crippling moment Karan was unable to continue. He was a sensible man, only once stirred by passion strong enough to usurp his governing sense of reason. He had feared Sonali's reaction would be extreme, that was why he had decided to broach the topic in Chhobi's presence.

The sisters were silent, waiting for him to continue. Sonali spat a peanut out of the window with an audible 'Pthu', Chhobi munched hard.

'It will be a very short contract, just a couple of voyages to tide us over. There is nothing available, absolutely nothing. As it is I should be grateful to them they are helping out. After all Beeji's mother and Mrs Bhai Sahibs' mother were sisters. Don't think I want to, there is absolutely no choice... The ships are very small and in a poor state of repair. It is not what I am used to... but...'

Sonali's driving was jerky, all the happy excitement vanished from her face.

'Talwar Shipping!' she said and looked at Chhobi in the rear-view mirror, their glances touching in mutual anger and humiliation. Beholden to Sonny. Sonali felt something snap inside. She was driving much too fast, foot thrusting down on the pedal as though goading the car with a spur. There was a sickening thud as she hit an Ambassador a glancing glow and sped past. Although it was the grey Fiat that was dented, the Ambassador increased its speed in angry pursuit.

'Slow down, Sonali!'

'Sonali, stop the car.'

The entreaties fell on deaf ears. She was forced to halt at the red light. The fat man in the Ambassador drew up alongside shouting, jowls jingling, all his massive flesh in enraged motion. Karan and Chhobi made placatory gestures, pointing at the red L on the windscreen. Sonali stared stonily ahead. Then as the light changed, she leaned out of the window and jerked up her hand, crooking it at the elbow, middle finger extended in a universally offensive gesture before racing away. The fat man was too astounded to react and his car stalled, holding up the traffic in a cacophony of impatient horns.

'Where did you pick up that?!' gasped Chhobi

'From the bo'sun on the ship, where else?' came the furious retort. There was a strange singing roar in Sonali's ears. She felt the reopening of a terrible wound inside her. She pressed harder on the accelerator.

'Never do that again,' shouted Karan as he grasped the wheel and made her stop the car to exchange places with him. Chhobi had gathered herself into a tight ball in the corner of the back seat. She was horribly embarrassed to be caught in the middle of this ugly spat, but for once was in perfect accord with Sonali.

Karan drove in complete silence, Sonali looked sphinx-like out of the window. Chhobi unfurled the empty paper cone, it was a sheet of newsprint. Dusting off the peanut bits, she began to read the paper with extreme concentration.

It was part of an article on nationalism, more specifically Mrs Gandhi's views on nationalism. There were excerpts from a recent parliamentary debate in which Mrs Gandhi had intervened to respond to remarks coming from one opposition Member of Parliament to the effect that India was 'many nations'.

'I strongly deplore the remarks,' Mrs Gandhi stated, 'India is one nation, it was one nation and it will remain one nation.' The article's next paragraphs reiterated the point. It mentioned Indira Gandhi's interview with the Yugoslav news agency, Tanjug, where she insisted the concept of the Republican nation state was a repudiation of the concept of nationality based on tribal, ethnic, regional and religious definitions. The letters broke off in mid-sentence where the page ended.

The words were jumbling together, running up against one another in a blur. Chhobi was unable to focus. Little paroxysms of indignation and anger were going off as flares in her mind. She hurled the page out of the window, Mrs Gandhi's words dissipating in the slipstream of the speeding car. Chhobi wanted to blurt out her objections, but bottled them instead – Oh God, oh God, this is what comes of marrying a poor relative, were they never to be free of Sonny?

Sonali gave Karan a look cold enough to freeze him.

'Don't think I will be sailing on a Talwar ship. If that's all you can manage, you go alone.'

'Of course, of course. I wouldn't take you on their ships. I have seen them in Bombay, they are rust-heaps and very small, not like our last ship with a separate day room and Austrian cooks. The Talwars only have three ships, you know, and two of them will be doing this same charter.' Karan's tone was one of extreme reconciliation, voice sprouting olive branches and white flags.

He continued, eager to restore harmony.

'It will be just a couple of voyages, not more than three while I look for something better. I should be back by February. Their ships are plying between the South Indian coast and the East, Cambodia, Malaysia – short trips. I asked Bhai Sahib about the cargo, but he was a bit vague. He said his nephew in Bombay was handling it. Must be tramping around. Cargoes are so hard to fix these days... I had to accept, just for some breathing time.'

Chhobi felt sorry for him. She wanted to reassure him that it was all right, desperate times called for desperate measures, but Sonali threw Karan a look that congealed his placatory speech, and extinguished Chhobi's clichés glimmering with good cheer. They lapsed into silence again.

book two

Two sister cargo ships belonging to the same shipping company, disappeared simultaneously in the Bay of Bengal without trace. The element of mystery and intrigue surrounding the case has only increased. Till last fortnight, there were still no definite clues as to the disappearance of the ships with their entire crew but maritime experts are convinced of foul play as are the families of the missing seamen.

– Extract from a report by Shekhar Gupta, *India Today*, 1985.

book two

one

Dadu and Ratan Kaku were drinking tea on the verandah. Ratan Kaku, in an expensive cream-coloured shirt and spanking new Quo Vadis Bata sandals, looked relaxed and healthy. It was that time of the year when they were both very homesick for Bengal. Mymensingh, lost forever in Bangladesh. A time when the rains were almost over, and the fields thick standing with the rice harvest, the white rush-like kash flowers edging ponds and rivers in full bloom. The dank greenness of the monsoon replaced by autumn tints of gold and bronze. Excitement mounting for the visit of the goddess Durga, riding on a lion, each of her ten arms bearing a weapon as she triumphed over the devil Maheshasura. This year both of them rehashed a letter from Ratan Kaku's brother in Calcutta. The letter described his son's visit to Bangladesh.

'Remember my brother Foni Da?'

'Yes, yes, used to be good at football.'

'Last month his son had gone to Dhaka with some business delegation… he is trying to develop new products in jute, you know.'

'Go on, go on, about Dhaka.'

'Foni Da had talked so much about Mymensingh, the beauty of

the Brahmaputra, that his son decided to hire a taxi in Dhaka, travel north and see his father's birthplace for himself.'

'Yes, yes... and?'

Kaku's eyes dipped downwards into the letter as if unable to comprehend.

'... He couldn't find any of the places mentioned by Fonida.'

'What!'

'After all his father had often pointed out the area to him, he still had maps of the place and photographs, talked about it so much that his son felt he would instantly recognise it. After roaming around for several hours, he gave up and turned back toward Dhaka. He stopped at a petrol pump and there an old attendant told him.'

'Told him?'

'Yes, Ramlakshmanpur had been renamed, it was called Ahmed Bari, and Kali Bazaar had become Islamic too, it was called Fatema Nagar. He could recognise no names in that area belonging to either his father's maps or his father's memories.'

Ratan Kaku and Dadu looked at each other, then retreated into the silent shell of their past. Did the reality of one's birthplace vanishing deny the truth of one's present existence?

Dadu's family used to have their own private celebration of Durga puja, a celebration of great pomp and splendour. They would commission a life-sized image of the goddess, vibrant life breathed into the idol of straw and clay during the four hectic days.

Of course, in Delhi nobody had private puja celebrations.

More than the beating of the dhak, the incense-wreathed aratis, the throng at the pandal, Chhobi loved the chanting incantation of the Chandipath a week before the pujas. The whole family would be up before dawn to gather around the old Bakelite radiogram to listen to AIR's broadcast of the hymn eulogising the Maha Devi's victories. A poem of twelve cantos from the Markandeya Purana supposedly recited by the goddess herself:

> ... In autumn, in October when ripen the fruits of rain
> Come to me and perform puja : I give children and grain.
> Those who have listened to this hymn will know me when they look

They know my triumphs of the past recounted in this book
....When you are lost, imprisoned, or exhausted, near starvation,
Recite this poem and I will work for your liberation
If you are on a ship at sea in danger and distress
Recite this hymn and I will be near you in happiness.

The last stanza, danger and distress at sea, was to prove prophetic.

The build-up to the festivities at this puja were interrupted by Karan's departure just before the holidays began. He would be flying to Madras on the weekend to join *MV Neel Kamal*. Another Talwar vessel, the *MV Jalaj,* had been chartered for the same cargo and had already left on its eastward ballast voyage. The charterers wanted them to load simultaneously and sail on their outbound journey together.

Karan was busy tying up loose ends. He was worried about Sonali. About how she would fend for herself in his absence.

Karan's love for Sonali had a simplicity and sincerity about it that the whole family recognised. With straightforward idolatry he had placed her high on a pedestal, unwilling to notice even the smallest hint of clay. She was lovelier to him than the first day he had been dazzled by her. His life in the last few months had achieved the grace of an idyll, despite the fruitless search for employment.

He worked hard at making their little flat comfortable, a home. He liked to busy himself installing mirrored cabinets in the bathroom, fixing soft shaded lamps in the living room. Once Sonali's friend Indu had watched him sort through a tangle of wires and attach them to speakers placed above the lintel in the corners of the room.

'You have made the place so cosy,' she had commented. Sonali had glared, she would have preferred a more chic description, but Karan had been well pleased with the word Indu had chosen.

Sonali had resumed attending classes, but college bored her. The hot classrooms irked her, the battered desks scarred with the initials of the girls who had already passed out. The smell of the chalk dust tired her, the gongs ringing at the dragging end of the dragging hours, the teachers dowdy and earnest, nagging about dates and words, the giggling classmates preoccupied with lipsticks and boyfriends, the cramping weight of books under her arm.

She was invited to a couple of engagements, arranged marriages, bride-to-be stiff in gold encrusted pink, groom, an awkward youth forehead streaked with a red tilak like a sacrificial goat. The couple being force-fed pure ghee sweets by an assortment of noisy relatives. Sonali felt so out of it all.

The four days of puja came and went. The weather was changing. Ma came down with viral fever, aggravated by an untimely cold-water bath. She worried ceaselessly about Sonali, dropping in to see her every other day on her way back from office.

There had been endless speculations about Sonali's safety. Everybody at home wanted her to lock up the flat in Karan's absence and return to sharing Chhobi's bedroom. Karan was not very keen. Although worried about her managing alone, he felt were she to move back to Dida's house, he would be relinquishing his importance as a husband.

'Won't you be lonely?' Chhobi asked.

'You are too young. What about your meals? You will be surviving only on bread, I know,' said Ma.

'The doors in those DDA flats are so flimsy, just one kick will smash them. Meera, why can't she stay at home with us,' objected Dadu.

Sonali was obstinate. 'I will be fine, just *fine*,' she replied with emphasis.

'Karan's installed a steel grill door and multiple locks and chains. She is married now, her husband wants her to live there, we can't interfere,' said Dida suddenly. So far she had been silent, sequestered they thought by her deafness, but as usual Dida could hear perfectly when she wanted to. 'Savitri will get somebody.'

Sonali gave everyone a seraphic smile; Dida's word would be final.

Savitri located an old woman from her village, more in need of a place to stay than a job. As wizened and wrinkled as a chimpanzee, she was a slow worker but competent enough, hands like a bunch of withered leaves, sweeping, stirring and swabbing. She was an indifferent cook, but Sonali had always been disinterested in food. At night the old woman would spread a roll of faded bedding under the Mona Lisa poster to sleep. Karan had taught Sonali how to open the door, cautiously, first peeping through the magic eye, before slipping off the safety chain. The Kumars downstairs were also requested to keep an eye on her, much to her annoyance.

two

It was the last day of October. Chhobi was at home nursing a toothache. Applications of clove oil on tiny wads of cotton wool only numbed her jaw for a few minutes, then the pain returned in shocking spasms. Dadu had peered into her mouth, diagnosed an abscess and said that she would probably require a root canal filling. She would have to visit the dentist as soon as the swelling subsided, meanwhile Dadu started her on antibiotics and an anti inflammatory painkiller. The left side of her face was puffy.

'They say labour pains and toothaches are equally intense,' Dida commented then added wryly, 'it must have been a man who said it, a toothache is nothing. Come on now, Chhobi, press this to your face.' She handed her a thick wad of cotton cloth. Chhobi winced as she pressed the makeshift heating pad to her cheek, recognising the remnants of Ma's tangail sari. Dida was warming the pad on the tawa and passing it to Chhobi through the service hatch in the kitchen wall. Chhobi felt tears smarting her eyes, there was no relief from the pain. She passed back the pad to Dida as it cooled. Dida was stirring a sour-sweet date chutney on the other gas burner.

'Try and distract your mind. The pain will subside as soon as the tablet takes effect. Read something.'

'Didaaa, how can I read?' groaned Chhobi. Rosemary had suggested the same thing when Chhobi had called to say she wouldn't be able to make it to office today. In fact Rosemary wanted her to read up on Mirza Azadullah Beg so that she could do a story on him. She wanted Chhobi to visit his home in old Delhi and describe it, interspersing the article with quotations from his ghazals.

'But who is Mirza Azadullah Beg, I know nothing much about Urdu poetry,' Chhobi protested.

Rosemary was severe, 'You write historical pieces about Delhi and you haven't heard of Ghalib?'

Ghalib could wait, along with his ghazals.

Dida looked at Chhobi sympathetically and told her to switch on the radio.

'Listen to something then, anything – Kishore Kumar, cricket commentary. Here take this, I will switch it on.' Handing her the reheated pad, Dida switched off the gas. The chutney was done. She wiped her hands on an old duster and began to twiddle with the knobs on the radio. There was the sound of static and the same mournful music being played on all frequencies.

'What's wrong? This is not going to make you feel any better... somebody must have died.'

Chhobi feeling half dead herself, administered another dab of cotton wool soaked in clove oil. Her lips were tingling and the room smelt sharply of the spice. She started as there was a loud knocking on the door, on the other side of which Mrs Chatterjee could be heard, calling out for Dida. She sounded excited, agitated.

'What is it now?' Dida was cross. She still had the mutton curry to prepare. She called for Savitri to answer the door. Savitri's hands were covered with flour, she was squatting on the kitchen floor, kneading dough. She was working the water into the hillock of flour, the brass plate with the upturned rim revolving with the vigour she put into the action. Dida gave her an exasperated look, then glanced towards Chhobi mournfully nursing her tooth and went to let Mrs Chatterjee in.

'Have you heard, heard the news?'

'No, what?'

Even through the mist of pain Chhobi registered Mrs Chatterjee's extreme emotion. Trouble, she thought, Mrs Chatterjee was always at her most agog during trouble – other people's.

'I have just received a call from London.' Despite the obvious importance of the news she had to impart, Mrs Chatterjee couldn't help putting the words 'call from London' in inverted commas.

'Montu called,' she paused, then the words burst out of her, 'Mrs Gandhi has been shot, shot this morning.'

'No!' Dida sat down on a chair as if her knees had buckled. Chhobi's toothache receded – the news was so shocking. Dropping the heating pad she questioned Mrs Chatterjee, 'What else did he say? Is he sure – is it a fact?'

'It has to be true. It was on BBC. Montu rang up to find out more details from *us*. She was shot by her guards – Sikhs, at her own residence.'

Chhobi was fiddling with the radio, nothing except the sad music. If the aerial wire was pulled to the window it was sometimes possible to tune into BBC. Chhobi was trying that now.

'Is she badly hurt? Where have they taken her?' Dida sounded shaky, infirm. Mrs Chatterjee shouted for Savitri to fetch water. She began theorising. 'These politicians, it might be a popularity stunt, remember when they broke her nose at some rally with a stone, and she won the election.'

Savitri's dripping hands were proffering a plastic tray with glasses of cold water. Chhobi, toothache forgotten, drank some before the water hit the inflamed nerve and the pain returned with a brain-penetrating jerk. She moaned a little and put the glass down. She went to the garage to tell Dadu.

By mid afternoon the rumour had spread through the city like a forest fire in peak summer. People gathered in clumps. Some shops were downing shutters and most office goers were impatient to return home. Ma arrived home early by auto rickshaw. She said there was a huge knot of people on the Ring Road outside the hospital where they had taken Mrs Gandhi. They were chanting *hai, hai* and beating their breasts. BBC had announced Mrs Gandhi was dead.

'I hope Sonali is back from college, we have to go and get her.'

Dadu reassured Ma. 'Sonali had called from the Kumars, she is okay, don't worry I have told her not to step out.'

Dida was sitting on the sofa. None of them had eaten. Dida was crying, tears running in rivulets down her cheeks. Chhobi had never seen her so upset before.

Dead. Mrs Gandhi gone. India is Indira, Indira is India. Chhobi remembered how people always said that years later they recalled perfectly whatever mundane activity they were occupied in when President Kennedy's death was announced. A moment frozen in their mind like a photograph. This was one of those frozen moments. Forever after Mrs Gandhi's assassination would twinge in her memory like a toothache.

By 6 p.m. they announced on TV that she was dead. The newscaster's voice had a break in it. She looked dishevelled – her usual mask of make-up was imperfectly applied, it was almost as if she were bedraggled from the inside. The half-opened rose she always tucked into her hair, missing.

⁂

By nightfall there was an undefined but gathering disquiet. Chhobi went up to the terrace for a better view, the roads looked deserted. She could hear a distant roar, something like the sound she heard when she pressed the white conch shell from Dida's puja thaal against her ear. A precursor to the rumbling build-up of tension that would erupt with volcanic incandescence over the next few hours.

Ma sent Savitri off early, Dadu checked the bolts on the doors and windows with more than usual care. Dida had gone to bed without bothering about dinner. Dadu was unusually talkative, recounting the horrors of 1947 and violence he had witnessed during Partition.

None of them slept much. By morning Chhobi's toothache had receded to a dull throb. She cautiously felt the sore area with her tongue. She must be careful to chew from the other side and drink no liquids, either hot or cold.

The morning bustle of activity was absent. Savitri hadn't turned up either. Chhobi went up to the terrace again. The streets were still empty, no children rushing with bulky school bags, no vegetable vendors pushing their wooden carts, no pajama clad figures carrying home unwieldy cans of milk from the Mother Dairy. Nobody. There was an acrid smell of something burning, a grey pall of smoke hung just below the sky as motionless as a shroud.

Dida finally got out of bed. Her face looked very tired, her hair stringy and uncombed. Ma and Chhobi both stayed home, staring at the TV in silence. It was showing the great throng of mourners filing past Mrs Gandhi's body. Sombre faced military men in full regalia stood stiffly to attention by her side. She looked courageous and aristocratic even in death, patrician profile bedecked with flowers.

Even Dadu, not very enamoured with the Nehru family was moved.

'A very brave lady,' he kept repeating. Ma commented that Mrs Gandhi had been foolhardy, if not downright reckless, to have Sikh security guards after the Blue Star debacle. She was literally asking for it.

Chhobi felt extremely restless. She walked into the garden which was dusty and dry. The champa flowers littering the lawn were turning brown. She began to water the plants with a garden hose. Washing off the dust and watching the fresh green emerge made her feel a bit better. Dadu had planted a bank of variegated leaves near the gate. The water hit them now turning them slick and wet, red and white and green. Drops collected at the centre of the large heart-shaped leaves, perfect circles like mercury spilled from a broken thermometer, like tears of crystal. What were the leaves called... Yes. Ma called them Bleeding Hearts.

Ma went into the kitchen to rustle up a kichchudi for lunch. Stocks of most things including cooking oil were very low. Dida normally replenished her rations in the second of the month. There were no green vegetables, just some potatoes caked with mud in a wickerwork basket. Ma was debating whether to rush to the market for some oil and powdered milk when the phone rang, jangling her nerves.

It was Mrs Chatterjee, with the latest bulletin from London. There were reports of the Sikhs celebrating. There had also been terrible visual images of Connaught Place in flames, red tongues lashing out between the symmetry of the white columns. Angry mobs were looting and attacking Sardars, anybody in a turban was unsafe.

A fresh wave of anxiety washed over Ma, thinking of Sonali all alone with no protection but that old crone and a jar of chilly powder. Karan should have at least ensured a phone connection. Chhobi was dialling Indu's number. She didn't know what to say but had to find out if they were all right. Perhaps Sonali had called them. She could not get through, it was continually engaged.

Ratan Kaku called. The taxi stand close to his house had been torched. The drivers had run away, but everything at the stand, parked taxis, their string cots, the little lean-to with the rickety table and telephone were gone. All burnt. He had seen the place blazing from his balcony. It was smoking, smouldering even as he spoke. He tried to call the fire brigade but there was no response. He had also tried the police station but they were not answering the phone. Kaku said they were expecting big trouble on the day of her cremation.

Ma was frantic.

'We have to go and fetch Sonali right now.'

'How will we go?'

'Why, the buses are still running, I asked Mrs Ghosh, her house is just opposite the bus stop. There are very few people, but they are running. It is not far, on the way back Sonali can bring her car.'

'And the old woman... we can bring her too, she will be useful with Savitri away and Dida like this.'

three

Dida seemed to have shaken off her grief. She was bathed and dressed in a white and black dhakai sari, a little pale but her old well-groomed self.

'I am coming with you,' she announced, as Ma and Chhobi were preparing to leave to fetch Sonali. Both of them protested, but she was adamant. Ma gave in, Sonali's apartment was only three stops away and they would be back soon. They passed the burnt-out remains of the taxi stand on the way.

The conductor was talking to Ma, asking her if they had far to go, telling her it was unwise to venture outdoors. They were the only passengers, save for an old man carrying a jerry can of kerosene. Chhobi could smell it from where she sat. Molotov cocktails, that was what mobs always used as weapons, crude fiery incendiaries that streaked tails of flame through the air, setting alight whatever they struck. She imagined the old man fashioning those bombs out of old soft drink bottles.

The conductor began telling Ma about Trilokpuri. He had heard there had been terrible bloodshed in that locality.

'Where is Trilokpuri?'

'Across the river. Men were pulled out of their homes by their

hair and slaughtered in front of their wives and daughters. The
police did nothing. They are cutting off their hair, shaving their
beards. After all it is a matter of life and death. Of course they
shouldn't have killed an old defenceless woman like that.'

Chhobi thought 'old and defenceless' such incongruous words
to be applied to Mrs Gandhi – she had always been so brisk and
vigorous. That swift walk so charged with energy.

Ma was directing the conductor, requesting him to stop the bus
so that they could alight just outside the gate to Sonali's apartment.
He blew his whistle obligingly. Chhobi and Ma got off and turned
to help Dida down. Dida hadn't stirred from her seat.

'Come on Dida, this is it. Hurry up, he has stopped in the
middle of the road,' said Chhobi impatiently.

Dida remained seated. She looked curiously detached but
composed.

'I am not getting off here, I am going.'

'*Chalo chalo* mataji,' interjected the conductor, giving a short
blast on his whistle. The driver turned around to see what was the
delay.

Chhobi and Ma stared at the Dida, dumbfounded, 'Where are
you going? This is the stop.'

'I am going to pay my last respects. I am going to Teen Murti.'
A pause, then she added, 'You carry on, I will just take a bus back.'

'But you don't even know whether this goes to Teen Murti.'

The driver blew the horn loudly, the conductor was
expostulating. Suddenly they were all so impatient. '*Jaldi karo, ye to
koyi stop bhi nahi hai.*'

Ma climbed back into the bus, she would make Dida get off by
force if necessary. The driver started the bus. Chhobi ran alongside,
shouting for him to stop, yelling at the conductor. Ma was arguing
with Dida. Dida looked serenely out of the window. She gave
Chhobi a little wave as the bus gathered speed.

'Take Sonali back at once,' shouted Ma from the window next
to the conductor, wisps of hair escaping from her bun, her
distraught face in complete contrast to Dida's cool one.

Chhobi was enraged. Dida and Sonali, both so troublesome, such... such... pests! Had she taken her insulin shot? Yes, she had. Dadu would be so agitated. She hoped Ma could make her get off at the next stop. All this was so unnecessary and dangerous.

The apartment blocks, so identical in design, a honeycomb normally alive with a bee-buzz of activity, were quiet. Doors and windows were shut and barred. There was a choking burnt odour in the air. Images of Beirut smoking and bombed out flashed through Chhobi's mind as she rushed up the stairs.

Sonali's doorbell wasn't working. After pressing it futilely several times, Chhobi hammered on the door. There was an interminable fumbling wait, as she heard the sound of a padlock being unlocked, then the door opened a crack. The old woman, Neyoti, peered out with a rheumy suspicious eye.

'Kholo kholo,' Chhobi commanded impatiently as the maid struggled to slide off the safety chain.

It was very dark inside, curtains and blinds tightly drawn. Sonali was still asleep. Chhobi went into the bedroom, which was filled with the darkness of rest and simple languor, heavy and ripe to the touch. She shook Sonali awake roughly. Sonali stirred like a lazy cat and switched on the bedside lamp. The Klimt poster began to glimmer above her head.

'What... What is the matter?'

'Don't you know what's going on in the city? How can you sleep? We have all been sick with worry for you. Mobs are rushing into people's houses, grabbing them by their beards and setting them alight. Tyre garlands... it's like those shanty town riots in some banana republic... rolling them to their death wrapped in burning tyres... and Dida... Dida...'

Chhobi's voice broke, she felt perilously close to tears.

'Dida? What's happened to her? Tell me... what's wrong?'

Sonali was sitting up now, the sleep driven from her eyes.

'She's gone off to Teen Murti, that's what, to take a last look at Indira Gandhi.'

'What … but what's the use of that? How could you let her? Is she alone?'

'How could *we* let her go? Since when have any of us had any control over her actions? Or yours, for that matter?'

'Has she gone off alone?'

'Ma is with her. Ma has been so worried about you. Hurry up, get dressed we have to rush back. Tell that old woman to pack her bedding.'

'Okay, okay.' Sonali threw aside the sheet and twisted her hair into a topknot. 'Not before I have had a cup of tea… Neyoti *chaa… doo* cup.' Sonali disappeared into the bathroom. Chhobi gave her an exasperated look and began straightening out the rumpled sheets, spreading the bedcover over them. She went into the kitchen to speak to Neyoti, who was busy brewing the tea in a saucepan. Luckily Sonali kept a tin of powder milk that should come in useful. Neyoti strained and liberally sugared two cups and handed one to Chhobi. Sonali began sipping hers in the living room, still wearing her flimsy nightdress. No point hurrying her, Chhobi thought, she wouldn't bestir herself until she had finished her tea.

Neyoti was rolling up her bedding with alacrity, happy to be going off to Mashima's house. Chhobi searched the kitchen, looking for food, anything edible. The fridge held only a yellowing cabbage and a couple of eggs. She found an unopened can of cooking oil and some instant noodles. Shoving them all into a plastic bag, Chhobi was reaching for the powdered milk when there was a loud knocking on the door. She froze in her tracks, a prickle of fear running through her. She was about to shout to Sonali to check before opening the door when she heard the bolt being drawn back, an old familiar voice, tone threaded with smiles, saying, 'Sonali, how are you?'

There was a long pause then Sonali's voice, just a decibel above a whisper said, 'How did you find this place?'

'Karan had given his home address in his joining papers. I've been meaning to drop in ever since. Then with this disturbance, I knew you were alone, I was worried. I came to see if you were okay.

How are you? You look well… very well. Aren't you lonely? Living all alone? I miss you.'

Chhobi burst into the living room, tin of milk powder clutched in her hand like a grenade.

'She is not alone, but it is best if *you* leave her alone.'

Sonny, the gleam in his eye dimming, smile fading, looked at her with annoyance, the old arrogant tilt to his head more pronounced then ever. His gaze slid over Chhobi and then Neyoti standing like a shadow behind with the same dismissive indifference. Then his head swivelled back to Sonali and raked her body with an insistence that ignited a fresh fury in Chhobi.

He held out a small gift-wrapped packet to Sonali who stood there stricken, mug of tea clutched in her hand.

'A belated wedding present. Go on, take it.'

Sonali did not move. Giving Chhobi another glance of annoyance, Sonny kept the packet on the table.

'If you ever need anything, anything at all, just contact me. We have to look after you in Karan's absence.'

Sonali said nothing, standing there stockstill in her flimsy nightdress.

Chhobi moved then. Wrenched the front door open and glared at him. Sonny impeccable as always, pearl-grey shirt, pleated trousers with their knife-edged crease, took his time. His expression as he glanced at Chhobi was one of complacent insolence, self-contained and backed by his father's rapidly amassed millions. It stirred an impotent rage in her. Sonny half turned and gave Sonali another long lingering look, one that burnt through the thin nightdress. Then he was gone, leaving behind an aura of wealth and expensive after-shave.

Chhobi crashed the door shut behind him.

'Why did you accept that? How dare he? He is so bloody arrogant, presumptuous.'

The wrapping paper was olive green, handmade, speckled with dried rose petals. Sonali was slowly unwrapping it, expression still blank.

It was a miniature painting, in a heavily chased silver frame. About four inches in length, it was painted in the Mughal tradition and depicted an exquisite woman in the process of adorning herself. She was naked but for a watery saffron veil across her breasts, and the pearl and gold ornaments on her fingers, throat, arms and girdling her waist. Her hair fell in a cascade of black to below her hips. She had a flirtatious half smile on her lips that seemed vaguely familiar. The smile was reflected in a small mirror she held up to her face. The jewellery and the thin fabric had a sensual air of suggestiveness – so that Chhobi could not just see but almost feel her bare breasts beneath the veil.

Suddenly the dark room was stifling, oppressive. Chhobi strode to the window and flung back the drapes. The light streamed in, a diamond haze, sunlit motes dancing. It passed through the flimsy nightdress like sand through a sieve. Chhobi could not just see but almost feel Sonali's bare breasts beneath the diaphanous garment, dark aureoles blooming like shadowy flowers under the voile. Her hair falling in a river of black to below her hips. Mirror images – laterally inverted.

Something inside Chhobi snapped. 'Put that down. Indira Gandhi's been assassinated, the city is burning, we are all half dead with worry for you and you... you are busy being a sex symbol. Don't you have a dressing gown? I mean, look at this painting. It's the painting of a courtesan. He obviously views you as an object of desire, that's all. Your nightdress is completely see-through.'

Sonali's rose-painted fingernails were slowly crushing the rose-speckled paper, crumpling it to a tight ball. Her face was like a mask, but for the narrowed slits of her eyes. Chhobi glimpsed with a slight shock, a flash of torrential fury. But Sonali did not give vent to it. She was self-possessed as she commented distantly, 'To be desired is a useful thing.'

'Oh, why were you so quiet, you should have smacked him on the face with that.'

'I wasn't expecting him. Why should I show him that I am bothered? Why should I react violently?' She tossed the painting down on the table as she continued. 'I know what he wants. I don't need to create a scene. Do you think he will get away with everything? Look at Indira Gandhi – even she had to pay... I am going now to change.'

Chhobi began to wrap up the painting of the naked woman, she wanted it out of sight. A gilt-edged sheet of notepaper was taped to the back. It was a certificate of authentication from the souvenir shop at the Meherangarh Fort, Jodhpur. It listed the natural pigments that had been used in the miniature. The gold of the ornaments was real, 24 carat, burnished to a high gloss. The painting had been executed on handmade paper that was a hundred years old. Chhobi noted with distaste that the yellow of the subject's veil was colour distilled from the 'urine of cows that had been fed with ripe mangoes.' She flipped the paper over and saw the bold 'Sonny' followed by a telephone number with the words 'My direct line' in brackets. This was one line Sonali didn't need to tangle with. Chhobi dropped the card into her bag.

The old Fiat, big red L on the front and rear windscreens, was uncooperative and refused to start. Chhobi, nerves frayed to tatters by the events of the morning, got out to push the car. A dull throbbing in her jaw announced the revival of the toothache. A Nepali servant boy from the ground floor flat lent a hand. The car sputtered into life as Sonali went directly into second gear. Chhobi ran alongside and managed to jump in, banging her knee. Neyoti clutching her bedroll in the rear seat was sitting bolt upright.

It was a day when tension stretched taut between all of them like the criss-crossed strings of a cat's cradle. Chhobi went to her bedroom and lay down trying to fight pain, fear, anger and hunger. Dadu was patrolling the area near the gate, muttering aphorisms about mob mentality. Sonali was on the phone with Indu, trying to find out if she had heard anything about the situation at Teen Murti. The BBC was flashing reports about violence and arson spreading as far as Bidar in South India. After calling up everybody for news and meeting only wild rumours, Sonali gave up and began to pace the verandah. Chhobi could see her walking up and down, her shadow moving with her, gradually growing taller and taller. The disappearance of Dida and the appearance of Sonny chased each other like spectres in her mind.

It was almost two and none of them eaten. Dadu and Sonali were contemplating taking the Fiat to search for Dida and Ma, but as usual Sonali had forgotten to fill up the tank and the fuel gauge needle was hovering just above E. At the best of times, the combination of the car and Sonali's driving was an unreliable one and Dadu, forehead puckered with worry, couldn't decide what to do.

Sick of the tension, Chhobi started to make some chow mein. She rarely cooked anything and read the instructions on the packet of instant noodles carefully while she chopped up the wilted cabbage and a couple of onions. She seasoned the whole dish liberally with tomato ketchup, which was a mistake for it now tasted unappetisingly sweet. She unearthed some soya sauce to add flavour – the liquid had dried to a hard black sediment at the bottom of the bottle. She was shaking it up with some water when she heard a motorbike stop at the gate.

It was Khokon. He had been foraging for fresh vegetables. Handing them three cauliflowers, he said he had found a farmer with a sackful of these near Tughlakabad. He began talking about the Trilokpuri carnage but Chhobi interrupted him to tell him about Dida. There was a pause as the news sank in, then he said in awed tones, 'Didima is really too great, yaar.' He put on his helmet and said he would go up till Defence Colony to look for them. He was back very soon. Army trucks were entering the city in convoys, there was talk of military rule. The town was virtually under curfew. He had seen a number of burnt buses, some still smoking. There was no sign of Ma or Dida. Khokon promised to drop by again later, his mother would be worried and he had to hurry home.

It was past five when a shout from an increasingly frantic Dadu drew them all to the gate. In the distance were two figures, so changed they scarcely seemed familiar. Two figures that were limping – crumpled, rumpled, and fractured by fatigue. Ma was dragging Dida forward, supporting her with an arm around her waist. Both of them had puffy bloodshot eyes, their hair tangled and coming uncoiled. Ma's feet were bare. Dida's sari had a flapping tear near the dusty hem. It was Dida's face that alarmed them. It had a leaden cast to it. Her eyes were rolling upwards, the pupils half hidden by the lids that looked so heavy. Her lips were cracked and she was trying to moisten her mouth with her tongue, repeatedly licking it with slow and feeble licks.

'Water. Get water. The sky is turning black for her. Her feet are numb,' Ma said.

The doctor in Dadu took over. Chhobi and he half carried Dida into the house, Dadu speaking in the incomprehensible vocabulary that doctors have – paresthesia, polydipsia, blurred vision.

He seemed to have unconsciously donned a white coat. Once they had got Dida to bed, he rushed to the garage to fetch his medical things.

Ma, dabbing at her feet with a wad of cotton wool soaked in Dettol, her head fragmented by pain, felt a little lighter with the relief of seeing Sonali safe, of reaching home, and of handing Dida over.

'We reached Teen Murti quite easily. The bus went past Ashoka Hotel. We joined a long queue of people waiting to see the body. Some commotion broke out after almost an hour. People began milling around, rushing, clambering over the gates. We were just carried forward. The police lathi-charged the crowd. Although we were far away we could hear the thwack of their batons hitting the bodies of the mourners who were literally panic stricken. I lost one sandal and threw away the other one. Then there was a terrible choking, burning… We could not see at all.'

There was a long pause. She began dabbing some antiseptic cream on her feet that were bleeding slightly.

'Why?… why couldn't you see?'

'We were teargassed.'

There was a silence.

This cannot be happening to us, it is all so unreal, Chhobi thought. We are like those people who have actually lived through history in the making, like all those people who went through Partition.

Sonali brought a plate full of chow mein for Ma who took one bite and was nauseated by it. She asked for a cup of tea and her migraine medicine.

They had walked all the way back from Teen Murti. There were no buses, no auto rickshaws running anywhere. Dida hadn't had much of a breakfast, and had begun to feel very faint. Luckily Ma found a couple of Cadbury's milk toffees in her purse and made Dida have them.

Nearing Mool Chand, Dida had been plagued by acute thirst and in desperation Ma had let her drink from one of those earthenware pitchers left under a tree for thirsty wayfarers. Just about to drink herself, Ma had seen some larvae wriggling in the water.

'Forget it Ma, just some mosquitoes probably,' comforted Chhobi.

The last three kilometres had been almost impossible, every step forward like climbing a steep mountain. Dida just wanted to collapse by the wayside, she kept complaining of numbness in her feet, of everything turning black.

Later they tiptoed into Dida's room. She lay in a stupor, hands tightly clenched. She was running a slight temperature. Dadu had given her an injection, fixed a saline drip. He would spend the night next to her on an armchair watching her frail face. He had prepared for his vigil with his medical bag beside him, a shawl around his shoulders.

❧

The phone rang at midnight. It was Karan calling from the ship. The connection was an awkward ship-to-shore one-way line. Sonali had to shout 'over' after she had finished speaking. Karan sounded relieved to hear her voice, and Sonali felt a surge of affection for him. Worry about Dida had taken its toll.

She began to ask him about the details of his voyage, the cargo he would be loading and the destination port. Maybe she could journey down to meet him there.

She looked a bit perturbed as she rang off.

'There is something odd going on. He was so guarded in his replies.'

A sleepy Chhobi echoed, 'Guarded?'

'Well, not guarded exactly but almost secretive... strange. He said he would call from land when they docked.'

'When are they reaching?'

'He wouldn't say.'

'Where are they going?'

'He wouldn't say.'

Chhobi was so exhausted, she felt quite unable to cope with any fresh worries, especially nebulous indistinct ones. All she wanted to do was to go back to sleep and never get up.

The fourth day after the assassination, Dida's fever abated. It was the day of Mrs Gandhi's funeral.

The shock and fatigue had emptied Dida so completely that she seemed bereft of substance. She felt white and blood-drained, empty of organs. The faces of her family gathered around her bed when she opened her eyes brushed off delirious visitations. Chhobi drew back the dark curtains. The pale golden November sun came through the windows in a luminous tide, bearing the flotsam of bird song, the petalled perfume of the haar singar and children's voices. Its light washed the room of night and nightmare. Dida sighed. She felt like a shipwrecked sailor who feels terra firma again, wild oceans swept away, deliverance miraculously gained.

four

It was late, just past midnight. Chhobi was struggling with English translations of Ghalib's ghazals which, she suspected, had lost much of their lyricism in the interpretation. Rosemary had asked her to intersperse descriptions of Ghalib's haveli with quotations from his ghazals. The magazine's photographer had seen the place – it was situated in a dusty by-lane amidst the hubbub of a crowded bazaar in Old Delhi and bore no trace of Ghalib or his poetry. Housed within the crumbling walls was a factory making electrical appliances. Matching his ghazals to that description would be hard.

Ghalib wrote at a time when living in Delhi did not nurture the interests of anyone involved in the writing of poetry, a pastime not appropriate even for the emperor Bahadur Shah Zafar II, himself a talented poet but the symbol of a dying empire. Delhi was at that time the focal point of the final conquest by the British, a time when the fabric of an entire civilisation was coming unravelled. Ghalib was, she read, surrounded by constant crises and carnage, yet obsessed with his own material means and personal insecurity. He wrote a poetry that not only spoke of tragedy but of endurance in a world growing increasingly unbearable.

Chhobi put down her pen, distracted as thoughts of the visit Rosemary had organised yesterday to one of the refugee camps came back to her. The camp had been hastily erected in one of the city's gurudwaras, where the normal tranquil atmosphere of prayer had splintered with a violent and jagged edge. Here was a world suddenly unbearable, personal security and a fabric of life that had not only unravelled but also been savagely ripped apart.

Rosemary had collected old blankets and clothes for donation, for so many of the riot victims had nothing at all, their homes doused in kerosene and set alight. Chhobi, lugging a big bundle, felt they were so inadequate that she had to avert her eyes in an odd mixture of shame and guilt.

Each survivor had his own tale of tragic loss, but in the majority the refugees were a bewildered, harbourless lot, addled by their defencelessness against the ferocity of the rampage.

One widow's, Simran Kaur's, tale seemed symbolic of the collective suffering. Even here, there were invisible boundaries marked on the floor. Their battered and burnt possessions, somehow salvaged, could occupy only so much space, no more. All around them were remnants of other families trying to remain within the lines demarcating their own area. Simran Kaur's younger son, recovered it seemed from the ordeal, raced a small dinky car around the periphery of their space.

'Vroom... Vroom... Vroom,' he growled, going round and round and round.

On the first of November every Sikh home on the lane where Simran Kaur lived gathered their kirpans and sticks and barricaded themselves in their homes. Towards evening the attack began. There were thousands outside, baying quite literally for blood. '*Khoon ka badla khoon.*'

Some front doors were smashed in, others were told to hand over the men. Even young boys were not spared. Simran Kaur, mother of two boys, eight and ten, had made a flimsy effort at defence. She had pulled off their turbans, put ribbons in their long hair and dressed them in frocks borrowed from their neighbours.

They clung to her as her husband was taken with other male neighbours and set alight. Their house was ransacked, even the stove emptied, for kerosene was a precious commodity. The little boys, pink ribbons in their hair, were spared.

Chhobi asked her hesitantly, 'Now what will you do? Move to Punjab?'

'Punjab? I have nobody in Punjab. My family and my husbands' came here from Sindh in Pakistan. They came here as refugees in 1947. Now more then thirty years later, we are refugees once more. Where will I go? I know only Delhi. I was born here, married here, had my boys here and here I will die.'

On the way back to office Rosemary and Chhobi passed the burnt-out remains of two buses, like the funeral pyres of some slow mammoth creatures. A half-sob rose in Chhobi's throat as she burst out, 'I can't bear it. We are supposed to be secular. After all what had all these poor people to do with Indira Gandhi?'

Rosemary answered, her cynicism for once tinged with compassion, 'What an idealist you are, Chandrayee. Do you think the mobs, God, it's become a generic term... yes, those mobs attacked the Sikhs out of love of Indira Gandhi or religion? It was an excuse to loot. Ethnic conflicts won't go very far without the impetus of commerce.'

'My grandfather says this reminds him of Partition.'

'Well, for the Sikhs it is, they have the same terrible insecurity, the same loss... but they will bounce back. They are a very resilient people.'

'Recover from this?' Chhobi was thinking of Dadu unable to come to terms with his loss after nearly forty years. 'At Partition, Punjab was divided and so was Bengal. The Punjabi and Sindhi refugees did so well – but in comparision the displaced Bengalis just did not flourish, especially materially. Why? I mean just look at my grandfather.'

This elicited a dry laugh from Rosemary. 'Bengalis have too much culture,' she said.

Chhobi saw the time with a start. It was a quarter to one and she had a deadline to meet. She quickly selected Ghalib's fifth ghazal and looked through the annotated notes.

> Waterbead ecstasy: dying in a stream;
> Too strong a pain brings its own balm.
> So weak now we weep sighs only;
> Learn surely how water turns to air.
> Spring cloud thinning after rain:
> Dying into its own weeping.
> Would you riddle the miracle of the wind's shaping?
> Watch how a mirror greens in spring.
> Rose, Ghalib, the rose changes give us our joy in seeing.
> All colour and kinds, what is should and be open always.

Strange how it made her feel better. It was after all an acceptance, perhaps even a celebration of change. Intangible clouds water the tangible rose, and both die into awareness at once existent and non-existent, the reality behind the appearance. 'The mirror greens in spring', the fourth couplet said – in Ghalib's time, mirrors were made of burnished metal and tarnished with changing seasons. The mirror being one of the oldest images employed in the Persian tradition of poetry. In the mirror, Chhobi read, both man's presence and his absence were clearly recorded; it was an impartial arbiter of truth.

Before closing her book, she thought of Mrs Gandhi, the face of her son Rajiv at the funeral, dark liquid eyes, so expressive in grief. A moment more cinematographic than any film. Acceptance of change, who was untouched by that?

five

The month of November passed uneventfully. The days were growing shorter, shadows longer. Rajiv Gandhi's face filled the newspapers and television screens. Young, so handsome, so untouched by the low level machinations of most politicians. Dida immediately transferred all her loyalties to him and began to follow his life, instead of Mrs Gandhi's, with a more fervent devotion.

Ratan Kaku, growing plump with his newfound wealth and health, was planning a trip to the mountains, to Darjeeling via Calcutta. He had discovered a latent, suppressed passion for the Himalayas. Dida and Chhobi would hear him discussing details with Dadu on the verandah. Dadu objected that it would be too cold, but Kaku wanted to see the sunrise over the white Kanchanjunga. Chhobi thought of Simla, her own Himalayan retreat, and wished she could make a quick visit. Kaku waxed eloquent about the beauty of Calcutta in winter and then nostalgia about Bengal winters gripped both of them. As usual it was food that flavoured the memories of their salad days.

They began to speak, tones dripping with greed, of the joys of drinking khejur ras or the undiluted sap of the date palm. Both of them had possessed fields fringed with date palms, land lost forever in Bangladesh. In late autumn when the other trees were beginning to lose their leaves and the earth caked into a dry mask, the date palms stood in serried ranks, earthen pots tied to their trunks to catch the sap as it trickled from the tapping cuts.

Chhobi had never tasted khejur ras. Her knowledge of the various stages of palm sugar or patali gur preparation was limited to an Amitabh Bachchan film, *Saudagar*, that had shots of his endless hairy legs climbing up endless date palms while a fat heroine cavorted coyly underneath.

Dida went out to join in the conversation.

'What about nolen gurer sandesh? I would love to make it, but in Delhi where is the new gur? If you go to Calcutta, you must get me at least five kgs of patali gur for my payesh.'

'Definitely, definitely, I shall accept no payment, but a bowlful of your khir every time you prepare it.' Kaku was being gallant; he was usually a bit nervous of Dida. He started telling her about jhola gur, a pure undiluted sweetness, gur sold in its liquid form at the beginning of the season, something like maple syrup only far more delicious.

Dida replied referring to a eulogy on gur by Bengal's very own Lewis Carroll.

'Sukumar Ray has described it in his poems, as topping the list of good but contradictory things in life. He has said better than the very best is jhola gur with bread.'

She began to recount the predicament, peril almost that the love of patali had landed Mishti in.

'Who is Mishti?' queried Kaku

'Mrs Chatterjee's daughter-in-law. Anyway Mishti was returning from Calcutta to the UK last winter with two discs of patali gur. She had wrapped them in an old sari. They stopped her at Customs and asked her what it was. She is so stupid instead of saying it was a sweet – a kind of burfi or laddoo, something which they had heard of, she said it was brown sugar.'

'Brown sugar!' Kaku's eyes gleamed in appreciation at this intoxicating twist in a sugary tale. 'Then what happened?'

'What happened? She was put in the lock-up for a day while they chemically analysed the gur and found it really was as harmless as sugar.'

Everybody laughed – it was one of those pleasurable moments when they all could take delight at a common friend's discomfiture.

❦

Kaku departed for Calcutta a week later, multiple mufflers and monkey caps carefully packed. By coincidence Chhobi's wish for a brief spell in the hills, her Simla sojourn came true in December. Soon after Kaku left they received an unexpected visit from their father's course mate from the NDA days. Now a colonel, he was posted in Simla and offered to book a room for them at the military inspection bungalow for the X-mas-New Year week.

Chhobi politely pouring the tea, offering namkeen and biscuits, jittered the cups in her eagerness for Ma to agree. Ma refused. Chhobi looked at her imploringly and tried to make her change her mind. Ma, the bleak look about her eyes, would not go. It was Colonel Yadav who intervened and said he would book a room for both the girls, Chhobi and Sonali – they would be very safe in his care.

Chhobi resolved that upon her return she would tell her family about the offer and her acceptance of the research assistantship at UCLA. She had finally, and not without considerable trepidation, made up her mind to go. Now the secret was becoming too difficult to keep, it was time to inform everyone that her horizons had widened, taken on more colour, excitement and reach. Yes, she would tell them, but after Simla. There she would prepare to leave behind her past and embrace the future.

Sonali meanwhile had been uncommonly hard at work, preparing for her degree, writing out all her tutorials, and assiduously making up lists of expected questions. She was glad to get away for a week.

They boarded the Himalayan Queen from New Delhi railway station bound for the transit town of Kalka at the foothills. The train arrived late at Kalka and they switched to the narrow gauge mountain train that would carry them to Simla, passing through the hundred and two tunnels that punctuated the track. Swooshing from darkness to light every time. Hundred and two times.

Chhobi felt absurdly happy, as the little train whistled to a stop at the midway point of Barog. The tiny railway station, a gem set exquisitely in the wintry mountainscape, was so Victorian England, it bore no resemblance at all to the tumult of the railway stations of the plains. Pulling a scarf tight around her neck, she slid up the glass window and gasped as the blast of crystal air drenched her. Chhobi watched the unforgotten landscape sliding lazily past. She began to smile as she looked at the curlicues of mist wisping around the pine trees, the golden sun slanting through the trunks, the valley unfolding below in a picture postcard vista. Her mood was rapidly changing to one of heady euphoria.

Simla, not the Shimla it is now, but the Simla of her school days remained a place where some of Chhobi's happiest times were spent. All she was required to do was study and grow up. She was good at the former and the latter was still bothering her.

Neither Ma nor Sonali shared her love for Simla. Ma could never forget the terrible day when their father died. It wiped out all the good days spent earlier. Sonali simply found it too dull and small-town.

Chhobi frequently made imaginary escapes to Simla. This was especially so in summer. June in Delhi was such a diminishing month. Plants shrivelled, tap water reduced to a thin trickle and pupils shrank to pinpricks in the blinding incandescence of the mid-day sun. At such times Chhobi would daydream about Simla's walks. The hillsides towards Chotta Simla and Mashobra entangled with wild roses of palest pink, and vines with red raspberries. In the monsoon, rills of water criss-crossing untarred pathways damp with maidenhair fern. The dreaded bichhu booti brushing bare legs in summer. The Himachali name so much more evocative of the deadly scorpion bite of the stinging nettle.

The Gaiety Theatre where they watched Shakespeare enacted by the Kendalls, stuffy but with perfect acoustics and swagged boxes around a horseshoe-shaped hall. It was supposed to have witnessed Rudyard Kipling enact a piece written by himself. Flooded with honeymooning couples from Punjab, it was difficult to reconcile the Mall with an earlier time when 'natives' were not allowed on it, and it was a promenade for grass widows and indolent hill captains. When the British journeyed up annually from the searing plains, what an upheaval it must have caused, especially before the Kalka-Simla railroad with its hundred and two tunnels was constructed.

The first inhabitants to greet the British must have been the monkeys. Simla's monkeys, the most enterprising, gibbering creatures. On the road up to Jakhu hill and near the Viceregal Lodge they appeared in groups, very active when the rhododendron was in flower. The ground was soon carpeted with the bruised blossoms as the monkeys snatched at bunches of flowers to suck the honey. Babies with their bright beady eyes clinging to their mother's teats, and aggressive male monkeys, their bottoms an angry red matching the flowers they discarded.

Chhobi remembered with affection the erudite antiquarian bookseller on the Mall with his collection of old lithographs and rare books. The church with its clock tower in the centre of the town where it was chronicled the Chaplain once preached a sermon in the 1870s, against the extravagance of crinoline gowns, the space they occupied to the exclusion of other would-be worshippers. It was also recorded that the next Sunday all the ladies appeared in their riding habits.

Well-remembered botany lessons and treks to Huttoo Peak came flooding back. The cheer pine, *Pinus longifolia*, which appeared in the lower reaches on the journey up from Kalka. The greenish blue *Pinus excelsa* whose blue colour was very marked on a breezy day when the spiny tufts were upturned by the wind. The hills of deodars with their pollen-laden cones staining porches yellow in late autumn, dispersing sneezes and hay fever with their sulphur-coloured powder. At Mashobra was yet another conifer, the spruce fir closely allied to the *Picea Peculiata,* and at Huttoo the silver fir which owed its name to the whitish streak on the underside of the leaf. These firs towered to a height of over 100 feet. The white and the green oak, and the yew, *Taxus Baccata,* which was supposed to provide the base of an extract for cancer cure, or rather cancer control.

Delhi was supposed to be the greenest metropolis, but Chhobi found it difficult to admire Delhi's trees in comparison to Simla's evergreens. The closest she came to it was after winter when the jamun trees around India Gate and Ashok Road put out tender new leaves. She wondered if after all Dadu's genes were dominant – both of them trying to retreat to places whose geography did not align with their history.

Yuletide hymns began to hum inside her...

Hark the Herald Angels sing,
Glory to the newborn king...

Sonali looked at the Chhobi's glowing face and smiled. She had been very quiet, beset by problems that seemed to be burgeoning beyond control.

'You know, there is something very odd going on,' she said softly, harking back to Karan's phone call on the night of Mrs Gandhi's funeral.

But Chhobi wasn't listening. She was back already in Simla, and ringing in her ears was the school choir. The perfect voice of the head girl singing *Ave Maria,* the *Aaave* rising and rising up the scale, soaring above the rest of the chorus in vertiginous ascent. Lifting her spirits until she was carried to the very summit of those blue mountains.

'I think Karan's ship is involved in some kind of smuggling.' Sonali had Chhobi's attention now. Her happy thoughts smashed with a jangling crash as she stared round-eyed at Sonali.

'Smuggling! What do you mean? Who said such a thing?'

'The horse's mouth,' came the terse reply.

'Stop talking nonsense. Karan has gone on a legitimate contract even if it is for those Talwars.'

'I wanted to go to meet Karan when the ship touched port. Initially he had been told it would unload somewhere in South India, and I could have easily gone. But Karan did not phone me after that call he made during the riots. Last week I received a letter from him. He has written that he suspects there is something very fishy about the cargo. That they had unloaded sealed containers in mid-ocean somewhere off the Andamans. In the dead of night. There were no normal port formalities, no bills of lading examined, no customs, no health and safety inspectors. In fact the *MV Neel Kamal* had unloaded while displaying lights that indicated it was waiting at anchorage. Silently fishing vessels had crept up to the ship's prow and the cargo was unloaded swiftly and surreptitiously. In the middle of the night.'

'May be Karan doesn't know all the details, after all it is the captain's decision.'

'But as the chief officer, he is in charge of the cargo, of the unloading and loading. Karan had also written that there was some uneasy talk amongst the crew. Talk that was immediately suppressed by the captain who shut their mouths with a hefty cash bonus. They think the containers held VCRs for the black market. There is such a huge mark up on them... Karan has resolved to sign off, break his contract prematurely after completing this last voyage. He should be here by end of January. Jobless again... but it is better to try for something else, I mean this business is so shady.'

'Karan and you are probably imagining things, the Talwars may be into all kinds of wheeling-dealing, but they couldn't be involved in something like that. Why, ministers are in and out of their house. Did Sonny ever tell you what their business was about?'

'Sonny never spoke of business.'

'You and he were together for almost two years, what did you talk about?'

'Nothing... Sweet nothings.' Sonali gave a wry smile.

'God, I really curse the day you met that Sonny and all his clan.'

Chhobi looked out of the window again. She refused to believe it. She no longer heard the music soar. It had collapsed into a monotonous click clacking. The wheels going round on the track, not a triumphant spiral but a tired chugging. Chug…chug… smug…smug… smuggling… smuggling. Journeying through the tunnels, light into darkness.

Chhobi had revisited Simla only once since leaving school, and that was in the year after she graduated, more than six years ago. In the intervening period, the Simla of her imagination had acquired the rosy patina spawned by longing, by love for those often remembered school days. Simla swung into view now, as festive as a multi-tiered wedding cake. Chhobi shrugged off black images of Karan handling contraband cargos in murky waters. She began determinedly to hum *Rudolph the Red-nosed Reindeer*. Sonali, about to blurt out her second, even more troubling concern, controlled herself. After all Chhobi had been so looking forward to this trip. Although distinctly half-hearted, Sonali joined in and both of them were singing aloud as the train pulled into Simla station, much to the astonishment of the Pahadi porter, still unchanged, with his brass badge and his rope-soled sandals.

six

On their first evening the colonel invited them to the club, the Green Room, historically the hub of Simla's Amateur Dramatic Club, located above the Gaiety Theatre. Over the years it had degenerated into a meeting place for card and not stage players. Most plays were performed by troupes travelling up from Delhi.

The colonel plied them with oily finger chips and seekh kebabs. They were soon joined by the club secretary , who took one look at Sonali, drew his chair up close to her and proceeded to monopolise her for the rest of the evening. She was looking quite arrestingly beautiful, hair pulled up into an intricate knot, dangling silver earrings dramatic against a velvety black jacket she had bought in Hong Kong. A golden yellow scarf made her eyes glow like lamplight. The secretary was puffing like a pouter pigeon. 'Did you know Rudyard Kipling wrote some verses on the opening of this theatre almost exactly a hundred years ago?'

Chhobi was interested. 'Of course everyone knows his *Plain Tales of the Hills* is based on life in Simla, but I didn't know he had specifically written about this theatre.'

'Yes, he had. Amateur dramatics were a very popular pastime,

and a hundred years ago the Simla stage was the most active one east
of Suez, why Suez, east of London.'

'Well, the foyer has some very interesting photographs. I have
always liked to look at them. There is one of Baden Powell dressed
like a Japanese, holding a paper fan, he is acting in *The Geisha*.'

'Simla was a hotbed of local British intrigue, extra-marital
affairs and gossip in those days. Wait, I have a copy of Kipling's verse
in my office downstairs. I will get it. Most amusing. We want to use
it in the brochure we are planning for the centenary celebrations.'

The colonel and Sonali shrugged and grinned at Chhobi.
Kipling didn't excite them. Sonali commented, 'I have only heard
about that poem *If*. We had it in school, a bit preachy it was.'

'What about *Kim*?'

'Yes, yes, that too, of course.'

The secretary was back with a typewritten sheet that he handed
to Sonali who did not look at it but passed it to Chhobi. 'There
certainly are very broad allusions to morals, or lack of them. Listen
to this bit:

> Why 'chaste' amusement? Do our morals fail,
> Amid the deodars of Annandale?
> Into what vicious vortex do they plunge
> Who dine on Jakko or in Boileaugunge?
> Of course it's 'chaste'. Despite the artless paint,
> And P-m's best wig, who dares to say it ain't?
> Great Grundy ! Does a sober matron sink
> To infamy through rouge and Indian ink?
> Avaunt the thought. As tribute to your taste,
> WE CERTIFY THE SIMLA STAGE IS CHASTE.'

Sonali looked slyly at Chhobi, 'Poetry and chastity, quite your
thing,' she murmured *sotto voce*.

Kipling and Christian virtues recurred again as Chhobi knelt to
whisper the Lord's Prayer at the Christ Church on the ridge. The
beautiful stained-glass window representing Faith, Hope, Charity,
Fortitude, Patience and Humility patterned the floor in jewelled

lozenges of light. The fresco surrounding the chancel window was the work of Lockwood Kipling, Rudyard's father. Chhobi had learnt these facts while still at school. She repeated them now to Sonali who gave an indulgent but long suffering groan.

'What a Raj Revival we are having. And you, what are you? A want-to-be born again Christian!'

Sonali laughed then, little knowing that she was about to enter the darkest period of her life. A time when Faith and Hope would be all but extinguished to the dullest flicker. A time when the whole family would have to draw very heavily on reserves of Fortitude, Patience and Humility, Sonali's being very meagre in any case. A time when they would be forced to rely on the Charity of near strangers.

⁘⁘⁘

The next few days passed pleasantly. It was cold, a bright and sunny cold. No chill winds or rain and the winter sun sparkling clear champagne. They did not discuss Karan or the Talwars. Sonali shut her mind to her other problem, postponed thinking about it until they returned to Delhi.

They went ice-skating, teetering and sliding, clinging to one another for balance, ankles wobbling in ill-fitting hired boots. Chhobi recognised the son of the Chinese shoemaker on the Mall who was performing on the ice for the tourists from the plains. Swerving and slashing, leaping over obstacles, blades knifing through the ice with swashbuckling skill.

The town had grown. Cheap hotels had mushroomed between the English cottages and the Gothic architecture of the government buildings. Baljees on the Mall still served a very British menu, eggs and sausages and chips, with scones and tea, but at every corner there was also a proliferation of fast food hamburger stalls and ice-cream parlours.

On the day before New Year's Eve, and just two days away from their planned return to Delhi, they took a bus to Mashobra about ten kilometres away on the road to Kufri. Both of them had wonderful memories of picnicking in the apple and greengage orchards, picking fruit straight from the trees, fingers smudging the bloom misting on them.

There were no apples on the trees in December, but Mashobra was remarkably unchanged. It remained thickly wooded with pine and oak trees. The russet leaves of the Virginia creepers as they twined around the pines added a touch of warmth to the wintry landscape. They wandered in and out of old houses that had been weekend getaways for the British. A sleepy chowkidar didn't object as they peered through the locked windows of one really imposing house. It was another time, another place. The rooms were filled with old furniture in carved rosewood and Burma teak. The doors to the ramshackle garage attached to the house were slightly ajar. Peeping in Sonali discovered it contained a probably priceless vintage car, carelessly draped in tarpaulin. When questioned, the chowkidar confirmed the house belonged to the raja of some erstwhile princely state in the Punjab. The family rarely visited, but a manager arrived at periodic intervals to stay and maintain the house and car. Sonali, very excited now, persuaded the chowkidar to open the garage so that she could look more closely at the car.

Chhobi sat on the steps leading up to the porch, picturesque even in winter with espaliered vines and a bank of hydrangeas. It was beginning to grow much colder and they should soon be starting back. She looked at the view melting into the distant plains and listened to the sounds of silence. Disparate notes randomly strung together to produce a most natural medley. A breeze stirred up leafy lyrics, a grasshopper chirped a background score in the overgrown hedge, keeping time was the rhythmic swish of a scythe as an unseen woman cut swathes of grass, there was a faint throbbing of twigs and telephone wires.

Chhobi blew on her fingers and looked at her watch. Sonali, cheeks flushed, eyes shining, ran up to her.

'Come and see, it is a Rolls, a Rolls Royce!'

'Is it? How do you know?'

'I have seen one like it in Delhi, at the Vintage Car Rally in February. It got a prize. I had gone with Sonny. I just sat in this one.'

'We must hurry back, it will be dark soon. What did you do? Pretend to drive it?'

'Drive it? No, of course not? I sat in the back seat and imagined I was the maharani.'

'The Maharani of Mashobra! It sounds like the title of a bad novel. Come on, let's get back.'

It was almost dark by the time they reached the Inspection Bungalow, where an urgent message awaited them. The colonel had come looking for them three times and had left a message for them to rush to his house near Chotta Simla as soon as they arrived. He had left a note, a little map and the bus number.

'What is it? Do you think something's wrong?'

'Probably wants to invite us for a New Year's Eve bash. Let's visit him tomorrow. I am sooo tired. I want to have a hot bath and get into bed.'

'He has printed VERY URGENT on the message. We better go. I think he will definitely offer us dinner.'

Sonali was resentful as they both trudged back again uphill towards the Cart Road to catch the bus.

'Hang on, slow down, I have got a blister on my foot. Oof, these hill roads. Don't Simla people believe in telephones? Why didn't we just call him?'

'You are right we should have... Just felt a bit worried. Look here's the bus, come on, come on, we will have a good dinner at least.'

The colonel lived just short of a stop called Strawberry Hill, one of Simla's finest houses, originally named after the Duke of Marlborough's residence in England. The painter Amrita Shergil had had her studio in the vicinity. Sonali wasn't interested in historical homes. An icy wind was blowing when they got off the bus. They had to climb up from the Cart Road towards the lower slopes of Jakhu where the colonel lived.

The wind cut through their jackets, turning their noses red, it almost hurt to breathe. Suddenly it was truly winter in the Himalayas. Sonali stared at the gradient with eyes that streamed a little.

'It's almost perpendicular, the dinner had better be worth it,' she gasped, hunching her shoulders, shivering a little, thrusting her hands deep in her pockets, the words collecting in a panting aura around her head.

The colonel and his wife greeted them, unsmiling and grim. Sonali flopped down on the nearest overstuffed armchair. There was a fire blazing and she extended both her hands greedily, tilting her whole body towards the flames.

'Is anything wrong?' Chhobi asked hesitantly, taking in their stone-faced expressions. Their teenage son was playing with a rubic cube near the fire, twisting and turning the coloured squares. There was a vase of improbably pink artificial roses on the mantel. Chhobi registered these facts automatically, a faint fear prickling in the pit of her stomach.

The colonel's tone was formal. 'I am sorry to say so, a message was passed to my office through the army headquarters this morning. The message was from your mother.'

'Are they okay… my grandmother, is she all right?' Chhobi broke in.

'Yes, yes, your mother, nana, nani are okay. The message was not a long one… I am not completely clear… It's become very cold, tomorrow we might have snow. Have some hot soup.'

Oh get on with it, thought Chhobi in a fever of impatience. What could be so urgent if everybody was okay. Why was he talking about the weather?

'You will have to return today.'

'Today?'

'Yes, there are some night buses to Chandigarh, change there for Delhi. It won't be as comfortable as the train, but it cannot be helped. I will speak to the driver and conductor. You will be quite safe.'

He just could not bring himself to utter the words. Chhobi

thought of medieval Europe when the bearer of bad tidings was put to death by royal decree. At that momement shooting the messenger seemed a perfectly plausible choice.

'But ... *what has happened!?*'

Finally he spoke.

'It's her husband, there has been some problem with his ship.'

Sonali rubbing her hands dreamily by the fire stiffened, then gave them a piercing glance. A log shifted in the grate, with a shower of sparks. The fire snapped and crackled, flames leapt and subsided, suddenly, throwing up ominous shadows.

'Problem... what problem?'

'I am not clear, both ships of the company were together, almost within sight of one another. Yesterday there was an SOS message from one of them. A Greek vessel intercepted it. The message broke off midway, but the operator managed to give the ship's position. It was somewhere in the Bay of Bengal. The weather was also fine... the Greek vessel immediately alerted other ships, the coastguard. It changed course to try and locate the Talwar ships but could not find them. The coastguard is still conducting its search. It's been forty hours but no sign of them, no wreckage, no life boats, nothing... not even an oil slick. It's quite a mystery. Where were the ships bound?'

'An island in the Andamans,' Chhobi replied mechanically.

'Most unusual, Andamans... What cargo could they be carrying there?'

Sonali stood up abruptly, facing them, her eyes staring – wide open – wild, wet honey.

'Missing! How can ships be missing? The Bay of Bengal is not the Bermuda triangle.'

The colonel's wife patted her shoulder, soothing. 'I am sure it's just a false alarm. By the time you get back, they will have been located, I am sure.'

Sonali wrenched away from her touch, the meaningless platitudes. They were offered dinner, soup, fruit and coffee, but hunger had vanished. The news was lying as heavy in their stomachs as an unexploded bomb. Chhobi wanted to telephone Ma but they had no time to book a call through the military exchange if they were to make the 9 p.m. bus. The colonel ferried them back to the Inspection Bungalow in a Willy's jeep. They packed their bags at lightning speed and left for the freezing chaotic bus terminal.

They were pushed into a half-empty bus. It was no luxury coach. The seats were plain slatted wood that dug into their backs. The window was cracked, the glass smeared. A faint smell of vomit emanated from behind them.

Sonali was absolutely still, completely quiet. Chhobi feeling on the verge of collapse at this Kafkaesque turn their holiday had taken, tried to eat a cold storage apple. Her teeth sank unpleasantly into the cloudy, powdery fruit. The bus was making its descent to the plains at breakneck speed, careening around hairpin bends on a pitch-dark road. Its headlights briefly lit up slogans hand-painted in yellow and black on projecting rock faces that bordered the road.

'IF MARRIED, DIVORCE SPEED.'
And
'GO EASY ON MY CURVES.'

The driver was completely oblivious to the message they conveyed. After four hours of lurching and rattling, stopping and starting, the winding hill road levelled out. They had reached the plains. It was still bitterly cold. Sonali huddled in a corner was staring blindly ahead.

'But *why* did you marry him?' burst out of Chhobi. 'This question has tortured all of us.'

Sonali began to speak, very slowly. 'I knew something was wrong. His last letter left me very uneasy… Why did I marry him?'… For a long moment she said nothing. Then, '… I don't know… When I was with Sonny… I thought, I felt it was the real thing…'

'Sounds like an ad for an aerated drink, I am not talking about Sonny,' said Chhobi dryly.

'But I am, I am. Shut up and listen before *always*, always qualifying everything…'

'…Okay… *okay.*'

'What I am saying is that when Sonny jilted me, I felt I just had to get away… Escape. I could not bear to be stuck in my old life… I felt like nobody… Yes, that's what I was. Nobody to nobody… and Karan, he offered me a way out, no explanations, no expectations.'

seven

Ma awaited them at New Delhi's Inter State Bus Terminus. It was past daybreak when they arrived, a cold dull day washed by shades of evening. Chhobi spotted her at once, her quiet face standing out bravely amidst the dingy chaos.

Ma who could never visit Simla because the hills resounded forever with the news of Bapi's sudden death. Ma who now waited for the bus from Simla, bearer of news that tolled like the echo of echoes. Khokon was with her. Over the rumble of countless diesel engines igniting, they could hear somebody's radio playing Kishore Kumar.

Ma had seen them now. Her face rose up like a shield, protecting them from the grimy disorder, the tattered bundles of humanity who huddled under piles of rags and newspapers, the aggressive touts for buses that seemed to be departing continuously for Meerut or Moradabad, the beggars who clutched at them with filthy hands. Khokon was hefting their bags, strange how they had come to rely on him, they quite forgot he was still a teenager. Ma normally quite undemonstrative just held Sonali for a minute, pressing her cheek against hers. She looked at Chhobi's inquiring expression and shook her head in negation. Sonali shivered slightly, lips trembling.

'There is no news is there?' Sonali asked, her voice flat and expressionless. Then as Ma wordlessly shook her head, Sonali darted behind a pillar and squatted on the ground. Bending her head, she retched painfully, bringing up bile coloured, vile smelling vomit. Chhobi held her shoulders till the attack passed.

Ma pulled off her own thick shawl and wrapped Sonali in it. Khokon drove up in Sonali's battered Fiat. He had only a learner's licence, but Sonali was in no condition to drive. Chhobi looked at her. She had taken this very hard, she must be more attached to Karan than they all realised. Or was it more the fear of being 'nobody to nobody ' again?

Ma spoke as they eased out of ISBT. 'The coastguard is still searching. They will keep up the search for another forty-eight hours. Yesterday I went to the Talwar's office in Connaught Place. The press was there, but nobody of any importance, or with any kind of information had come to the office. Only the secretaries and junior accountants. They didn't seem to be doing much work, just attending to secretive phone calls in an inside cabin. The old man, the managing director or whoever, his secretary kept saying that Talwar Shipping's office is in Bombay. That in Delhi they do other business – rice exports, hand tools and auto parts. The whole problem is that they are all so evasive. One journalist was commenting that the owners had been very tardy about informing the rescue agencies, especially since owners are normally in touch with their captains on a daily basis.'

Ma might have left Sonali and Chhobi with a great measure of independence, allowing them to grow up very much unscolded and unfettered, but now in this terrible moment of crisis she was asserting herself. 'Colonel Yadav has been most kind, he has called twice from Simla. He said he knows somebody in the coastguard… one Admiral Verma, he is in close contact with him, we will know as soon as there is anything.'

Khokon carefully negotiated the traffic on the road running parallel to the undulating grounds of the Shantivan, overlooked on the right by the ornate arches of Red Fort's Rang Mahal.

Chhobi realised dully that it was a Sunday for the weekly flea market was setting up its makeshift stalls all along the two kilometres stretch behind the ramparts of the Fort. They stopped at the traffic lights. She could see an old woman trying out used dentures from a pile that lay grinning like macabre disembodied smiles on the pavement. Behind her the second-hand carpet sellers were spreading out their rather well-worn wares in bright squares of geometric disarray. Chhobi felt a sudden longing to escape into that vivid kaleidoscope of colour, movement and sound. She had to restrain herself from wrenching open the car door and losing herself in the melee. The light turned green and they moved forward.

Ma waited until they had started breakfast before telling Sonali, 'Karan's mother had rung up yesterday. She is on her way, she will be arriving early tomorrow morning. Poor lady, she was very distraught, Karan's father is unwell again she said. She will be staying with you at the flat.'

Sonali blanched, then shrank back in her chair, pushing away her plate. She had done little more than pick at her food. 'Rahu and Ketu. She will blame me, I know. I know she will. I am not going to stay alone with her. I simply cannot.'

'Rahu and Ketu?'

'Yes, my horoscope. She had it made when Karan and I went to Hoshiarpur. She said my stars were unlucky, inauspicious. That they would align to form an eclipse.'

The words enraged Dida.

Dida, who seemed to have exhausted all her generous reserves of hope and optimism. Dida, who had been unusually withdrawn and quiet, snapped now with a return to her old acerbic self – 'Eclipse! What nonsense! How can your stars cause an eclipse?'

'I think she meant metaphorically,' Chhobi interjected.

Ma, who had heard it all before, ill luck and unfortunate stars said firmly, 'Then we have nothing to fear for the darkness of an eclipse will soon pass. And of course you won't stay there alone with her. Chhobi or I will go with you. The important thing is not to be hopeless, ships don't disappear into thin air. The coast guard is still searching.'

Dida ignored her. Going to the glass-fronted bookcase, she scrabbled amidst her books, tossing aside the tomes by and on Nehru. She pulled out a book with a faded jacket. It contained the sayings of Swami Vivekananda. Leafing through it, she paused at a page. Muttering 'Where are my glasses,' she handed the book to Chhobi, pointing at a paragraph. 'Read that,' she said.

'Do not put your faith in planets and stars… if a star disturbs my life it is not worth a cent. To be tricked by twinkling stars is a shameful condition.'

Meanwhile Dadu and Ratan Kaku were sitting on the sofa, pouring over Chhobi's old school atlas, fingers stabbing at the Bay of Bengal. They were talking knowingly but with complete ignorance about ocean currents, treacherous squalls and navigation by stars. Stars again. A strong undercurrent of despair tugged at their words.

The phone rang. It was Colonel Yadav for Ma. Everybody froze, watching her with gut-wrenching anxiety. They could gauge little from her monosyllabic replies. When she turned to face them, it was a face touched by the faintest glimmerings of hope.

'The colonel has just spoken to the coast guard. It may be nothing at all. A Japanese fishing trawler saw a light on the waters in the early hours of the morning. The position of the light almost coincided with the last position flashed by the radio officer before the ships went missing. The Japanese tried to follow the light, but they were headed in the wrong direction. By the time they turned, the light had vanished into the horizon. They were aware of the alert for the Talwar ships and immediately informed the coastguard, who have sent a very fast vessel and a helicopter to reconnoitre the area… However, at best it could only be a small dinghy, the Japanese confirmed it was not large enough to be a lifeboat. The coastguard should be informing us very soon, he has given them our number.'

All of them were quiet, feeling hope surge like a foaming wave-crest. Only Chhobi waited uneasily for a great wall of water to smash down on them. Dadu and Ratan Kaku got up to pace the lawn, Sonali was suddenly too exhausted to react. Ma herded her into her bedroom and they both lay down, tucked into a sun-streaked quilt. Chhobi and Dida sat on opposite ends of the drawing room and muttered prayers. Dida from the *Krishna Karnamrita*, and Chhobi...

'...Oh Thou protector of cows! Ocean of mercy! Husband of the princess of Sindhu land! Destroyer of Kansa!'

'... Hail Mary, full of grace, the Lord is with thee... Blessed are thou and blessed is the fruit of thy womb, Jesus.'

'Thou art my Life, my life's support, granting me grace, granting me all I desire, granting me insight, granting me lordship. Oh Lord! Thou art my God! Nought else...'

'Holy Mary, mother of God, Pray for us sinners, now and at the hour of our death...'

Chhobi stared in dismay at Mrs Chatterjee, a galleon in full sail zooming past their gate, set on a collision course with the two old men who reared back to see her. They hastily stepped aside as she did not falter, merely nodding at them imperiously as she swept past. Chhobi thought it was odd how all her thoughts were finding expression in nautical lexicology. Reluctantly she got up to let her in, Mrs Chatterjee brushed her aside and addressed Dida in stentorian tones. 'What is wrong? My maid Helen met your Savitri at the Mother Dairy milk booth yesterday. She said there was a calamity.'

Calamity put it so succinctly, Chhobi thought, waiting for Dida to reply. But Dida chose to turn her deaf ear and, eyes closed, continued murmuring to Krishna, awaiting his divine intervention.

The phone rang. Chhobi rushed toward the instrument, just beating Ma who came running from the bedroom. Kaku and Dadu hovered near the door. It was a wrong number. Everybody receded, resuming his or her original position. Mrs Chatterjee, who had watched the flurry of activity with surprise, turned now to Chhobi. 'What is the trouble? There was a message from her husband's ship – what does he say?'

She is just like a fat vulture, Chhobi thought, always circling when things go wrong. Dida stopped muttering her prayers and said loudly, 'Mayday, Mayday, Mayday.'

'No, no Dida, that's not for ships. On ships it's SOS.'

'SOS? I know it means trouble, but what do the letters stand for exactly?' boomed Mrs Chatterjee.

'Sunshine Over the Seas,' Chhobi replied rudely.

The phone rang again and this time it was an impersonal coast guard official. He came to the point immediately.

'Not good news… I am sorry. Admiral Verma informed me that they have thoroughly searched the area, taking a very wide radius and deploying three boats. Finally, one of them picked up a small blip on his radar. By that time it was full daylight. Visibility was good. Ocean flat calm. They soon found the light. It was a signal buoy which had somehow got adrift and floated out to mid-ocean.'

Chhobi interrupted urgently, 'A signal boy? Only a boy, what about the rest of the crew?'

'Not a b-o-y, but a signal b-u-o-y. You know those nautical objects moored to mark channels, or navigational hazards. Nowadays most of them are fitted with lights. Well, this one had broken free of its anchor and floated away. I am sorry. There was no sign of the two Talwar ships. It's very mysterious. Admiral Verma said that it is very perplexing that apart from one indistinct, incomplete message there has been no other signal. An instrument called the auto key which should have automatically transmitted a distress signal on its own as the ship went down, did not do so for either ship. Why are the Talwars so evasive? There is something fishy about the cargo as well.'

Chhobi could no longer hear his words. The sound of breakers smashing and hissing roared in her ears. Nudging her sharply, Dida demanded, 'What does he say? What does he say?'

Chhobi signalled for quiet and tried to focus on the voice that was displaying curiosity now, for it was a mystery in the Bermuda tradition. 'Where were the ships coming from? What were they carrying? These answers will definitely throw light on the mystery.'

By now the anxiety in the room had swelled to deafening proportions. Chhobi hastily said, 'Thank you so much. Is the coastguard still searching?'

There was a long pause, and then he said, 'No, they have called it off. I am sorry. Please do not give up hope, it is now a matter for the intelligence agencies, perhaps you should try to contact them. It is a time to be very brave.'

eight

Indu dropped in on the second of January. She brought with her the breezy insouciance of the holiday season and the brightness of a bouquet of yellow roses for Dida.

'What's wrong?' she asked, looking at the family slumped in sepulchral silence. Dida's deaf ear heard her. She shot the rest of them a warning look and answered sharply, 'Nothing, nothing at all. Thank you for these flowers.'

'But why are you so grim?'

Grim, Chhobi thought bitterly. Nineteen eighty-four had come, after all, to an Orwellian close, with the clock striking thirteen. Sonali got up abruptly, 'I am going inside to lie down. I have a terrible headache. Karan's...' Catching Dida's glare, she finished, 'Karan's mother is coming to visit us tomorrow.'

'Oh,' Indu nodded, completely understanding the reason for the gloom. She followed Sonali into the bedroom and began to talk about an Xmas party she had attended. Sonali wasn't really listening until she mentioned Sonny.

'He was alone, already sick of his wife. His behaviour was weird. He was quite high – really knocking down the drinks. He cornered me and demanded, absolutely demanded to know where you were.

So insistent, he grabbed my arm, there was a bruise the next day.'

Frowning, curiosity vying with disapproval on her face, she lowered her voice and asked, 'Have you been meeting him after... Karan?'

Sonali stared at her apathetically, and then shook her head in negation. Faintly surprised at her disinterest, Indu glanced over her shoulder almost surreptitiously. 'He was bragging, no exaggeration, that he had got rid of Karan... said he had contacted him and fixed him up with some job on a ship where wives were not allowed.'

Sonali remained motionless, only the briefest flash of fire under those thickly lashed lids indicated that she had heard. Her hands concealed by the shawl she was wearing, dug into one another, the finger nails gouging red crescents into her palms so tightly clasped across her belly as though to suppress the secret growing within.

⁂

With the arrival of Beeji, it was no longer possible for the Talwars to avoid meeting them. Beeji spoke to Mrs Bhai Sahib from a public call booth, before carrying her small suitcase upstairs to the flat. Sonali, who has been dosing herself with Ma's tranquillisers, was being cosseted by Dida at home. So it was Ma and Chhobi who awaited Beeji's arrival at the flat.

At first they were surprised to see her looking so calm but later when they asked her if Karan had mentioned anything in his letters, her composure cracked. They saw the terror burning in her eyes, bruised by distress, scarred by foreboding. The invisible constant presence of panic.

Mrs Bhai Sahib had told her to meet the Talwar brothers at Sonny's house at 4 p.m. It was more conveniently located in South Delhi, she said. It would save them the trouble of journeying to Rajender Nagar where Bhai Sahib still lived, close to the first factory he had acquired soon after Partition. Do not go to the office, she emphasised.

Beeji came away looking reassured, 'Bhai Sahib knows the mantriji, all the bade aadmi, the high-ups. He will surely help, after all it is his responsibility, Karan is like their son. His wife must come with us. Where is she?'

Both Chhobi and Ma murmured excuses. Chhobi wondered if this was the moment to tell them about the smuggling letter. The thought of Beeji's scandalised rebuttal of the merest hint that her Karan, or Bittoo as she called him, could be involved in something as unsavoury as smuggling made her hesitate and finally she said nothing.

⁕

Sonny's house seemed to have acquired a magnified magnificence in the late afternoon sun. The grounds had been newly landscaped and undulated in gentle hillocks skirting a lily pond. An army of gardeners and security guards was toiling with unusual zeal. The verandah was massed with rows of tiered flowerpots blooming with late chrysanthemums and early dahlias. A curled profusion of bronze and gold, and burnished copper.

Feeling like a bunch of unwanted tourists from a poor country peopled only by women, they sat rigidly in a row. Beeji, Ma, Chhobi and Sonali sitting on a narrow couch in the entrance hall at the bottom of the sweeping staircase. Chhobi's thoughts were running dramatically ahead of real life as usual – it was like a scene from a Raj Kapoor film, you almost expected the 'Thakur Sahib' to descend the stairs. Chhobi remembered meeting Karan for the first time, sitting on the very same spot and drinking coffee, trying to clear the alcohol-induced clouds in her head. And Sonali, so radiant on Sonny's arm. Where was he? Chhobi turned to look at Sonali. She was unrecognisable as the girl of a year ago. The trials of the last few days had gnawed away at the opulence of youth and natural beauty. The last time she had been in this house, she had looked born to silk and satin. Now, huddled in a shapeless shawl, a shabby salwar kameez, unwashed hair loose tangled, complexion muddied by lack of sleep and confidence, she resembled a servant girl.

Through the parted drapes to her right, Chhobi could glimpse Sonny's mother in a lavishly appointed room. She was speaking discontentedly to a man who wore the placatory apologetic air of a minion who has failed to please. Chhobi could overhear them.

'But what about the view, Mr Sarin? You designed this water garden, but I am beginning to regret it. The lilies do not bloom in winter. It takes the malis two hours to clean the scum that floats on the surface every other day. I have sacrificed my space reserved for the winter flowers just to look at this muddy pond. My view is important – it makes all the difference to this room. You can see this wall is sheer glass.'

'But madam, I assure you it does look beautiful and so different. Besides, madam, in water gardens, we have to keep one thing in mind – reflections. Reflections are so important, with the changing seasons at least one edge should be planted with some tall bright plants that will be mirrored in the water.'

'Reflections?' Sonny's mother was thoughtful. 'Well, what can we do now, it is too late to plant anything.'

Relieved at averting a crisis, Mr Sarin hastily stood up, saying, 'Just leave it to me, madam, I will see to it just now. Some flowering pots camouflaged so that they look as though growing naturally along the edge. Just leave it to me.'

The four women continued to sit silently outside the room where flowers and mirror images were being debated. Chhobi slid into a brown study. How strange to be involved with views and reflections, not cudgel one's brains with missing persons, life and death, sink and swim.

The brothers, Sonny's father and uncle, had obviously been conferring together on the first floor, for they were coming down the stairs now. Both Sonali and Chhobi looked up quickly to check if Sonny was with them, and were relieved to see he was not.

What struck the tense group at the bottom of the stairs were the smiles on the brothers' faces. Meaningless smiles, in no way threatening but going on for far too long. They stood together now on the last step but one and continued to smile in unsmiling persistence, Cheshire cat smiles, smiles without meaning or pity.

Beeji's reserve snapped. She rushed forward to clutch at Bhai
Sahib moaning, 'Hai, hai', the panic visibly pulsating in her throat
as she desperately tried to claim kinship, help, comfort... anything
at all. Ma and her daughters flinched. The scene was more
reminiscent than ever of a B-grade Bollywood film. Bhai Sahib
recoiled sharply in distaste, jerking at the sleeve Beeji clutched,
brushing her off like a repulsive insect. The smiles vanished now.
Gold-rimmed glasses glinted angrily as he told her roughly in
Punjabi to calm down.

They were ushered into a cold beautiful glittering room, a
cavern of green ice, where Sonny's mother still sat looking at
pictures of gardens. Her eyes swept disinterestedly over the
group, then she got up and drifted away, murmuring something
about tea.

Ma tried to pat Beeji who was still wailing loudly. Sonali's
mouth was clenched, her face white. She pushed herself behind
Chhobi into the very corner of the brocade-upholstered couch.
They all waited for Beeji to stop crying. Sonny's father was running
his finger around the collar of his Nehru jacket which seemed too
tight above his closely shaved jowls. He had none of the tired
elegance of his wife. No preoccupations with landscapes and
reflections here, his view was simple, telescoping towards a more
and more affluent future.

Ma spoke now, softly, with a quiet dignity, 'As you know, the
search has been called off. But we require some answers. This
disappearance without a trace does not make sense. Admiral Verma
of the coastguard has told me that if the ships had not flashed their
position as the Bay of Bengal, then it would have been assumed that
pirates in the Singapore Straits had attacked them, such a thing has
happened before. But they had safely made *that* passage. Where
could they go in flat calm weather? What were the ships carrying
and where were they bound?'

The brothers looked at one another, the meaningless smiles
back in place. Then Sonali burst in childishly, 'They were smuggling
something to the Andamans.'

The men stiffened. Chhobi saw a shift, a sharp reaction in Bhai Sahib's so-far Sphinx-like expression, the glasses glinting again as he rapidly reassessed the opposition. Ma was not going to be fobbed off as easily as the distraught Beeji. He decided to attack.

'That is a very serious thing you are saying, young lady. What do you base that statement on?'

Ma, who was even more aghast than them, spoke desperately now. 'Sonali, what are you saying? If you knew something why didn't you tell us?'

Beeji had followed that a momentous statement had just been made. She stopped sniffing, alert now, eyes darting back and forth between Ma and Bhai Sahib like a spectator at a tennis match. Bhai Sahib meanwhile had noted the obvious confusion between the four of them.

Chhobi spoke up then. 'We didn't want to worry you, but last month she received a letter from Karan in which he said that the cargo was being unloaded in mid-ocean in complete secrecy. That no proper port formalities were taking place. He felt that they were smuggling VCRs into India.'

There was a release of breath. 'Ahh… VCRs.' Chhobi saw the brothers relax perceptibly and lean back against the cushions. She was rattled, conscious of a misstep, a mistake… but what? Sonny's father signalled now to a servant lurking in the doorway, then a tea trolley was wheeled in. Outside the glass picture window, a group of gardeners and Mr Sarin were bustling about, rearranging plants.

Then Bhai Sahib said, 'Show me the letter.'

Chhobi looked anxiously at Sonali, willing her not to say the letter was lost. She wished they had rehearsed this. It was wrong to be so unprepared with such hard-nosed businessmen.

Sonali said nervously, 'I have misplaced it.'

From being the questioners, they were now the questioned. Chhobi observed Bhai Sahib mentally dismiss the danger. The servant was proffering the teacups, eggshell thin and rimmed in gold. The brothers were trying to bring the interview to a close.

Bhai Sahib said smoothly, 'You have misunderstood your husband, young lady. We are even more concerned than you, after all you are only worried about one person, we have sixty-seven lives and two ships to worry about. The whole matter is very inexplicable. I have spoken to the minister for surface transport. He will be commissioning an enquiry very soon. As for details regarding the voyage, I am afraid no shipping business is conducted from here. The office is in Bombay not directly under my control. You could enquire there, but it is better to wait. Let the authorities decide. We will contact you as soon as there is anything.'

Beeji put down her untouched cup of tea. Emotion was getting the better of her again. 'But Bhai Sahib,' she exclaimed breaking into frenzied Punjabi again, 'Bittoo is my only son, why did you let him go on that ship if it was not safe. Pehenji should have prevented it.'

Bhai Sahib's face and voice were bland as he told her to go back to Hoshiarpur and wait. He said he would do his best to get to the bottom of the mystery, that next week he had an appointment with the minister.

Beeji began to insist, 'I will come to the mantriji with you.'

Finally Bhai Sahib compromised, 'Wait for my meeting with the minister then we will reassess the situation.'

Sonny's father said in conclusion, 'After all no news is good news.'

At that Beeji broke into a fresh flood of noisy weeping. The rest of them lapsed into depressed defeated silence.

The *Zielverkoopers* of the Dutch East India Company beckoned with false promise before Chhobi's eyes. She had read about them in that second-hand book she had picked up behind Plaza Cinema.

It was in the seventeenth century when the Dutch trading company would conduct an annual muster for its fleet. Out-of-work slum dwellers and backward peasants would be rounded up and herded into the company's imposing office where an orchestra played a siren song. The men who marshalled the recruits were known as *Zielverkoopers* or soul sellers, for it was known that at least a third of the recruits would not see Holland again, victim to disease, shipwreck, attacks by pirates and privateers. Nothing, but nothing seemed to have changed till today she thought bitterly

Bhai Sahib stood up, signalling that the audience was over. Ma helped a shaken Beeji to her feet and towards the door. Chhobi could see the lily pond clearly as she walked to the door. One bank was massed with rows and rows of tall scarlet poinsettias in full bloom. The dying sun backlit them with a crimson brilliance multiplied in images trapped perfectly on the still water. Then suddenly a stone, or it could have been the wind, disturbed the surface and the picture broke into pieces, smashed like a molten mirror running in beaded globules of red, frantic and shivering – blood on the water.

nine

Ten days went by. They had started subscribing to extra newspapers for any leads. Beeji spoke to Mrs Bhai Sahib every other day, urging her to prod officialdom. Nothing. The much-awaited interview with the minister had not transpired, he was away visiting his constituency. Apart from a single report in *India Today* that covered the bare facts of the ships vanishing, but did not explain why, there had been nothing further in the news. Not a hint, not a clue. It was as if the disappearing ships had never existed. Even calamities require fresh developments to sustain the interest of readers.

A week back, Chhobi, unable to bear the suspense, unburdened herself at office. She shrank a little as Rosemary's plucked brows climbed her forehead. There was an expression lurking behind the incredulous surprise in her eyes that Chhobi did not like. A touch of gleeful enjoyment. It was after all a strange unsavoury tale that unfolded – missing ships, contraband cargoes and in the centre a beautiful, wilful girl. Perhaps it had been a mistake to confide in her.

Rosemary, who never liked being at a loss, questioned her carefully on what the coastguard had to say. 'Contact somebody in the intelligence agencies? Hmm… let me think. I will have to speak to Frances... my brother-in-law, the one in the foreign service. He is posted at Tokyo – I will book a call this evening. He is bound to know somebody. What a mystery! How did your sister get involved in all this? She is not like you at all, is she?'

Chhobi had murmured something in a vague fashion, finding it hard to deal with a situation that was suddenly such an open question.

※

Sonali and Beeji were on a bus hurtling toward Mehrauli. Beeji had handed her a cloth bag with two coconuts and a tin of pure ghee that she had brought from Hoshiarpur. Ghee clarified from the milk of her own cows. She was going to offer special prayers at a temple at Chattarpur. A temple with a wishing tree. Both of them were fasting. Sonali had been wrenched out of her bed and the stupor induced by shock which had so far anaesthetised her, at first light.

Beeji didn't seem to need much sleep. She spent most of the night sitting upright on the cushions under the Mona Lisa on a Plate. In fact as the days passed, the division between night and day grew blurred for her. Chhobi would wake up in the middle of the night and find her making carrot kanji spiked with pepper, shelling bowlfuls of peas or reorganising the kitchen shelves with a clatter of tins and pots. She could not abide the sight of Sonali – her voice when she spoke to her struck a jagged chord, there was a spitting crackle to her speech like the sound of papads being lowered into boiling oil.

During all the transmission hours, she kept the TV on, volume turned up. Both girls grew as sick of hearing about Karan's childhood as they did about the travails and trials of Nanhe and Badki, characters in India's first soap opera, *Hum Log*. Listening to the little homily by Ashok Kumar as he summed up each episode became a ritual, for it was a programme to which Beeji was addicted. It was the only time she left off her frantic wondering and waiting.

The bus was jolting through potholes that belonged to a moonscape, it was a patch of road left unattended since the monsoon. To her left Sonali could see the Qutab Minar outlined against a sky of darkling blue and scudding clouds. One of Chhobi's earliest pieces on Delhi had been on the Qutab Minar. She had begun the article by writing that in the twelfth century Qutub-ud-Din followed by Iltutmish had together drawn a vertical alif in Delhi's sky, first letter of Allah's name. 'Qutab' also meant axis, and there was a Kufic inscription carved into the stone that referred to the minaret casting the shadow of Allah over east and west.

What had actually sprung up in its shadow was the huge temple complex toward which they were headed. Concrete mandaps and mandalas with towering domes and innumerable carved niches, and most of the gods in the Hindu pantheon.

Sonali felt a fever coming on as she got off the bus. She was shivering. Beeji had insisted on a ritual purifying bath at the crack of dawn. Her still-wet hair was coiled on the nape of her neck, as heavy as the coconuts she carried in her hands, entwined with garlands of saffron marigold. Nausea gnawed like a rat at the pit of her stomach. She pressed a corner of her dupatta to her mouth to suppress the retching. More cleansing as Beeji made her wash her hands and feet in the icy water gushing from the row of taps outside the gate. They received numbered plastic tokens in exchange for the safekeeping of their shoes. Bare feet and head covered with dupattas, they made their way to the wishing tree.

Sonali stopped short. It was a bizarre and terrifying sight. A real tree but without any leaves, the lack of them not just a seasonal winter loss. The hundreds of thousands of desperate hopes tied to little rags burdened every branch with disappointment and frustration and left no space for a true leaf to grow.

Wishes for a child from the barren, a son from those with daughters, the health of a spouse, success in an exam, the revival of a failing trade, the return of an unrequited love. All linked together in a fluttering multi-hued foliage of pain. Strips of sari aanchal, dupatta ends, pieces of turbans, handkerchiefs, each wish clasped to a stranger's in a fragile chain of expectation. Hoping against hope.

Sonali and Beeji tied their own leaves, two handkerchiefs with coins wrapped in them, to the ragged canopy. Beeji began to pray, eyes tight shut in a web of wrinkles. Sonali just watched her, then the eyes opened and focused on her with such an expression of malevolent hatred, that Sonali snapped out of her daze, thrust the garland-festooned coconuts into the old woman's hands, and made her own wish.

※

Meanwhile, Rosemary called Chhobi into her cabin at office, a conspiratorial tone lacing her voice. Her brother-in-law Frances had spoken to somebody she said, who was in a position to throw light on the mystery. The only thing was that he was sensitive about meeting the press, so he was willing to speak only to her mother, not to Chhobi. Picking up the phone she made Chhobi call Ma, who was to meet him at a neutral place. Rosemary had suggested the Taj Mahal hotel.

'But what is his name and how will I recognise him?' said Ma baulking at the thought of meeting a perfect stranger in the posh, plush surroundings of a five-star hotel. 'Who is he?' Rosemary took the phone from Chhobi and said , 'Well, he is making a flying visit to Delhi so you must meet him today, he is the cultural attaché at our embassy in Sri Lanka.'

'Cultural attaché in Sri Lanka?' Ma repeated faintly, muddled.

'Well, that is the title he goes by, but we all know the cadre these cultural attachés belong to, especially in a hotspot like Colombo. I actually contacted him after Chandrayee said the intelligence agencies needed to be reached. He hinted that our friends in Jaffna might have something to do with the disappearance.'

'Jaffna,' echoed Ma again, hearing the boom of gunfire, the shatter of shrapnel. She felt as though she was drowning, floundering, out of her depth. It was time to sink or swim.

'Yes, yes, Mrs Dutt, now pay attention. I do not want to repeat these things on the telephone. And Mrs Dutt, I would advise you at this stage to keep this completely to yourself, do not speak to anybody. Rai, for that is his name, has emphasised the need for secrecy. Remember this meeting does not really take place. The press must not get a whiff of this, Mrs Dutt? Mrs Dutt are you listening?'

'Yes,' whispered Ma.

'Okay, good. Meet Rai in the lobby at 5 p.m. today. He will recognise you, wear something pink.'

'Pink?' parroted Ma, voice tailing to a squeak.

'Yes, yes pink. I told Rai pink,' finished Rosemary impatiently, clearly thinking Ma was quibbling about details.

Ma replaced the receiver. Pink. Jaffna. Cultural attaché in Colombo. Cold seeds were sprouting in her belly, the germination of nightmares. She went to her cupboard to search through the colours hanging there. There was a marked absence of them. Slate and stone, salt and pepper, drab and dun, mole and mouse. No pink. She possessed pink saris but they were packed away in the wooden boxes that were stacked in a minaret in the garage, and she did not have the energy or inclination to dismantle any towers. Maybe the girls would have something. She found an entirely unsuitable Lucknowi kurta folded on Chhobi's shelf. It was far too flimsy for January and besides she wore only saris. There was also a Gurjari shawl – magenta heavily studded with tiny mirrors. Ma took it out doubtfully and wrapped herself in it, peering into the bathroom mirror. As she swung the shawl around herself the ceiling glittered in a chaotic stream, the Milky Way as the mirrors collected shooting stars of light. She unwrapped herself hurriedly.

It was four-thirty when she hailed an auto rickshaw for the Taj Mahal hotel. Dida and Dadu, already perturbed at the recent events and her prolonged leave of absence from work, followed her to the gate. Dida had noticed her attire.

'Meera, where are you going? Why are you dressed up?' Dida kept asking as Ma climbed without replying into the auto. She had finally worn Sonali's gift. The pale pink mohair cardigan embroidered with tiny pearls, made in Japan, matched with an ivory silk sari swirling with dull pink and grey paisleys. Looking back through the rear window veiled by a sheet of smeared plastic, she could see her bewildered parents growing smaller and smaller as the distance increased, growing it seemed, older and older.

She was ten minutes late as she rushed up the entrance stairs of

the hotel. A turbaned giant of a doorman swung open the glass
doors for her. Her cheeks were flushed with the cold of the ride in
the rickshaw, hair escaping from her bun in little tendrils. She felt
as though she had blundered into one of her detective novels, this
jagged acceleration to her daily life leaving her quite breathless. She
tried to unobtrusively gaze around the lobby, icy marble underfoot,
glowing enamel-work overhead. She wished Chhobi could have
accompanied her.

Rai materialised silently by her side as she was looking at her
watch and looking around with huge drawn eyes. Looking very
much in the pink, as a matter of fact, although unaware of it.

'Mrs Dutt?' was the query.

Rai was a small powerful man in his late forties, who smelt
pleasantly of tobacco and eau de cologne. Later when she got to
know him better, Ma came to appreciate his stone-faced humour,
that turned life and death dilemmas into commonplace events with
a cool wryness.

The coffee shop where he headed her had an Indian jungle
decor. The walls were covered in life-size painted murals, a
Rousseau-esque rendition of Kanha. A tropical heat oozed from the
walls in that January chill. Monkeys chattered and leapt through the
air, parakeets screamed overhead. Sword-shaped grass, dark green
and gold parted to reveal the striped heads of tigers.

Ma sat down nervously at a table for two next to a wide window
of sheer glass overlooking a turquoise pool. Glancing around
diffidently, she almost expected to see Jim Corbett priming his rifle at
the next table. She turned to find Rai's eyes on her, assessing, shrewd.

'Tell me, Mrs Dutt, how did your son-in-law get a job with
Talwar Shipping Company?'

Ma prepared to reply, and then as he nodded at her reassuringly,
suddenly felt close to tears. Her voice when she spoke had a break
in it.

'My daughter is only nineteen. She married him very suddenly,
we know nothing much about him. He was working for a British
company, but with this recession, that company went into

liquidation. He was jobless, applying everywhere, found nothing. Finally he contacted the Talwars, they are related to him somewhat distantly.'

'Oh... related... I see. The Talwars have been very careful till now, they always use the same trusted senior crew members. Both captains have been with them since inception, in any case they use a skeletal crew.'

'But what has happened? Rosemary said you have some knowledge about what actually transpired. This silence, this uncertainty is killing... The Talwars might be related but they have done nothing, absolutely nothing to help. In fact they were almost offensive and very evasive when we met.'

'You must realise, Mrs Dutt, the Talwars do not have a good reputation in shipping circles. The ships are very poorly maintained. They routinely bribe the safety inspectors to certify the vessels as fit for sailing.'

'Do you think they sank because they were not in good condition? Even so what happened to the lifeboats... Some survivors...' Ma interrupted.

'No, I am coming to that. The Talwars are not only unscrupulous in matters of safety, they have no qualms about the kind of cargo they carry. They go, especially in these times of recession, where the returns are highest, legal or illegal.'

'Illegal,' repeated Ma, then she told him about the smuggling letter.

'Where is the letter?' enquired Rai, eyes alert, pushing away his cup of tea.

'Lost,' she returned despondently, 'lost,' feeling close to tears again. What was wrong with her, she thought.

'Okay, okay, forget it, it doesn't matter. I wish it had been as simple as blackmarket VCRs. At least the crew would have been alive today. We suspect something far more serious.'

'Serious?' She gulped quickly at the tepid tea Rai refilled her cup. All she could think of was that he felt the crew was dead. Dead. Widowed. No hoping against hope.

'Yes, we suspect the involvement of the Tigers.'

Ma looked up uncomprehending. Behind Rai's head loomed the face of a stalking tiger. Royal Bengal, green eyes glinting, pupils narrow vertical slits. The jungle foliage, the lianas, the tall grasses, the leafy branches swam in and out of focus, she was getting that familiar drowning feeling.

'Mrs Dutt, Mrs Dutt, are you all right?' Snapping his fingers at the waiter, Rai was telling her to drink some water.

She pulled herself together. 'I am okay, please continue,' she said firmly taking a sip of water. She noticed her hand was rock steady. 'I just don't understand.'

Rai looked at her, wondering whether to continue. She nodded vigorously, 'Go on, please.'

'I am referring to the Tamil Tigers, the LTTE. We feel the Talwar ships were carrying arms for them.'

'Gun-running,' she whispered dully. Ma's response was mechanical. She felt so numb, nothing registered beyond the death. What did it matter what the ships carried if Karan was dead. Now she understood fully the earlier reference to Jaffna. She stood up, the jungle closing in on her. With a muttered thanks, she began rushing away, out of the restaurant, through the lobby past the elaborate flower arrangements and the liveried bellhops, through the glass doors, a startled Rai following behind her, his stride stepped up to a run. Outside night was falling in shadows like sadness.

'Let me drop you. Please. You are upset. Come. I insist.'

She stared at him wildly, habitual calm completely deserted. No more hoping against hope. Did Sonali love him as she had loved Bhaskar? 'Who are you? How do you know all this and are you sure he is dead?'

Rai took her elbow, shepherding her towards a waiting taxi.

'Take it easy, Mrs Dutt, we won't talk anymore. No, I am not sure, these are all conjectures, but yes, I am afraid and very sorry, there is a strong possibility. I shall speak to the Coutinhos tonight, please calm down.'

ten

Ma did not meet her daughters that evening. She was afraid of the onset of a migraine, but the turmoil of worries occupied every crevice, every corner of her head, leaving no space for any pain to intrude. She spent the night huddled under a quilt in the planter's chair, next to the tall standing lamp in her room. Her favourite place, where she normally relaxed with an Agatha Christie or Dick Francis novel. Tonight the lamp was switched off. Dida eased the door ajar to peep in at midnight, worried, but Ma did not reply to her hesitant questions.

Towards the early hours of the morning she fell asleep, at first fitful and cramped in the chair, then cold and stiff as she shifted to her bed, curling herself into a foetal posture. It was the not knowing... with Bhaskar the nightmare had stilled with finality. There was a body to mourn over, rituals to perform, friends and relatives making condolence calls. This time... what had Sonali embroiled them in... a ferment of international intrigue... the terrible, terrible uncertainty of it all. She resolved to speak to Chhobi in the morning, she could not shoulder this alone.

Dadu in the neighbouring bedroom was lying absolutely still and tense with apprehension. Finally his eyes closed at that hour, when for him, dreams of a lost place preceded dawn. For the past week there had been no welcome escape, no journey back to Mymensingh and his terrible need for a history that nurtured. It was with relief that night that he surrendered himself to sleep.

He dreamt of water. Not a violent ocean, boiling and turbulent, but the tributory of the Brahmaputra spreading silver beyond his home. A river always lapping at the edges of his consciousness. His body relaxed in a visible slackening of tension as the river waters carried him back to the spring tides of his life.

He was standing on the steps of the ghat, stained green with slime and moss, looking out across the swift flowing river swollen by the mountain rains. The surface glassy grey with the darker force of the current visibly rushing beneath. He shaded his eyes with his hand as the river caught the setting sun in a flash of fire and squinted to focus on the boats. The boatmen were poling the riverbed, shouting insistent messages at one another. All the men of his large joint family were gathered on those boats. Father, uncles, numerous cousins all frantic – searching, searching.

A dry-throated sob sounded next to him and he turned to see his aunt, towering above him. He must have been very young, five or six perhaps, for she had been scarcely five feet in height. Her hand tightened on his arm, Dadu's dream getting nightmare-tinged in that incubus grip. Her son, truant swimmer was lost that day to the Brahmaputra's strong current.

The boy was never found. Dadu saw him clearly now. White skull rolling on the river bed, tiny fish entering empty eye sockets, hair floating free like weed, bone fingers snared under a rock.

He jerked awake, switching on the light. The clock stretched its arms in an insomniac's embrace – a quarter to three.

'What...what's happened? What's the matter?' Dida asked sitting up, her skin as wrinkled as crumpled silk. In her eyes, smudged with fatigue, he saw his aunt's face, the panic pulsating underneath, and the absolute conviction of another vanishing. Yet still hoping against hope in an illogical suspension of disbelief.

Ma received a call from Rosemary very early the next morning. Silent and withdrawn she was drinking her first cup of tea. Dida had wisely decided to leave her alone when the phone rang.

'Mrs Dutt, yes, how are you? This is bad business. Rai spoke to me. He is returning to Colombo tonight. He has offered to drop by at my place this evening. You must be there, around five o' clock. Let's try and work out a sensible course of action.' Rosemary's tones were crisp, commanding, and very much in charge.

Ma's voice was suddenly as firm. 'Thank you for your help, Rosemary. I will be there but Chandrayee will accompany me. I need her. After all she is very discreet.'

There was a small pause, then she agreed.

Cold and haze hung over the city when they left for Green Park, the blue exhaust from the cars shivering the buildings and traffic lights as in a mirage. January was such a dreary month. Ma and Chhobi lurched and jolted together in tense silence. The auto needed to be manually cranked at every traffic signal when the engine would sputter and die as soon as the lights turned to red. The driver would jump out and lift up the seat, sticking his own in the air as he scrabbled with wires, nuts and bolts. Chhobi was still dazed by Ma's choked utterances, the probable conjectures about the improbable vanishing. The thin veneer of serenity on her mother's face so brittle and cracked, the despair pulsating beneath. She wondered if she would ever be able to make her own announcement about her departure to America. All the documents had arrived, she had formally been offered the research assistantship, but she doubted now whether she would be able to depart at all. She didn't see any solutions to Sonali's situation.

Rosemary had painted the area outside her front door a pale blue. It was still lit up with a huge cardboard star of Bethlehem. A light breeze made the perforated illuminations tremble. Stabbing at the doorbell with her finger, Chhobi felt completely out of place standing under that twinkling cerulean mantle, her dark mood an absolute contrast to the Christmas cheer that still persisted.

Rosemary's husband, Alban, a detached man quite content to leave the running of all things to his wife, opened the door. Chhobi felt suddenly self-conscious as Rai, already there, rose to greet them. Dapper in a double-breasted blazer and silk tie, he ushered Ma solicitously to a chair, even as she was murmuring an introduction. Both men returned to the small talk they were making about the absent Frances. Chhobi turned her head towards the kitchen from whence Rosemary was beckoning, sticking her head out of the swing doors.

'Where is your daughter?' Chhobi asked as she joined her.

'Oh, I sent her to the park with the ayah. I know it's cold, but we wanted no interruptions. I have found out more about this Rai, Frances confirmed it. You do know who he is, don't you?'

'Isn't he the cultural attaché at Colombo?'

'That's only a... what do you call it? Misnomer, no, no... alias. Yes, an alias. He is actually with the RAW.' Rosemary's voice had switched to a sibilant hiss, her eyes were shining with excitement. She was quite bustling with efficiency, now deftly arranging teacups on a tray, rectangular chocolate biscuits on a flower-patterned plate. Chhobi supposed dully that it was exciting, if one wasn't so closely connected. Rosemary, checking to see if the water had reached boiling, looked at Chhobi, a little disappointed with her lack of reaction.

'You know what RAW is, don't you?' Chhobi was expressionlessly wiping already gleaming teaspoons with a kitchen towel. Rosemary lowered her voice, trying to be blasé, as she said in an offhand manner, 'It's the Indian secret service, the Indian CIA, MI5.'

'I know,' said Chhobi quietly. 'He is undercover, not using an alias.'

'Oh,' Rosemary poured the water into the pot, adjusted the tea cosy embroidered with hollyhocks in buttonhole stitch, and handed Chhobi the plate of biscuits, motioning her to lead the way in deference to her closer connection with the calamity.

'It's a question of geography, and demography.' Rai was speaking, Chhobi realised, about the situation in Sri Lanka, ethnic conflict again. Alban who must have just returned from office, looked at the tea tray hungrily. 'Some snacks Rosemary…' he murmured.

Chhobi sat down, interjecting abruptly, she was sick of vague theories and generalisations. 'Excuse me, Mr Rai, a couple of questions have been bothering me ever since I heard about the supposed gun-running. First of all, aren't all the LTTE sympathisers located in Tamil Nadu? How does a North Indian family-owned company suddenly forge contacts with a guerrilla outfit? Then if the Talwars *were* carrying arms for them, they were doing them a service. Why should they harm *their* ships? It doesn't make any sense.'

Rai stopped addressing himself to Ma and turned to look at Chhobi, reassessing her rapidly. She had obviously scored a point.

He spoke slowly, measuring his words. 'What I am trying to explain to your mother is that separatist groups which act in a calculatedly violent manner can only be called terrorist organisations. With the LTTE, terrorism is its core, much due to the nature of its leadership. Velupillai Prabhakaran is very cruel, bloodthirsty and pitiless, he has been compared to Pol Pot, if not in scale but definitely in the intensity of his brutal acts. He will order his Tigers to ruthlessly eliminate anybody who could be an informer or collaborator or even if they do not, should he suspect, respect his diktats.'

Alban handing him a cup of tea nodded intelligently and commented, 'Tiger tyranny.' Rosemary shot him a look of annoyance. Chhobi put her cup down, carefully placing it on a papier-mâché coaster painted with a chinar leaf. House-proud Rosemary hated rings on her polished wood. Rai was continuing.

'The second thing to realise is that in recent years the LTTE army has swelled in numbers. They are comparatively large and well-equipped, and the question of finances to maintain them is a huge problem.'

'I thought sympathetic groups, you know, the Tamil diaspora communities in the US and Canada fund-raise for them. Sometimes under duress,' said Alban.

'They do, of course, and on the contrary, a lot of that fund-raising is quite voluntary but it's inadequate. They are now placing reliance on other sources of money and narcotics, for one, is gaining importance. In fact we have definite proof that they are an important link in a wider narcotics trade that comes down from Afghanistan, Pakistan to India and then to Sri Lanka.' Rai stopped, glancing at Ma in concern. She had visibly paled, fingers gripping the china cup so hard Chhobi feared it would be crushed in her grip... Gun-running *and* narcotics.

'Mrs Dutt, don't... don't, there is no discernible narcotics link in this case. Please. I am just trying to educate you about the background scenario. To tell you that if you choose to do business with a group that has no scruples, no law, then you cannot also expect the normal safeguards offered by international law.'

Alban was nodding, 'If you play with fire you are bound to get burnt.'

It's cliché time, Chhobi thought grimly. 'Okay so if you do business with the devil you end up in the deep sea. But what happened to the ships? Did they sink them or what?'

'Ah. This is the moot point. One reason why the Talwar ships were chosen was their size.'

Moot point? Thought Chhobi incredulously, people actually spoke like this? All this was so far removed from their lives, it was hard to fathom what had overtaken them.

'What is the moot point, Mr Rai? We still have to get the point.'

Rosemary glanced at her, Ma frowning too at her impatient tone. Rai continued coolly unruffled.

'The Talwar ships are small, little more than trawlers. The Jaffna peninsula has a very indented coastline, with isolated coves. These provided both security and access especially for small vessels. Why charter a vessel when you can own it? The Talwars cannot take recourse to any action since they are involved in something so illegal any way. The ships must already be repainted, renamed and provided with forged documentation, new port of registry papers, etc.'

'But how much weight can be placed on these theories, for that is what they are,' asked Chhobi.

Refusing Alban circulating with the chocolate biscuits, Rai continued, 'The interesting point is where the ships loaded – in Cambodia. Cambodia is an open arms market, originally started with stockpiles left over from WW II and the Vietnam war. Now, of course, all kinds of arms are freely available.'

Chhobi remarked slowly, 'Well... yes... Karan's letter mentioned unloading in the dead of night, in mid-ocean... no port formalities... Okay, suppose it's possible, but why the Talwars? There are other ship owners with small ships surely.'

'I cannot answer that question,' said Rai. 'I don't know them, perhaps they have other business in South India and developed contacts. In any case, we know the Talwars are motivated purely by profit, always operating on the fringes of the law. Perhaps a combination of several factors, not easily being able to fix cargoes with the slump. It's expensive to keep a ship idle.'

'Oh God!' Chhobi exclaimed. 'Sonny's wife! He had to marry her because of her business connections. Her family have a dealership network of hosiery goods or something in South India.'

'Well, there you have it.'

Ma spoke finally, voice a little tremulous with emotion, 'Can't we go to the government, the police or somebody, they can't get away with putting so many lives in such extreme jeopardy. It's murder.'

Rosemary snorted, 'My dear Mrs Dutt! Where is the proof? Who will you go to, they probably have ministers in their pockets.'

Rai continued, 'Yes, nothing happens in Delhi without political sanction, unofficial or official. In any case Indira Gandhi's government has always been sympathetic towards the Tamil separatists. It's a dangerous policy. One that will backfire in the near future. I mean, we have actually trained the Tigers.'

'What?' said Rosemary and Chhobi simultaneously in shocked surprise.

Rai lost a little of his composure. 'That's digressing,' he said quickly.

Ma spoke again. 'But what *can* we do?'

There was silence. Rosemary's thin brows met over the bridge of her nose, fingers drumming on her knee in frustration. Rai was frowning too. He spoke very slowly. 'Well... basically you need something – some documents... some taped conversation, anything to confront them with. They will be shaken by the fact that you know, but you will need some kind of evidence.'

'Confront them with what, after all he is dead,' Ma said, a hopeless finality in her voice. Rai was quite clear – 'In any service when a wife loses her husband, she is looked after, resettled. They have to help your daughter. They owe her that responsibility.'

Chhobi wasn't listening anymore. Taped conversations, secret documents, cameras in bow ties, he was truly the secret service. It seemed it was all going to boil down to a question of money in the end. Or the lack of it.

Rai looked at his watch, then at Ma.

'I want to introduce you to a colleague, well... he is also a friend. He can offer assistance, send messages in the diplomatic bag to me, any time you need advice. I will phone you as soon as I get your message. In the meantime maybe the mother-in-law, I believe she is also related to the Talwars, is the best person to unearth some facts, evidence, anything.'

Beeji! Thought Chhobi and Ma in unison, recalling how Sonny's uncle had brushed her off like a speck of dust on his sleeve.

Rai was standing up. 'Shall we?' he said to Ma, then as she looked at him bemused, he continued, 'My friend... he lives close by in Lodhi Estate, I just want to introduce you as you will have to deal with him personally. It will take just half an hour before I drop you back, then I must be on my way to the airport...'

'Yes, yes, Mrs Dutt, carry on. It's only ten minutes away. Chandrayee will wait for you here,' said Rosemary in bracing, brightened tones, relieved that at least some action was taking place. Ma got up hesitantly, giving Chhobi a look of entreaty. Chhobi felt a flash of rage at Sonali for having landed them in such dislocation.

Outside a fine drizzle had begun to fall. Rosemary's daughter came rushing in just as Rai and Ma reached the door, filling the room with a noisy buzz like a swarm of flies let loose in a mithai shop, and attacked the chocolate biscuits.

There was an official car waiting for Rai. Ma shivered slightly as she got into the cavernous back seat of the white Ambassador. She brushed the fine droplets of rain that had collected on the hairy fluff of her old wool cardigan, making it somehow almost pretty, a sprinkling of pearl dust. She shivered again. Rai giving directions to the driver, looked at her, then leaned forward to pick up his overcoat folded on the front seat. Unfolding it, he draped it around her, ignoring her embarrassed protests.

The car slowed to a stop, caught in a snarl of traffic at the foot of the flyover. Ma fingered the plaid woollen lining of the coat, red and tan and black, luxuriating in its warmth. For a brief span, she forgot about Sonali and her troubles. The coat smelt dry-cleaned with a faint lingering aroma of tobacco. She imagined the empty sleeves encasing strong arms, wrapping around her. Imagined them crushing her against a chest sprinkled with dark hair, heart pounding against heart. Synchronised in close embrace. It had been thirteen years since a man had held her. Thirteen long years. Days spent trudging the treadmill of trivia and endless lonely nights. She turned her head to look at Rai, thinking, I know nothing about him. He caught her gaze and smiled in response. Colouring slightly, Ma murmured, 'We are very ordinary people.'

⁕

Back at Green Park, Rai was the topic under discussion. 'A good man,' Alban was telling Chhobi, as he mopped his plate of leftover curry with a slice of bread. Noticing Chhobi looking at his heaped plate he added, 'Sorry, missed my lunch today.'

'Can we rely on Mr Rai's theories – they do sound far-fetched, and more to the point, make life so hopeless,' Chhobi said, feeling despondent again, once removed from Rai's aura of potent energy.

'Of course, of course, he is a very astute analyst, doing very brilliantly. I have been finding out about him.'

'How do you find out about anybody in the secret service?' Chhobi returned dispiritedly, glancing around to look at Rosemary stirring Bournvita into a bright plastic mug of milk. The ayah had taken the little girl in to take off her damp jacket.

Alban was still on the same subject, 'My brother Frances knows him for the last fifteen years. I spoke to him to crosscheck, after all we are depending on his assessment of the situation... a brilliant man he said, just brilliant.'

Chhobi wondered what they would do. What *could* they do? She got up restlessly and began to look at the scores of New Year cards still ranged on the mantle, the gleaming occasional tables. All these greetings... 'Happy New Year' the refrain began ringing in her ears as unpleasantly as an attack of tinnitus.

'What about his family? Are they in Colombo?' she asked.

'He doesn't have any family. I mean not an immediate one, he never married. I believe some tragedy in his past. His fiancée died just before their wedding and he threw himself into his work.'

Nobody spoke of comedies in their past, only tragedies, Chhobi thought, Rai's unbreachable strength becoming coloured suddenly by a great red bloom of pain.

Rosemary finished her ministering and joined them. 'What are you all talking about?'

'Rai,' said Chhobi shortly.

'Rai... He is what you call a masterful man,' Rosemary gave a little giggle, a glimpse of the teenager she must have been, 'old but ...' then leaning close to Chhob,i whispered, '... sexy.'

Chhobi reared back, 'He is no James Bond.'

Alban who had finished eating, said sympathetically 'I wanted to ask, Chandrayee, how is your sister Sonali, how is she? How is she taking it... A terrible business this terrorist connection.'

Chhobi felt a prickling in her eyes. She bit her lip to control the trembling. Rosemary had the grace to look a little abashed. She had been so preoccupied with separatists and secret service men that Chhobi's sister had been quite forgotten.

'Sonali doesn't know. She only thinks the ships are missing. We haven't told her about the LTTE yet. We really don't know how to. Already she is taking Calmpose, sleeping pills. It is too much to take, ordinary people like us.'

Her outburst silenced both of them. Rosemary still looking shamefaced murmured softly, 'Not ordinary, never ordinary. So young, your sister, and really her beauty is extraordinary. Take her off that medication. This will pass. No pills.'

The problem both Chhobi and Ma grappled with on the way home was how to tell Sonali and Dida. Chhobi kept mentally phrasing and rephrasing the words, but however delicately she put it she could not temper their shocking impact. Rai had advised Ma to say nothing to Beeji after listening to her account of Beeji's unimportance in the Talwar scheme of things.

Reaching home, they hesitated undecided on the verandah, looking in through a chink in the curtains. The brightly lit room, so familiar, but both of them peering in as though at an unknown stage set. Dadu and Ratan Kaku were devouring bowls of jhal moori – puffed rice garnished with tiny green peas, onions and cubed potatoes, spiked with pungent raw mustard oil. Dida and Sonali were talking, watching Runa Laila on TV, Dida rubbing oil into Sonali's scalp, her hair spread about her shoulders in a blue-black mantle. For a moment Chhobi felt as though she had slid back in time to the pre-Karan period, the lazy regimen of one uneventful day following another in uncomplicated assurance, and felt a sharp pang of longing. If only they could slip back into the inertia of the past.

Ma and Chhobi stared at each other helplessly, loath to enter that calm domestic tableau. What was more real? The scene inside as everyday as a family watching evening television or they, lurking coldly outside, burdened by knowledge at the same time so melodramatic and terrible it seemed to belong in the nightmare of a psychotic theatre artiste? Looking at Ma tight-lipped in pain, Chhobi felt a familiar stab of anger. Sonali, the cause and effect of so much distress was being pampered by Dida indoors. Roughly she pushed the door open, letting in a blast of icy air, and marched in to the background score of *Damadam Mast Kalandar*.

eleven

They waited for Ratan Kaku to leave, for Dadu to finish checking and crosschecking all the bolts and locks and latches before going to bed, for Dida to finish clearing away the leftovers of their dinner. Ma had only picked at hers, pushing away her thaal unfinished and getting up to rummage amongst Dida's albums. She hadn't looked at them in years. Now she stood dusting the one she wanted, silverfish shooting out of it like miniature lead missiles. Later Chhobi found her sitting on her chair under the red silk shaded lamp, the flattering illumination wiping out years and terrors in the pink light that pooled under the shade. She looked at Chhobi, then continued to turn the leaves of the album.

She stopped at an enlargement of the three of them. It was a summer shot. Chhobi at four years wearing a white petticoat embroidered in lazy daisies, leaning her head on Ma's shoulder. Ma looking gravely at the camera with six-month-old Sonali, fat, beautiful and quite naked on her lap. Then Chhobi saw a dark stain appear on the page, Ma was crying, tears sliding noiselessly out of her eyes.

'It's ruined, just like us,' she said brushing at the damp blotches on the page. Chhobi moving closer saw the silverfish had been at it, eaten away the pupil of Ma's eye, riddled another irregular daisy chain on her slip. Baby Sonali was untouched.

'Give it to me,' she said gruffly, close to tears herself, 'I will try and get it restored, our art department should manage.' Ma smiled a little through her tears, sadness threaded through with irony. She handed her the album, wiped her eyes and said, 'Call them, I will tell them now. No need to disturb Dadu.'

It was going to be a mobilisation of sorts, as frail as an assemblage of Adam's ribs. Three generations mustered together in a feminine foregathering. Sonali immediately got into Ma's bed, crumpling the bedcover in an untidy heap, pulling the faded quilt up to her chin. Dida took Ma's place on the planter's chair, wrapped in her old but exquisite katha shawl, silk with a sun motif in saffron, crimson and rose emblazoned across the back in minute quilting. She looked almost regal, Chhobi thought, and very expectant, sitting with straightened spine. She had sensed and resented the exclusion of the last two days. Ma and Chhobi ranked themselves at the foot of the bed. Chhobi began folding the bedcover into a neat rectangle.

For what seemed like aeons they just stared at each other, Chhobi looking anxiously at Ma, willing her to speak. Finally Sonali asked, 'Yes Ma?' She seemed to have thrown off the sad languor that had enveloped her since the New Year. Some of the golden Sonali sheen had returned to her skin and eyes.

Ma was straining to form the words. They seemed to be burning in the pit of her stomach, she was afraid they would scorch her tongue, singe her lips as they left her mouth. She did not look at Sonali, carefully addressing Dida's deaf ear to lessen the impact. Her words were soft and very brief, she did not mention the Tamil Tigers, speaking only of Karan's likely death.

What Ma saw with a dismayed recognition of shock was the complete lack of it displayed by her mother and daughter. They had begun the process of adjusting to the loss before she had even begun to accept it.

Dida did not stir, had she heard everything clearly? It hit Ma hard, this calm acceptance of Karan's permanent absence. She doubted whether Sonali fully understood the implications, or whether it was Ma herself who misunderstood. Ma who even after thirteen years woke up in the middle of unending nights, to search the bed for the man who was lost to her forever. Her daughter's reaction left her reeling, unable to believe she had whelped this unlikely flesh.

Ma did not mince her words then, sugarcoat the syntax – everything came spilling out, the LTTE, the probable gun-running. The truth as perceived by Rai, terrible and violent.

Sonali looked quite uncomprehending, then said shakily, 'I thought it was VCRs they were smuggling.' She sounded thirteen, not nineteen. A not-too-perceptive thirteen-year-old who wanted to block out the present. She started to speak quickly, telling them about her visit with Beeji to the Chattarpur Mandir, the desires she had added to the wishing tree. For a moment both Chhobi and Ma were almost frightened to watch her lovely mouth jabber as though no grief had transpired at all.

'What was your wish? Did you pray for his return?' asked Chhobi abruptly.

Sonali faltered, but only for a second.

'No,' she said, a faint note of defiance creeping into her voice. Unconsciously she straightened her back, alert now, watching their reaction to the statement she was about to make. 'I wished I was not pregnant.'

The wish that had turned into a mantra, one she repeated hundred and eight times a day, but her menses did not start.

For the past two weeks, she had tried every old wives' tale she had ever heard of. She had confided in Savitri and the taciturn old woman had brought her raw papayas, critically watching her gag and choke, as she made her swallow the unpalatable milky white flesh. Sonali had skipped furiously on the terrace until her limbs trembled with exhaustion, she had hefted Dida's heavy grinding stone in the kitchen, but her period did not come.

She could conceive of no part that a baby could possibly play in her life. She, who had been so careful during all the months she had spent with Karan, except for that one time the night before his departure, when she had allowed his desire to overthrow all caution. Always rooted in reality, she visualised now a bleak future, Ma's life repeating itself.

Today she had sneaked into the garage, when Ma and Chhobi were away meeting Rai and had gone over Dadu's medical books. The pictures of the baby growing day by day in the womb had dinned a kind of realisation into her. Nine weeks overdue.

An abortion was the unspoken option and Sonali looked now at Ma and Chhobi, their faces grey and still as though hewn from stone. She turned away towards her grandmother, relying as always on her support. Dida would arrange it somehow. Hoping against hope.

The hope died instantaneously as she saw her expression. Gladness flooding Dida's face, her lips trembling in a welcoming smile – a child. Nine weeks would grow to nine months.

Reasons jumbled through Sonali's head as she tried to reassess this miscalculation. Dida who had longed for a large family, Dida who had suffered the pain and disappointment of three miscarriages, and Dida who had spent the tedious months of her own difficult pregnancy confined to her bed, a row of bricks ensuring the mattress was upraised at her feet. Dida... a child.

Sonali so brilliant at fresh starts would have to see this through to the very end.

For the first time in her life she resented her sex. To be caught in such a female trap... a prisoner of gender.

Dida found her voice first. When she spoke her Bengali was rapid-fire and decisive. 'One thing is definite,' she said, 'that Beeji must not come to know. We cannot have her interfering in Shona's life. She comes back here. We will tell Karan's family we cannot afford the rent... It is the truth. Shona needs looking after, we must prepare for the child. Let us think, I am going to make us something to drink,' she said as she rose, rewrapping the shawl around herself. The silk shimmered in the lamp's ruby glow, the embroidered sun radiating red and gold and orange. It undulated on her back as she turned, as gorgeous as the plumage of some fantastic bird.

Definitely the phoenix thought Chhobi flabbergasted, risen from the ashes.

Ma was shaking, Chhobi saw. She went into the bathroom to rifle through the pills and potions in the cabinet behind the mirror. Suddenly mindful of Rosemary's allusion to drugs, she took down the worn Duckback hot water bottle hanging from a nail behind the door. Good for shivers, good for cold feet.

As she moved towards the kitchen to fill up the bottle, she saw Sonali was playing an old game. She had always transformed childhood sick beds into magic landscapes, the bedclothes moulded into mountains and valleys. Her slim fingers would sometimes advance like marching armies, or sometimes twist and pirouette, a Bollywood heroine on outdoor location in Kashmir.

In the kitchen, Chhobi saw with a little spurt of dismay, that Dida was stirring spoonfuls of sugar into four mugs of Horlicks. Chhobi had been hoping for some tea, somehow she always associated this grey malted drink with periods of convalescence. The taste sat thickly on her tongue like a sickness. Chhobi so far numbed by the revelations of the day started to speak slowly, just thinking aloud. 'How is she going to manage? We just can't exploit any advantage we might have...'

'What advantage?' pounced Dida.

'Well... we do know the Talwars were involved up to their necks in something so illegal. That is definitely a weakness, but how do we make use of it?'

Dida pursed her lips, narrowing her eyes. Chhobi left her there meditatively stirring. She returned to wrap Ma in a blanket, tucking it around the hot water bottle she placed at her feet. Ma was looking absolutely drained, fatigue resting on every line of her body. Her eyes were as black holes punched into a dingy sheet.

Dida resumed her place on the planter's chair, face wreathed in wisps of Horlicks fumes. Her kitchen cogitations were about to bear fruit, Chhobi saw. Dida always thought best in the kitchen, it was the cramped hotbed of all her schemes. Chhobi and Ma were both almost too tired to care. Sonali was blowing on her drink, careful not to meet anyone's eyes.

'We must understand the law if we are to find out how they are liable. I just remembered Mishti's uncle is an advocate with the Delhi High Court. Doing very well. I met his family during the Durga Puja last year, all the women could have been weighed in the gold they were wearing.'

'You want to take them to *court*! How can you talk like that? Don't you have any hope? He is still presumed missing. It's barely been a month,' cried Ma.

'No, missing and presumed dead,' Dida said baldly.

Meanwhile Chhobi was murmuring. 'Mishti... Oh, Mrs Chatterjee's daughter-in-law.' She had a sudden vision of Bhai Sahib in the dock, gold spectacles glinting, every hair in place, and them in black robes, as accusing as a pack of crows shrilly intoning 'Your honour' with every breath.

'I have heard his charges are very high, his fees, I mean. I suppose he will give us a discount if we go through Mrs Chatterjee, but I am not going to ask for one,' Dida continued in a practical vein, selectively turning off her impaired auditory faculties as usual.

'But what will we achieve?' asked Chhobi valiantly, the scene of them visiting a legal eagle with a wild theory and nothing else straining at the limits of even her imagination. 'Lawyers deal in facts, and they cost a lot of money.'

Ma struggled up in a tangle of blankets and hot water bottle, now tepid. 'Enough,' she announced, 'I am going to bed.' Then looked around undecided – this was after all her room and her bed they were all sitting on. History repeating itself because they had not learnt from it. Just as she had married Bhaskar in her teens to escape the poverty pulling them down after Dadu had been forced to leave Dr Mitra's clinic, now her daughter free-falling on a parallel path because her mother could not provide her with enough. A daughter not qualified in anyway to support herself or a child. She felt unable to squeeze out even the thinnest sliver of enthusiasm for her coming grandchild.

Chhobi was speaking now, fearful and frantic, but trying to sound reasonable. 'Punjabi businessmen! We cannot tackle them without putting up a front which they will find threatening. They think nothing of us – law-abiding Bengali women – for them we do not exist. That is why we need Mishti's uncle. He will confront them for us... but we do need some kind of evidence to prove they were involved in something illegal... so far Rai's theory is mere conjecture.'

Sonali put down her empty mug on the bedside table with an audible thump. 'I will get the evidence,' she said speaking with a desperate resolve. 'Tomorrow I will get a message across to Sonny that I want to meet him... and then if there is anything, I will get it.'

'You will not!' exclaimed Ma, horrified at Sonali's immediate seeking of compensation in catastrophe. Ma looked at her with impotent anger, 'You, Sonali, you get down to your books at once... Do you hear me? At once. I want a first division even if it means slogging day and night.' It was as though Ma was working up a rage to construct a semblance of sane thought. Sharp arrows were shooting into the right side of her brain, radiating down her shoulder and back.

Sonali wasn't listening. 'He is the beginning and he will be the end... The weakest link, the breaking point,' she spoke with theatrical aplomb, her eyes dreamy and distant.

'Stop talking like a Bengali Javed Akhtar. This is not a screenplay. This is our life,' Ma screamed, her head splitting down the middle like schizophrenia, but Dida's eyes were lit up with the light of vengeance. She was not listening either, budgeting expenses in her head, 'A loan, we need a loan to invest in this period.'

They all stopped in mid gesture, as though someone had yelled 'Statue', but this time the voice calling out the command was Dadu's. He had pushed open the door to Ma's room, bewildered by the hysterical loud babble that had woken him. He was shocked to find his daughter, habitual serenity departed, standing up and facing the rest of them, wild eyes staring, hair dishevelled.

'What has happened? Why does nobody tell me anything?' He tried to infuse a note of authority in his voice, but he had neglected to wear his dentures and what came out was an unintelligible mumble. His mouth fallen in like the opening of Dida's drawstring cloth purse sucked at the words he spoke, and they kept slipping back into that wrinkled orifice. His wispy white hair normally slicked back, was awry, he looked very old. Dida wrapped in her golden shawl, appeared at least a generation younger.

Dida told him. She did not bother to soften the impact of her words by wrapping them in silence or in convoluted phrases. She was harsh and to the point.

Dadu stood at the doorway, looking as though his knees would buckle. He clutched at the doorframe for support, his large stomach sagging against it. He was backlit by the blue tubelight in the passage and appeared as an extra on the periphery of a stage set, outside the circle of warm pink light. Ma rushed up to help him, but he pushed her away. His daughter widowed. Her daughter behind her, huddled in a quilt, widowed. And a child coming.

Ma was attacked by blinding spasm of pain and held on to the doorframe to prevent herself from falling down. She pressed her fist into her right temple, bright sparks exploding red behind her eye. Dadu facing her also hanging on to the door for support, put his hand up to touch his own head in a mirror image. Then he turned and shuffled away down the corridor, worn Bata slippers flip-flopping with every step.

❧

Later when they were finally ready for bed, Sonali stood looking at herself in the bathroom mirror.

'On the ship he used to brush my hair every night, never hurting me at all,' she said, 'He loved my hair. He loved me.'

Now she was spreading toothpaste on her finger, her toothbrush was at the flat keeping Beeji company. Sonali gave a small shudder as she got into bed, 'I couldn't have borne it anymore

– Beeji's presence. She blames me you know – because I didn't chant those mantras.'

'Go to sleep,' Chhobi muttered, plummeting into a well of exhaustion. It had been a day of apocalyptic disclosures. The final revelation, that of Sonali's imminent belonging to the unnamed society of motherhood was too much... it pushed Chhobi into a state of oblivion where everything was quite numb.

Sonali was thoughtful. 'Sonny has been trying to urgently get in touch with me.'

'What!'

'Yes, first he rang up Indu, then twice he was waiting in his car outside college just as I was going in. I didn't speak to him. But it will be easy.' Then with real hatred underlying her voice she told Chhobi about Indu's Xmas encounter with Sonny. She did not mention her pregnancy. It was as though by not thinking about it, Sonali denied the very existence of the child growing within her.

twelve

Dadu refused to get out of bed, or attend to his clinic the next day. Taking refuge as always in the past, he lay on his bed, an oversized brown shawl slightly riddled with moth holes wrapped around him. Dida, worried though unwilling to admit it, kept going into the room on the flimsiest of pretexts. She could evoke no response from those open, unseeing eyes.

It was winter Dadu was thinking of, winter in Mymensingh, not this grey lonely cold of Delhi in January. It was the image of a huge sunny courtyard he retained like a relic. All afternoon the women of that sprawling family would sit and talk, their backs to the sun, drying their long tresses, some would be stitching winter quilts in minute katha designs. Afternoons lazy and convivial and so comfortably predictable. He wondered if the courtyard still existed, if that warm afternoon sun remembered the idle chat of the women, whether the flagstones of the yard still felt the wet drip marks of their freshly washed hair.

The sound of Savitri washing clothes in the adjoining bathroom disturbed him. It was bed sheets she was tackling, energetically beating the wet, flowered bundles with a wooden bat. The dripping water running into the rinsing bucket and the rhythmic thump,

thump, intruded, causing a momentary lapse. He burrowed deeper into the stratified layers of his memories, every motion of Savitri's arm pressing the grey soapy water out of the sheets and driving his thoughts deeper into Mymensingh, lost forever in Bangladesh.

He returned to the women again, farm labourers this time, he was watching two of them using the dhenki, the traditional Bengali instrument for taking the husk off the rice. They were dehusking the winter harvest.

He clearly recalled the dhenki, a long wooden board that had a short pedestal, like a see-saw, in the middle. One end of the board was equipped with a pestle built into the underside, which was positioned over a large shallow depression in the ground where the unhusked rice was kept. One woman was turning the rice in this depression, crouched on the ground in back-breaking labour. The other woman was standing at the end without the pestle pressing down on the board with her foot. As she released her foot, the board dipped down, the pestle hitting the rice, separating the husk from the grain. Again and again the pestle rising and falling, in tune to Savitri's thump, thump. Drudgery, so infinitely time-consuming.

Dadu was gulping hard, the vein in his neck pumping. The pictures appearing with perfect clarity on his retina. The woman kneeling on the floor, ceaselessly turning the rice for a fresh batch to be dehusked looked up. With a shock of recognition he saw that she was Meera, and the younger, lithe girl at the other end stepping on and off the board with such sinuous grace, her skin the colour of ripe sun-stippled grain, yes she was Sonali – golden Sonali.

Eventually even Dida felt too acute a prickle of alarm to be ignored, when he refused food. This was something he had never done, not even when he lost his job with Dr Mitra, or during the '71 crisis when Bhaskar had died. Dida tried to tempt him with a thin fish jhol redolent of panch phoron with slices of purple aubergine and white florets of cauliflower, but he shook his head complaining of aumbol, that peculiarly Bengali version of acidity. Towards evening Dida went in to telephone Ratan Kaku, then afraid that Dadu would overhear, replaced the receiver as the first ring went through. She told Savitri, who was finishing off a late lunch of leftovers that she would just be back. Dida hurriedly changed her sari and began to walk down to Ratan Kaku's house.

Dida and Ratan Kaku shared a somewhat formal relationship, Kaku afraid of the biting edge Dida's sharp tongue often lent her words. But today she was worried, and confused. It was not one of those moments when she could rely on quick instinct to initiate equally quick action. Both her husband and daughter appeared near collapse. She looked at Kaku's house as she approached it. The hoarding with the giant wheel overshadowed everything on the lane. At night when she had last seen it, only the neon illumination was visible, lending the structure an airy, if bizarre, look. During the day it was revealed in its full ugliness. The angled iron gridwork propping up the hoarding had begun to rust and lay crouched on Kaku's rooftop, the discoloured bones of some pre-historic creature of reptilian ancestry.

All down the long walk through Kaku's lane, Dida nurtured the faint pity that stirred when she reflected how unfortunate Kaku was to be forced to live with such an unaesthetic embellishment to his rooftop, but up close she also registered the freshly painted gate, the weedless lawn, the topiary work that had tortured the mehndi hedge into undulating waves. She found Kaku at home, planning the itinerary for the trip he was going to take as soon as it warmed up a little. Pamphlets of Kulu and Manali were spread on the dining table, glossy red apples ornamenting orchards in the Kulu valley, the Rohtang Pass all ice and blue sky. Goel had painted Ratan Kaku's stained walls, plastered over the crack in the bedroom. Maybe not willingly, under duress from the cricket team, but Kaku no longer feared him. The cosmetic repairs to the house apart, it was the money that had cushioned his terrors, real or imaginary.

Why, he is looking years younger, thought Dida, who never really looked at him at all. His eye contemplating the Himalayas had a distinct sparkle, the dyspeptic pallor of old quite vanished. He was almost ten years younger than Dadu, but today the gap in their ages appeared more like twenty.

Kaku had hired the Bihari dhaba help who used to bring him packed meals, and he shouted for him now to make tea. A new tea set, she noticed, teapot warm under a batik tea cosy, and a plate of thin arrowroot biscuits arrived almost immediately. Dida felt an irrational rage as she looked at the neatly laid tea tray. Ratan appeared to have successfully got over his bad times, he looked positively happy. 'I cannot drink this, I don't have my saccharine,' she refused a little churlishly, then hastened to hide her anger. Softening her tone, she harked back to the days when Kaku and Dadu had both lived in Mymensingh. The words mawkish and sentimental issued forth a little unnaturally from her lips, but overwhelmed Kaku all the same. There is nothing to hide from Ratan Kaku, Dida kept telling herself as she recounted yesterday's events. But the old habit died hard of putting a brighter, lighter complexion on a truth that was dark and ugly. She could not bring herself to tell him any more than an abbreviated version – that in every likelihood Sonali's husband was dead, Dadu needed Kaku and that he needed hope.

'Just leave it to me,' Kaku reassured her. 'I will be there within half an hour.'

Dida got up to leave, folding her hands in a formal namaskar. On the way home she made a small detour, stopping at Mrs Chatterjee's. She asked her to fix up a meeting with Mishti's uncle, the advocate at the high court. She was tight-lipped as she made the request, leaving Mrs Chatterjee goggle-eyed with curiosity.

When she got home, Ratan Kaku was already there, hesitating on the verandah.

'Come in, come in,' she told him peremptorily, suddenly feeling the weight of problem solving. 'Just one minute,' she added as she moved swiftly into her bedroom. She shook Dadu who appeared to be dozing, looking distastefully at the white stubble covering his face. 'Ratan is here, go on, wash your face, fix your teeth,' whisking off the quilt, flinging a shawl at him. She twitched the bedcover in place, ashamed suddenly of the contrast presented by Kaku's home, so spick and span. She looked around the room to see what else needed tidying up. A pale tangle of washed saris was twisted together on the stand like a nest of albino snakes. Spreading a sheet over them, she tried to wipe the powdery dust that lay thick enough to write upon on the dressing table.

Dadu a bit unsteady on his feet, got back into bed, hair slicked back with water, teeth in place, so used to doing Dida's bidding that now he obeyed her automatically. Kaku came in and perched like an anxious bird on the edge of his chair, beady eyes focused on his friend.

Withdrawing quietly from the room, Dida went to the kitchen and began to organise the dinner. A delicious fish kalia, Dadu's favourite. Food, the most important metaphor in her lexicon, recipe for her to display her anger, or record her pleasure.

Measuring out the steel katori of dal and soaking it, she shouted for Savitri who was still sweeping the terrace. She wondered what Kaku was saying. Softly, she eased open the kitchen door and moved silently to stroll past the bedroom where the two old friends sat, but Kaku had shut the door. Only a faint murmur was audible, even though she cocked her good ear. Although she didn't like to talk about it, her hearing was deteriorating steadily though she had begun to lip read quite proficiently. Suddenly the door opened, too late for her to withdraw. She tried to cover up the fact that she was so obviously eavesdropping by inquiring if they wanted tea. Kaku shook his head, asking for water and a little flattened rice with milk for Dadu. This time he didn't shut the door.

The cold foggy days of early January, days when sometimes the sunlight barely filtered through, were over. It was spring that Kaku was talking about, Basanta, the two months of Falgun and Chaitra, mid-February to mid-April, according to the Bengali calendar. A time for renewal, rebirth. Also a fleeting time with summer's terrible heat waiting to pounce. A time when the sunshine is lambent, the breeze balmy, a time when trees take on a new irridescence. So Kaku continued in almost poetic vein, 'Bad times pass, like winter.'

'Why are you talking like an Angrez? Bad times in Delhi are the summer months, not winter,' said Dadu with unusual acerbity.

Dida loitering outside wished Kaku would not employ quite so oblique a method to bring home the point. Kaku was talking now of that official harbinger of Basanta, Saraswati puja, when special prayers are offered to the goddess of learning.

Dadu did not bother to disguise his bitterness. 'What has the worship of Saraswati brought us? It's true what they say – those who worship Saraswati never receive the favours of Lakshmi... In my days widows were banished to Kashi, begging for alms to make a living, heads shaved.'

'But she is so young. This will pass... anyway times have changed.'

Dida, still outside the door, could barely restrain herself from bursting in. How could they forget that the household was running on Meera's earnings?

Kaku was trying a new line. 'Look at me, last year I was as good as dead. Some things are taken care of by providence, destiny. Have faith in God and be a little optimistic.'

'We don't have a spinning wheel churning out rupee notes on our roof top.'

'If there is any need, you know my money is your money. I have no family. If Sonali requires it, it is there for her. Believe me this spring, this Basanta, will see a change in the ill luck. I have a premonition.'

Dida had never made much of Kaku, but she thought now that he truly was a good friend. She began budgeting expenses in her head. After all, Ratan was a rich man now, with no family. Dadu had saved his life by fixing that Goel and taking him to the hospital in the nick of time. As he said, Shona was as good as his own grand-daughter. He could pay for the lawyer... a loan of course. They would be hard pressed to prepare for the birth of the baby... a child, miracle of love and creation. The thoughts raced through Dida's head.

Dadu interrupted pessimistically, 'Basanta, Basanta... don't forget what else the word is synonymous with in Bengali.'

'What?'

'Remember Basanta in Bengali also means smallpox. It is the time when outbreaks of dreaded diseases strike,' Dadu said grimly, refusing to let even the smallest ray of hope puncture the dark cloud of gloom he was wrapped in.

Dida lost her temper and her patience. Turning around she marched back to the kitchen. With an angry clatter of dishes, she put away the fish that was defrosting. She told Savitri who had just prepared the flattened rice with milk and sugar for Dadu to empty the bowl in the garbage pail. Then she counted out some notes and sent her to the market to buy bitter gourd and white radish, she would make sukhto, a dish Dadu disliked. Bitter food to feed his bitterness.

thirteen

Indranil Mukherjee was a senior advocate at Delhi High Court. He was tall for a Bengali. Something about him reminded Chhobi of Satyajit Ray, though his eyes were very different, a shrewd glint slanting across his spectacles whenever a useful point was made. Mrs Chatterjee had made the appointment for them, the importance of her connections making her bloated body swell even further with pride. Ma and Sonali did not go. They were busy closing chapters, trying to finish off unfinished business. Today they were seeing Beeji off at the ISBT. Bhai Sahib and clan had successfully managed to elude her. Ma had given notice to the landlord and pushed Sonali off to the library. They would vacate the flat by the end of the month.

For a while Dida and Chhobi had wandered the corridors of Delhi High Court, looking for Mukherjee's chamber. Dida remembered her last tangle with lawyers, almost thirty years ago when she had to bail Dadu out in that criminal case, after selling her ruby and gold necklace to pay the expenses. Things had gone downhill after that – now they seemed to be accelerating faster into a nadir of hopelessness. Ever since Sonali had got married so impulsively, she felt the family could not keep pace with the momentum of their changed lives, so charged with mishap.

Chhobi meanwhile leading the way up the stairs felt she had blundered into a black and white montage, a collage of penguins. Everywhere were lawyers conferring or hurrying to make court appearances, robes flapping behind them like raven's wings.

Mukherjee dismissed the case in a few brief moments. It was a simple legal point. Chhobi had barely started explaining the case when he interrupted, drawing the Bermuda triangle analogy like everyone else.

'Where is the company registered?' he asked

'In Bombay.'

'Then you will have to go there. I cannot do anything. It is not in this jurisdiction. You will also probably have to consult a lawyer qualified in maritime law.'

'But we were hoping we could attack them on the illegal trade they were involved in,' said Chhobi hurriedly, a note of desperation entering her voice, 'after all they are liable for somebody who may have died in their employ.'

'That kind of liability can be dragged on in the courts for years. Do you have any proof, documents? Anything at all to prove their malpractices?'

'No,' Chhobi answered reluctantly. 'Well then, my advice to you is to first get hold of some kind of evidence, then go to Bombay.' Looking at their crestfallen faces, he added, 'Well, show me the evidence and I will make an appointment with somebody suitable in Bombay,' waving away their offer of a consultation fee.

It was a dejected duo that walked toward India Gate to board a mini bus. They squeezed into the last seat, a fat woman smelling of onions obligingly making place. Dida stared despondently at the floor.

She did not hear the bus conductor clicking his metal ticket dispenser, shouting out the stops in a hoarse voice or banging on the dented body of the bus to attract passengers. Finally she looked at

Chhobi, her hands clenched around the metal bar in front of her. 'We cannot let them get away scot free,' she said.

For once Dida seemed unable to seek refuge in her deafness, or in Krishna. The tightly coiled whorls into which she normally withdrew were resounding today with a desperate message. One that impelled them to *do something*.

Sonali ran out to meet them as they unlatched the gate. 'What happened?' she asked, although the answer was evident in their dashed expressions.

'We need evidence,' muttered Chhobi pushing past her towards their bedroom. 'You better not neglect your studies,' she said sternly to Sonali, who had followed her in.

'I better not neglect my appearance,' Sonali retorted, as she picked up a comb and began running it through her hair. 'He is sick of her. Beeji told me. He has sent her back to Ludhiana.'

'What? Ludhiana? Who?' Chhobi was sharp, not in the mood for Sonali's nonsensical fiddle-faddle.

'Sonny's wife – she is fat. Indu attended the wedding, she told me that she was very healthy.'

'So what?'

'And she is in disgrace with the family for introducing this very dubious business connection. It's been a huge loss. There appears to be some problem even with claiming insurance.' She looked at Chhobi through the shining skeins of her hair.

'I suggest you think about your degree instead of Sonny's wife. Even if she has gone, it must be temporary.'

But Sonali wasn't listening. She was blueprinting the details of a scheme. One that had been incubating in her mind since the night Ma broke the news. It was a simple plan that she hatched, the Seduction of Sonny.

She would contact Sonny again, draw him out, play on his attraction for her and coax him into unearthing some evidence. It was important that she should portray her quest as concern for her own fate... weary of endless waiting for Karan. The elder Talwars must not know. No need to involve Ma either, or Dida, she said, drawing Chhobi into a small tight knot of conspiracy. Chhobi looked around. Suddenly the room seemed all listening ears and silently watching eyes.

Chhobi thought then of Ma, Ma who moved slowly these days as though an iron band was constricting her heart... For Ma's sake and for the baby she would have to help her sister.

Chhobi began searching frantically through her bag, tipping out the contents on to the bed. Library cards, letters to be answered, seldom used lipsticks, pens and old movie tickets tumbled across the bed, but she did not find it. She was bedevilled by confused thought as she began rifling through dusty drawers crammed to overflowing with notes on Delhi's monuments. She threw an irritated glance at Sonali, who was listening to the old radiogram, a seraphic expression on her face as Akashvani played Kishore Kumar.

Finally she found it under notes on the Jamali Masjid. Her next piece for the magazine, on the mosque attached to the tomb of sixteenth century poet Jalal Khan, who wrote under the nom-de-plume of Jamali. She had one page of notes on the tile ornamentations and tucked right under it she found it. Sonny's card, which had been placed with the wedding gift he had given Sonali. The one with his direct telephone number.

Sonali's eyes glowed as she saw it. Then she began the fine-tuning of her scheme. To be realistic, chances of unearthing anything incriminating were slim, but it was all they had.

She must look different, no trace of Behenji like the wife... More western and sophisticated... more exciting. She must be wrapped in an aura of mystery, of magic.

Sonali didn't need much tutoring as far as her dress sense went. She concentrated on the contents of her cupboard. It was still quite cold. Finally she made a selection of clothes culled recently from Simla's Nixon's Bazaar. Not a real bazaar but a nickname strangely acquired. In the early seventies someone had found a coat with a nametag 'Richard Nixon' stitched into the inside collar. Ever since then the pavement market had been called 'Nixon's Bazaar'.

It was where the Tibetan refugees disposed of surplus woollen clothing donated by the 'First World'. How Chhobi hated the term 'Third World'. It sounded so despairing as though they were inhabitants of some inescapably dark lower world akin to Hades.

The clothes were generally very good quality, donated by rich and generous Americans and Europeans. The Tibetans hardly used them, preferring to sell them in piles, tossing and jumbling the clothes like colourful mixed salads spread out on the pavement. Sonali foraged with a keen eye – unlike Chhobi, she was not squeamish about donning second-hand clothing. There were others like her, a lot of them well-off tourists from Delhi and Punjab, all sifting somewhat surreptitiously through the piles, carrying away their gleanings to cars parked nearby. Sonali swooped like a cheel on Italian labels, she liked the styling. She was laying the clothes on the bed now, making her choice. Narrow black trousers and a burgundy lambswool cowl neck. She paused for a moment. All her clothes still fitted snugly over her wasp-waisted body. She suffered a pang as she thought of what the baby would do to her figure. She refused to worry about it now. Tomorrow she would call Sonny on his direct number.

When she did call, a bored and fed-up Sonny literally sat up, throwing off the tedium of the long day so heavy with ennui. He thrilled to the sound of her voice, instinctively pitched deep and low.

'Draw him out like a fish on a hook, promising, hinting... then when he is gasping for air... reel him in,' thought Sonali viciously.

fourteen

Sonny replaced the receiver. He looked beyond through the smoked glass partition to the inner office where his father sat, conferring with someone on the telephone. Soon he would be summoned to Bhai Sahib's office in the next building.

Sonali... God he had missed her. The thought of her under the mango tree filled him with lust. Skin to skin, filling him, thrilling him in sweet musk. What a bore marriage was, Bubbly lying inert under him like a dutiful log. Fat spilt on the sheets like a bedspread. And this mess they were in, her father had something to do with it.

He got up restlessly, looking again resentfully at his father. The pattern of the days since the vanishing was being repeated. His father picked up the jottings he had been working on and got up, locking the door of the office behind them. What was happening? Nothing good, Bhaiya had to flee Bombay, he was holed up somewhere in Bangalore. Of course nobody told him anything.

Sonali... he would have to lose weight, he thought, looking critically at his reflection in the plate glass. Definitely paunchy... those fried snacks Bubbly stuffed him with at every opportunity. Must work out every morning, jog in the park.

Sonali... how glorious her hair, so much of it... glittering jet black around that face... those brandy-coloured eyes, quite intoxicating. A man felt proud to enter a party with her by his side. Heads swivelled, yaar. Bubbly looked like a bloody yawn.

Sonali... going through hell too... he knew she had married on the rebound. Now they were both in this mess, thanks to Bubbly's father.

Why did nobody tell him anything? A bloody glorified peon, they treated him as... Zero decision-making he had, everything was always decided by Bhai Sahib. What was the use of this fancy office, that fancy schooling, Bhai Sahib was always in charge after attending some pathshala in Sialkot.

Some shady smuggling-wuggling, that's what the ships must have been involved in. The whole crew was probably in jail in some foreign country, ships impounded with their cargo.

He walked to the window of their tenth floor office. Connaught Place was growing steadily skywards. The tenth floor was just not what it used to be, he felt dwarfed by the building across the road, towering above them in an expanse of concrete and glass. Not long ago it had been an old-fashioned single storey bungalow with palm trees and a beautiful lawn. All around him other bungalows were being smashed and bulldozed, new structures rapidly taking their place, stretching tall. Even the American Centre down the road was beginning to look less imposing when compared to the new buildings. He was beginning to feel left behind. It was time for a change in management. He must talk to Bhaiya privately. *Where was Bhaiya?*

Bhai Sahib was after all a senior citizen, time for him to retire and look after the gardens in his Mehrauli farmhouse. Sonny moved back to look at his silhouette in the plate glass again, running his fingers through his coxcomb hair, holding his breath and turning sideways as he sucked in his stomach... hmm ... not bad.

Sonali... Yes! He began to whistle tunelessly. Did he need a change! He was picking her up for lunch tomorrow.

Smashed hopes were what remained on Sonali's plate since she had last been with Sonny but although she little knew it then, the intervening period had led him on a rapidly downhill road as well. He was bored beyond belief by his wife, frustrated and resentful at work.

⁕

Dida and Sonali were alone, both the other women having gone into work. Sonali had just one class that they had decided she should bunk. Sonali had confided in Dida, her constant ally, though not in Ma. She was meeting Sonny for lunch, he would pick her up from the local market.

Dida, as was her habit when tense, was energetically cooking something elaborate. Today she was rather aptly making dhonkar dalna, a dish popular at funeral feasts as a vegetarian substitute. She was supervising Savitri who was pounding away with the grinding stone, pummelling soaked split peas and spices to a fine paste.

Strange that Dida had chosen this dish, the word dhonka meant hoax. Possibly the squares of pressed ground dal were meant to deceive the person eating into thinking they were eating fish, a dish of red herrings, perhaps.

Sonali popped her head round the kitchen door as Dida was preparing the gravy for the dhonka, lowering cumin and bay leaves carefully into the hot oil.

'Am I looking okay?'

'Don't stick your head in here, your hair will absorb this fried ginger smell. Wait outside, I am coming,' she said, adding a blend of ground ginger, coriander, yoghurt and sugar to the oil. The kitchen was filled with an explosion of sputtering, a rich commingling of spices.

Dida looked at Sonali critically, wiping her hands in a kitchen towel.

Sonali had lost weight since the New Year. The fine lines of her jawbone and throat rose out of the burgundy wool, breathtaking in their beauty. She had coiled her hair up tightly, adding a pair of dangling silver grape earrings at the last moment.

'Take those off,' Dida said. 'Wear no jewellery, those baubles add nothing. Remember not to appear cheap or frivolous. You will do,' she added in satisfaction. The events of the past year had left their stamp on Sonali's face, an adult restraint now replacing some of the callow coquettishness.

Handing Dida the earrings that jarred, Sonali swung a tiny embroidered black bag on her shoulder and began to walk to the market. Looking back once over her shoulder she felt the empty lane thronged with ghosts, the strong presence of her family propelling her forward, even Dadu and Ratan Kaku were present, a shadowy but encouraging backup force.

For a moment she could not spot Sonny, and looked at her watch thinking she had arrived too early. But he was there – she had been misled because he had a new car, not the red Datsun she was familiar with, but a silver-grey Toyota. Part of the dowry, no doubt she thought disagreeably, then recalled the purpose of this meeting and Dida's prompting – speak to him sweetly, sweetly, focus your whole gaze on him. Dida was relying on Sonny's vainglorious estimate of his own abilities. He had put on a lot of weight since October she saw.

'Hi,' Sonali said, a little breathless with tension. Sonny got out of the car quickly to greet her, his eyes doing a radar sweep to see if anyone had noticed. He saw Sonali watching him with an appraising air and flicked his hair in that peacock gesture she knew so well, sucking in his stomach at the same time. A crow sitting on the roof of the Mother Dairy shop nearby suddenly cackled, it seemed to him in derision. He thrust Sonali towards the car, getting in hurriedly and stepped on the pedal, eager to speed away from the vicinity of her house where they might be spotted. He was very conscious of her gaze on his profile.

Damn, he hoped she wasn't going to create a scene, he thought, remembering how she had raked his face with her talons once. His spirits lifted as she asked him softly, sweetly,

'How *have* you been, Sonny?'

Suddenly the cumulative dissatisfaction of the past year erupted into defiance. He looked sideways at her without turning his head, just the pupil of his eye swivelling to the corner of his eyelids. She looked very beautiful. He did not care who saw them together. In fact he would take her for lunch to Bhai Sahib's favourite restaurant. Yes, he would take her to Gaylord's in Connaught Place. Cock his snook at them by entertaining her in the place most frequented by them and their business cronies.

⁘

Connaught Place was slowly spinning, a white-rimmed wheel carrying a steady stream of traffic. Not the frenetic rush hour of the morning but a relaxed revolution of afternoon shopping and mid-day luncheons. Sonny parked the car and took her elbow, ushering her past the crowds outside Regal Cinema, festooned with garishly hand-painted hoardings of matinee stars.

Zeenat Aman towered above them. The artist had exaggerated her already impressive cleavage, turning her body into a mountainscape thinly veiled in pink.

Sonali moved away as pavement vendors thrust snow-white handkerchief packs, toy cobras that sprang out on collapsible stands, a pocket flashlight that momentarily blinded her. Sonny uttered a curse and steered her into Gaylord's.

Inside it was quiet, etched glass, snowy damask and gilt chandeliers. The walls were an apricot shade of peach, embossed with ivory Plaster of Paris wreaths, tendrils and vines. They were no free tables, but the maitre d' recognised Sonny and the frequency of his custom. He immediately placed them at a table reserved for somebody else. Sonny leaned back, looking around. Nobody he recognised. He looked at Sonali from under half-closed lids. She was looking at him adoringly. Her new thin elegant face overlaid by the memory of the younger one abandoned under the mango tree. Dappled light and shade passing through the branches, glinting on her hair and breasts,

~241~

freckling her naked body with a leopard skin. Honey in her eyes, a whole beehive of it. Flowers crushed between their bodies. It had been the most erotic moment of his life.

He ordered Kingfisher beer. He would begin whittling down his belly tomorrow, luxuriating for the present in the expanse of peach and cream, gold bubbles winking in the glass before him. The waiter who recognised him too, was bowing obsequiously.

Sonali, as tightly coiled inside as a spring, was feeling faintly sick. She rather abstemiously ordered a soup. Sonny asked for a tandoori chicken, rogan josh and mint parathas.

Sonali ran a finger down the back of his hand. Just once. Withdrawing her hands and folding them on her lap almost immediately. His eyes leapt towards her face.

Their meal arrived. Sonali nibbling fastidiously at a bread stick stared a little surprised at Sonny's plate. The feeling of nausea intensified as she looked at the mutton swimming in a sea of red chilly and oil, the parathas glistening in concentric rings of fat, the chicken artificially coloured a lobster orange. He was still very handsome, but grown coarse with over indulgence.

For a split second Sonny caught a distorted glimpse of Sonali through the bottom of his glass as he emptied it, her face appearing refracted and curved giving him a pang of disquiet, but when he lowered the glass she was sweetly smiling. 'What happened to the ships?' she asked interjecting a piteous note in her voice. It wasn't hard. She was feeling quite sorry for herself.

'I don't know,' he replied briefly. She felt a cold clutch of panic, why had they imagined she would be able to make him talk?

'But your brother's heading the company,' she persisted.

His anger spilt out, the feeling of exclusion, the real and imagined slights heaped upon him by the rest of his family and, most of all, this unfortunate marriage he had been forced into.

'Bhaiya's gone underground. I haven't spoken to him.'

Sonali was astonished. This they had not foreseen, that Sonny himself was equally in the dark. She looked at the brown moustache streaked with a daub of rogan josh and tried again.

'I just want to get on with my life, and I cannot if I don't know whether he is dead or alive. Karan had written that he felt they were smuggling VCRs.'

She had his complete attention now. He pushed away his plate, appetite suddenly satiated. Dunking his greasy hand in the finger bowl, he began to meditatively smash the wedge of lemon turning the water a cloudy grey.

'I suspected as much. For all you know the ships and crew could be arrested somewhere.'

'Arrested? But how can they keep something like that quiet?'

'Arrey, Bhai Sahib hasn't been cultivating these mantrijis for nothing. Anything can be suppressed.'

Sonali went in for the kill, sensing the damage to his self-esteem. 'Sonny... *you* can surely find the truth, don't you want to? For me... please... I really need to know. Why should you not be told? After all you will one day be the owner of at least one of the Talwar companies? You mean you don't have access to all the files and things?"

A frown gathered on Sonny's face, but the seed had been planted.

A hollow note of bravado entered his voice. 'Of course I have access. Let's see,' he said, 'I will try and find out.' Then, looking at his watch, said, 'Come, I will drop you back.'

Sonali bit her lip, fearing she had overdone it. She took his arm briefly as they left. Just a touch, looking up at him from under her lashes.

'I really missed you, Sonny,' she whispered.

fifteen

It took another surreptitious rendezvous for Sonny to quell his unease. Let desire overthrow caution.

Sonali was at Indu's copying down notes of missed lectures when he called. Chhobi had answered the phone. She recognised his guarded voice but pretended not to, merely replying that Sonali would be home for lunch without inquiring who was speaking.

Chhobi, who had been working on visual ideas for the commemorative book, felt her concentration ebb away. Rosemary was difficult to please and expected such unfailing brilliance. She looked down at the foolscap sheet on which she had been jotting down ideas. Springtime in Delhi – a blooming Lodhi Gardens. Sikander Lodhi's tomb rising out of a frieze of February flowers. Important historical dates scratched to resemble the graffiti on the black dome had been an inspired touch, she felt. She closed her eyes and thought of the gardens. She shook her head, as couples embracing on the benches and behind the bushes presaged her vision of the tombs. With chameleon cunning they all transmuted into Sonny and Sonali.

She scored a line through her scribbles and began to worry instead. Her departure for America loomed imminent and so much needed to be done. She would have to tell them soon but it would mean leaving home at a time when Sonali and Ma needed her most. She tried to return to working on a fresh visual. Ideas shuttlecocked to and fro and crystallised into clarity by the time Sonali returned home, her arrival announced by the crashing and grinding of gears in the grey Fiat that had begun to resemble the jalopy which circus clowns drove, falling apart at the end of the act.

Chhobi carefully put away the sheet of paper, a surreal sketch of an idea stolen from Salvador Dali. She had seen a photograph of a painting of his, one which had a cloud of butterflies floating in and out of the Eiffel Tower. She had replaced the tower with Delhi's own minaret, the Qutab Minar, suggesting sepia tones for it with a cumulus mass of polychromatic wings beating in the foreground. Springtime in Delhi, as bright and short-lived as a butterfly.

Sonali breezed in looking as colourful as a butterfly too in a loose tie-and-dye kurta. She was humming a little ditty with an insouciant air. Chhobi remembered Charles Dickens' words – 'butterflies are free'.

'Sonny called,' she said watching her sister's face become immediately arrested into a freeze frame. 'He will be calling again any minute, you better decide what to say.'

'He is not really ready to do anything as yet, take any kind of risk, I mean. I will have to meet him again to convince him to do some digging. It's most unexpected, his ignorance.'

'Remember what they say about playing with fire.'

Sonali only shrugged. When she did speak to Sonny, she was careful not to ask to meet him, or ask for any information about Karan or the missing ships. She spoke only about her depression, how she was giving up her flat. She mentioned in passing that she would be there from early on Sunday morning, the last weekend in February. She had to finish packing and shifting her stuff before vacating the place on the first of March.

Dida sent Savitri along with her on Sunday. Ma had already shifted the heavier things, the refrigerator, the bed and most of the clothes. The few possessions which remained of Karan's, were packed with mothballs into an old black painted wooden box that had belonged to their father. Ma had sent Sonali to the next room when she emptied Karan's cupboard. Her hands were shaking as she folded the shirts into the box, mind flashing back to Simla in '71 when she had washed and ironed Bhaskar's clothes before packing them as though he would be returning to wear them. Black boxes neatly stencilled, crammed with the garments of missing men.

Savitri energetically tackled the kitchen, her own area of expertise, wrapping the plates and glasses in old copies of *The Times of India* before handing them to Sonali to place in brown cardboard cartons. Tiring of it after a while, Sonali who was tingling with anticipation, one ear cocked to hear the doorbell ring, went into the balcony to see if the silver-grey Toyota was approaching. It was not. They finished the kitchen utensils, then started on the curtains and the woven cane chicks, the dust trapped between the slats making Sonali sneeze. There wasn't much left to do except wait for Khokon who would be arriving by lunchtime with a tempo to load the stuff. Obviously Sonny was not going to show up. Savitri spread out last month's copy of the *Sunday Times* on the kitchen floor and lay down for a nap, her head resting on Sunil Gavaskar's.

Sonali went into the bathroom and began to wash away the dust smears on her face. She unwrapped the dupatta she had tied around her hair to protect it. Her face was pale above the black T-shirt. He was definitely not coming. Bhai Sahib must have warned him to steer clear of her. She looked at her reflection in the mirror. Behind her through the open doorway she could glimpse the entwined couple in the Klimt reproduction, she had forgotten about her two posters still scaling the walls. This one reminded her now of Karan and herself making that fleeting trip to Vienna. They had dashed there one weekend when their ship had entered dry-dock in Poland. Unaccountably she felt her eyes fill with tears. It had been *fun*. Travelling to all those countries, sailing across oceans of never ceasing motion.

She uncoiled her hair, spreading it about her shoulders. It reached down way past her waist, glittering in the afternoon light, merging into the pitch of her shirt so that she seemed clothed in it. Stripes of jet and ebony and blue-black Indian ink. She began to toss her head from side to side, watching the hair whirl around her.

The doorbell rang. Must be Khokon, he would take down the posters for her. She opened the door and stared into Sonny's face. Her eyes widened at the sight of him, pupils expanding in the dark fringed topaz depths. Sonny felt a faint stirring of confusion, a tiny uncoiling of disquiet. Then she smiled and desire washed over him as powerful as a tidal wave.

'Sonny,' she said, voice husky with relief that he had turned up.

'All packed?' he asked walking into the bare room, the Mona Lisa on a Plate standing out as the only occupant besides them. Good, he thought, they were alone.

'Almost, just a couple of posters to take down,' she answered quickly twisting her hair into a rope to coil it on top of her head.

His arm shot out to stop her, but she only laughed and slipped away, the rivulets of hair firmly gathered into a heavy knot.

'What else?' he asked.

'Nothing... and what's up with you? Any news?'

He shook his head in negation at the same time feeling a snigger build up inside, girls always asked what's up?

Sonali had her back to him now, stretching on tiptoe to try to remove the thumbtacks pinning the poster to the wall. Sonny walked up and stood immediately behind her, fitting his body to hers, spoon-like. She stood still, balancing on her toes, arms outstretched on the wall, his arms reaching out to remove the thumbtacks, flanking her. The pins tinkled to the floor, La Gioconda's enigmatic smile half hidden by the curling top of the paper as it flopped against her breast. His quickened breath was audible and hoarse in her ear.

'No!' she cried turning around, jerking her arms to break the restraining circle of his limbs. He was quicker, his arms encircling her waist, his weight crushing her against the Mona Lisa. She heard the paper tear with a twinge of dismay.

'I can't, Sonny, not until I know what happened to him,' she whispered.

Sonny continued to press his body against hers with renewed force as though he hadn't heard.

'Didi moni?'

Savitri was at the door. With a start Sonny let go of her and turned around. The old woman was standing stock still, eyes narrowed to watchful slits. Sonny was speechless, his face thwarted and dark.

'*Theek achay*, Savitri,' Sonali said, quickly tearing down the ripped poster flapping against the wall. She rolled it into a tight torn cylinder and told Savitri to put it into one of the kitchen cartons. She tried to look at Sonny, careful not to be observed to be looking at him. He was a glowering, seething presence.

Trying to conceal the surge of satisfaction she felt that he wanted her so badly, Sonali moved up to him, steps swift and sinuous, opened her eyes wide and gazed into his face, willing the hum and swarm of mango blossom and musk deer kasturi ittar to engulf him.

'It's not that I don't want to... but I cannot until I know what's happened.'

'Okay,' he said grimly, 'I will go now, and I *will* find out for you.'

Sonny planned on the following Sunday. Bhai Sahib had invited some neta type, ostensibly to see the first spring flowers at his Mehrauli farmhouse, but it must actually be to strike some deal, involving kickbacks and commissions as usual. The whole family was expected to be in attendance. Sonny would make some excuse and steal away at the last moment. The coast would be absolutely clear, and Sonali could join him at the office. She had suggested it. At first he had demurred, but she had looked at him so adoringly that he had eventually acquiesced. It would be very safe. Nobody would be there on a Sunday but a couple of security guards. They knew him well enough to let him in without disrupting their usual game of cards in their poky little cubicle.

He had kissed her last time after lunch, very briefly in his car, her lips opening like a cardamom-scented flower under his, quickening his body with that immediate unsatisfied arousal. Who knew? Daddy had a wide, comfortable sofa in his office... already he could feel her kisses raining on him like applause. After he had found proof that Karan was safely out of the picture for some length of time, he would help her to plan her future, closely linked to his, of course. Maybe she could retain her flat. The rent was not much. She would be so grateful. She would forgive him completely for this alliance with Bubbly, once he explained how he had been coerced into it for business reasons.

But first he had to get hold of the information, time to seize the day. Besides he wanted to know, dammit. There was bound to be something locked in the safe in his father's office. His mother had once commented with fine irony that Bhai Sahib was careful not to keep anything incriminatory in his own office – it was Daddy who was the scapegoat, keeper of his brother's shady secrets.

Sonny thought back to the day he had first joined office, more than five years ago. His father had been sentimental that day as he welcomed him into the building. He had been introduced to the staff, taken on a tour around the office. As a grand finale his father had taken him to that sanctum sanctorum, his own office. In an expansive frame of mind Daddy had painted a very rosy picture of the future. The virtues he had stressed were discretion and an ability to grasp every opportunity. He must make use of this advice now.

Finally his father had taken down the painting hanging in a spotlit niche on the wall. It was abstract art, one of those contemporary fellows patronised by his mother. Useful as a clever camouflage for Daddy's confidential chronicles, Sonny had realised. He had watched with attention, for the painting concealed a wall safe, which his father opened with a key dangling on his key chain. He needed the key now. He would have to lay his hands on it somehow.

sixteen

Sonny woke in the early hours of the morning, not long after midnight. A full moon hung low and yellow outside his window.

His eyes opened briefly then closed again. The branches shook, the light moved slow colours over her face. Sonali suspended in a stray sunbeam, enclosed in an amber dream.

He visualised her with almost hallucinatory lucidity. Amazing how an accident of circumstance had provided those mango trees. A setting so perfect for future recollection, that whenever his plump and placid wife lay beside him, he lingered gratefully in the green gold shade of memory. Wrapped around him were those silk and honey limbs. Sonali's face beneath his tasting of innocence and an unexpectedly thrilling candour. The possibility of the event recurring left him parched and trembling.

His parents would be entertaining friends at a bridge lunch today. He would get hold of Daddy's bunch of keys and extract the one he needed somehow and get a copy made. One of those tala chabi walas at Bhogal or Kotla Bazaar. It shouldn't take longer than half an hour and Daddy would be too busy concentrating on his cards to notice anything amiss.

Later that afternoon Sonny was driving down to Kotla Bazaar through Defence Colony with all the urgency of one who carries with him a message of crucial importance. The key burnt a hole in his pocket. His emotions were as jumbled as the elements on a stormy day.

Kotla meant fortified citadel. The narrow road leading into the bazaar could have, but for the cars, resurfaced several centuries ago, in the fifteen century when Kotla Mubarakpur was first built. Of course the last wall of the fortification had crumbled some fifteen years ago, now only part of a doorway and the name remained.

Cursing, Sonny negotiated his shining car between a bullock cart that had stopped by a street vendor squeezing sugarcane juice and a row of makeshift butchers' stalls. Goat carcasses dangling from huge iron hooks, doomed chickens squawking in split cane cages, the open drains running with blood and entrails made him wrinkle his nose in distaste. Flotillas of discarded poly bags sailed slowly through the murky drain water. What was he doing here? This place was meant only for servants and slum dwellers. The smell... an exquisite shudder of expectation shook him as Sonali's nude body flashed before his eyes and brought back his resolve.

Behind a man sleeping on a charpoy almost in the middle of the narrow road and two boys who were industriously boiling dye in copper vats to colour dupattas, he spotted a four-foot board propped at an angle of sixty degrees. It was hung with locks and keys of every conceivable size and shape. Sonny stopped his car and tried to edge it until it was overhanging the filthy drain. He hoped he could make it home without scratching his car. The two dyers stretched the freshly dyed dupatta in front of the board and began to make undulating wave-like motions to dry it, so that at one instant the board was visible, at another veiled by bright red muslin. Sonny eased himself gingerly out of the car. There was no sign of the key-maker.

In response to his query, one of the boys prodded the sleeping figure on the charpoy. Obviously, business was anything but brisk.

The key-maker looked at Sonny, at his expensive clothes, at the car parked in the middle of the road and mentally inflated his bill. He peered closely at the key, glancing sharply upwards at Sonny but saying nothing. Then he rummaged in an old tin trunk under the charpoy and took out several iron hoops closely hung with keys. Each hoop must have held hundreds of keys. Some shiny and new, others rusted with age. A magpie collection gathered to dredge up an erratic livelihood.

He quickly selected two keys most closely resembling Sonny's, and unwrapped a cloth case fitted with a set of steel files. The key had three indentations and he began with the topmost one, filing and shaping the discoloured rust-stained key, until the edges gleamed bright. The rasp of the file grated on Sonny's nerves and he glanced back to see if the car was all right. The man was dextrous and soon the irregular head was a perfect match. Sonny peeled off notes from a bulging wallet that made the key-maker regret not pitching his fee higher.

Sonny turned towards his car and stopped in midstride as he saw two urchins make a dashing retreat. His chromium-plated hubcaps, those four shining-silver oscillations of which he was so proud, had been prised off.

seventeen

While Sonny was storming the fortress of Kotla, Ma and Chhobi were forced to face a new challenge. Mrs Chatterjee, emboldened and intrigued by her success at fixing the appointment with the advocate, rang their bell insistently just as they were finishing tea. Ma was looking fatigued, she had rejoined office after a long absence and was struggling with the backlog of work, struggling too with the weight of her depression. She exchanged a glance with Chhobi, both of them simply too enfeebled and bone-weary to deal with another of their neighbour's inquisitions.

Dida coming in from the kitchen saw how much both of them wanted to avoid her. Letting Mrs Chatterjee in, she tried to steer her towards the sagging sofa but Mrs Chatterjee refused to change course. She pulled out a dining chair which creaked in protest as she settled her massive girth, and rested her forearms on the table. Chhobi saw how thin Ma had grown, her wrist lying on the table next to Mrs Chatterjee's looked so fragile that it seemed inconceivable that both arms related to the same section of human anatomy.

Mrs Chatterjee launched on her mission to discover the truth, beginning with the obvious.

'Well, Meera, you will need all your resources to clear this mess of Shona's making. Of course, I do not know all the details,' she paused hopefully but when no explanations were forthcoming, continued in a slightly piqued manner. Sonali studying in the bedroom, peeped in to see who was talking about her, made a face at Chhobi and hurriedly withdrew.

'Yes Meera, you must remember your duty, you have an another daughter, an elder unmarried one – Chhobi here. What are your plans for her? You must settle her now.'

Chhobi inwardly flinched, a familiar anger possessing her, tempting her to turn her back upon this conversation with a tart rejoinder. Dida's retort pre-empted the sour riposte rising to her lips.

'We are quite aware of our duties,' Dida said grimly, her Bengali as formal as Mrs Chatterjee's. The latter ignored her, unstoppable now in her role of Good Samaritan.

'I have found a boy for her,' she announced, then opened her purse, took out her spectacles and a black and white photograph that she peered at, before passing it to Dida.

'A good Calcutta family, they have also heard of Meshomeshai's family, the Talukdars of Mymensingh,' then with an air of triumph, as though conferring a knighthood on Chhobi, pronounced, 'he is a doctor.'

'Oh, doctor?' said Dida not very impressed.

Mrs Chatterjee glanced at her – they could see her recalling Dadu's profession in that moment.

'No, no, a specialist, an onc... onc... oncologist,' she enunciated sow-like, her tongue tripping over the unfamiliar word giving it a porcine intonation.

'What's that?' Dida asked, appraising the photograph with a critical eye. Both Ma and Chhobi sat silently like observers in a comic drama.

'A cancer specialist.'

'Cancer...' Dida let out a sigh, losing interest. 'Not cancer, it's too hopeless a job, can you imagine what kind of companion he would make at the dinner table every evening? Like Yamdoot always dealing with death.'

Mrs Chatterjee bridled indignantly. Really, she thought, what an attitude, still thinks she is rich Ira Dey living in a mansion on Elgin Road, Calcutta. Such a qualified boy, and no demands.

Chhobi stood up, she had had quite enough, and she too had her own announcement to make.

'No "boys" for me,' she denounced putting the word in parentheses, giving a disparaging, dismissing look at the harmless photograph. The boy in question looked at least thirty with his incipient jowls and thinning hair.

'I am leaving for America after summer. I applied for my passport last month, soon after I received an offer of research assistantship at the UCLA. I will be starting a Ph.D. programme there. The assistantship is quite generous and it's what I want.'

Mrs Chatterjee's face darkened at this peremptory cancellation of a ritual of centuries, while Ma's lit up with an astonishing radiance.

'Really, Chhobi, truly?' Ma smiling at her with such sweetness, asked to see the letter. As Chhobi went to fetch it, Dida, whose eyes had been darting from mouth to mouth, trying to lip-read what her deaf ear couldn't hear, looked questioningly at Ma. 'Did she say she is leaving for America?'

'Yes, she did, for a doctorate,' Ma continued to smile gently.

'Put that away,' said Dida to Mrs Chatterjee, tossing the photograph towards her, 'Our Chhobi is going to be a doctor herself.' Chhobi saw something of Ma's glowing face reflected in Dida's expression but mingled too with a hint of trepidation. America – so vast, so distant.

The phone rang. Dida, Ma and Chhobi continued to smile at each other, the full importance of the news penetrating their thought, unfurling tiny pennants fluttering in hopeful celebration.

Shifting her ponderous mass, Mrs Chatterjee sniffed as she picked up the rejected photographs. Sonali rushing in to answer the phone exclaimed, 'Why can't someone pick up the telephone? I am trying to study here.'

'Listen, Shona, listen there is great news!' Dida was grasping her arm in excitement, as she picked up the phone.

'Call from *where?*'

'Yes, yes, operator this is 6412488, from where? Who wants to speak?' Holding the phone gingerly, Sonali turned a bemused face at them.

'Call from Sri Lanka, Colombo for Ma.'

'Colombo!' said Mrs Chatterjee and Dida together as though Colombo was the Congo.

Ma, face tight with tension again, spoke a hesitant 'hello' into the receiver. The rest of them stared at her, Mrs Chatterjee and Dida straining good ears and deaf ear to overhear.

'No news, nothing as yet, yes... We are simply trying to come to grips with the situation.' They saw her relax her white-knuckled grip on the telephone with a little dissipation of tension.

'Pardon? Oh, tea, yes, I see... Well, thank you.'

'Yes, I am well.'

'Yes...'

'Really? Soon?'

'I see.'

'Maybe Delhi? That will be nice.'

Chhobi and Sonali standing still watched the pink steal up to their mother's face. Mrs Chatterjee sat there lumpishly, her mouth pursed tight, the downward flicker of her eyelids unable to conceal the hard glitter of curiosity. Dida gave her an irritated look.

Ma murmured a flustered good bye and replaced the receiver. The radiance was heightened manifold. She said nothing, merely looking at the circle of questioning faces for what seemed an epoch. Finally she spoke.

'That was Rai,' she said a little unnecessarily, who else would be calling from Colombo.

'Oh,' said Chhobi, thinking of Rosemary's description – sexy Rai.

'Did he have any news?' asked Sonali and Dida in unison.

'No… That's why he had called, to find out… He is sending us some tea from Sri Lanka.'

'Tea,' said Dida blankly.

'Tea?' echoed Sonali

Tea? Thought Chhobi, talk about carrying coals to Newcastle, quite amazed that Ma had found an admirer.

'Tea,' said Mrs Chatterjee firmly, adding in a distinctly patriotic tone, 'I would like a cup now, not some Sri Lankan swill, but our own Brooke Bond Red Label cha – strong and sweet. And now tell me,' she demanded 'who is this Rai? And what is he doing in Colombo?'

Dida, a hundred questions quivering on her tongue, rose reluctantly to go to the kitchen. She was feeling unnaturally confused and it appeared Mrs Chatterjee was going to be difficult to dislodge.

Much later, after dinner had been cleared away, Chhobi answered Dadu's questions, his finger following the indentations of the California coastline on the old school atlas. He consulted a yellowed address book to locate distant relatives who had immigrated to America at least a decade ago. Leaving him as he started on letters to them, Chhobi stole away and peeped into Ma's room.

Ma was sitting there in her glimmering pool of pink light, combing her hair. All her fatigue seemed to have dropped away. For a moment Chhobi just watched her. Her unbound hair slightly wavy lay in glistening threads around her head. A luminous halo. She saw Chhobi and the brilliance entered her eyes. Normally quite undemonstrative she rose and folded Chhobi in a brief embrace.

'The thought of the life ahead of you, filled with purpose, grand places and people has literally flooded me with happiness and hope.'

'I won't go unless Sonali's problem is sorted out,' Chhobi replied feeling like the one that got away.

Ma gripped her arms. 'Nonsense. You will go, no matter what. We will manage. Something will work out for Sonali. Things have to get better, why, today they have. For years I have waited for something to change our destinies and today my prayers are answered. From today I feel the odds and the Gods are with us.' She hugged Chhobi again. 'It will be very lonely without you Chhobi, very lonely.'

Chhobi felt a fresh infusion of guilt swirl inside her. She said at a tangent, unconsciously trying to bridge the loneliness yawning like a gorge before Ma.

'This Rai, he seems to be a helpful sort. Only thing Colombo is so far away.'

A coral glow crept up Ma's face, discernable even in the pink light.

'Actually he is expecting his posting back to Delhi soon,' she murmured. 'That's what he said today.'

'Oh,' said Chhobi then added as she got up, 'I like him.'

eighteen

Sonny contacted Sonali on Friday.

He offered to pick her up on Sunday but she replied that she would make it on her own, arranging to meet him outside his office, in the embrasure where the lifts were, on the ground floor.

Sonali replaced the phone and began to await Chhobi's return from office with simmering impatience. She could hear Dida, Dadu and Ratan Kaku in the next room, talking about food as usual. What was it about food and Bengalis?

Ratan Kaku had been very attentive since Dida had sought his help. He would arrive every other evening holding a plastic packet tied with a rubber band, or an earthenware container with some sweets or savoury to uplift Dadu's spirits. He was speaking now – 'Our sweets are unique, the rest of the country has some version or the other of halwa or solidified khir, but our paneer-based sweets are so special.'

Dida suddenly interrupted, 'Did you know that in all the poetry and songs describing Lord Krishna's childhood, he is depicted as stealing cream and butter, but never paneer. In those days it was considered inauspicious to curdle milk with anything acidic, cheese was after all unknown.'

'Well, we all know that both sandesh and rosogolla were only invented in the mid-nineteenth century, obviously Krishna had not tasted them.'

'It was K.C. Das,' said Dadu loudly, joining in the conversation, 'actually his father, who created rosogolla.' Dadu was referring to Calcutta's most famous sweet shop.

'Who created sandesh?' asked Kaku. 'Bhim Chandra Nag,' replied Dadu whose knowledge of Bengali sweets suddenly appeared encyclopaedic for he was continuing, 'he also invented ladikanee, that most delectable mouth-watering version of the gulab jamun. He was challenged to create a new sweet for the Vicereine's birthday, Lady Canning, and he came up with this.'

'Oh, is ladikanee really Lady Canning? I didn't know.'

Sonali pacing the floor in the next room felt a wave of irritation engulf her, this pointless talk of comfits and confectionary, however harmless, was getting on her nerves. She realised that it was going to be now or never on Sunday. Sonny was not going to be easy to fob off a second time. Amazing how she felt no attraction for him at all, just a constant sharp prickle of anger. She had but one dominant thought in her head drumming away, fraying at her nerves, beating as relentlessly as her heart – have to get out of this mess... out of this mess... get out. Even Chhobi was going away...

Chhobi walked in flinging her bag on the bed. She went straight into the bathroom and began to vigorously wash her face. She could feel a subterranean rash lurking beneath the surface of her skin, her face always erupted at the onset of summer. Soon Dida would be making bitter infusions of neem leaves for her to steam her face with. Sonali unblemished in every season had no such problems. Chhobi looked at her now, sensing the tension in her. She had been hovering outside the bathroom door, humming tunelessly but insistently, like a stressed-out bumblebee. Right now she looked like one that had lost its sting.

'What's the matter?'

Sonali told her, the tension making her a little incoherent.

'Let me think. We have Saturday to work something out. At least you will manage to get into that office.'

'He won't be satisfied with a kiss or two this time, it is now or never.' Then, uncharacteristically imploring, 'Help me get out of this mess. I won't be able to evade him all alone on the tenth floor.'

'Calm down... We have to play it by ear. Let me think.'

Unbidden a picture of Sonny and Sonali together at Connaught Place appeared before Chhobi. Why had he agreed to meet her at the office? Chhobi's imagination superimposed on what Sonny's might be, began to riot.

Undoubtedly it was the recurring vision of Sonali naked in his father's office that haunted him. She seemed transfigured into a symbol of his lost freedom, she lifted him from a coarse basic want to an almost lyrical plane. With the singlemindedness of a cartoon character, no doubt he imagined the office resounding to the sounds of their illicit lovemaking. Sonali swivelling boldly on the chair behind the imposing teak wood desk, one golden delicious leg bent flagrantly at the knee. Gold eyes gazing at him with desire. Her flesh warm against his, her breasts flowering under his touch like blossoms, her long hair like so much lascivious black lace draped around her. It was this scene, Chhobi was convinced, that was goading him into this betrayal.

Chhobi rose early the next morning and looked at her sister sleeping soundly on the next bed. Her own sleeplessness weighed on eyelids that felt cast out of lead. She had a vague semblance of a plan in her head. It had entered her mind like a brief sparkling light before night departed. Much of its execution depended on circumstance – Sonny's reaction to Sonali's actions.

She took the key from Dadu and went towards the garage cum-clinic, holding her morning cup of tea in her hand. She carried a pen and paper in the other. Sorting through Dadu's dusty medical textbooks, she began to search for one specific ailment, visions of a schoolmate, gasping for breath, the nuns like a flock of anxious penguins gathered around her, flashing before her eyes. She jotted down a brief list of symptoms on her paper.

She got Dadu alone, sitting on the verandah with his newspaper. Spinning out a simple but entirely untrue story that completely satisfied him, she got him to unsuspectingly write out a prescription for her.

Carefully recalling the poor girl's plight and incorporating the other symptoms she had read about, Chhobi locked herself in the bathroom, trying to replicate the attack. Her gasping and groaning woke Sonali who after studying late, had gone to bed in the early hours of the morning. She hammered on the bathroom door in alarm, shouting.

'Are you okay? What's the matter?'

The girls were cloistered in their room all Saturday, weighing pros and debating cons. They ventured out in the evening to the chemist's to use the prescription written out by Dadu. They told the family nothing.

The events that followed were to haunt Chhobi. It would be years before she would find some acceptance of her actions, by giving the day a farcical twist, turning it into the climax scene of a comic thriller, the sequence of events unfolding in vaudeville glee. Prompted by some desperate demon she had taken on the lead role simply because there was nobody else to cast. Her movements dictated by a plot so entirely in the present tense that trepidation and shame were completely deferred.

　　　　　　　　°°°°°

They were late setting off on Sunday, nervousness robbing Sonali of her customary panache in selecting the right clothes. She changed twice, settling finally on jeans and a T-shirt. She was driving more erratically than normal, lurching forward at every traffic light as it changed from red to green, her fingers tightly clenched around the steering wheel. The car hadn't been cleaned for weeks and at one traffic signal Chhobi got out to wipe the encrusted rear windscreen with a piece of newspaper. The film of caked dust was wiped off like a ripped veil and she could see Sonali's face, biting her lips, in the rear-view mirror.

A MIRROR GREENS IN SPRING

Sonali glanced hopefully at Chhobi as she got back into the car. 'What do you think our chances are of discovering anything?' 'Anything?' 'Anything incriminating.' 'Oh… Low, I think… Yes, quite low.' 'How low…? As low as zero?' 'Right now I suggest you concentrate on playing up the power of helplessness. One thing is certain, he won't be at all pleased to see me.'

They lapsed into silence. Chhobi, her mind blank, tried to focus on the signs of summer already invading Delhi, spring had been unusually brief this year.

The thanda pani man was pushing his cart towards a bus stop, a sweaty film beading his forehead. The familiar round earthen pot containing cold water was draped in wet red muslin, mouth garlanded with mint and roses to stave off flies,the long brass ladle singing with bells as it hung by the side. Along the sidewalk near Panchsheel vendors had erected a tattered awning of bright blue plastic, giving the road a carnival air. Heaped under the shade were pyramids of early watermelons, some small spherical and bottle green, others elliptical and striated. Triangular pink wedges of cut fruit were an effective advertisement for the pleasures that awaited willing customers. At a makeshift stall two men were repairing room coolers, stuffing padded rectangles of yellow wood shavings into slatted iron frames.

The roads widened into the area of Delhi Chhobi loved best, the tree-lined boulevards past the Oberoi Hotel. Each avenue had its own separate botanical identity, the jamuns around India Gate with new leaves of satiny green, the neems on Aurangzeb Road and the arjun trees on Janpath.

Connaught Place was empty, easy to negotiate even for Sonali. No throng of unceasing, endlessly circulating crowds. No multitude of unknown faces burdened by umbrellas, shopping bags and deadlines. No synthetic sari clad secretaries and telephone operators, their mouths outlined in cheap maroon lipstick. No ragged canteen boys carrying wire basket trays slotted with smeared glasses of sugary tea. No businessmen in safari suits all set to slay paper tigers.

Sonali found the twelve-storey building without any difficulty. She parked the car right in front, under a 'No Parking' sign. Chhobi looked at her watch – 11.10.

'He is bound to be late¸ he usually is,' said Sonali tightly.

They walked towards the deserted entrance, not a soul around. No security guards, no telephone operators with maroon lipstick, no canteen boys with glasses of tea… Just a solitary businessman holding a briefcase, waiting for the lifts in the dim enclosure beyond the open lobby. Chhobi wondered if Sonny was on his way. The businessman was looking at them. She noticed that out of the four lifts only one was operational since it was Sunday, the little red numbers on the display window above the door indicating its descent.

Moving closer, their eyes adjusted to the dimmer light and Chhobi realised with a shock that the businessman with the briefcase was Sonny. He was furious to see that she had accompanied Sonali. Her thick handloom kurta and grim expression gave her the demeanour of duenna. Without intending to she looked very much her sister's keeper.

⁕

It was only three-quarters of an hour later that they were back in the lobby. Chhobi felt completely drained as though actually battling a chronic disease, choking on her tongue wrapped around her heart for the past so many minutes. It was Sonali now who was all frenetic motion, urging Chhobi forward, running toward the parked car, wrenching the door open and firing the ignition like the getaway man in a bank robbery.

As always Sonali was awkward while reversing and she did so now with great vigour. There was a jarring clang and Chhobi turned in alarm to see that they had backed right into the neat 'No Parking' sign. The grey and red painted metal sheet was leaning forward in a drunken incline. The iron pipe holding up the sign seemed to have inexplicably but inextricably fused with the bumper of the Fiat.

'Let me get out and see,' said Chhobi

Sonali shook her head determinedly, pressing down firmly on the accelerator, changing into first gear with a whinging noise. There was a reverberating sound of tearing metal. They heard a shout, and Chhobi turned to see the security guards, their card game abandoned, running towards them. The car moved forward in a lurching motion, a scrape-like screech announcing the crushed damage to their rear. The 'No Parking' sign smashed down on the asphalt with ringing finality. Sonali was grinning as the speedometer needle gamely went up. She put down her window glass as the car turned towards the main exit, stuck her hand out and waved to the speechless guards.

Her exultation was dimmed somewhat as they pulled in midway into a quiet leafy lane, stopping under a mauve-blue jacaranda tree in full bloom. Flowers the colour of Krishna's skin. Lilac blossoms trumpeting springtime's swan song.

Chhobi removed the photostat pages tucked into the waistband of her salwar and flattened them, trying to smooth the uneven crinkles. Sonali stared at them bemused then said in disappointed tones.

'They are mostly figures, not even in English but in…'

'It's German.'

'German! What connection can the LTTE have to German?'

'What were you expecting – letters in Tamil signed V. Prabhakaran with a letterhead done in tiger stripes?'

'Don't be sarcastic. This was my only chance.'

'Look, we are not qualified to understand these. They are obviously worth something or they wouldn't be in that safe. Then this handwritten page is in English,' said Chhobi examining it closely. It was lists of figures divided into four columns.

'Let me see,' Sonali pulled at the paper, examining it, thinking aloud. 'These are shares of something. See the totals are given – maybe money… Yes, divided between the two brothers. Sonny's father and uncle. Those are their initials on the top... But it doesn't help us at all. Useless. All that effort, planning... Entrapping Sonny,' her voice tailed off into a wail.

Chhobi was frowning, feeling lightheaded, her veins still clamping in spasms with her heightened pulse. 'We will get translations. Look, there are telephone numbers of some banks on this page – account numbers again.'

Chhobi carefully smoothed the sheets, folding them together. She rummaged in her bag and found a used envelope into which she tucked the papers. She unzipped the inner pocket to place them and started as there was a rapping on her window. Thrusting the papers deep into the pocket, pulling the zip in one swift motion, she turned her head. It was spinning slightly with the excess of adrenalin coursing in her blood. A pockmarked face swam into view behind a large steel plate that carried curving white and cinnamon coloured sections of fresh coconut. A fleshy cooler gleaming wet with juice. She stared wordlessly at the zebra crescents arranged in a lotus flower design. Darkness and light, Rahu and Ketu. Umbra and Penumbra.

The vendor moved to Sonali's side of the car. Shifting his plate closer he began extolling the virtues of the fruit that had probably been rinsed in water thick with germs. The empty space in the centre of the plate reflected the sun in a sudden scattering of light, blinding her for an instant, and then bursting into every cranny of her mind with the heady tang of realisation, filling her with a luminous transparency. In a voice ringing with confidence she said to Chhobi, 'Did you see Sonny's reaction when he saw these? His eyes were popping out. These are not useless, they are not.' Her sister, completely limp after the event, lifted her head dispiritedly, then sat up to see Sonali so jubilant.

'Just a minute,' Sonali added, jumping out, shooing the coconut seller away, running to the back of the car to see the damage. One side of the bumper had been wrenched loose and was hanging dented and askew. She gave it a little kick, and then another much harder one, expecting it to crash to the ground but it did not.

She began to painstakingly remove the red L signs that were stuck fast to the rear windscreen, grimacing a little as a sticky residue of gum and dirt caught in her fingernails. Slowly clean L shapes emerged from behind the red tape clearly visible on the dirty glass like remnants of her novice state. Throwing away the curling bits of red tape, she tried to push the bumper back into place.

Chhobi feeling completely depleted, too tired to turn her head, adjusted the rear-view mirror to see what Sonali was upto. A light breeze agitated the leaf-light, a point of focus on the mirror. Like Ghalib's verse it was green as though with mildew or tarnish, a harbinger of change in spring perhaps, but a stain nevertheless.

Chhobi collapsed on the last leg of the journey home. She had only just begun to realise the consequences of their actions. Her legs trembled as she imagined Sonny's father making a chance visit to the office, even while she was photocopying his most secret papers. Or worse, the violence simmering beneath the surface of a scene where Sonny and his security guards caught them red-handed.

Sonali's high spirits, meanwhile, were lending their journey the faint air of a victory drive. She began to smile at Chhobi, humming a little tune, leaning back against the seat, oblivious of the clank and rattle at the rear. She said with a little giggle, referring to Chhobi's prominent role in the charade, 'You deserve an Oscar.'

As they took the right turn into their colony, Sonali stuck out her hand to acknowledge somebody waving vigorously. Chhobi swivelled around to see Helen, Mrs Chatterjee's adivasi Christian maid in her Sunday best, returning from church with a gaggle of her friends all waving and smiling. Sonali grinned back at the rows of shiny white teeth. With their sari pleats arranged in accordion precision they made an unlikely squad of cheerleaders, but as they disappeared from view, Sonali thought, the multicoloured hues of their sari pallus had the look of flying colours.

nineteen

They spent the month of April in a state of limbo. Sonali vacillating between hope and hopelessness, despondency and enthusiasm. Ma looked at the papers, handling them gingerly, finally locking them deep in her cupboard, hiding them in the shelf where her good shawls were kept. She had found them impossible to assess. She felt a helplessness steal over her, unable to keep pace with the new momentum of their life. Brusquely she told Sonali to stop building castles in the air and to get down to her books. For a week Chhobi and Ma debated what to do, they needed somebody who could see the whole picture. Somebody more able to pinpoint accurately the extent of the Talwars' liability. Somebody who would be able to advise them if the information they had could be utilised by them, and how.

Somebody like Rai.

In the end Ma went to see Rai's friend who lived at Lodhi Estate, and handed him a letter for Rai to be sent to Colombo through the diplomatic bag. Her letter was very brief, betraying none of the confusion or anticipation they were all experiencing. It was couched in guarded words, after all his was a sensitive appointment, may be others examined his mail. Chhobi snorted a little with laughter, imagining a team of secret service agents prying and hunting for hidden meanings in Ma's letter. They were there, but would be hard to find. As the missive was winging its way southwards, they all felt a slackening in tension, enjoying the temporary abeyance in decision-making. Ma's depression lifted, and Chhobi too allowed herself to float away, dreaming of America. Dadu and Dida had been told nothing about the papers.

Dida was very preoccupied with Sonali's health and exams slated to begin at the end of April. She would wake her up at 4 a.m. to rub the sleep out of her eyes with a cup of black tea. Later she would grind a paste of soaked almonds into her milk to improve her memory. Dadu had prescribed vitamins and folic acid for her and Dida ensured that Sonali took the tablets.

The peaceful lull was soon punctuated, the respite gained little longer than a comma when they had been hoping for a full stop. Rai phoned from Colombo, pressing the need for secrecy, urging Ma not, absolutely not, to send the papers to Sri Lanka. He would be coming to Delhi by the end of April he said and would then help sort out the problem.

The days were spent then in waiting for Rai. Mid April and the mercury had already climbed to peak summer heights. The sun beat down flat and hard. A brown pariah dog with sad eyes black-rimmed as though with kohl, tunnelled dark patches of wet earth under the Kamini shrub near their gate, and cowered there motionless, tongue lolling, thin ribs panting. Walking to the bus stop became a trial for Ma, burdened with her summer load of water bottle and parasol. Even so she felt any exposed skin shrivel. The water in the pipes had already reduced to a thin trickle. Despite the rising examination fever and the intense occasional bouts of morning sickness, Sonali took time off from her books to spend the dwindled remains of Karan's money on a pair of smuggled dark glasses.

Rai contacted Ma on the very day of his arrival in Delhi. She invited him home, speaking to him in words that like her letter were precise and formal. He agreed to come over the next evening. Ma went to inform Dida who was in the kitchen boiling arrowroot powder to make starch for crisping their cotton saris. Savitri had already finished starching the first batch and had gone to stretch them flat on the terrace, weighing down the corners with old bricks. Border designs coming together along the edges of the saris, merging to form a crazy carpet underneath the unrelenting sky.

'Mr Rai will be coming to look at some documents tomorrow evening,' Ma said without preamble, unsure as usual about how much Dida knew, had guessed or conjectured. She continued, 'You know Rai, that helpful diplomat introduced to us by Chhobi's editor.'

'Yes, yes, tea from Colombo. I know. Those documents?' she said stirring energetically, bangles jingling, 'that the girls got from Sonny?'

Ma stared at her. She was so matter of fact, strangely she did not seem to be terribly interested in the evidence they had acquired. 'So Sonali has told you. We cannot understand them. They are not in English.'

'They are in Punjabi?'

'No, no some official papers, in German I think, maybe some bank accounts in Switzerland.'

Dida stopped stirring. The ladle slipped against the edge of the pan, and the arrowroot began to boil and curdle in opaque light grey bubbles. Her eyes narrowed and she gazed into the distance as though locating new horizons.

'That's illegal,' she said in the heartened tone of one who has finally turned up trumps.

'Well, it's too soon to say. We cannot understand much. There is nothing about the missing ships at all.'

'And Rai – this Rai, you are confident he will be able to understand, to know what to do.'

'I… yes, I think so. Yes.'

'Good, I will have to tell your father before Rai arrives. Don't go into any details with him. Leave it to me.' The arrowroot paste had dried to a glutinous rubbery ball. Savitri bringing back the empty bucket, stared at the pot, then lunged past Dida to switch off the gas.

Later, Dida was thrown into an agony of indecision about what snacks to serve for tea.

'Snakes!' laughed Ma to Chhobi, she was thinking of her army days, the parties thrown by the commanding officer, the mess waiters circulating with snakes as they called it – fried peanuts liberally garnished with raw onions that made polite conversation impossible, and small dry shammi kebabs as hard as bullets.

Dida was thinking aloud. 'Something salty and westernised, no dripping syrupy sweets for him.'

'Dadu and Kaku will also be there.'

'Will they? Yes, I suppose they will, but we have to cater to him first.'

'Don't get carried away,' Ma interjected. 'Just tea and biscuits will do nicely.'

Her suggestion fell on fallow ground. If Rai was the man then Dida was going to rely on that sole contribution to Bengali food that two hundred years of British rule had made. She was going to make mutton mince chops. A misnomer really as it was not a chop at all, but a round potato cake stuffed with spiced mutton dipped in egg and breadcrumbs and fried crisp. It was normally served with 'kasundi', that peculiarly pungent mustard sauce which stood virulent and green in its rectangular glass bottle right next to another old favourite – Telephone Brand flea seed husk – isabgol for indigestion. Chhobi always said you needed it after kasundi.

twenty

Rai appeared taller and more authoritative than Chhobi's first impression of him. He was dressed with a quiet elegance, in a cool shirt the colour of a pigeon's wing, matching the hair greying above his temples. He looks, well, distinguished, she thought.

Barely had he entered than Savitri, looking unusually spotless, was circulating with a tray, bowing deferentially but vaguely in his direction. He was faintly taken aback to be handed a plate by Dida, almost as soon as he sat down. A pair of chops gazed up at him like bulging eyes, the pool of kasundi spreading and opening like a third eye between them. All around the room other eyes were trained on him.

Ma and Dida in Bengal cotton saris too stiffly starched were gliding about the room, their movements resembling those of old fashioned clockwork dolls with invisible feet. Dadu and Ratan Kaku sat bolt upright on pulled up dining chairs. Chhobi was sitting on the planter's chair that had been dragged from Ma's room, with Sonali perched on its arm. Ma took her place at the extreme edge of the sagging sofa where Rai sat.

Balancing the plate on his knee, he ran a finger around his collar, which suddenly seemed too tight. Ma gave him a reassuring smile then placed a small table near his knee. She handed him the envelope with the papers and took his plate. Dida fussing with a brand new bone china teaset borrowed from Mrs Chatterjee, stopped moving, and like everybody else in the room watched Rai's reaction with unblinking attention.

Rai was frowning as he glanced through all the papers quickly, then turned back to the first one. Taking out a slim leather case fitted with a calculator he began to stab at the buttons with a gold-capped Schaeffer pen. There was complete silence in the room broken only by the click of Dadu's dentures, ill-fitting of late, he had lost the last molar on which they were anchored. Dadu was the only one concentrating not on Rai but on his plate. He seemed to want to disassociate himself completely from the proceedings.

As the digits ascended on the little window of the calculator, Rai began to smile. For a long moment he did not speak as he stared at the final figure. He was grinning when he looked up, then he turned to the handwritten page and his smile broadened.

'We have them. These are dynamite.'

Ma spoke hesitantly. 'But there is no connection to the missing ships at all, we cannot tackle them about the loss of her husband on the basis of these.'

'Look,' said Rai tapping the papers with his pen, 'Let's get a few things straight. We know that *they* knew the risk in doing business with a terrorist organisation. For monetary gains they lost the lives of so many men and are therefore very guilty. What we have is proof of their illegal deposits in what is probably a Swiss account. The name of the bank is not there, but somebody has on this last page very kindly noted down the fax number. There also appears to be a phone number, although the code is not given. Should be no problem tracing it. We will try Zurich first. I have counted no less than twelve accounts and fixed deposits of various kinds. The numbers are there and the money deposited quite sizeable. If you cannot get them for the crime where you have been wronged, then get them for another that will put them away for many years. I will trace the bank before you approach them.' He folded the wrinkled pages and replaced them carefully in the envelope before handing them back to Ma.

Chhobi looked around at her family. Ma was pale and tense. Sonali was listening intently but had not like Ma flinched at the talk of missing men. Karan... a man whose absence had taken on a permanent presence in their lives.

Ma spoke up again. 'But that will be... I mean... that's...'

'Blackmail?' Rai was grinning again. 'Call it whatever you like. Let them make her a generous financial settlement or else threaten to go public with the papers. The authorities, the income tax, the enforcement directorate.'

'Threaten!' repeated Chhobi, quailing at the thought of speaking to Bhai Sahib let alone attempting to blackmail him.

'No! No... we cannot... not blackmail,' Ma whispered, her horrified expression reflected in the dismayed faces of Dadu and Ratan Kaku, both of who had stopped eating.

'The lure of lucre... however filthy,' interjected Chhobi. Everybody ignored her weak attempt at satire. There was a strained silence.

'I will do it.' Sonali's face was set in determined lines, her tones whiplash, transfused with a new resolve now that the papers had proved to be what they were. Rai looked at her as though just noticing her, the protagonist, for the first time. He had not met her before. He was curious to see the daughter who had played the role of catalyst, jerked this family from their ordinary safe lives and spun them into fast forward. He stared at her, then asked in the crisp commanding way he had, 'Forgive me for asking but how did you get involved with such a family? After all, your husband was related to them.'

Sonali said nothing, pouting, looking for a moment not so winningly winsome. She sensed that Rai was a man not immediately dazzled by her. She looked at him from under her lashes and murmured, 'A chance encounter and one thing led to another.' Her expression was so incongruous in the circumstances that Ma and Chhobi both glanced sharply at Rai, anxious to see his reaction.

Rai was continuing expressionlessly, 'I don't think they will take you seriously. Besides it may not be very safe. They are essentially middlemen, wheeling and dealing. You do not know the levels of corruption that have permeated their lives.'

Dida, handing Rai a cup of tea and urging him to eat the untouched chops, spoke up then. 'Advocate Indranil Mukherjee of Delhi High Court will do it. They will take him seriously. As for harming Shona, we will have to work out some safeguards.'

Rai bit into the deliciously spiced chops, feeling the keenness of the kasundi stinging in a rush up his nostrils, and took out a handkerchief to wipe his mouth. 'These are excellent,' he told Dida who turned pink with pleasure. 'This advocate, he is personally known to you?'

As though on cue, the doorbell rang. They looked through the parted curtains of the window to see Mrs Chatterjee standing there looking larger than ever, bristling with curiosity. She had noticed the car parked at their gate. Getting up to open the door Ma felt quite unable to summon a welcoming smile. She knew Dida shouldn't have borrowed that teaset. Mrs Chatterjee, unable to stay away, had arrived now on the thin pretext of showing them some new snapshots of her grandchildren. For once Ma was firm, she took the heavy arm and guided her toward the dining table as far away from Rai as was possible.

Mrs Chatterjee glared at Ratan Kaku sipping his tea, expostulating some theory to Dadu, a shower of spittle giving expression to his excitement. He had not, like her, been excluded. Dida distracted her by handing her a laden plate and she began to eat with unsuppressed eagerness. Dida watching her eat thought she had the appetite of a rakshash. In Calcutta, as a widow, she would have to subsist on insipid vegetarian fare.

When Ma had resumed her place on the sofa, Rai shifted closer to her and, lowering his voice, spoke softly almost into her very ear. The rest of the room watched them covertly.

'My reading is that with the very hint of exposure backed by this actual evidence they will be in a hurry to hush up the matter. Do not forget you are dealing with men of no conscience. Certainly they are not people who have been swayed by remorse or sentiment.'

Rai's final analysis of the Talwars resounded in Ma's ears like an unpleasant echo. It sounds as though he is talking about Sonali, she thought – 'unswayed by remorse or sentiment'.

Ma felt a coldness crystallising in jagged icicles around her heart. The description fitted Sonali – the tight hard core of her – that selfish streak which was quintessentially the essence of her penetrating to the pith... to the very soul. What a beautiful baby she had been. Perfect strangers would stop to admire her going for a stroll in her pram. Only nineteen. She had failed her somehow, there was something lacking in her upbringing. Ma felt the sharp prick of tears in her eyes. Rai watching her was trying to fathom the cause of her sudden and acute distress.

'You are worrying they will harm her? I suggest a safety net. Something like the advocate telling them that should any unforeseen accident take place, the papers and a fully signed affidavit will reach the press and the authorities.'

Chhobi spoke finally... 'But blackmail? I mean can we ask an advocate?'

Mrs Chatterjee's ears pricked up, she looked up from her plate, signalling imperiously to Savitri for tea, then shouted across the room, 'What advocate are you talking about? Indranil Mukherjee? He is my sambandhi, he will help, I will see to it.' Rai who had not been introduced to her raised his eyebrows again. 'My mother's friend,' Ma said sotto voce.

Chhobi was asking Rai, 'But why should they, specially Bhai Sahib, even agree to meet the advocate?' It was Mrs Chatterjee who replied, 'I don't know all the details but if it is anything legal...'

'Or illegal,' interjected Chhobi with a slight shiver, trying to make a separation in her head, reminding herself that all this was after all for Karan's child. Karan who had so easily been repudiated as an object of grief.

Mrs Chatterjee was continuing boastfully, 'Whatever it is, he

will manage.' Chops finished, her gaze sharpened as she stared at
Rai but postponed her queries for later.

⁕

Once Rai charted the course of action, Ma insisted on postponing the
plan whilst Sonali cleared her examinations. For the next month they
did nothing, except hang on to inaction a bit longer. Nothing except
do all the things that were such daily tribulations to get through each
burning day. In every summer's repeating pattern, Dadu was in
charge of the water chores and would patiently await the morning
gurgle in the water pipes signalling the coming to life of the dead taps.
The room coolers needed to be filled, the empty buckets gaped in the
bathroom, the plastic tub in the kitchen yawned, the thirsting grass,
the parched plants all required quenching.

Dida would unfurl the dark green lined chiks that protected the
verandah like eye shades, drawing tight the heavy curtains across the
windows so that not a chink of the blinding day entered. Chhobi
coming indoors from the bright white heat would blunder moth-
like banging into the dark furniture till her pupils expanded and she
could see in the cool dimness.

Looking back on that month, Chhobi thought that during that
period of expectation the house was like a giant womb, Karan's
disappearance squinting in unexpected corners like phantom
foetuses, incubating in that warm darkness, made fluid by the moist
cooler-driven air. The undoubted finality of his vanishing taking on
such solid substance, growing larger by the day, waiting to burst
forth into the light with a raucous cry.

The dim indoors, and outside the dust storms that turned the
sky a metallic grey, the sun not golden but silver white and perfectly
round like Savitri's aluminium thali. Later what Chhobi
remembered were the pigments that coloured those waiting days.
Technicolour memories. Dida meditatively stirring ice into pale
yellow glasses of mango panna clouded with cold milk. Sonali
spreading snippets of crimson silk, satin and tissue on the bed –
Indu had suddenly got engaged and wanted her to design the

wedding lehnga. The five-petalled flamboyance of the gulmohar tree outside the advocate's house in Neeti Bagh, leaves feathery, doubly compounded with yellowing leaflets and flowers a flaming orange-red as though the branches were spontaneously combusting.

Sonali was very preoccupied with Indu's approaching nuptials. The family had arranged the match with a distant relative, a businessman with a chemical factory located in a suburb of Bombay. He had taken Indu for tea at Claridges and when they returned home they agreed to get married, to the mutual satisfaction of both families. Indu – guitar-twanging, gum-chewing. Indu – frayed jeans and with an insatiable appetite for bun andas. Indu – suddenly so demure in embroidered chiffon saris.

Sonali was out shopping with Indu when Ma telephoned the advocate, Chhobi standing with her next to the phone like a prop. Dida was watching Rajiv Gandhi on TV, addressing a rally in one of the north-eastern states, looking startlingly handsome despite the elaborate and faintly ludicrous tribal headgear he was wearing.

Indranil Mukherjee remembered their case once Mrs Chatterjee's reference was made. Ma asked for an appointment hinting that they had acquired some evidence pointing to probably illegal transactions.

'Has anybody knowledgeable seen them?' he questioned.

'Yes, somebody in the government has examined them and found that they are incriminating.'

'Okay, do not come to my Delhi High Court chamber, come to my office at home tomorrow, 6 p.m., Neeti Bagh. Take the Siri Fort road.' Ma replaced the receiver and began to doodle on the pad she had written the address on – a series of interlocking diamonds turned into a shoal of fish eating fish. 'I think we won't take Sonali along. Let's see what he has to say first.'

Dida interrupted, deaf ear catching Ma's words over Rajiv Gandhi's. 'Who is the client?'

'Client?' repeated Chhobi.

'Yes, I remember my father had filed for recovery against a company that had supplied him with defective components.

Lawyers handle cases for their clients, who have to sign some legal documents at the outset – Vakalatnama, I think it's called. So her presence is definitely required, besides she may have some important points to make. He is expensive, so I suggest you decide on some firm course of action at this meeting. Do not worry about the money, your Dadu has spoken to Ratan Kaku for a loan.'

Ma stiffened, so did Chhobi. Dida looked at both of them. Ma was frowning, shoulders slumped helplessly, thinking of the fine balance of the monthly budget. Dida continued, 'It's only a loan,' she repeated. 'Wait.' Switching off the TV, she went into her bedroom. They could hear the creak as she opened her Godrej cupboard. She had a tightly stapled wad of notes in her hand when she returned.

'Ten thousand,' she said, 'it should do. Fix the charges for the whole case – lumpsum.'

A Nepali servant ushered the three of them into a long narrow room where an elderly typist clattered at a legal brief. Half an hour elapsed before they were summoned to Mr Mukherjee's office, a book-lined room, leatherbound spines of legal journals glinting with gilt-embossed letters. The desk was placed in front of a large window, so that the light streamed onto the faces of the visitors, the clients, and kept the advocate's in shadow. He looked now at the three flustered faces. Sonali still fuming from the drive there, the Fiat was becoming impossible. The pick-up was so slow, and a circular knocking sound indicated some serious malfunction. Whatever was the outcome of this meeting, she wanted a new car, she thought. She *needed* a new car.

Ma, trying to stick close to the line prompted by Rai, began with a background to the case. Mukherjee cut her short, nodding at Chhobi, saying he remembered the facts well.

'On the phone, you had mentioned some documents?'

Silently Ma handed them over. He was a long time examining them. Unlike Rai he did not grin, but his eyes gleamed behind his bifocals when looked up.

'These are account numbers... overseas, the bank...?'

'We have traced the bank from the fax number given on the last page, it is a Swiss one.'

'Quite careless of them to make these handwritten notations.' He began to ask a great many questions about Karan's age and earnings. Ma was unable to restrain herself.

'How will you make them respond to these? After all, they are not directly connected to the case?'

Mukherjee was confident as he replied, 'They will respond all right. If we use these, they will all be inside.'

'Inside?' repeated Chhobi, unable to comprehend. Sonali understood at once.

'How many years will they get?' Her eyes were cold, gold and malevolent.

Mukherjee clicked on the angle-poise lamp on his desk. A dust storm was darkening the sky outside, the room inside. They saw his face clearly now, spot lit. Then he adjusted the arm of the lamp so that the light fell on Sonali.

'You don't understand. The point is not of how long. With the connections they must be having they will soon be out on bail, however, no doubt about the damage to their reputation, their business. I will prepare a letter to them. We will keep these numbers confidential, fill them up by hand after the letter is typed.' Then looking directly at Sonali he asked, 'What do you want?'

For a moment Chhobi and Ma were both confused. Sonali answered in a voice laced with venom, 'I want them to pay.'

'Yes, yes, but we must fix a number.'

'Maybe I want them to pay for it in Tihar Jail,' said Sonali implacably. In that moment of realisation of her own power she was suddenly prepared to give no quarter. From zero to hero.

'Tihar!' Chhobi gasped. Immediately a picture of Sonny, his father, and Bhai Sahib dressed not in their impeccable business suits but absurd in striped regulation prison gear, haggard with unshaven chins, flashed before her eyes.

'Sonali!' protested Ma flinching as the weight of her hatred slammed into them. Sonali did not respond, holding Mukherjee's gaze steady, relentless. Mukherjee's eyes were shining, he thought she wanted vendetta for her husband's disappearance and almost certain death, but Ma and Chhobi knew that it was in retaliation for everything that had befallen her since Sonny had spurned her.

He was gentle when he spoke. 'These are only for bargaining with,' he said tapping on the papers. 'If you report them you get nothing. We will only threaten with these. Now what do you want?'

At first she didn't answer. It was as though finally the invisible surge of spleen had eaten away the toughened cicatrice that had grown over the fact of Karan's vanishing. It lay now completely exposed, a raw wound. She sat back, unclenching the hands turned to fists in her lap. 'Okay,' she said taking a deep breath.

'I want to study fashion design, clothes. I want my own label, my own outlet in a good area. The outlet must be owned not rented... I want a new car.'

Ma and Chhobi swivelled around to stare at her. Such a litany of wants. Mukherjee returned Sonali's look with upraised brows, his expression tinged with respect. From zero to hero.

'Yes, well, that can all be worked out... We will ask for money.' He named a figure that boggled their imagination and rendered them speechless.

twenty-one

Mukherjee gave the Talwars seventy-two hours to respond to his notice after it was received.

On the third day after the letter had been despatched, the phone rang as Chhobi and Dida were sitting down to lunch. It was Sonny asking for Sonali who was spending a few days with Indu. His voice, vibrating with frissons of anger tinged with fear, was raised just short of a shout. Immediately Chhobi felt engulfed with satisfaction, the threat was going to work.

'Where is she? I need to speak to her urgently?'

'Sorry. I don't know where she is.'

'Look, just call her to the phone.'

'She is out, busy.'

'What do you mean busy? She has to be somewhere.'

'Why do you need to see her? I don't think she wants to see you,' Chhobi said blandly.

With an effort Sonny lowered his voice, she could hear someone prompting him to speak calmly. 'The matter is very urgent, please tell me when she will be back.'

'I don't know. What is this urgent matter? Is it a question of seventy-two hours?' She couldn't help gloating, sick of the active suspense that had distilled the hours down to these final seventy-two.

There was a tense silence, prelude to the explosion that followed. 'You… You bitch, you and your fake asthma… I never did trust you, you put her up to this…' A volley of profanity pelted into her ear. She was about to bang the telephone down, when the voice changed. It was Sonny's father.

'Hello? You are Sonali's elder sister? Yes, good, please give her a message. You know she moves around in that old car, well, please tell her to take care, as old cars often meet with accidents.' The voice was smooth as Kanjeevaram silk, but the threat was not even imperfectly veiled. Chhobi blanched, but was well prepared, coached by Rai and Mukherjee.

'Mr Talwar, thank you for your concern, but my sister and indeed the whole family has taken precautions as advised by our counsel. Should *any* mishap to *any*one take place, a notarised affidavit and a set of some documents you are familiar with, will reach the authorities and the press. If you have anything else to convey to my sister, please do so through her lawyer. Bye.' She replaced the receiver, softly, carefully, her hand trembling slightly.

Ma was much more shaken up when she heard, and immediately rang Mukherjee, speaking to him in an agitated fashion about Sonali's safety.

'Calm down, Mrs Dutt, they are not going to add a sensational murder to their list of crimes. After all the matter is in the open, in legal hands. They have appointed a counsel who has requested me for an extension of three days. Tell your daughter to speak to them agreeing to meet us in my high court chamber on Friday. Mention the safety net.'

It was Chhobi who contacted Sonny and informed him about the meeting. They continued to get blank calls on the telephone for the next two days, Sonny desperate to speak to Sonali. Chhobi or Ma would pick up the receiver and answer hello, there would be no reply, just the hurried click of somebody replacing the phone. On the third day even Dida began to stiffen with tension whenever the phone rang, and mutter to herself about police protection.

Sonali returned home on Thursday morning. She looked quite unruffled when the three of them, Ma, Dida and Chhobi started on their harangue about the latent goonda tendencies of the Talwars.

'What did you expect? Stop worrying,' said Sonali, looking at her hands, as were all of them.

'Who did that? It's a very intricate design,' asked Chhobi.

'Yesterday was Indu's mehndi ceremony. They had called the mehndiwali from Hanuman Mandir. It was a pain to get this done, but fun too. All of us sat with Indu for hours, the mehndiwali kept dabbing some solution to make the colour darker, while Indu's mom kept stuffing mithai and pakoras right into our mouths.'

Ma looked at her helplessly. 'How could they let you apply henna? It will take weeks to wear off... don't they ask you about your husband? Don't they ask about Karan, don't *you* wonder about Karan!'

Sonali's long fingers clenched and unclenched. She shrugged. 'I haven't told them anything... That he is missing or... and actually they only talk to me about clothes. They rely on my taste. I have been practically living in Ushnak Mal's for the last week.' She was smiling pensively, abstracted but pleasantly. She stretched out her hands to admire the henna patterns. The orange brown lattice work tracery looked as though she had pulled on a pair of lace gloves crocheted in fine silk.

'I want to show you something.' She returned with a sari box, inside which lay a sari wrapped in layers of white tissue paper. Carefully, carefully those ornamented hands peeled off the paper. The rest of them stared as she unfurled the shimmering six yards of stiffly sequined fabric. Her stomach would be well disguised.

'Indu's mother gave this to me to wear at the wedding.' Sonali draped it around herself and looked at them, head tilted back, eyes narrowed. The last time she would look as gorgeous before her body swelled, grew heavy and ugly.

For once Dida was speechless.

Dadu entering the room stopped short to see her swathed in the translucent cloud of fabric. The silken threads dark green touched with gold. Sequins caught the light with a momentary spark of phosphorescence.

Sonali twirled lightly, the sari floating out behind her, sparkling in the dim evening light.

'Fireflies,' said Dadu in a tone of reedy wistfulness. He took an involuntary step back, closing his eyes.

…He was a small boy running through the damp orchards on his estate. The trees in the twilight lit by green embers, fireflies floating through the groves by the hundreds, tails winking on and off with white-green flashes of cold fire. He opened his eyes as Sonali left the room. A glittering stream of fireflies flickered in his memory. Never seen in the dry dust of Delhi. Fireflies, lost forever in Bangladesh, living now only in the imagination of a man long past his youth.

⁕

When Ma spoke to Mr Mukherjee that evening, he mentioned in an offhand way that the Talwars had approached a very close friend of his, a retired Justice, to speak to him on their behalf. They wanted a private meeting with him, 'without any of the ladies' but Mukherjee had refused. He added that they had appointed a senior advocate to conduct the negotiations.

'They are worried. The very fact that they have approached my friend means they are shaken up. Come half an hour early to my office in Delhi High Court. We will go up to Agarwal's chamber.'

Ma said a bit doubtfully, 'Why should we go to their lawyer's office? They should come to yours.'

Mukherjee gave a dry chuckle. 'The venue doesn't matter. Their lawyer is senior to me. I plan to deadlock the meeting. It will be easier to do that in his office. I cannot very well walk out of my own office.'

twenty-two

Mukherjee warned them to let him do the talking. Sonny and his father were already there in Agarwal's chamber when the three of them filed in behind Mukherjee. The room was very small and cramped with so many of them. Chhobi sat on a stool near the door, Ma and Sonali flanked the Talwars while a peon pulled up a chair for Mr Mukherjee.

All three of them had dressed carefully for the occasion. Ma looked cool in a lavender and white printed crepe de chine sari with a string of pearls, not her usual starched tangail. She had tried to recall how the senior army officers' wives would dress for their coffee mornings. Chhobi had also worn a sari, looking much taller and slimmer than she did in the shapeless handloom kurtas that were practically her uniform. Dida had nodded at her approvingly. She had subconsciously selected a black and white sari as though to reinforce their litigious mood. Sonali had turned many heads as she walked down the long corridor on the first floor of the high court. She was wearing a simple but well tailored knee length black skirt with a slit at the back. She had teamed it with a leaf green shirt that made her eyes glow catlike, dark pupils defined in the tawny depths. Her hair was pulled up high, revealing the proud length of her neck. She wore Dida's gold stars in her ears. Now that they were going to ask for so much money, it was important to look as though they didn't need it at all.

Mukherjee had decided on the offensive. Scarcely had he sat down, a barrage of aggressive allegations all couched in convoluted legalese issued forth from his lips. The Talwars, looking aghast, found that their own lawyer was quite unable to penetrate the thick fusillade of words.

Sonny was staring fixedly at Sonali. She did not look at him, but made a steeple of her fingers, resting her elbows on the desk. Both Mr Agarwal and Sonny seemed fascinated by her hands. The henna meshwork quite obscured the real lines on her palm, the patterns web-like – a twisting wreath, a filigree braid, a net in which so much seemed ensnared. Sonali's gaze rested in fastidious disdain on the untidy stack of dusty files piled on the floor behind Agarwal's desk, then she began to contemplate her hands again. Those paradoxical hands, so bridal, touching each other as though cementing a union.

Sonny's father was unable to take any more. Without waiting for his lawyer to speak, he interjected, attempting to sound avuncular, 'We quite realise the little lady here has been under financial and mental strain and we are willing to make some compensation on a monthly basis. You must realise the investigation is still on. After all, we too have suffered a heavy loss. We are prepared to assist her monthly expenses.'

Mukherjee stared at him, then said, 'Not monthly, a one-time lumpsum settlement.'

'Lumpsum?' said Agarwal speaking finally, surprised at the strength of Mukherjee's assurance. He was beginning to feel that his clients had divulged but a fraction of the truth to him.

'Yes, lumpsum,' repeated Mukherjee. He mentioned the figure, lowering his voice as though to soften the impact of the amount.

Ma and Chhobi felt a shrivelling sense of shame, but Sonali raised her head and stared stonily at Sonny.

There was a stupefied silence from the Talwar camp for a few moments, then Sonny's father threw back his head and gave a bellowing laugh.

'Good joke!' he said laughing uproariously. He took out a monogrammed handkerchief and dabbed at his eyes, which were streaming a little like a crocodile's. Still laughing he added, 'I was thinking of offering her a couple of thousand a month, but your expectations…'

Now the laughter was stilled. His brows snapped together behind a hard and offensive gaze. Looking directly at Ma so silent, he said loudly, 'This is … you know what this is…'

'Blackmail?' supplied Chhobi in anger, furious that he had unerringly fastened on Ma, so fatigued by the anguish of broken habit, and this enforced adoption of behaviour so alien that it was beyond cognition. The blood drained out of Ma's face, her lips turned white, her fingers dug into the leather of her handbag. She did not speak.

Mukherjee stood up and gave them all a warning glance. He looked at Sonny, then at Agarwal, neither of who was laughing. Withdrawing an envelope from his pocket he handed it to them.

'Come on, Mrs Dutt, this meeting is meaningless. We will see them in court,' he said in a rude arrogant manner as he swept out.

The three of them were caught unawares at his speedy exit, pushing back their chairs, stumbling a little to catch up with him. Sonali dragged her foot as the strap of her sandal came undone. As she knelt just outside the chamber to refasten it, Sonny hurtled through the door like a missile. She rose and began to walk quickly down the corridor. Mukherjee and Ma had already started down the stairs and only their rapidly descending torsos were visible. Chhobi awaited her near the stairs.

'Sonali, wait,' said Sonny, and then as she started to walk faster, stepped in front of her to bar the way. He looked at her. Images swam before him… a vision of her – a golden sheaf, a bouquet of wild laburnum and mango blossom, scented through with musk deer kasturi ittar, arms and legs wrapped around his body in a yielding embrace.

A couple of senior advocates looked at them curiously. Like Mukherjee and Agarwal, both of them were theatrically garbed in the Queen's Counsel gowns. Chhobi, angry at the way the meeting had turned out, grew furious at the sight of Sonny. She started to walk back, brushing against the billowing black robe of one of the advocates. God, she thought momentarily distracted, glancing at the multitude of pleats and the double back on the gown, I thought these robes went out with the British Raj.

Then she glared as she heard Sonny say, 'Sonali, don't you walk out on me, dammit!' Anger, confusion and a desperate desperation all vying for space on his face, until it looked as though it would disintegrate. Chhobi grasped Sonali's elbow. Sonali's face was blank and glassy-eyed. Chhobi faced Sonny squarely and said, 'Just leave us alone. Come on, Sonali.'

Sonny turned on her fiercely.

'You... you planned it, you are the mastermind. Why don't you let me talk to her? *You* leave us alone. Just f.o.'

Then a pleading note entered his voice, quite wiping out the arrogance. 'Sonali, don't kick a man when he is down, dammit!'

Chhobi smiled scornfully to see his lack of poise and the look of contempt that crossed Sonali's face and fired her eyes with a golden flame.

'She is my sister,' Chhobi answered simply, and then added, 'Karan was your brother.'

He stared at her dumbfounded. Karan... He had quite forgotten him. Karan ... a man whose absence was taking on such a looming presence in his life.

'Karan,' he said. For what seemed like an epoch the two syllables of that name remained suspended between the three of them. Chhobi felt quite unsteady on her feet, then she was whirling backwards into a medieval battle scene. Spears slashing the air, swords clashing, richly caparisoned elephants trampling soldiers under foot. The Mahabharata and Karan killed by his brothers.

Shaking her head to dismiss the grisly picture she snapped, 'Tell your father we have uncovered the link to the Tigers.'

'Tigers... what Tigers? What the hell do you mean? Stop talking in riddles.'

'Just tell him,' she repeated giving him a look like a dagger, then unable to restrain herself she said, 'You *Zeilverkooper*!'

Sonny gathered from her tone that she was being acutely insulting, but he was more baffled than angry. 'Zelv... what... you bitch... talking double Dutch.'

Chhobi did not reply. Steering Sonali away down the long corridor, she resisted the urge to look over her shoulder and instead swallowed the repartees rising so quick and so thick on her tongue.

You've got *that* right she thought. It is Dutch after all.

<hr>

As post-mortems went, there wasn't much to analyse. Their mood oscillated as before between hope and despair, despondency and euphoria. Ma felt that Mukherjee might have been too ambitious and melodramatic. All of them were shaken at the mirth displayed by Sonny's father. Ma spoke hesitantly to Mukherjee the next evening and he advised her to be patient. They were going to crack, he felt. Rai called from Colombo again, cheering up Ma, telling her to have faith in her lawyer, he would be back in Delhi before the monsoons.

He was right, as a matters turned out. Mukherjee, deadpan as always, called them on Monday evening. 'There have been some developments. Mr Talwar likes to haggle, I don't. You know that envelope that I handed to their lawyer?'

'Yes,' said Ma.

'It contained a photostat of one of the pages of evidence, I had printed *the name of the bank* on it. It worked.'

Ma, who had been told about Chhobi's mention of the Tamil Tigers to Sonny, thought it was probably that which had worked but now she kept quiet. Mukherjee was continuing.

'I have got an offer from him, half of what we asked for. More will be difficult. Should we accept?'

'Yes, yes,' said Chhobi.

'Yes,' said Ma.

'What?' asked Dida.

'Definitely not,' said Sonali, 'it's not enough.' Capricious turned avaricious.

Negotiations between the lawyers continued for another five weeks before the final figure was agreed upon. The amount upped somewhat, but not substantially despite the intensive haggling. Sonali was indefatigable, mulishly pushing up the figure bit by bit. It was a process that depressed Ma immeasurably, quite breaking the remnants of her spirit and exhausting the rest of the family.

A date for the final meeting with the Talwars was agreed upon. They needed some time to arrange for the money, they said.

twenty-three

Save for Dadu and Sonali, the rest of them did not get much sleep. It was a night grown big and heavy with the new day.

Just after first light, Chhobi got up and went into the drawing room. It was dark, the dawn sky unable to penetrate through the thick curtains. She wandered around touching familiar objects. She started as Ma came into the room.

'What are you doing, Chhobi?'

'Nothing... just trying to get in touch... with our old life.'

Ma who was unbolting the front door, grew still for a moment when she heard that, then threw open the door letting the light stream in. It was a beautiful morning, palely golden. Ma tried to give Chhobi her smile of extraordinary sweetness, but it slipped a little, her face tremulous with foreboding. She kicked off her slippers at the edge of the verandah and began to walk barefoot across the lawn silvered with dew.

The rest of the household was stirring. Dadu came out in his lungi looking for the newspaper, muttering under his breath when he saw the boy had hurled it under the car again. Chhobi took his umbrella with the curved handle and crouched down to extricate it, holding on to the car's bumper for support. Dida was clinking the teacups in the kitchen, they could hear Akashvani's opening notes as she switched on the old radiogram. Sonali was still asleep.

Today, like always, Dadu sat at the head of the table half-hidden by *The Statesman*. Chhobi tried to read the headlines from across the table, but just then the paper was laid down. Ma, slowly stirring the sugar in her cup to dissolve it, put down her spoon as Dadu stiffened and spoke in an agitated manner.

'Listen Meera, there's been a big burglary, just down the road, in Greater Kailash. With the air conditioners on, the family could not hear the thieves breaking in. We must install the steel grills in the windows at once.'

Dida interjected immediately, 'We have no air conditioners.'

A sharp pang, the flash back to another morning over a year ago, shook Chhobi. Nothing seemed to have changed. The feeling evaporated as Sonali entered the room. She stumbled to the sofa with the broken back, pushing the hair and sleep out of her eyes, 'Chaa Dida,' she called. Her shape in the thin faded kaftan was quite visibly pregnant.

Chhobi looked at her. She felt oppressed by a heart-sinking heaviness. Ma's face mirrored her own. They were both worrying about the meeting that had been fixed for 5 p.m. in Mukherjee's chambers that evening. Only Ma for this final encounter with the Talwars would accompany Sonali.

Chhobi and Dida remained behind, so tightly strung that evening that the stress visibly vibrated along every line of their bodies. Dida, especially, began to get very restive towards nightfall. She had been gate watching from the verandah, muttering to Krishna for the past hour. Chhobi sitting on the edge of the lawn began to feel an irrational irritation against her. Not one to enter lightly into theological debate, nevertheless she expressed her doubts now.

'But, Dida, how can you rely on him? Krishna's activities are so mysterious and unfathomable... so... so ungodlike! He breaks his promise in the Kurukshetra war by taking up arms to save Arjuna. He persuades Yuddhishtra to tell a lie for mere tactical gain. He aids in the abduction of his own sister Subhadra. He uses deception to retrieve the five arrows meant for killing the Pandavas given by Bhisma to Duryodhana. He... butter thief, practical joker...'

Dida looked at her without replying, continuing to murmur to herself, this time passages about Krishna as the true god, as Vishnu's prefect avatar.

Savitri came out looking for her slippers that were normally parked sentinel-like outside the front door. Abruptly she told Dida.

'I am off. The masala is ready. What about dinner?'

Dida's eyes distant, preoccupied, focused on her with difficulty.

'Yes, yes, go now. I will make only kichchudi tonight.'

They heard the heavy rattle of the bolts as Dadu began to lock up his clinic. Sighing, Dida got up. Chhobi followed her in with a last backward look at the gate. No sign of them.

Dida said suddenly, 'This is one of the moments we will look back upon in the future and laugh.'

'Sometimes it's difficult to wait for the future,' said Chhobi, racked by insidious tension. She was watching Dida deftly assemble the dinner.

Dida was carefully wielding a pair of orange kitchen scissors, cutting flat white papads made of rice flour in half. She was the only person that Chhobi knew who did that, whole ones occupied too much space on the thaala she said. Chhobi watched as she lowered the semi circles into the semi circular kadhai bubbling with hot oil. The papads turned creamy and crinkly at the edges at once. Just like ears, she thought. Dida's papads like Dida's deaf ear dancing on the hot oil, listening for the sound of their return.

⁂

It was past nine when Ma and Sonali finally walked in. The car had broken down and had had to be towed away for repair. Although the Talwars had paid up the promised sum, a strong feeling of anticlimax seemed to slam into all of them.

Ma, who looked terribly tired, had not so far mentioned the money. She stopped picking at her food as Sonali, somewhat revived, began to make plans for buying a new car. A Maruti on the black market. No six-month booking queue for her. Dida demurred, advising her to save for the child. Sonali laughed, and then commented that she could now buy two dozen cars if she wished.

Her words made Ma flinch and she lost control, the tears glazing her thaal as she looked down at it, the colours on it blurred like an artist's palette. The mound of yellow kichchudi studded with green peas, and arranged around it the crispy brown fried fish, the round slices of fried aubergine, the cream coloured papads all mingled to mist in their steam and her tears.

'But are we any different to them?' she cried, the strain of sitting on a knife-edge all day coming through with jagged edge. Sonali barely heard, having glided away to a dreamworld far beyond the realm of irony.

Ma got up, pushing away her thaal, turning away from her daughter. Chhobi made as if to follow, but Dida motioned to her to continue eating as she intoned,

'You and I Arjuna
have lived many lives.
I remember them all:
You do not remember.'

Counselling words, not hers but Krishna's.

There was a flicker on Dadu's face, a flash in those cataracted eyes, as blue-grey as the Brahmaputra on a dull day, but it was almost immediately extinguished, and he spoke only to ask for a second helping. Sonali shrugged.

'Don't!' Ma exclaimed almost shrilly as Chhobi switched on the light, bright and so hurtful that she immediately flung an arm across her eyes as though to ward off a blow. Chhobi saw that she had not bothered to change into her night things but lay crumpled in her Murshidabad silk sari, her handbag and shoes jumbled together on the floor by the bed.

Chhobi felt helplessness gain on her, a crippling impotence in her inability to deal with the situation. Desperately she searched for words to comfort Ma, but they hung blue and clustered just beyond her lips, as teasing as Tantalus' grapes.

'Ma...' she whispered.

Ma spoke up softer now, but bewildered. 'I do not understand the happening of things which leave no trace... it is as though for her Karan had never been.'

There was a horrid gaping hole of silence as they both remembered Karan's twinkling glance. Chhobi wanted to talk about many things, the expected arrival of the baby, that quickening urgency of change in their lives that had drowned all sense of regular direction, but she remained quiet, discouraged and inarticulate as she glimpsed the pain in Ma. A shame, raw and pink. Words flared and died inside her and speechlessly she rushed out of the room and into her own. She began to feverishly scrabble through the clutter in the drawers of her desk, searching for something to bridge that yawning gulf of inadequacy. The manila envelope Chhobi had been searching for swam into view and she snatched it up running back to Ma, laying it gently on her lap.

'What is it?' Ma asked listlessly as she opened the flap.

The photograph slid out. It was a summer shot. Chhobi at four years wearing a white petticoat embroidered in lazy daisies, leaning her head on Ma's shoulder. Ma looking gravely at the camera with six-month old Sonali, fat beautiful and quite naked, on her lap. Ma noticed the careful restoration, the artwork that made the picture perfect, but her rejection of it was instinctive and immediate. The stony look on her face depleted Chhobi, the sweet serenity so vanished that it gave her a most confusing sense of dislocation.

'Patched up, huh?' she commented as she slid the photograph back into its envelope. For a few minutes neither of them spoke, then Ma said, 'You never saw him, so how can you remember?'

'Who? Whom didn't I see?'

'Dadu's father, my grandfather. The memory of him is so clear. After they fled Mymensingh, they were living in a small rented house in a very crowded part of North Calcutta – Goabagan, the area was called. The walls of their house were painted a most hideous shade of blue… in between cobalt and turquoise… ' Her voice tailed off as though she meant to hide her face in meaningless detail.

'You were saying – about your grandfather?'

'Yes,' she continued, 'I remember him sitting very upright in one of those rooms so heavenly blue, he was dressed impeccably in a starched muslin kurta. The sleeves crushed by the dhobi for a wrinkled chiffon finish, gold buttons glinting at his neck. He had lost everything in Partition, except for a sense of who he really was. No, he never forgot that… He died soon after that last visit of ours. We never saw him again.' There was a long pause, then she said, and there was a closed finality in her tone,

'Switch off the light, Chhobi, when you go.' There was something so irreversibly sad in her voice, at the same time a firmness that prohibited further trespass on her thoughts.

One by one, all the lights of the house were switched off and everyone, quite enervated by the tension of the day, lay down to rest. Both girls were awake, but silence cleaved the space they shared. Chhobi, still shamed by her own ineptitude and Ma's distress, felt quite unable to explain the paradox of Karan, who in his departure had released such chaotic forces while at the same time memories of him had receded so rapidly. He had become so soon a dim and faded figure, despite inciting in them such desperate behaviour.

For the first time she allowed herself to think back to the events of that gut-wrenching day when they had so blithely set off for Sonny's office. What an improbable plot and so hastily constructed. The minutes, so vital in retrospect, such a blur of agitated motion then. The complete disbelief with which she had watched Sonny take down that oil painting. Somehow a steel safe hidden behind abstract art seemed so vintage James Bond. Today she found it hard to remember the reasons for their actions, beyond a dread of conflict and a faint disgust at her own role in the sequence of events that had unfolded with such comic timing.

She relived the moment when she lay on the floor gasping and wheezing with her attack of fake asthma, fright pounding with hammer blows in her temples. The inhaler on which the whole plan hinged seemed so very flimsy and improbable in hindsight. How incredulous it appeared now that Sonny was galvanised into a panicked dash to fetch the inhaler from the car, parked ten floors below. All this while Sonali overdid her Florence Nightingale act.

One moment still stood out with cinematographic clarity. Chhobi remembered snatching the folder from Sonali's hand and rushing to switch on the Xerox machine. Even as it had hummed to life, she was spreading the sheets, two pages juxtaposed and face down on the black glass. She had actually felt the jolt of the bright cylinders of light slide across the paper as though across her impatient body. Then as the machine began to belch out the copies she had seen that they were smudged along the edges as though with tell-tale finger prints. As she was copying the last page Sonali's raised voice in the corridor had alerted her to Sonny's return and she had retained the last handwritten sheet in the original.

Chhobi sighed as she flipped her pillow, laying her head on the cool side, looking at her sister in the dim light. Sonali was asleep, her breathing even and regular. At that moment Chhobi was conscious of a deeper understanding of her sister, of reasons that provided their own defence of her. Sonali, with such a lively appreciation of the present. She wanted to be no part of a heritage that allowed no space for caprice or adventure. She believed in no fatiguing struggle against her own desires. Honour, not a genteel virtue in her vocabulary, but just a word bordering on obsolescence. For her, it was the rejection of the past that began the process of recuperation.

epilogue

Chhobi packing away her paperbacks in cardboard cartons saw that the books, except for the words they contained, hardly looked worth preserving. Jackets dog-eared and spines so worn as to be nameless. Anonymous. A familiar smarting started in her eyes. She heard Dadu answer the phone in the next room. The call he had booked to the USA had finally come through. A friend of Dr Mitra's would receive her at New York and put her on the bus for Connecticut, where she was going to spend some time with her uncle, Bapi's brother's family, before joining the university. Dadu was speaking to New York now, instinctively raising his voice to a shout as though to bridge the vastness of the distance spanning oceans.

'No, no, the name, I repeat, is Chandrayee... what? Oh spell... C for Calcutta, H for Hooghly... No, H for Hooghly, A for Agra...'

Dida interrupted, clucking in annoyance, 'What can't you simply say C for cat, H for hat, A for apple?'

The tears slid down Chhobi's face. The names of those cities so rooted in the realities of immediate geography, would soon, like her, become unknown in American surroundings. She began to check her passport, ticket and traveller's cheques for the umpteenth time.

It would be her maiden flight. A take off in a *Virgo Intacta* state. Still making a big issue about that little bit of intact tissue. Hadn't even left home and was already so homesick.

Ma, carrying a Hawkin's pressure cooker that she had bought from the military canteen store at a discount, came in. Her face so wracked by tension during the last few months, looked serene today. Worry lines smoothed away, happy in Chhobi's future happiness. Dida followed close at her heels holding out two jars of her mango chutney, hot and sweet.

'Pickle is unlucky for travel they say, but chutney should be fine. Pack these inside the pressure cooker. How *will* you eat that bland food?'

Sonali emerged from the bathroom, wet hair wrapped in a towel. She moved very awkwardly now, swaybacked, her time was near. Looking at the piles of discarded handloom kurtas, the hard-topped VIP suitcases nearly full of new clothes, she began to hum the John Denver number, 'All my bags are packed, I'm ready to go…'

Dida asked Chhobi, 'What do you want to eat for dinner?' A quaver betrayed the emotion she felt at the finality of this decision. 'Last Supper, eh!' quipped Sonali, trying to grin, but she too looked distinctly woebegone. Chhobi lost control then. All four women looked at each other, the tears starting in their eyes in unison.

For Chhobi, leaving India would mean such a disbanding, a forsaking of the company of women. Alone, adrift. She felt a rent as though she had lost her moorings and was quite suddenly cut away from such daily intimacies as sitting down to a meal cooked by Dida, or have Savitri massage her head with coconut oil.

Ma was thinking back to '71. To another parting. When Bhaskar had died, she had wanted to as well, and felt herself grow brittle with the responsibility of staying alive for her daughters… Now they were grown, she was still alive, and had raised them without dying after all. She moved to sit beside Chhobi on the bed.

Chhobi spoke in a choked voice, 'Ma, I am scared, everything will be so unfamiliar, a strange world, and I so strange in it.'

Sonali paused at that, 'That will be so interesting.'

Ma was moved to speak gently, breaking out of her customary reticence, smoothing the top of Chhobi's head.

'The last year was strange too and very difficult, we would have never got through it without you. You will make friends. Then there is always the library, just take out some book you have read before, go through a few pages, you will find things are not so alien. Go now, wash your face.' Ma smiled, her expression once more calm and almost cheerful.

Mrs Chatterjee and Ratan Kaku congregated after dinner to wish Chhobi good-bye. Kaku shyly slipped her an envelope. 'Buy something for yourself at the duty-free shop. I arranged this through my travel agent who organises my holidays to the hills,' then in a whisper, 'he deals in black market dollars.'

Chhobi, peeping into the envelope, felt a fresh wave of emotion – it contained a hundred-dollar bill.

Mrs Chatterjee had a long list of names, addresses and phone numbers. She had included those of acquaintances of acquaintances in America.

'I have ticked three names, they all have unmarried sons,' she boomed. They were all sitting on the verandah, the girls on the edge of the floor bordering the lawn. Dida was handing out glass bowls of khir. She had saved a large helping for Khokon who would be arriving at midnight to accompany them to the airport. Departure was at 3.45 a.m.

Arrival and departure, Chhobi wandering as always between titles of familiar books. Rai had called to wish her too, he would be landing in the very same airport next week, returning to Delhi for a long stint, he hoped.

'How long will it take for you to finish your Ph.D.?' questioned Mrs Chatterjee.

Chhobi felt her depression recede as a familiar feeling of irritation took over. 'A minimum of four years,' she said shortly, expecting to hear a sermon about her old maid status. But Mrs Chatterjee was distracted, asking again about the brand new red Maruti parked in the driveway.

Sonali had wasted little time in getting rid of the old Fiat. As she had resolved, she waited in no six monthly booking queue for the new car, but paid the black market premium in cash, for immediate delivery. They would all be piling into it, to drop Chhobi off at the airport. Sonali and Khokon, Ma and Dida, it would be quite a squeeze.

Dadu who remained behind decided to sit for a while on the verandah. The flight path of airplanes travelling west crossed directly overhead and as he settled his weight in the creaking cane chair he thought he would watch out for Chhobi.

Soon, however, his eyes grew heavy-lidded and he slipped into a familiar landscape.

He appeared to float despite his girth into a moonlit garden, wondrous and magic. As he paused on a narrow path flanked by dark shrubs, they sprang skywards, rather like Jack's beanstalk. Suddenly they put forth a thousand flowers. Invisible buds unfolding into thick inflorescence in seconds as in an animated film. Milkwhite Chandini and ivory Kamini, so tender in that argent light.

Seasons merged into one single flowering as he walked down the path. All the trees and all the shrubs, decked it seemed with silver frosting, in one simultaneous blossoming, dictates of orbits of the sun and moon quite obliterated.

Swarms of honeybees clustered on the spherical blooms of the kadamba, climbing over each other in greed. The creeping jasmine awakened in a spangled scarf of shining stars. Around him were strewn the gold-hearted champa's sweet odours. Such abundance. He stooped to pick a flower from the creamy banks of tuberoses at his feet, and as he did so, looked back along the pathway paved by the moon. Looked back at his home.

The house appeared grainy and indistinct, almost like a picture imperfectly remembered,the air shifting with the perfume of the flowers. He waited confidently for the colonnaded courtyards of Mymensingh to swim into focus.

A waist-high shrub of gardenia doubled in size before him, completely obscuring the view, alabaster flowers palely shining. He pushed aside a branch and began to hurry, run almost, down the path, impatient now and eager for a sight of the house. Footsteps thudding in his ears, like his stethoscope listening to the palpitations of an agitated heart.

Then his vision cleared as though looking through a break in the clouds. He saw the house. His jaw slackened in surprise.

It was a modest one, set not like a solitaire amidst jewelled orchards ripe with fruit, but a single-storied one, set in the corner of a narrow lane with rows of similar houses. These were lime-washed yellow, rose pink and Mrs Chatterjee's a dubious shade of pistachio green. His was white, streaked with grey, verandah half smothered in the grasp of an unpruned jasmine.

He walked slowly now, but surely. He reached the verandah and sat down in the cane chair placed there. It creaked in protest, as he settled his weight more comfortably as though onto the lap of Morpheus. His eyes closed and he fell asleep, deep and restful.

credits

While all the books I have read as part of my background research are too many to mention, a few authors must be singled out: K.M. De Silva for his works on ethnic conflict and politics in Sri Lanka; Chitirita Banerjee for her wonderful book on Bengali cuisine; Dr Narayani Gupta and Gordon Risley Hearn for their works on the history of Delhi.

Following are the sources of quotations:

P. 24: Verse from *Gita Govinda* of Jayadeva, 'Love Song of the Dark Lord', translator and editor Barbara Stoler Miller, Columbia University Press, 1977.

P. 137: Extract from Shekhar Gupta's report in *India Today*, India Today archives, New Delhi, 1985.

P. 140-141: Verses from the Chandipatha from *An Encylopaedia of Myth and Legend: Indian Mythology* by Jan Knappert, Diamond Books, London, 1995.

P. 164: Ghalib's V ghazal, translation by Thomas Fitzsimmons, edited by Aijaz Ahmed, Oxford University Press, 1994.

P. 174: Verse from Rudyard Kipling on the Gaiety Theatre, from *Simla Past and Present* by Edward J. Buck, Sumit Publications, 1979, Delhi.